MURDER
BY THE
WAY

OTHER BOOKS AND AUDIO BOOKS
BY BETSY BRANNON GREEN:

KENNEDY KILLINGSWORTH MYSTERIES
Murder by the Book
Murder by Design

HAGGERTY MYSTERIES
Hearts in Hiding
Until Proven Guilty
Above Suspicion
Silenced
Copycat
Poison
Double Cross
Backtrack

HAZARDOUS DUTY
Hazardous Duty
Above and Beyond
Code of Honor

OTHER NOVELS
Never Look Back
Don't Close Your Eyes
Foul Play

MURDER
BY THE
WAY

A NOVEL

BETSY
BRANNON
GREEN

Covenant Communications, Inc.

Cover image *Traffic Cones* © Mark Evans, iStockphotography.com

Cover design copyright © 2012 by Covenant Communications, Inc.

Published by Covenant Communications, Inc.
American Fork, Utah

Printed in the United States of America
First Printing: June 2012

17 16 15 14 13 12   10 9 8 7 6 5 4 3 2 1

ISBN 978-1-62108-123-4

To Abbie Grace Acker—
who made me a grandmother

ACKNOWLEDGMENTS

THANKS FIRST AND ALWAYS TO my husband, Butch. He is not only my romantic interest—he is the best person I know. I couldn't accomplish anything without his patient support. Everything good in my life is in some way a result of my wise decision to marry him. I have been blessed with eight nearly perfect children and (so far) four nearly perfect in-law children. I am eternally grateful for them and the way they enrich my life. And there are no words wonderful enough to describe my grandchildren—eight and counting. My greatest desire is to be with them all forever.

I also appreciate the encouragement and plot suggestions I receive from my extended family, friends, coworkers, and faithful readers. You'll never know how much I appreciate you!

I am particularly thankful for Kirk Shaw, the best editor ever! And for Christina Marcano, an artistic genius. And all the other folks at Covenant who help to make my books the best they can be. May we still be working together for many years to come!

CHAPTER ONE

MY SECOND WEDDING DAY WAS off to a perfect start. The July weather, which had been seasonally scorching for weeks, tempered itself that morning to merely hot. My something old was my grandmother's wedding dress. It had survived the dry-cleaning process and was hanging in my closet ready for me to wear on what I hoped would be my final walk down the aisle. My something blue was a little garter loaned to me by my sister Reagan. It was on my dresser beside the new gold ring that would soon be on Luke's finger. So I had all the superstitious bases covered. However, since in my life nothing ever goes perfectly, I was expecting trouble, but I never dreamed that I'd get involved in another murder.

My name is Kennedy Killingsworth, and I have always lived in Midway, Georgia (which until a few months ago was the dullest place on earth). My current residence is an apartment above the office for the Midway Store and Save—a self-storage facility. After the wedding I'll be moving into an apartment in Atlanta with my new husband, Luke Scoggins, where we will both be students at Emory University.

The wedding plans started two months earlier when I told my parents that I was going to marry Luke. This announcement was met with limited enthusiasm. My father's reactions are always reserved. If he ever had any strong feelings about anything, forty years of living with my mother has extinguished them. My mother is very opinionated and always feels free to share what she thinks on any subject. She was raised to despise the Scogginses, a name long associated with scandal and criminal activity in Dougherty County. If I married Luke, not only would the Killingsworths be legally linked with the Scoggins family, but I would actually be one of them. And this was not an easy thing for my mother to accept.

But one of Mother's many good qualities is her resiliency. After she had a few days to think about it, she decided that my being married, even to a Scoggins, was preferable to my being alone and not producing any grandchildren. So she jumped into wedding planning with both of her dainty little feet.

I pictured my marriage to Luke as a very simple affair. We'd say our vows in my parents' living room. I'd wear a nice Sunday dress, and Luke would wear the suit he'd purchased for his uncle Foster's funeral. Afterward we could adjourn to the kitchen, where my mother would serve light refreshments to those who had come to witness the event. Then Luke and I would leave for our honeymoon. I didn't care where we went as long as it was far away. I wanted to spend quality alone-time with Luke—and that wasn't ever going to happen in Midway.

But according to my mother, it would be the end of the world if we didn't get married in a church. I was prepared to dig my heels in and fight her on this. I'd already done the whole church-wedding thing once to please my mother, and I didn't feel that I owed her a second one. Then Luke remarked that he kind of liked the idea of watching me walk toward him down a church aisle. So I reluctantly agreed with the understanding that it will be small and simple.

Mother said if we wanted to offend people by limiting the number of guests we invited, that was up to us. But some things were just expected and could not be worked around no matter how "simple" we wanted to keep things.

One of these minimum standards was that wedding invitations *had* to be engraved on high-quality cotton paper. Another was that the sanctuary *had* to be full of flowers. We *had* to have a traditional wedding cake with at least four layers (she assured us that anything less was reported to be bad luck and would definitely look funny in the pictures).

She said we absolutely *had* to have a full-blown reception in the church's fellowship hall after the ceremony. There, in addition to the aforementioned tall wedding cake, a vast array of finger foods would be served to guests because heaven forbid that we send anyone home hungry.

But the most annoying of my mother's minimum requirements was that all immediate family members *had* to be given a significant role in the ceremony. As a result I ended up with two matrons of honor (both of my sisters), two ring bearers (both my devilish nephews), and three flower girls (two of my nieces and one of Luke's). Since juvenile delinquency runs in both families, we couldn't trust any of our junior attendants with jewelry. So it was decided that Luke and I would carry the rings ourselves.

When we arrived for the rehearsal the night before the wedding, it was obvious that my desire for small and simple had been completely ignored. The church was decorated from top to bottom with flowers, candles, ribbons, and bows in a medley of summer colors. And although I hated to admit it, everything looked nice.

The rehearsal went well. The children were no more unruly than usual, and the dinner afterward, which Luke had catered by a barbecue restaurant in Albany, was delicious. When it was over, we sat on the front porch swing at my parents' house basking in the unexpected success. Neither Luke nor I had been particularly lucky in our lives up to that point. So we marveled a little—and even expressed some concern—that our current state of happiness was too good to be true. We decided to hope that double bad luck would cancel out—the way two negatives make a positive.

While sitting on the porch swing, Luke had said that he needed to tell me something important. I braced myself, expecting the worst. Then he announced that after a thorough investigation of the Mormon Church, he had decided he wanted to become a baptized member. He'd asked how I felt about it.

Although surrounded by religion my entire life, I have never felt spiritually engaged. The Scogginses are famous for repulsing religious overtures (with shotguns if necessary). So Luke's desire to align himself with any congregation was surprising and a little confusing to me.

I didn't mind that he'd chosen the Mormons over the Baptists (who unquestionably deserved to save him since they'd been futilely pursuing his family's souls for generations). My sister Madison was a member of the Mormon Church, and I'd attended their meetings several times. So I knew the Mormons were good Christian people.

My only objection (which I kept to myself) was that I felt excluded. Up until that point we had been unified in our opinions of the important things like politics and religion (we didn't care for either one). Now Luke was joining a church and embracing a new religion, leaving me in spiritual no-man's land alone.

My mother, however, was a different matter entirely. She believes that all the world should be Baptist, or at least Protestant, to keep things from being so confusing. She was horrified when Madison married a Mormon and then joined his church, but over time she had come to accept it. And she had gotten used to Luke, in spite of his embarrassing family history. But a Mormon Scoggins might be beyond her tolerance limit. So I suggested that he wait until after the wedding to inform my mother of his religious plans. With a smile, he agreed.

I felt like we had passed the final big hurdle. But fate was just lulling me into a false sense of security.

I woke up early on my wedding day and took a relaxing bubble bath. I could hear my mother and Luke's niece, Heaven, talking in the kitchen. I hoped my mother was telling the child, who was nothing like her name, not to do anything outrageous at the wedding. I'd already offered a bribe but figured a few words of warning from Mother couldn't hurt.

I finished my bath and was lounging around in my bathrobe, waiting for Farrah, my mother's beautician, to come and fix my hair when the doorbell rang for the hundredth time. We had been receiving deliveries all morning so I didn't pay any attention—until I heard Luke's voice.

Naturally I stood and walked toward the door. But when Mother saw me coming, she slammed the door in Luke's face.

"The groom can't see the bride before the ceremony on the day of the wedding!" she cried. "It's bad luck!"

"I didn't see Cade on the morning before our wedding," I pointed out. "So maybe that's not a tradition we should put too much confidence in." Then I reached around my mother and clasped the doorknob.

She didn't budge. "I'm serious, Kennedy! You shouldn't invite trouble."

My mother can be very stubborn, but I can be more so. I was about to continue the argument when Luke spoke from the other side of the closed door.

"I'm sorry, Mrs. Killingsworth, but all superstitions aside, I have to talk to Kennedy." His tone was polite but insistent. He makes every effort to please my mother, and I knew he wouldn't upset her if there was any choice. Something was wrong, and I needed to find out exactly what it was before my heart pounded out of my chest.

"I'm afraid it's an emergency," he added to further terrify me.

Completely unconcerned about my mother's wedding-day superstitions, or the fact that I was wearing a tattered terrycloth robe and no makeup, I pushed her out of the way and yanked the door open wide. There on the front steps stood a soldier I had never seen before. His nametag identified him as Lt. Dempsey. Beside him was Luke, the love of my life, my future husband. Unless he had come to his senses and was here to tell me that he didn't want to get any more closely involved with my family and was therefore calling off the wedding.

I pointed at Luke and commanded, "Say you still love me!"

His face relaxed a little. "Of course I still love you."

I reached out and drew him into the living room away from the prying eyes of our nosey neighbor, Miss Ida Jean. "Then I can handle whatever terrible news you've come to deliver."

"I hope so." He didn't sound sure. And I noted that Lt. Dempsey followed him inside without an invitation.

"Who is your friend?" I asked, hooking a finger at the lieutenant who was still hovering near the front door.

"I'll explain," he promised grimly as we sat down on the couch.

Mother stood near the kitchen, wringing her hands. I looked over at her and said, "Could we have a little privacy?"

Mother pivoted and disappeared into the kitchen. Since she couldn't get me to bend to her will, I felt sure she would go straight out the back door to the garage, where my father was giving my old truck an oil change. She would report my misbehavior and demand that he convince me to be sensible.

I turned my eyes to the lieutenant by the door. "Can you step outside so we can be alone for a few minutes?"

His answer surprised me. "Sorry, ma'am," he said. "I have to keep Corporal Scoggins in my sight at all times."

"All times?" I repeated.

Lt. Dempsey nodded.

I clasped Luke's hand and demanded, "For how long?"

Luke looked pained when he replied, "A week, maybe two."

"Two weeks?" I repeated.

"Lt. Dempsey is a Marine version of a subpoena," Luke explained. "He's come to escort me to Camp Lejeune."

Now I was confused as well as alarmed. "But you're not in the Marine Corps anymore."

"Actually, that's not true," the lieutenant clarified. He had a prominent Adam's apple that bobbed as he spoke. "Corporal Scoggins was returned to active duty effective at eight hundred hours this morning."

I ignored the lieutenant—who was now firmly on my bad side—and whispered, "Luke?"

"It's true. My former commanding officer has been accused of war crimes—" Luke began, but Lt. Dempsey stepped forward and cut him off.

"Discussing any aspect of the case with civilians is a violation of the Uniform Code of Military Justice!"

Luke frowned. "Lt. Dempsey is a military lawyer, so I guess he knows what violates military code. But I can tell you that they've called me up so I can testify at a court-martial."

"Can't you refuse?" I whispered.

Luke shook his head. "The lieutenant is authorized to use any means necessary to get me to Lejeune."

I turned to stare at Lt. Dempsey. He was a small, unimposing man, and it was unlikely that he could force Luke to do anything.

"If he doesn't come voluntarily, I'll have to put him under arrest," the lieutenant said with complete seriousness. "I've already spoken to the sheriff, and he has agreed to provide assistance if needed."

"Besides, I want to help my CO," Luke told me. "He's a great guy and a good friend. He never committed a crime in his life—let alone a war crime. It stinks that he's being framed."

The lieutenant cleared his throat. "Corporal Scoggins," he warned.

"How could I live with myself if I don't help my friend?"

My heart sunk. "I guess this is what I get for marrying someone honorable and loyal."

He smiled. "You make that sound like a bad thing."

"At this moment, it feels like a bad thing," I admitted. "When do you have to go?"

I was prepared to hear that our honeymoon was going to have to be cut short. But I was not prepared for his shocking answer.

"I have to be there by five o'clock this evening. The lieutenant has a military transport plane waiting at the airport in Albany."

"The wedding," I managed. Since it was scheduled for two o'clock, obviously things couldn't proceed as we'd planned.

"I hope your mom won't be too upset," he said with a nervous glance toward the kitchen. "Maybe some of the decorations and things will last until I get back."

I shook my head. "We won't need the decorations when you get back because we're going to be married before you leave—just in case."

"Just in case what?"

"Just in case your plane crashes or you get thrown in military jail along with your friend," I clarified.

"Which is why we shouldn't get married before I leave," he countered.

I swallowed the growing lump in my throat. "I'm going to allow Lt. Dempsey and the U.S. Marine Corps to take you away from me on my wedding day." I cut my eyes over at the lieutenant, and he had the decency to look ashamed. "However, I will be your wife before you go!"

"I can give you until three o'clock this afternoon," the lieutenant said. "But that's as long as we can hold the plane."

"What plane?" my mother asked from the kitchen doorway.

I turned and saw both my parents standing there. My mother looked indignant, my father looked wary.

"The Marines have called Luke back to active duty so he can testify at a trial," I explained. "He has to be on a plane by three o'clock this afternoon so we need to move the time of the wedding up to . . ." I glanced at the clock on the mantel, "now."

Mother wrung her hands. "Impossible!"

"How about noon," Luke offered as a compromise.

"That's still impossible!" Mother replied. "Even if we could get everything ready—which we can't—no one ever changes the time of the wedding at the last minute!"

Under certain circumstances I can be as stubborn as my mother. I put my hands on my hips and said, "I'm going to be married to Luke before he leaves. So either we start the wedding early, or I'll get Brother Jackson to come here and perform the ceremony in your living room."

Given these options, Mother decided moving up the time of the wedding wasn't impossible after all. "Okay, but we may not be able to reach everyone to let them know about the change."

That was the least of my worries. "Then they'll miss it," I said firmly. "Luke and I will be there—that's all that really matters."

"The cake has already been delivered to the fellowship hall at the church," Mother continued. "But some of the other food for the reception may not be ready yet."

This did not faze me in the least. "I don't care."

My mother said, "Well you should care. What are we going to do with all the food that won't be ready until two o'clock?"

"The reception can continue after I leave," Luke pointed out. "So anyone who is hungry can wait for the rest of the food to arrive."

Mother nodded absently, her mind racing on to another thing to stress about. "Morning weddings are more formal, so the tuxedos should have tails."

I didn't even try to hide my exasperation. "Mother, we can't worry about silly little details!"

Mother folded her arms across her heaving chest. "We'll just have to make sure that no one starts down the aisle until at least one minute after noon so that *technically* it will still be an afternoon wedding—if anyone asks."

I rolled my eyes. "That might be the most absurd thing I've ever heard." And having lived in Midway my whole life, I've heard some absurd things.

Luke leaned down and whispered into my ear, "One minute won't make a difference to us—so if it is important to your mother . . ."

His lips brushed my neck, and I was powerless against him. "Okay," I relented. "We'll start at 12:01."

My mother seemed inexplicably relieved by this stupid concession. "I'll call Zelda and explain the situation. Then she can have the church ladies start calling the guests."

I nodded. The preacher's wife would provide both practical and emotional support for my mother in this time of need—and keep her occupied, which might preserve what was left of my sanity.

Mother shifted into fast gear. "We won't have time to wait for Farrah, so your sisters will have to fix your hair." She turned to her husband. "Russell, call Madison and Reagan and tell them to hurry. Heaven can go ahead and put on her dress, but be sure she doesn't over-accessorize!"

I wanted to suggest they check her for hidden weapons, but my mother was already upset enough.

My father rushed off—partly to do her bidding and partly just to get away, I was sure.

"Your sisters ought to be here," my mother ranted, as if they should have anticipated the Marine Corps's determination to ruin my wedding. "We've got so much to do in such a little bit of time." She started toward the kitchen. "Go home and get dressed, Luke. And Kennedy, you'd better do something about yourself!"

So Luke left, followed closely by his unwelcome escort, Lt. Dempsey. I went back to my childhood bedroom to improve my appearance. I've never taken much interest in hairstyles or cosmetics, so this would have been a big challenge anyway. But since I couldn't keep the tears from leaking from my eyes, putting on makeup seemed impossible.

And then my sisters arrived. I don't remember another time in my life when I've been so glad to see them. They started with my hair, applying products and then using straighteners and curling irons in seemingly opposing efforts, but the result was impressive. While they worked they told silly jokes and soon my tears dried up. Then, garnering all their artistic abilities, they transformed my blotchy, tear-stained face into an almost-radiant bride.

By the time my mother came in to check on us, I thought I looked incredible.

Mother gave me a critical examination and declared that I "would do." Then she added, "Now let's put your dress on before Myrtle gets here with her camera."

The dress was a simple column-style made of silk and embellished along the hemline with French lace. It was beautiful and sentimental, but it was also very old, and my biggest fear was that it would rip and I'd be dressless.

We managed to get it over my head without tearing it or messing up my hair and makeup. I considered that a major accomplishment. I was sucking in my stomach so my sisters could fasten the row of tiny buttons that ran up the back when Heaven opened the door to my room, without knocking of course.

"Photographer's here!" she announced. Wearing a white eyelet dress, with her blonde hair pulled up on top of her head and secured with a ring of daisies, Heaven looked like the angel she wasn't.

"Thank you, darling!" my mother told the child with a smile. "Tell Miss Myrtle to come in here and take a few pictures of me putting Kennedy's veil in place."

"Mother . . ." I began testily. We'd already discussed the fact that we had all the traditional wedding poses made for my first marriage, and I didn't want this to look like a rerun.

She carefully placed the veil on the back of my head. "I just thought it would be nice to have a picture of you with your sisters and me."

How could I argue with that? So Miss Myrtle, who fancies herself a professional photographer since she occasionally gets one of her snapshots published in the local paper, came in. There was no time for posing. Mother and my sisters really were securing the waist-length veil that matched the dress as the pictures were taken. I looked at our reflection in the mirror. The veil was yellowed and frayed with age but still beautiful. My mother and sisters were working hard to make me look my best. And I was overcome with tenderness toward them.

I caught my mother's hand as she pushed a stray curl from my face. "Thank you."

She smiled. "See, girly-girls can come in handy sometimes."

The camera flashed. "That's a good one," Miss Myrtle said.

Mother moved toward the door. "Okay, ladies, the air conditioning is running in all the cars. Everyone gather your families and meet in the living room. Then we'll divide up into vehicles and head to the church."

As I walked from my room to the front door, I tried to forget that Luke was going to North Carolina and just feel the excitement of the moment. For once I was glad that I looked like a Killingsworth girl, and I could hardly wait for Luke to see me. And in less than an hour—we'd be married. With a smile I lifted my skirt and stepped out into the warm Georgia sunshine.

CHAPTER TWO

THE RIDE TO THE MIDWAY Baptist church took less than two minutes. As we climbed back out of the car, I teased my mother that we should have walked.

"And mess up your hair?" She was aghast.

I had been kidding, but before I could explain this to my mother, Miss Ida Jean Baxley met us on the church steps. Instead of offering congratulations or commenting on how nice we looked, she said, "I never in all my life heard of someone changing the time of a wedding on the very day!"

I was ready to uninvite her on the spot, but my mother intervened.

She tried to soothe the hateful old woman by saying, "It is an unusual circumstance that comes from having a war hero in the family."

Miss Ida Jean frowned, making herself even more unattractive—which I wouldn't have thought possible. "What hero? Isn't she marrying one of those no-good Scogginses?"

Now I knew I was within my rights to let Miss Ida Jean have what had been coming to her for years. I took a step toward her and opened my mouth, but again, Mother blocked my way.

"Kennedy is marrying Luke Scoggins," she confirmed politely. "He has already served this country bravely and today, just minutes after his wedding, he is going back into military service, protecting the freedoms you and I enjoy."

I didn't correct this slight overstatement of the facts.

Apparently Miss Ida Jean realized she had finally gone too far. She put a boney hand on Mother's arm and said, "I like soldiers just as well as the next person, Iris, but since Robby can't leave his duties at the prison until after lunch, he's going to miss the wedding and he really wanted to come."

Miss Ida Jean made it sound like her son was a prison official instead of a recently released inmate. Robby hadn't been home a month before he broke into the Jiffy Mart and stole a flashlight. He committed the crime not because he needed a flashlight but to get sent back to prison. Apparently he missed his friends there (and was probably tired of being with Miss Ida Jean all day—who could blame him for that?). So the sheriff arranged for Robby to work in the prison cafeteria to keep him from earning his way back into permanent residence.

Miss Ida Jean continued. "Robby was disappointed when he found out Kennedy was getting married, but I told him he shouldn't get discouraged. There's always the chance that she'll get divorced again."

I was sure that this rude, insensitive remark would push Mother past good manners. But as usual, I was wrong. She just smiled and turned to my father.

"Russell, will you get Miss Ida Jean seated in the sanctuary?" she asked sweetly.

Without waiting for her consent, Daddy took Miss Ida Jean by the arm and led her away.

As we watched them leave, I whispered to Mother, "How can you be so nice to her?"

Mother's eyebrows drew together in a dainty frown. "What do you mean, dear?"

"I mean that Miss Ida Jean is a hateful, horrible person, but you always treat her with the same kindness you would a nice person."

Mother laughed. "Do you really want to know the trick to dealing with Miss Ida Jean?"

I nodded, feeling like I was being inducted into a secret sisterhood. I leaned my face close to hers so this privileged information wouldn't be overheard.

"I just don't pay a bit of attention to anything she says," Mother whispered.

It was brilliant in its simplicity. "I can do that."

"Of course you can," Mother agreed.

I was basking in this new, insider knowledge when Heaven pulled on my arm.

"Isn't your wedding dress going to get all sweaty?"

"Oh yes, let's get out of this heat!" Mother cried. She ushered us into the foyer where it was not only cool, but also quiet. I felt calmer immediately.

The flowers Mother had put literally everywhere smelled wonderful. The sun streaming through the stained glass created colorful patterns on the marble floor. Mother smiled. "I love this old church. Once you're married, I'm hoping you and Luke will sit on our pew with us every Sunday."

This might have been a good time to mention Luke's intentions to become a Mormon, but I just couldn't do it to her. So instead I looked around and very honestly said, "It is a beautiful church."

* * *

Miss Zelda started playing the organ, and mother rushed us into the waiting room attached to Brother Jackson's office. Closing the door that was normally propped open, she said, "We don't want our guests to see the bride before the wedding."

I didn't know if there was luck attached to this little tradition or not, but based on my run of bad fortune so far that morning, I didn't dare argue. So I stood by the door and looked through the small window into the foyer.

My sisters' husbands were ushers, along with a couple of cousins Mother had drafted into wedding service. Through the little window in the door I watched them greet guests and then seat them in the sanctuary. And I had to admit that the tuxedoes Mother had insisted on looked nice—even if they didn't have tails.

I checked my watch. It was nearly noon. I moved away from the door and made a point to speak personally with all the children in the wedding party. I reminded each of them about the significant amount of money I was offering to all who behaved during the ceremony. They nodded solemnly. I'd finally found the key to success with them. Apparently money really does talk, at least to the children in my family.

At eleven fifty-five Octavia Hitchcock, my mother's friend who had volunteered to direct the wedding, rushed into the waiting room. She gushed over how nice we looked for a few seconds. Then she told Mother it was time for her to be seated on the front pew so the wedding could begin. Mother gave me a careful side-hug and hurried out. I watched through the little window as Madison's husband, Jared, tucked Mother's hand through his arm and led her into the sanctuary.

In the meantime Miss Octavia was lining the children up by age. At exactly twelve o'clock noon, she led us to the side of the door where we could wait without being seen by the wedding guests. The music changed to "Canon in D," and Miss Octavia motioned toward my sisters. Madison and Reagan, accompanied by their husbands, each stepped out in turn onto the antique blue runner and started down the aisle.

After a minute, when presumably they'd had time to reach the front and take their positions, Miss Octavia sent Heaven and Major. I held my breath. Either one of them was capable of creating an embarrassing incident, but together it was almost a sure thing. I realized that disaster had been averted—at least temporarily—when Miss Octavia pulled forward my niece, Maggie, and her brother, Miles, and sent them on their way.

Daddy and I stepped closer to the door. I could see just inside as Maggie carefully scattered pink and yellow rose petals on the runner. They moved out of my line of sight, and we moved into place at the entrance to the chapel. I saw all the people seated inside and realized that Mother's concerns about a low guest turnout because of the time change were unfounded. I breathed in the flower-scented air. Then I looked at my father standing beside me in his tuxedo and went weak in the knees.

What was I thinking? I'd tried this once before with horrific results. Only an insane person would put themselves in this same position again. I couldn't possibly walk down that aisle and get *married*. I had to get out of there. I pulled back, but my father's hand at my elbow stopped my retreat.

"Look at Luke," he urged.

Nearing a panicked state, I looked to the front of the sanctuary.

I was peripherally aware of my sisters and nieces, Heaven, and the preacher. Luke's brother, Nick, who was the best man. But my eyes locked on Luke, and I gasped in surprise. He was supposed to have on one of the tuxedos my mother had picked out. But instead he was wearing his dress uniform—the dark blue coat, accented by a row of shining buttons. The light-blue pants with a gleaming sword at his side. The stark white hat tucked under his arm. Standing ramrod straight, he looked like all that was good about the United States of America. My knees buckled again—but this time in a good way.

"Steady now," Daddy whispered.

"I wasn't expecting him to be in uniform," I managed to reply.

"He was a civilian when your mother planned the wedding," Daddy said. "Now he's a soldier. And he's about to be your husband."

The music changed again. At the first introductory chords of "Here Comes the Bride," Daddy urged me forward. It seemed to take forever to reach the front of the room, passing pews full of people one after another. Fortunately the sight of Luke was enough to compel me onward.

It wasn't just the uniform that made him so appealing, although it helped. His solemn green eyes encouraged me, conveying love and loyalty. The dimple in his cheek told me we'd laugh about this later. The little chip out of his front tooth reminded me how hard he'd fought to reach this moment of happiness in his life. Even the beads of sweat on his upper lip were endearing. I knew it wasn't just the heavy dress uniform. He was standing in front of a room full of people who had been gossiping about his family for generations. We could have married in my parents' living room. But not one to do things the easy way, he had chosen to claim me in this painfully public manner.

When we arrived at the front of the chapel, Luke stepped forward to meet us. He took my free hand and leaned down to press a kiss to my lips as the final, triumphant strains of the organ music ended.

Brother Jackson teased, "Kissing the bride comes a little later in the ceremony, son!"

During the polite laughter from the assembled guests, Luke kept me close and whispered, "I can't believe this is really happening. I'd pinch myself, but if it's a dream, I don't want to wake up."

"It's real enough," I whispered back. "And with Heaven and Major here—it might be about to turn into a nightmare."

He grinned as the preacher cleared his throat to regain our attention.

Once we were both looking at Brother Jackson, he smiled and said, "Who gives this woman away?"

Daddy said, "Her mother and I do." Thankfully he didn't add, "again." Then he kissed my cheek and went to sit beside my mother, who was watching avidly from her place of honor on the front row.

Brother Jackson shook a warning finger at Luke. "Now her father and mother have given her away, but I haven't given her to *you* yet, so no more kissing until I pronounce you man and wife!"

There was more laughter from the crowd, and Luke's face turned pink. I glared at the preacher. He looked a little startled, but he stopped teasing Luke. He cleared his throat and read a few scriptures. Then he lectured us on the sanctity of marriage. I was pretty sure this was for my benefit, but with my hand clasped in Luke's while he was wearing that incredibly handsome uniform, I couldn't be mad at anyone.

Once this little sermon was over, the soloist sang an arrangement of "The Lord's Prayer." It was so beautiful that tears came to my eyes, and I almost never cry.

Finally the preacher got to the vows. Luke and I both said our "I dos" at the appropriate moments and then, at long last, Brother Jackson declared us husband and wife. Luke grinned, showing his dimple. I smiled back. Then I flung my arms around him and gave him a proper kiss that drew polite laughter and a few whistles from our more boisterous guests.

Brother Jackson called out, "May I present to you Mr. and Mrs. Luke Scoggins!"

Miss Zelda at the organ began playing an enthusiastic rendition of "The Wedding March." Luke held out his arm, and I clasped it, feeling all soft and feminine. It was a nice moment.

Then Luke said, "Here we go." And we walked from the sanctuary as quickly as my old-fashioned wedding dress and his ceremonial sword would allow.

Miss Myrtle followed us all the way to the fellowship hall, snapping pictures like a mad woman. We went straight to the wedding cake, and my mother joined us there.

"Go ahead and cut the first piece so we can start serving," she commanded.

Luke raised an eyebrow in my direction as Mother rushed off to boss someone else.

"Don't give me that look," I told him. "She's your mother-in-law now and you can't ever say I didn't warn you." I pushed a piece of cake into his mouth.

Miss Myrtle got a picture of his startled expression.

Then I jammed a piece of cake in my own mouth and turned for her to catch the obligatory shot on film.

"Now that's something you don't see everyday," Miss Myrtle remarked as her camera whirred.

Luke laughed and pressed his lips to mine. I didn't think his kisses could be improved, but a layer of buttercream frosting made them something close to miraculous.

Miss Octavia came up at that point and gave me a stern look. "Your mother said to stop playing with the cake and receive some guests before your husband has to leave for the airport."

I clung to the joy I felt at hearing Luke referred to as my "husband" and tried to ignore her untimely reminder that he was about to leave me on my wedding day.

The Iversons were first in line to congratulate us, with a new foster baby temporarily named Penelope. I remarked that their children were, as usual, perfectly well-behaved.

"Thank you." Kate smiled at Emily and Charles. "And I noticed that your nieces and nephews were model citizens during the wedding."

"Yes, how did you manage that?" Mark asked. He had seen Madison's children and Heaven in action on many occasions.

"I bribed them," I admitted without a trace of shame. Desperate times call for desperate measures.

"I showed them my sword," Luke added. "And I told them it wasn't just for decoration."

I was impressed. "I thought they were greedy, but apparently they were scared for their lives. You might survive in my family, after all."

Kate laughed. "Now that you know that sword has special powers, you should keep it on hand for future use."

Mark nodded. "Like Sunday at sacrament meeting."

"A sword in the chapel," Kate murmured. "There might be such a thing as encouraging reverence *too* much."

The Iversons moved away from us to the cake table. They were followed closely by Miss Eugenia and, unfortunately, Miss George Ann Simmons. First Miss George Ann announced, a little louder than necessary, that as a wedding gift she had made a generous donation in our names to her favorite charity. After graciously accepting our thanks, for a little longer than necessary, she walked on over and helped herself to the food table.

Miss Eugenia waited until Miss George Ann was out of hearing range. Then she lowered her voice and said, "If you think that her stingy wedding gift is the worst of it—I have bad news for you. She's also been telling everyone she's a close friend of your family."

I couldn't control a grimace. "It seems like she has been 'close' a lot lately, but 'friend' I'm not so sure about."

Miss Eugenia smiled. "I gave you a Crock-Pot, but my real wedding gift will be taking her home as soon as I can drag her away from all this free food."

I caught Miss Eugenia in a hug. "Now that's what I call friendship!"

Cade and his wife of one month, Hannah-Leigh, were next in line. He exchanged a civil, if a little cool, nod with Luke. Then he directed his best wishes in my general direction and stepped aside.

Hannah-Leigh seconded his well-wishing but did not move on. Instead she stood there, blocking the guests behind her, and looking embarrassed. Finally she said, "I have a little favor to ask."

This was unexpected. "What kind of favor?"

She pointed toward the door of the fellowship hall, and my eyes followed the direction of her finger. Standing just inside the entrance, beside Luke's guard Lt. Dempsey, was Hannah-Leigh's two-man camera crew.

"It's kind of a slow news day—or slow news month, to tell the truth," she explained nervously. "So my producer told me to ask you if we could get some footage. It would make a nice human-interest piece for the weekend news, a military hero being called up by the Marine Corps on his wedding day, then rushing off to serve his country and all that."

I wasn't thrilled with the idea of pictures from our wedding making the local news, and I didn't like being put on the spot. But Hannah-Leigh had done me some favors in the past, so I felt obligated. I told Luke if he didn't mind, it was okay with me.

He nodded. "It's up to you."

Hannah-Leigh flashed us a smile and waved her camera crew forward—apparently anxious to get her film bite before we came to our senses.

"Just look adoringly into each other's eyes," she said.

I turned to Luke and didn't find that hard at all.

"How about a little kiss?" she suggested.

We complied and when my lips touched Luke's, I forgot about Hannah-Leigh and her camera crew. I nearly forgot about the whole room full of wedding guests.

Cade brought us back to reality. "Okay, enough."

I moved away from Luke reluctantly. "For the news cameras, anyway," I murmured and Luke grinned.

"This is perfect!" Hannah-Leigh enthused. "I'll do my part outside in front of the church so we won't cause any more disruption at your reception. And I hope you'll both be very happy!"

"Thanks," I said to her back as she rushed out, followed closely by her news crew.

I couldn't help but feel sorry for Cade as he brought up the rear—less important than the camera guys.

My sympathetic moment was interrupted by Miss Myrtle. She sidled up to me. "Usually when I'm asked to photograph an event it's understood that I have the exclusive," she said as if she were at the Oscars instead of in the fellowship hall at the Midway Baptist church.

Fortunately Mother stepped over to handle the situation before I could say anything unforgivable.

"You're the *official* photographer," she assured Miss Myrtle. "Hannah-Leigh just needed some footage for the news. You know it's important to show the sacrifices our soldiers make and help people keep their patriotic spirit."

Miss Myrtle seemed appeased. "Oh, well, that is important."

Mother bragged on Miss Myrtle and then encouraged her to take a break and eat some wedding food. She'd just gotten rid of one annoyance when another arrived. Miss Ida Jean walked by carrying a plate piled high with wedding cake and finger sandwiches.

"I'm taking this food to Robby," she explained. "Since you made him miss the wedding, I figured it's the least you could do."

I could think of several other things we could do relating to both Miss Ida Jean and her son—like ban them from all future Killingsworth family events.

But my mother kindly said, "Tell Robby we hope he enjoys the food and we're sorry his work schedule made it impossible for him to attend." I noticed that she cleverly worded her response, putting responsibility for Robby's absence where it belonged—on him—so that Miss Ida Jean had no room to complain.

Miss Ida Jean scowled for a second and then nodded. "I'll tell him."

After Miss Ida Jean left us, Lt. Dempsey walked over and said quietly, "I'm sorry, Corporal Scoggins, but it's time for us to go."

I was both shocked and disappointed. The time we'd spent receiving guests had been more entertaining and passed more quickly than I expected. Dread overwhelmed me. "So soon?"

The lieutenant nodded. "Sorry, ma'am."

I told Luke, "I'm coming with you to the airport."

"They won't let you come inside the fence," he warned.

"I understand," I said. "I just can't say good-bye now. Not yet."

Wordlessly he leaned down and kissed my forehead.

Mother took my arm and led me away from Luke. "Kennedy, your sisters are waiting for you in the ladies' room. They'll help you get out of that dress and change into your going-away outfit."

I wanted to object to all of it. I didn't want to change out of my grandmother's dress, thereby accepting that the wedding was over. I didn't want to change into a "going away" outfit, thereby accepting more from my parents who had already spent way too much on this, my second wedding. I didn't want to leave my reception and take Luke to the airport so he could testify in a trial. But since I had no choice, I stood there silently while Mother addressed Luke.

"Are you going to change?"

He shook his head. "No, I'll wear this to Lejeune. I want to make a point with the Marine Corps."

She nodded. "Wait by the front entrance with your . . ." she looked at Lt. Dempsey and searched for the right word. Finally she settled on, "friend. It will only take Kennedy a few minutes to change, and then she will drive you to the airport in that horrid old truck of hers. I begged her to borrow my car, but she refused."

"I like her old truck," Luke said as he released my hand and started to walk toward the entrance. Left without any reasonable alternatives, I trudged over to the ladies' room. As Mother had promised, Madison and Reagan were waiting there for me.

While they unbuttoned my dress and unpinned my veil, they congratulated me on how nice everything had been. Grief-sticken, I watched them fold my wedding finery and store it in a large white box. I couldn't believe the wedding was over. This event had loomed before us, taken on a life of its own—the only thing that stood between me and my separation from Luke. Now it was finished. Completely gone.

Oblivious to my distress, Madison pulled a beautiful blue-and-white sundress from a clothing bag. "Isn't this gorgeous?" she demanded as she held it up for my review. "It's from Corrine's!"

I had to admit it was spectacular—like something Hannah-Leigh would wear. And I had no doubt it was also expensive since it came from the exclusive little shop in the neighboring town of Haggerty. My only reservation was that my parents had already spent too much money on my combination of weddings.

Madison relieved this concern by saying, "It's a gift from Reagan and me. We wanted Luke's last look at you to be a good one." She realized how this sounded and stammered, "I mean, well, you know what I mean."

"Kennedy knows," Regan assured our sister as she took the dress from Madison and handed it to me. I stepped in and zipped it up.

"It fits perfectly!" Madison handed me a pair of white sandals. "These match," she stated the obvious. "I got them from Edith's Shoe Emporium."

As I strapped on the really cute sandals, I saw the price tag. I could have put two new tires on my truck for the same price.

Once I was dressed, my sisters touched up my makeup. They took down my hair and brushed it out. Then Reagan handed me a pair of sunglasses with navy-and-white-polka-dotted frames. "These match too." She pushed them up into my head like a casual headband.

Finally, after a very critical review, they deemed me ready to go.

We left the restroom as a group, but once we were out and I saw Luke standing by the front door, I abandoned my sisters and rushed over to join him. One of the church ladies who had helped with the reception approached us shyly. She presented Luke with a to-go plate for the plane.

Dabbing her eyes with a hanky, she claimed, "This is the saddest, most romantic thing I've ever seen—you rushing off to war right after your wedding."

"Actually I'm going—" Luke tried to explain.

But Mother and Lt. Dempsey objected at the same time.

"You *will* be serving your country," Mother said.

"You're not at liberty to discuss the reasons for your return to active duty," Lt. Dempsey added.

We all ignored him.

Mother leaned in and hugged both Luke and me. Then she told us to be careful as if I was leaving with Luke instead of coming back to spend my wedding night alone.

Miss Myrtle followed us outside where our guests blew bubbles as we passed by. In the distance I saw Hannah-Leigh and her camera crew, recording the moment for the Channel 3 weekend viewers to see.

My father had guarded my truck to keep it from being "decorated." However, I noted that there were several cans tied to the trailer hitch—so either he hadn't been vigilant or he had allowed this small announcement of our newlywed status.

Luke opened the passenger door of my truck and I slipped inside. Then he hurried around and climbed in under the wheel. Lt. Dempsey pulled up behind us in a dark gray sedan. Our little caravan moved away from the church parking lot to the frantic cries of Midway residents wishing us the best and the cans rattling behind the truck.

As we drove down Main Street I noticed that most of the few merchants still in business had put American flags out to fly. Some even stepped out to wave as we passed. A couple of Veterans, wearing their old uniforms, were standing in front of the library. Luke pulled the truck to a stop and got out to give them a salute. Then he made use of the stop to cut off the cans with his ceremonial sword before we continued on toward Albany.

Once we left the Midway city limits, I leaned back against the seat. "Wow."

Luke smiled "Wow is right. You look awfully nice, Mrs. Scoggins."

I slid across the seat and kissed his cheek. "Thank you, soldier."

His face turned a little pink, and he cleared his throat. "Maybe you should move back over to your side of the seat so I can concentrate on driving."

I nuzzled his shoulder. "I'll be still if you'll let me stay."

He looked a little nervous but nodded. "Just remember that Lt. Dempsey is right behind us."

"Now that's something I wish I could forget," I muttered. Then I rested my head against his shoulder—thankful that I almost never cry since I wouldn't want him to arrive at Ft. Lejeune with tearstains on his uniform jacket.

CHAPTER THREE

The Southwest Georgia Regional Airport in Albany allots a portion of space to the armed forces. So when Luke and I arrived, we were directed to a parking area on the far side of the airport used by owners of private planes. The parking lot was separated from the tarmac by a serious-looking chain link fence. Through it we could see a small green military jet, ready and waiting.

Luke parked my truck and then turned to face me. He gently removed the sunglasses and said, "I want you to know that having you take my tattered name, knowing that you are my wife, has made me happier than I ever dreamed I'd be. I hope we still have lots of good times together—like a honeymoon and children and sitting in rocking chairs when we're old. But if this is as good as it gets, if my life is over now, I will die a happy man."

I grabbed his jacket and said, "I have much higher expectations out of life that *this*!" I waved to vaguely encompass the inside of my old truck. "You'd better come home soon and *alive*, because if you don't I'll do something terrible!" Just to be sure he was taking me seriously, I threatened, "Like remarry Cade!"

He pressed his lips to my forehead. "If I needed any more incentive—I have it now."

Mostly oblivious of the July heat, we shared a few more sweet kisses. Finally he moved back a little and said, "I have a favor to ask. I hate to, but . . ."

I couldn't imagine him asking anything I wouldn't be glad to do for him. "I'll do anything." I leaned forward and nuzzled his neck. "I'm your wife."

We were both more affected by this comment than either of us anticipated, which resulted in more kissing.

Then he pulled back slightly and said, "While I'm gone, will you visit my father?"

So he did find something to ask that I would not be glad to do. "In prison?"

He nodded. "I go every Wednesday. I don't have time to explain all this to him, and he'll be disappointed if nobody comes."

It was not fair. Luke's father had never done anything for him, and certainly not for me. I didn't like him and didn't want to see him anywhere, let alone in prison. But under the circumstances, I couldn't refuse Luke anything. "I'll go."

He rewarded me with a sweet kiss. Then we climbed out of the truck. He grabbed his bag from the back and put it over his shoulder. Holding hands, we walked together as far as the fence where Lt. Dempsey was waiting.

He touched the brim of his uniform hat and said, "It was nice to meet you, ma'am. And I'm sorry about . . . everything."

I couldn't force myself to say it was okay, but I nodded.

A guard stepped out of a little booth and walked toward us. He checked Lt. Dempsey's identification and passed him through the gate. Then he turned to us and regretfully told me I couldn't go beyond that point. Luke gave me one more quick, hard kiss. Then he released my hand and approached the gate. The guard checked Luke's ID and waved him inside.

I stood there clutching the chain-link as he and Lt. Dempsey trotted toward the green airplane in the distance. They climbed the metal stairs, and just before he ducked inside, Luke turned to give me a little wave.

I smiled brightly (if not sincerely). Then I watched as the door was closed to separate us. The plane's engines revved, and it began to taxi slowly down the runway. A few minutes later I saw the plane rise into the sky and disappear from my view. It was a bad moment.

Leaving seemed like deserting Luke, so I stayed by the fence, staring at the clouds that had taken him from me. Finally I noticed the guard fidgeting. It was probably against the rules for someone to loiter there. I didn't want to force him to order me to go, so I let go of the fence and trudged back to my old truck.

I was surprised to find both my father and Cade waiting there for me.

"What are you guys doing? Were you afraid I might drive off a cliff or something?"

"You shouldn't be alone at a time like this," Daddy replied. "Cade offered to bring me here so I can drive you home."

I hate situations where expressing gratitude to Cade is necessary. So I said a quick, "Thanks."

Cade scuffed the heel of his steel-toed boot on the concrete parking lot. "It wasn't any trouble." He took a step toward his sheriff department car. "I guess I'll go on. Hannah-Leigh will be wondering where I am."

Daddy shook his hand and said, "I appreciate the ride."

I gave him a little wave as he walked over to his car.

I handed my father the keys and opened the passenger door of my old truck. Once we were settled, Daddy followed Cade out of the parking lot. I curled against the back of the seat, closed my eyes, and gave in to self-pity.

* * *

A while later I felt Daddy coming to a stop and knew we couldn't be home yet, so I opened my eyes. Through my truck's dirty windshield I could see smoke billowing across the highway. I turned to my right and located the source—a car had crashed into a line of oak trees that framed the road. I sat up straighter.

Then the smoke cleared enough for me to see a large white Dougherty County Correctional Facility van turned over on its side in the median. Men wearing orange jumpsuits were helping each other out of the van's only unobstructed door. There was also an old pickup truck parked on the side of the road that didn't seem to have been involved in the wreck. The driver was pacing on the shoulder of the road, talking on his cell phone.

"It looks like it just happened," I whispered, noting the still-spinning tires on the car in the trees.

"That's how it looks," Daddy agreed.

Cade screeched to a stop on the shoulder, and Daddy pulled in right behind him. Cade jumped out of his car and didn't even bother to close the door. "Call 911!" he hollered to us.

The young man on the side of the road held up his phone. "I already did!"

"Call them again, Kennedy!" Cade commanded. Then he took off running toward the smoking wreck.

While we got out of my truck, I called to report the emergency. My conversation with the 911 operator was punctuated by the insistent beeping from Cade's car, warning that he had left the keys in the ignition and the door open.

Daddy cupped his hands beside his mouth and hollered over to the passengers of the van who were now out and milling around, apparently unharmed. "Everybody okay there?"

The only one not wearing a jumpsuit, presumably the driver, nodded. He had a cloth pressed to a nasty lump on his head with one hand and was holding his cell phone to his ear with the other. "We're all right."

Reassured on this point, Daddy started down the grassy slope toward Cade, who was now almost to the wrecked car. "Stay here," he told me.

I followed right behind him. It wasn't so much defiance as just an automatic reaction. And Daddy was too distracted by the dangerous situation to notice that I had disobeyed. We only made it a few feet before Cade saw us.

"Get back!" he yelled. "This thing could go up in flames at any minute!" Then like an idiot, he closed the distance between himself and the potential inferno.

My father might have continued on to assist Cade except for my presence. Once he realized I had followed him, he had no choice but to protect me from danger. So instead of helping Cade, he pulled me away.

With Daddy's arms firmly around me, I watched Cade reach inside the car's broken window and unlock the driver's side door. Then he yanked the handle, but nothing happened. It took several tries but finally the door swung open. His next challenge was to unlatch the seat belt. The tilt of the car and his position on the ground combined to make this awkward. After a few nerve-wracking failed attempts, he pulled out a pocket knife and sawed through the straps.

The hissing and smoking intensified, indicating that the car was about to burst into flames. I felt my father stiffen and knew he had come to the same conclusion. I watched in horror, knowing I was about to see Cade burned before my very eyes. And in this moment I realized that my relationship with Cade was very complicated. I had loved him and I had hated him. Then I had tried to be ambivalent toward him. But for better or worse, he was part of my life and I would always care. I was not completely comfortable with this discovery.

As these thoughts were racing through my mind, Cade dragged the limp body of a woman from the car and started carrying her back toward us. There was a loud popping sound and the car caught fire. A few more pops and flames engulfed the vehicle. The heat repelled us and the smoke blocked our view.

"Cade," I whimpered as I tried to step forward. But my father's arms prevented me.

Then miraculously Cade emerged through the haze, carrying the crash victim with him. His eyebrows were singed and his face was red, but otherwise he seemed fine. I went limp with relief.

Cade put the woman onto the ground and began CPR. As he worked I willed the woman to take a breath. Her clothes were soaked with blood from a nasty cut on her head and more on her face and arms. Her curly brown hair was fanned out behind her head. She was very pale and alarmingly still.

Finally Cade rocked back on his heels. "I think she's dead."

We heard the sirens of emergency vehicles approaching.

"Keep trying," Daddy advised. "Let someone else make that determination."

So Cade went back to alternately pumping blood and breathing since the woman couldn't do either for herself.

The sound of the sirens intensified until the blare was right behind us. I turned and saw two ambulances, several police cars, and a fire truck. Firemen jumped off the truck, unwinding water hoses, and raced down the slope toward the burning car, pulling their hoses along with them. They pummeled the car and surrounding trees with pressured water. The fire went out, leaving the air heavy with smoke and steam.

A paramedic, escorted by Albany police officers, rushed down the slope to join us. The paramedic checked out the victim.

Cade stood watching, and as the examination began, he said, "Is she dead?"

The paramedic confirmed this. "Yes. She has a broken neck besides all the lacerations and certainly some internal injuries."

Cade was visibly shaken. "Can you tell if her neck broke during the crash or if it was something I did when I got her out of the car?"

"One thing's for sure," the paramedic replied, hooking a thumb at the blackened trees behind us. "If you'd left her in that car, she'd be dead no matter what. You did all you could to save her."

This seemed to relieve Cade some. "I hope so."

Then another paramedic came over the hill, followed by the Albany police chief. I recognized him from his frequent television news interviews. He was a tall, thin man with bright red hair and a perpetually sour expression. Something I didn't know before, but learned quickly, is that he yells. A lot.

He started by yelling at the firemen for blocking his approach with their equipment. Then he yelled at the paramedics. He wasn't mad at them. He just wanted a report on the accident victim. Once he got the news that she was dead, he rounded on Cade.

"Deputy, were you the first law enforcement officer on the scene?" the chief hollered.

"Yes, sir," Cade replied.

"Then why didn't you secure those convicts?" The chief waved toward the highway behind us.

"I thought it was more important to get the woman out of the car," Cade replied reasonably.

The chief looked over at the victim. "The dead woman, you mean?"

Cade's face was already red from exposure to the car fire so I couldn't be sure if he blushed, but he was definitely embarrassed. "I didn't know she was dead when I was pulling her out of the car," he explained, "but I did know the car was about to blow."

The chief's bright-red eyebrows shot up. "You can predict the future? What are you, some kind of a soothsayer?"

Cade looked flustered as he shook his head. "No, sir."

"Well, that's a real shame," the chief continued, "because we could use someone with psychic powers to help us find the two work-release prisoners who are now missing—thanks to you!"

"I'm sorry," Cade stammered. Then he attempted to defend himself. "I had to make a quick decision, and trying to save the driver of the car was the most important thing."

I thought it was a good response—for Cade.

But the police chief shook his head as if Cade and his reaction were both unfathomable. "You've been around too long to be making rookie mistakes," he declared loudly. "I expected more from one of Sheriff Bonham's deputies." Now that he had thoroughly humiliated Cade, he turned to the paramedics. "So the only occupant of the car is dead. Did either one of you think to examine the van driver to see if his injuries are serious?"

"Concussion," one of the paramedics said promptly. "He needs to go to the hospital."

The chief considered this for a few seconds before shouting, "Then let's get him to the hospital! And load up this body so we can clear the roadblock. We need to get traffic moving on the highway and organize a double manhunt. So why is everyone just standing around?"

No one answered this semirhetorical question, but everyone started moving—at least trying to act busy. While the firemen loaded up their equipment and the paramedics transferred the body to a stretcher, the chief focused his attention on my father and me.

"You two witnesses?" he yelled at us.

Daddy shook his head. "We got here after the wreck. All we saw was Deputy Burrell's courageous attempt to rescue the victim."

The chief glanced briefly at Cade but didn't comment.

I pointed toward the road. "There was a guy standing by an old truck when we got here. He might be a witness."

The police chief nodded. "We're questioning him now. I probably won't need to talk to you again, but I'll send someone over to get your contact information just in case." Then he stalked away from us, presumably in search of someone else to scream at.

We stood there for a few awkward seconds until a harried-looking young officer rushed up and asked for our names and phone numbers. Daddy provided them succinctly.

After the officer left, Daddy said, "I guess we'll head back to town." Addressing Cade, he added, "Are you coming?"

Cade's eyes strayed to the victim, now covered with a plastic sheet and being wheeled toward the waiting ambulance. "I think I'll hang around for a little while."

I almost never feel any sympathy for Cade, but he looked so forlorn that I forced myself to say, "You did your best to save her."

Daddy added, "In fact, that may have been the bravest thing I've ever seen."

"I wish it had been enough," Cade said.

Besides not saving the victim, he was upset about letting the prisoners escape, I was sure, and about being yelled at by the police chief. And there was the possibility that he would get yelled at again when Sheriff Bonham found out about it. But I couldn't think of anything to say that might make him feel better. So when Daddy took my arm and pulled me toward the road, I didn't resist.

We trudged up the slope and walked to my truck. The hot asphalt burned my feet through my expensive sandals. Several grim-faced policemen were now guarding the remaining convicts huddled beside the overturned van. Police cars with lights flashing blocked the road on both sides, and a fire truck and ambulance added to the light show. Fortunately the roadblock was set up right behind my truck so we were able to pull onto the road and proceed toward Midway. As we drove slowly away from the fray, I looked back at Cade. He was standing a little apart from the other law enforcement officers. Not a contributor to the scene, just an unwelcome observer.

Long after the wreck disappeared from sight, I continued to look out the truck's window at the lush forests and green grass and wildflowers that lined the highway. A little while ago I had been discouraged. I'd felt sorry for myself because Luke had to leave so soon after our wedding—ruining our honeymoon plans. But now I had a new perspective. Luke was gone, but he would be back. I was still a part of this beautiful world, but that poor woman Cade tried to save was not. I had a lot to be thankful for, and I determined to focus on the positive more in the future.

Daddy called my mother as he drove so by the time we reached my parents' house, most of Midway knew about the wreck and the missing prisoners. Mother met us in the driveway. Miss Ida Jean, who had been watering her lawn, dropped her hose to stand beside my mother.

"Is it true that Cade let convicts escape?" Miss Ida Jean demanded the second we stepped out of my truck. Her tone and expression indicated that I was somehow responsible for my ex-husband's actions.

"Cade didn't have anything to do with the escaped prisoners," I replied tightly. "They got away after the prison van was hit by a car—before Cade even arrived at the accident scene."

"Well, I don't know how Christian ladies like myself are supposed to sleep at night when our virtue is at risk!"

I stared at Miss Ida Jean. Imagining anyone who would pose a danger to her virtue was, well, unimaginable. And wholly repulsive. Remembering my mother's wise advice about how to handle Miss Ida Jean, I merely said, "I don't think you have anything to worry about."

"I'm sure the Albany police will find the missing prisoners soon," Mother added with a comforting smile. "But in the meantime it is probably wise for you to stay inside your house with the doors locked. Now if you'll excuse us, Kennedy needs to rest. She's had quite a day." And with that Mother started leading me to the house.

Then I remembered my promise to Luke regarding his father. I had to visit the prison, and Robby Baxley was my best resource for that. So I turned back and asked, "Is Robby home?"

Miss Ida Jean shook her head. "Not yet."

"Well, when he gets here would you tell him I need to speak to him?"

"About what?" Miss Ida Jean demanded.

"Just tell him, please." Then I followed my parents into the house.

Usually I find my mother's smothery kind of love overwhelming, but after all that had transpired, I needed it. I got into bed and she sat beside me, stroking my hair as I told her about saying good-bye to Luke and the wreck.

"So Cade is okay?" Mother asked.

"He's fine physically," I reassured her. "But he's upset that he couldn't save the driver of the car, and he's in trouble with the Albany police chief because he let those two prisoners escape. I've never seen him like that before. I'll admit I'm a little worried about him."

"Cade can take care of himself," Mother pronounced as she stood and pressed a kiss to my forehead. "Now you take a little nap. It will do you a world of good."

I knew this was her way of saying I looked terrible, so I curled onto my side and buried my head in the pillow. Then I dozed off to sleep and tried not to think about how a person's wedding day is supposed to be the happiest of their life.

I woke up a couple of hours later. I rolled over onto my back and stared at the ceiling in my old room. I was married to the best person I'd ever known and unquestionably the handsomest—and he loved me. Every hour he was gone brought me closer to his return. So I tried to look at his departure as progress and focus on the fact that our separation was temporary.

He'd promised to contact me as soon as possible—which gave me something to look forward to. And since he'd told me that my courage was sustaining him, I figured I'd better at least act like I had some. So I got up and walked into the living room.

My mother was sitting by herself, sorting through wedding gifts. She looked up from her lists when she saw me. "Well, there's my Sleeping Beauty."

I smiled and held up a fistful of my wrinkled sundress. "I know I look a sight."

"You've had quite a day," Mother said, excusing my slovenly appearance. Then she waved her hand at the room full of wedding gifts. "But you are the proud owner of six new Crock-Pots!"

"I've never used a Crock-Pot in my life." I sat beside her and she showed me her list. She was cataloging all the gifts to make the thank-you writing process as easy as possible. She had a column for the gift and one for the giver (including a description of *who* they were if she didn't think I'd know).

Overwhelmed by the stacks of stuff in the living room and the names neatly written on my mother's list, I returned it to her. Then I picked up two identical toasters. "I can't understand why we do all this."

"It's a show of support for the bride and groom," Mother explained. "In the old days people used to actually give the new couple something from their own household—a plate or fork or pot or quilt—whatever they could spare. That's how the custom started."

"*That* makes sense," I said. "But six Crock-Pots make no sense. It's gotten out of control."

Her mother frowned. "The thought is still the same. People want to help and wish you well."

"I hate to say it." And I really did. "But Miss George Ann Simmons might have the right idea, after all—donating to a good cause in our names."

Mother laughed. "I never thought I'd see the day when you'd agree with Miss George Ann."

"Me either," I muttered. "It took six Crock-Pots to push me to such an extreme."

We laughed together and then Mother said, "Don't worry about the extra Crock-Pots—or other appliances. I'll take all the duplicates back to the stores where they were purchased and deposit the money in your account."

That changed everything. "Money is something we can use!" With both of us in school at the same time, finances were going to be tight.

She nodded. And then, inexplicably, Mother was wiping tears from her eyes. "I'm sorry to be such a big baby, but all this talk about weddings and traditions—even Miss George Ann—all reminds me of my wedding. It doesn't seem that long ago that I was sitting with my own mother, looking at my gifts."

Even more recently she'd been sitting here with me, looking at gifts given to celebrate my marriage to Cade, but we were having a nice time so I didn't mention this.

"Many things change," Mother continued, "but traditions help to tie the generations together. Wedding gifts are a good thing—even if you get six Crock-Pots. Just be glad no one gave you an old used spoon."

I looked around the room full of unopened gifts and murmured, "At least not as far as we know."

Then my phone rang and I was saved from counting can openers or blenders or possibly even a few used spoons that the kind people of Midway had given us.

CHAPTER FOUR

I DIDN'T RECOGNIZE THE AREA code on the number that showed up on my phone, and I answered it hopefully, thinking Luke might have gotten a chance to call me. But although the voice coming through the phone was familiar, it was not Luke.

"I hear congratulations are in order," Drake Langston said.

"Thank you, Drake," I managed.

"I saw on the news that your husband left for active duty immediately after the wedding. That really stinks."

"I couldn't agree with you more," I assured him.

"I wish I could do something to help your husband get home sooner."

"I wish you could too."

"Unfortunately, I have no power over the military," he said. "And I'm sorry to disturb you on what I know has been a difficult day already, but I need your help."

I was astonished that the great Drake Langston needed help from anyone, let alone me. "You need *my* help?"

He chuckled, acknowledging the ridiculousness of this, but in a friendly way. "We finished our latest renovation project a couple of weeks early—which isn't enough time to do a full-blown town makeover, but we decided to squeeze a mini-renovation into our schedule. So we're coming back to Midway."

I was extremely surprised by this. "I thought we'd missed our chance at modernization."

"Good fortune has truly shined on Midway," he replied. "It is against my personal policy to go back to a town that . . . uninvited us.

But because of the circumstances, I felt this would be a good time to break my own rule."

The most eloquent response I could come up with was, "Wow."

"My renovation team will be arriving in Midway tomorrow. I've already talked to the new mayor and the preacher at the Baptist church. We've even arranged with your boss, Mr. Sheffield, to rent some storage units, and he's going to let us park our equipment at the Midway Store and Save. And since your husband has been hijacked by the Marines, I thought you might be interested in helping my team, if the Midway library can do without you."

"The library is already planning to do without me since I'm supposed to be on my honeymoon," I told him. I was proud that my voice only trembled a little. "But if you have a whole team, why do you need my help?"

"I've learned that hiring a local person to work with my team is beneficial—especially with acquisitions. Someone familiar with the community can advise us about locations and traditions and personalities of the people involved. If we'd had help from a local the first time we were in Midway, we would never have planned a housing development that required Foster Scoggins to sell his land."

I couldn't argue with that. "True. But if you're looking for someone who knows everything about Midway, you need my mother—not me."

He laughed. "You have access to your mother's knowledge. And as I recall, you talk to her regularly."

"That is certainly true," I muttered with a glance toward the living room.

"And you're the one with extra time on your hands."

I sighed. "I do have time, but no experience."

"My staff has plenty of experience. What they don't have is your knowledge of the community. You'll be helping to smooth the way so my well-qualified team can accomplish their assignments in Midway," Drake continued. "And 'smooth' is especially important since this time we're in a big hurry."

"Will you still do everything you started before?"

"No, we've scaled back our plans a little to fit the time frame. We'll finish up the sidewalks and general overhaul of downtown

Midway. We'll build a family center for the Baptist church like I promised. I still think new housing will bring in fresh residents who can do a lot for Midway, but I want to avoid the whole issue with the salvage yard. So we'll build just one subdivision, and it will be on south end of town. The bulk of the land we need is owned by Erskine Hodges, and he's already agreed to sell. There are just a few other small landowners that we need to approach."

"And what if they don't want to sell?" I asked.

"Since my last visit to Midway, I've incorporated backup plans— so if someone doesn't want to sell, it doesn't ruin the whole deal."

"That's wise." I was pleased that Midway had effected a positive change in the way Drake did business and tried not to think about the price Foster Scoggins had paid for this progress.

Drake continued. "The acquisition phase is the best part. You get to meet with the people from whom we want to purchase land and present them with our offer."

"And convince them to sell their homes?"

"Our offers pretty much eliminate the need for convincing," he replied. "I've learned that if I make a strong, almost irresistible offer from the first, I save a lot of time and headaches and even money in the long run. You can read over the specifics yourself, but in a nutshell we offer them a house in one of our new subdivisions to replace the one they are selling to us, at cost. Then we give them fifty percent above market value for their house and property. So they'll have a nice new house and money with which to send their kids to college or travel or whatever they've always dreamed of but couldn't afford."

"That is an amazingly good deal," I murmured.

"Don't you think delivering all that good news sounds fun?"

"It does sound fun," I admitted.

"Rand Roebuck is the legal expert for my team, and he handles acquisitions. He is a genius at planning new communities and drawing up the paperwork. But he has an acerbic personality that doesn't always work well with potential sellers. And I want to be particularly careful with the Midway residents after what happened last time." He paused briefly and cleared his throat. "Anyway, what I really need is a pretty face with lots of Southern charm to go around with Rand while he makes purchase proposals."

Ordinarily I would object to being referred to as a "pretty face," but Drake is extremely handsome, so I always cut him a little slack. "I'm not sure that I qualify on either of those requirements."

He chuckled softly. "I think you have plenty of both beauty and charm."

I would have demurred further, but good manners would have forced him to keep insisting. "I remember how excited most everyone was last time, so I doubt you'll have a problem finding willing sellers. My only concern is the people on the north side of town who thought they were going to make lots of money and didn't because of Foster. They might feel cheated if you come back and buy other property instead."

"To avoid that we are reinstating the original offers made to the people north of town as well. If they want to sell, we will buy their land."

"What will you do with all that land?"

"I won't lose money on it," he assured me. "Some of it we'll just deed back to the county and receive a nice tax write-off for it. Some of it we'll hold on to. Once the area builds up a little, the land will appreciate and we'll be able to sell it at a profit."

"Well, it seems like you've thought of everything."

"I've tried," he assured me. Then he quoted me a "consulting fee" of a thousand dollars.

I'm not a greedy person, but I'll admit that the money was attractive. Luke and I were about to plunge ourselves into educational poverty, so a nest egg would be comforting. And I certainly had some time on my hands.

I was already convinced when Drake added, "And I've saved the best selling point for last."

I wondered what could be better than earning lots of money by making people's dreams come true.

"Most women find my project manager irresistible," Drake enticed me.

"Who is the project manager?"

"Your hero, Sloan," he said.

Sloan had saved my life—twice—so I guess he could be considered a hero, if an unconventional one. "Sloan will be my boss, huh?"

"Is that a yes?" Drake pressed.

"I guess it's a yes, unless my husband objects."

"What could he possibly object to?" Drake asked reasonably.

"Probably nothing," I admitted, "but I need to check with him anyway."

"Well unless you call and tell me otherwise, I'm going to consider you hired."

"Unless you come to your senses and decide to hire someone with actual experience."

Drake laughed. "You'll be great."

"I'll do my best, anyway," I said. I tried not to worry about my lack of, well, every possible qualification.

"Sloan just left Atlanta and he's meeting the rest of the team in Midway tonight. I've reserved a block of rooms at the same hotel we stayed in before right outside the city limits. There will be daily team meetings in the conference room there that you will need to attend. The first one is tomorrow at 7:00 a.m."

"This is moving very fast." The change from deserted bride to Drake Langston employee was sudden and a little startling.

"When you only have two weeks, every minute counts," he pointed out.

I'd been attending church with the Mormons—which my mother considered just marginally better than not attending at all—to help my sister, Madison, with her passel of horrible children. So I said, "Will the meeting be over in time for church? I'm not a religious zealot or anything, but if I don't go we'll both be in trouble with my mother."

"I don't want that," Drake assured me. "If the meeting goes on too long, feel free to leave so you can get to church on time."

"Then I'll be there," I agreed.

"You're welcome to use one of the rooms at the hotel," Drake offered. "That way you'd be with the rest of the team."

"Thanks, but I'll just stay here."

"Suit yourself," he said. "The mayor insisted on having a little ceremony at two tomorrow afternoon to welcome us back to Midway. He's invited the local press, and we can't miss an opportunity for good publicity. I want the entire team to be there for that. Then you and Rand will start making acquisition visits. Since there are just a few, by tomorrow night we should have all the sellers under contract. After we take care of the legal paperwork first thing on Monday, construction can begin."

It was a little mind boggling but exciting. "And then I'll be finished?"

"Well, the acquisitions phase will be finished, but I'd like you to be on call in case the team needs your advice or assistance in another area. Will you continue coming to the team meetings until the project is finished or your husband returns—whichever comes first?"

"I will."

After saying good-bye to Drake, I sat for a few minutes, holding the phone. In spite of my separation from Luke, I found myself almost looking forward to the next week. I needed something that was consuming and satisfying to keep me from going crazy. And it seemed that Drake had provided the perfect solution.

I sent Luke a quick text telling him about Drake's offer. I didn't expect an immediate reply, but my phone rang just a few seconds later.

Luke's voice traveled the many miles that separated us. "Hey, Kennedy." The connection was so good that he could have been in the next room.

I wanted to I laugh. I wanted to cry. I was afraid my heart would pound out of my chest. "Hey, yourself!" I told him breathlessly. "Did you have a nice flight?"

"Not really," he replied. "But it's over."

"So what now?" I asked.

"I'm headed to my quarters, where I'll be sequestered until Monday, which is when I'll start testifying to the military equivalent of a grand jury."

"Where is Lt. Dempsey?"

"Oh, he's right here too," Luke replied. "He'll be my roommate throughout this process. It's his job to make sure my testimony is untainted by the media or my fellow Marines or even you. I can't watch television or listen to the radio, and all my phone calls and texts will be monitored."

This new invasion of our privacy was infuriating, but before I could start a well-deserved rant against the Marine Corps, Luke told me how much he loved me and how thankful he was for my bravery.

I didn't feel very brave at the moment, but I couldn't disappoint him. So I pretended like I was being a real trooper.

"How was your afternoon without me?" he asked.

"Eventful." I told him about the wreck we saw on the way home from the airport and our collection of Crock-Pots. "But don't worry about where we'll store all the Crock-Pots in our tiny apartment. Mother said she can return the extras for cold, hard cash."

He laughed. "That's a relief. Now tell me about this job with Drake Langston."

I gave him the basic details, including that Sloan would be the project manager.

When I finished, he said, "I can't say I'm thrilled about the idea of you getting involved again with Drake Langston."

"I won't have much involvement with him," I said. "I'll be working mostly with the team lawyer buying property from ecstatic residents. I'm coming home every night and sleeping in my lonely apartment—waiting for you to return and take me away from the drudgery of Midway."

"Midway and its drudgery sound pretty good to me right now." He did sound a little wistful.

I was determined not to cry, so I said, "I'm going to ask Miss Ida Jean's son Robby to help me arrange a visit with your father."

"Thanks. I really appreciate that."

"When can you call again?"

"I don't know," he replied. "Before when I was a Marine, I wasn't sequestered or married."

I sighed. "I wish fate had brought us together sooner so that during all those days in Iraq you would have had me to love and call and dream about."

"Oh, I loved you and dreamed about you," he assured me. "I just never thought we'd actually be together. Sometimes I still can't really believe it."

"Well, you'd better believe it, soldier. And you'd better get back soon so we can go on our Florida honeymoon."

"No one is more anxious for that than me. But Lt. Dempsey and I have been talking about our honeymoon, and we think you deserve an upgrade."

This was unexpected. "To what?"

"How do you feel about Hawaii?"

"I feel really great about it, but can we afford it?"

"Well, with the money you're making working for Drake Langston and my active duty pay . . ."

"And the money Mother will get for returning all our Crock-Pots," I added, just to make him laugh. Which he did.

"No, we can't forget those Crock-Pots. So since we have extra money, we could cash in our plane tickets to Ft. Lauderdale and fly to Hawaii instead. We've checked out a few airlines, and with my military discount, it won't be much more."

I could barely breathe. "You're serious."

He laughed. "I am completely serious. I'll handle changing the plane tickets if you'll look online for a reasonable hotel."

"I'd love to!"

He laughed again. "I have to tell you, Kennedy, it's a lot more fun being here knowing you're waiting for me there."

I blinked back tears. "Well, it's *not* a lot of fun for me here knowing you're there—but I am waiting for you, and we're going to have a wonderful honeymoon when you get back."

"I'll hold you to that," he said with clear regret in his voice. "But for now I've got to go."

"Call me again soon."

"I will," he promised. "And you can text me whenever. I'll text or call back when I can."

"I love you."

"Me too." His voice was like a tender caress. "Remember, in a few days we'll be walking around on a tropical island."

"That thought just might pull me through."

After we ended our call, I opened my laptop and looked at hotels in Hawaii until my mother called for me to come eat some dinner. I didn't want to stop my search, but I also didn't want to upset my mother more than absolutely necessary. So I closed my laptop, gathered my courage, and went into the living room to give Mother the good news.

Mother was in the kitchen organizing leftover wedding food. She had already fixed a plate for me. I sat down at the table and ate a few bites while I told her about Drake's return to Midway, the job he had offered me, and how this was going to translate into a Hawaiian honeymoon. I expected her to be at least mildly enthusiastic—since the Baptist church was getting a family center.

But she was subdued during my announcement, and when I finished, she said, "I don't really want you involved with Drake Langston."

"I don't want to be 'involved' with him either," I retorted. "I do want to help him improve Midway and make some money for my honeymoon in the process. And I want to have something to think about besides how much I miss Luke." My voice quivered a little, and Mother reached out to pat my hand.

"I understand the reasons you want to take the job, but Mr. Langston brought a lot of misery here last time."

"Drake only tried to bring good things to Midway. It was greed that brought the misery. But he has new policies in place now to avoid problems with unwilling sellers. So when he leaves this time, everyone should be happy." Then I cleverly added, "Drake said Brother Jackson has approved the plans for the new family center at the church."

"I'm sure the preacher knows what he's doing," Mother murmured. "But if it were up to me, I'd forget about the family center and tell Mr. Langston to move on to another town."

I was surprised that she was holding a grudge. Forgiveness is a Christian requirement—as has been pointed out to me innumerable times. Therefore I turned the tables on her. "You can't hold the past against Drake. Jesus said so."

Mother nodded stiffly. "I'm required to forgive Mr. Langston, but that doesn't mean I have to trust him. Listen to your mother. Call him back and decline that job."

I was amused by her determination to thwart Drake. "I can't back out now. It would be rude. Besides, Luke is all excited about going on a Hawaiian honeymoon, so I've got to make extra money to pay for it." I glanced at my phone to check the time. "The rest of his team is already on the way here and our first meeting is in the morning. Then the mayor is having a little welcome ceremony for Drake in the afternoon. It's going to be televised so I've got to pick out what I'll wear since I know you'll want me to look my best."

She took the bait. "You should wear that lavender suit you got at Corrine's. Just make sure it's ironed."

"I swear!" I held up my hand as if I were about to testify in court. Mother didn't smile.

"So, are you and Daddy going to come to the ceremony?"

"I think we'll just watch it on television."

My mother considers attending town functions her civic duty—so her decision to stay home during the welcome ceremony was almost astonishing. And it indicated that my mother's resentment toward Drake Langston was deeper than I had previously thought.

"You didn't eat anything," she fussed while looking at my barely touched plate.

"I had a few bites," I corrected. "And I need to watch my figure since in a few days I'll be wearing a bathing suit in *Hawaii*."

"I have to admit that I'm disappointed that you're going to be so busy while Luke's gone," she said softly, her eyes downcast. "I was hoping we could spend this last bit of time together before you move to Atlanta."

I laughed. "Atlanta is only a few hours away. You can come and visit with me there whenever you want."

"What about your thank-you notes?" she pressed.

"They can wait until Drake's project is over and I'm back from my exotic honeymoon."

Mother is nothing if not persistent. "I've already asked Miss Ida Jean to come over tomorrow and help us."

I love my mother, but I knew I'd go insane if I sat around writing thank-you notes for Crock-Pots and dealing with Miss Ida Jean. So this comment only strengthened my determination to work for Drake.

"I'd love to spend some time with you, but I've given Drake my word. I'm thankful for the opportunity to make some extra money and be involved in something meaningful while Luke is gone." I bent down and gave her a quick kiss. "It will be fine, I promise."

My mother nodded, as if accepting my decision, and then immediately made another demand. "There's no reason for you to go home to a dark, empty apartment every night. You should stay here instead. I can have a hot meal ready for you and your laundry done every morning."

I know that refusing such a kind offer sounds ungrateful, but if I don't at least try to keep my mother at arm's length, she'll be all over me. And I suspected this was her way of monitoring me during my brief employment with Drake.

"Thanks, but I'll stay at my apartment," I said. "I still have some packing to do, and I don't want to disturb you and Daddy by leaving early every morning and coming home late at night."

Mother clasped her hands together in obvious anxiety. "Oh Kennedy, I can't stand the thought of you out late at night, working with strangers who aren't even trustworthy! I wish you would reconsider."

"I've made up my mind, but you don't have to worry. I'll keep Daddy's gun with me at all times!"

"I guess that was supposed to make me feel better?" She sighed in resignation and added, "At least let me send some of this wedding food with you. Daddy and I could never eat all of it."

I waited with dwindling patience while she filled disposable containers with leftovers from the reception. Then she packed them neatly in a cardboard box. As she handed it to me, she said, "I'll call you tomorrow!"

This was a completely unnecessary announcement since we both knew she'd call me several times before the next evening. But to be kind I didn't point this out.

"I won't take time to stop by the garage, so will you tell Daddy good-bye for me?"

She nodded and I walked outside. I was so lost in thought that I didn't notice Robby Baxley standing beside my truck until I almost ran into him. I never thought I'd consider seeing him a good thing, but that night, I did.

"Hey, Robby."

He looked down, bashful. "Mama said you wanted to talk to me."

I didn't want him to get any false hope that I might be interested in him (picture me shuddering here) so I said, "I need some information about visiting the prison."

"Oh yeah! I can tell you anything you want to know about the prison." Not something most people would brag about, but then Robby wasn't most people.

"Now that I'm married to Luke," I began, figuring it wouldn't hurt to remind him of that fact since he'd missed the wedding, "I thought I would visit his father. He usually goes on Wednesdays, so I was wondering if I can just show up or if I have to make an appointment or something."

"To see an inmate you have to call and get on the visitor list a week in advance so they can check you out and make sure you're not a criminal or anything," he said.

As much as I didn't want to talk to Parnell Scoggins, especially in prison, I really did want to keep my promise to Luke. So this week-in-advance requirement was disappointing.

"But I'm friends with the warden," Robby was continuing, "so I could probably get them to make an exception in your case. They might not have to do a background check and all that—since I can put in a good word for you."

Now I was more than just happy to see Robby—I was actually happy to *know* him. "That would be great."

"I'll check with the warden and then I could call you, if you want to give me your cell number."

I wasn't *that* happy to know him. So I said, "I'm going to be in some important meetings over the next few days, and I can't have my phone going off in them middle of them. So I'll call you."

He looked a little disappointed but nodded.

I put his number in my phone. Then I opened the door to my truck.

"Mother said you sent all that food from your wedding home for me." He blushed. "Thanks."

I smiled, wishing—not for the first time—that I could strangle Miss Ida Jean. "You're welcome. See you later." I situated the food inside the truck and climbed under the wheel. As I backed down my parents' driveway, I was fully aware that Robby was watching my departure. I guess I should have felt bad about using his crush on me to my advantage, but I didn't. I figured it served him right for pining after a married woman.

CHAPTER FIVE

I HAD DRIVEN LESS THAN a mile before my phone rang. I hoped it was Luke but guessed it would be my mother. It was Sloan.

"Where are you?" he demanded. "I'm at your place, but you're not."

I groaned. "Don't tell me you climbed in through my bedroom window again."

"Okay, I won't tell you."

I didn't find this the least bit funny. "Don't be surprised if one day you climb into the wrong window and get shot!"

He laughed at my concern. "I'm like Superman—faster than any speeding bullet—so you don't need to worry about that."

I tried not to let him charm me out of my reasonable annoyance. "How could you be here already? Drake said you were just leaving Atlanta!"

"Didn't I just mention my superhuman speed?" he teased. "And Drake may have been a little off on my departure time. Now, we've thoroughly discussed my whereabouts. Let's talk about yours."

"I'm just pulling up," I told him as I passed through the entrance to the Midway Store and Save. I saw a sleek, black Ford F-250 truck parked in my normal spot. Suspicious that this was not an accident, I parked beside him. The lights were on inside my apartment, and I could hear the television. Apparently Sloan had made himself right at home.

My phone rang again. This time it *was* my mother. I assured her that I had traversed the half mile between her house and my apartment safely. Then I climbed the wooden stairs that led up to my front door. Sloan opened it for me.

I was prepared to give him a piece of my mind about driving too fast and the dangers of breaking and entering, but honestly the man is so beautiful that when I saw him, I couldn't be mad. His glossy black hair was parted in the middle and tucked behind his ears. It just brushed the collar of his blue polo shirt, which had "Langston Association" embroidered tastefully above the pocket. With white teeth, sensual lips, and startlingly blue eyes—he was gorgeous in a dangerous sort of way.

"Welcome," he said with one of his smart-aleck smiles.

"Thanks." I smirked and walked into my own apartment.

He gave me a long, careful once-over and then nodded. "You're looking good."

I fixed him with my sternest glare. "That is a lie. My dress is wrinkled, my mascara is smeared, and my hair is sticky from too much hairspray."

"And you still look good!"

"Do I need to remind you that I am a married woman?" I held my hand up so he could see the ring on my finger as proof. "Even if my husband has been hijacked by the Marines?"

"I'm sorry," Sloan said with a smile that didn't look apologetic, "about your married status *and* your missing husband."

I frowned. "Thank you, I guess."

He took the box from me. "I hope this is food. I'm starving, and your cupboards are more than bare. You don't even have Diet Pepsis!"

"I wasn't planning to be here right now so I didn't get groceries," I said. "But you know my mother won't let me go hungry."

"I love her!" Then he put the box on the kitchen table and started unloading it. "Your television gives new meaning to "high definition" because it has *no* definition! And you don't have cable."

I tucked a clump of sticky hair behind my ear. "I was aware of that."

"Which means I've been sitting here without anything decent to watch *or* eat."

Although it made no sense, thanks to my mother I felt like a bad hostess. But I wasn't going to admit that to Sloan. "Then think twice the next time you decide to break into my apartment."

He flashed me a smile as he unloaded finger sandwiches and a huge chunk of wedding cake. "Things are definitely looking up here—food-wise anyway. We can eat before we head to the hotel."

I plucked a chocolate-covered strawberry from the container he was holding. "I'm not staying at the hotel. That would be ridiculous since I live in Midway."

Sloan shrugged. "Sometimes unexpected things come up and we need to have impromptu meetings—so it's nice for the whole team to be together. And Drake has already rented you a room."

"Well he can un-rent it," I replied. "I'm only a few minutes away. If you decide to have a meeting, just call me. You're not the only one who can get places fast, Superman."

Sloan didn't smile at the joke. "Drake told me to pick you up and bring you to the hotel."

"Well, that was presumptuous of Drake," I said. "He should have asked me *before* he gave you that instruction."

Sloan's expression turned smug. "Your husband doesn't want you to stay at the hotel, right?"

"Luke doesn't know anything about the hotel, but he probably would prefer for me to stay here. And I'm more comfortable here anyway."

Sloan looked around in disbelief. "That's not possible."

"Besides, my mother is already unhappy about this little short-term job. If I told her it included a stay in a hotel, she'd die."

Strangely, this seemed to be my strongest argument. Sloan said, "So you're not coming to the hotel tonight—even just to meet everyone?"

"No. I'll meet everyone at the team breakfast meeting in the morning." I pointed to the containers full of food. "Eat as much as you want before you go or take it with you."

Sloan shook his head. "If you're staying here tonight, then I am too. We'll drive to the meeting together tomorrow."

I laughed. "I think I can safely say that both Luke *and* my mother would like that arrangement even less than me staying in the hotel!"

"If you come alone, you might have a wreck on the way. Since I'm the project manager Drake would hold me responsible. So I have to stay here. But if your husband doesn't trust you, I'll sleep in my truck."

"Now you're just being ridiculous. Of course Luke trusts me." Luke trusting *Sloan,* of course, was another matter. But I didn't say that. "And I won't have a wreck on the way to the hotel. But if I do—it wouldn't be your fault."

"I've been assigned to keep an eye on you," Sloan said. "So wherever you are—I have to be there too." He frowned at the TV. "Even if that means no ESPN."

I felt a combination of annoyance and appreciation. "That's very nice of Drake, if completely unnecessary."

"I'm just following orders."

I sighed. "Well, obviously I can't let you sleep outside."

"I could sleep on that couch downstairs," Sloan proposed. "It will be like old times."

This was a socially acceptable arrangement—just barely. So I said, "You can stay in Mr. Sheffield's office tonight since for some reason you think I'm incapable of making it from here to the edge of town alive without your help. But after tonight, you're staying at the hotel. I'll speak to Drake myself if you want me to."

Sloan smiled. "Nah, I'll tell him you are refusing overprotection. Now, do I have to go downstairs immediately or can I watch your terrible television and eat your wedding food until bedtime?"

I waved at my old couch. "I'm tired but I'll give you thirty minutes."

He sat down on one end and I took the other. While he ate we talked about Luke and the wedding and him being reclaimed by the Marines. When I finished my voice was quavering and Sloan shook his head.

"You have worse luck than I do."

"Not a distinction I treasure," I murmured.

He grinned.

After a few minutes of companionable silence, I asked how life had been now that he wasn't with the FBI anymore.

"Working for Drake is great," he replied. "And not working for him *and* the FBI at the same time is much less complicated."

"But you miss the FBI?" I guessed.

He shrugged. "A little sometimes—especially when I'm trying to pick up ladies. There is something about being an 'agent' that drives them crazy."

I shook my head in mock disgust. "I'm not sure it's possible to 'pick up' *ladies*—even if you're a secret agent."

He laughed. "Now you're just being petty."

"Let's talk about the Return to Midway Project instead of your love life," I suggested.

"That's a good idea since I haven't had much of a love life lately," he said. "I'm glad to have you onboard with the revisited Midway renovation."

"You don't seem that excited about it."

"I'm just confused. We rarely have projects that don't work out, but when we do—we never go back."

"Drake said this was a first," I acknowledged.

Sloan frowned as he continued. "We have this two-week gap that we could use as much-needed downtime or to iron out details for future renovations. Instead we're running ourselves ragged to help people who kicked us out." He raised his shoulders and spread his hands. "It doesn't make sense."

"Unless Drake just doesn't like unfinished business," I proposed. "Or downtime."

Sloan sighed. "He probably doesn't like either one. And don't get me wrong—I'm not complaining. Drake pays me the same amount no matter what town we're working on. But on this one we don't have any room for complications."

"Like a murder?"

He frowned. "We don't have time for a flat tire, let alone a murder. From my standpoint, getting everything on Drake's agenda renovated or built in two weeks will be a nightmare. But I don't expect any problems from your area—acquisitions—since we already know that all the landowners are willing to sell."

Before he could reply, there was a knock at the door that startled me into dropping my plate of half-eaten wedding food right onto the apartment's ugly brown carpet. Guests are rarely able to sneak up on me. Walls without insulation and the creaky wooden stairs combined to make a perfect—if primitive—early-warning system.

But while Sloan and I sat eating wedding food and discussing the new Midway project, someone had made it all the way to my door without us noticing. I could think of several good excuses. The old window air conditioner was blowing for all it was worth, the television was on, and I was distracted by Sloan. Still, it was unnerving.

Another knock jolted me out of my disturbed musings. I picked my plate up off the floor and called out, "Who is it?"

"It's me," my ex-husband growled. Then, as if he had the right to ask, he demanded, "Whose truck is parked out here? Have you got somebody in there with you?"

Sloan shook his head and moved stealthily to the door that led down to Mr. Sheffield's office below my apartment. He opened the door and paused long enough to put a finger to his lips.

I nodded.

Then he slipped through the door and pulled it closed, hiding.

I didn't have time to figure out why Sloan wanted to keep his presence a secret, because Cade was pounding on my front door again. Then he hollered, "Kennedy! Are you okay?"

"For heaven sakes!" I cried as I yanked the door open. "Of course I'm okay!"

Cade frowned as he stepped inside, completely uninvited. His red face and singed eyebrows reminded me of the wreck, and I was prepared to feel sorry for him until he demanded, "Who's in here? I heard a man's voice!"

I gestured toward the ancient television. "I'm watching the news."

He still looked suspicious. "And the black truck?"

Ever since that drive-in incident I haven't felt obligated to be completely honest with Cade. "It belongs to Drake Langston. Mr. Sheffield is renting him space here for his equipment." This was true if not the whole truth.

"So you heard that Langston is coming back to Midway?"

I nodded again.

Cade muttered under his breath, "The sheriff just told me—like this day wasn't bad enough already." He stood there deep in thought for a few seconds. Then his eyes turned to the two plates of food on my rickety coffee table. "If you're alone, why are there two plates here?"

I laughed and sat back on the couch. "I couldn't get all I wanted on one plate." I pointed into the tiny kitchen. "Mother sent tons of leftovers. Fix yourself a couple of plates and join me."

Cade tried to stay focused on his suspicions, but the lure of my mother's cooking proved too much. He went into the kitchen and forgot about the extra plate, the man's voice, and the strange truck parked below. He returned a few minutes later with a plate of his own piled high with reception food.

Once he was settled on the other end of the couch, he fished a few pictures out of his uniform pocket and passed them over to me. They were from the wedding, and when I saw Luke's handsome face, my lips trembled. I clamped them firmly closed to keep from sobbing out loud.

Cade saw my unshed tears. "I didn't mean to make you cry! I thought you'd be glad to have the pictures."

"I am not crying," I assured him. "And I do appreciate the pictures."

He took a big bite of a cream puff, still watching me warily. "I won't pretend that I like Scoggins, but it was a shame that he had to leave right after the wedding. Time goes by fast, though. He'll be back before you know it."

Our separation had already seemed forever, so I knew the time would not pass quickly for me. But I knew Cade was trying to help, and he had brought me pictures from the wedding, so I didn't argue.

Cade leaned back on the couch. "And since you've got some extra time on your hands while he's gone, I have a little favor I'd like you to do for me."

Now it was my turn to be wary. With limited enthusiasm I asked, "What kind of favor?"

"That wreck this afternoon has really been bothering me."

"Me too," I said. "You could have been killed."

"I've been hearing that all evening from Hannah-Leigh. Don't you start in on me too."

I decided to let his new wife handle everything about Cade, including his disregard for personal safety. "Is it because the Albany police chief was so rude to you?"

"Nah, I'm used to that kind of stuff. All the city cops think they're better than us country boys."

"Because you couldn't save the victim?" I guessed again.

He shook his head. "The paramedics convinced me I'd done everything I could have to save her."

There was only one other possibility. "You're bothered because two prisoners escaped?"

"That does bother me," he acknowledged, "but it's not why I'm here."

I was out of guesses. "I give up. Why are you here?"

"Because I'm not sure the wreck was an accident. Maybe I've been hanging around you and Miss Eugenia too much lately, but it felt a little suspicious to me."

Cade is not known for overthinking things. Ever.

"How?"

"The only witness was that guy driving in the truck behind the victim. He said all of a sudden she accelerated and ran into the Correction Department's van. The impact forced her off the road and into that line of oak trees. And she must have had a full tank of gas because her car burned fast and hot."

I shuddered at the memory. "And you think it wasn't an accident because . . . ?"

Cade leaned forward and said softly, "The missing prisoners."

His point became clear, and suddenly his suspicions seemed justified. "You think the victim *purposely* caused the wreck so the prisoners could escape?"

He nodded. "I'm sure she didn't mean to die. It was her bad luck that the spot she picked for the wreck was the only place on Highway 17 where you could run off the road and hit a line of oak trees."

"I guess it could be just a series of coincidences," I murmured cautiously. "But it should definitely be investigated."

"Now that's a problem," he said. "Since the victim died inside Albany city limits, they have jurisdiction. Sheriff Bonham says they've ruled it an accident."

"You need to tell the police chief your suspicions so they can un-rule it an accident."

Cade winced. "I can't do that without any evidence. If I'm wrong, I'd look like an idiot."

I thought, *It wouldn't be the first time.*

"So that's my favor."

I didn't remember him asking for one. "What?"

"I need a connection between the victim and the prisoners who escaped before I approach the police chief in Albany. Can you check for one?"

I was truly astonished, which doesn't happen often. "Me? You want *me* to investigate a possible crime?"

He had the decency to look sheepish. "Well, you've had some success lately, solving cases people didn't think existed."

I stood and put my hands on my hips. "And, if you'll recall, you tried hard to talk me out of investigating both of those cases!"

He waved for me to sit back down. "I know, I know! And I still don't like you being involved in police work. But what I'm asking you to do is just Internet research and maybe a few phone calls. Nothing dangerous like talking to criminals or sneaking around crime scenes."

Normally I look for any opportunity to tell Cade no, but I found myself mildly intrigued—both by the possibility that a crime had been committed and by his willingness to ask me for help.

So I settled back on the couch and nodded. "I guess I can check it out for you."

"I'd really appreciate it," Cade said.

"I'll need everything you've got on the victim and the missing prisoners."

He pulled several folded sheets of paper from his pocket. "All I have is the accident report, but it lists everyone by name. The victim's name was Nola Finkle. I printed off her DMV record."

I scanned the information quickly. "This is enough to start. I'll see what I can do."

Like most people in my life, Cade always demands more. "We can't wait too long. So do you think you can research it by tomorrow morning?"

This was ridiculous, of course, but then many things associated with Cade are. "I'll try."

With his hand on my doorknob, he said, "If this turns into a real case, I can bill the county for your time, but if not, I may not be able to pay you."

I waved this aside. Thanks to Drake Langston and my new short-term job, I could afford to be generous. "If it doesn't become a case, I won't charge you."

Cade seemed pleased by my response. "Great. Well, okay. Thanks."

"You're welcome."

"I'd better get home. Hannah-Leigh will be wondering where I am. But call me. Tomorrow."

"I will."

He walked down the stairs, and I saw him look hard at Sloan's truck as he passed it. Then I closed and locked the door. Sloan was standing behind me when I turned around.

"Well, you're getting job offers right and left," he said.

"Cade was asking for a favor, not offering a job."

Sloan reclaimed his plate from the coffee table. "I'm surprised you agreed to do it."

"Me too," I acknowledged. "And I don't plan to give him a lot of time. I'll do some Internet research and see what I can find out about the victim and the missing prisoners." I opened my laptop and spread the accident report out on the coffee table. "I want to be through with this favor for Cade when I start work for Drake tomorrow."

Sloan cleared the plates off the coffee table and then sat back beside me on the couch. "I'll help."

I raised my eyebrows. "You're going to help me? And, more importantly, *Cade*?" My ex-husband had made a bad first impression on Sloan when Drake's team came to Midway the first time.

He shrugged. "I can't stand watching another minute of your poor excuse for a television. I'd probably help the devil himself just to avoid it."

Smiling, I turned my laptop to face him. He scanned the accident report and then started typing on the keyboard. Soon Sloan was gliding through secure servers and private databases with terrifying ease.

"You can access all that?" I asked.

"My previous experience as a government agent has more benefits than just picking up girls," he murmured as the screen filled with data about Nola Finkle. "The victim lived in Templeton, a little town about forty miles south of Atlanta."

I looked at Sloan. "Isn't Atlanta *your* hometown too?"

He lifted one of his well-muscled shoulders. "I have a condo in Atlanta, but there's no place I really think of as home."

I frowned. "Not even your parents' house?"

His fingers continued to work as he replied, "They divorced when I was a kid. I feel welcome when I visit them, but not at home."

The old Killingsworth farmhouse where my parents live might be in constant need of repair (and is unfortunately situated right beside Miss Ida Jean), but from my earliest memories it was home to me. It was my beginning, my base, a refuge if there was nowhere else to go. It bothered me that no such place existed for Sloan.

"Everyone needs to have a home," I told him. "It's like an unwritten law."

"Then we'll call the office downstairs my home."

"I'm serious," I said. "If you don't have one already, you need to establish a home of your own. You should get married."

He laughed. "I don't have time for a goldfish—let alone a wife. And I don't even believe in marriage."

"What's not to believe? Two people meet, fall in love, and naturally want to spend the rest of their lives together."

"In my experience, love is never that permanent."

I hadn't seen this cynical side of him. "Love can last forever."

"I have my doubts, but maybe you and your Marine can prove that to me." His tone expressed no confidence. "Now that's enough talk about me. Let's concentrate on invading Nola Finkle's privacy."

I smirked at him and then turned to read from the computer screen. "She was forty-four years old when she died, never married, no kids."

"But she had a lot of cats," he said as a legal document filled the screen. "Twenty-seven at the time this complaint was filed by her neighbors." He looked over at me. "Twenty-seven *cats*! In one house!"

I continued to read. "Nola was employed by a veterinary supply company in Atlanta, but for the last year or so she has worked from home. In the evenings she volunteered at the local animal shelter. Apparently she took home the feline overflow." I pointed at the screen. "And at the hearing she convinced the judge that she was a responsible pet owner, caring for each and every one of her cats, and the complaint was dismissed."

"You're saying it's normal to have twenty-seven cats?"

"Twenty-seven is an excessive number of cats by anyone's standards," I conceded. "But I admire someone who can't say no to an animal in need. Don't you?"

He shivered. "I hate cats."

"Can you find a picture of her?" I asked. "I'd like to see what she looked like before the accident."

Sloan located a photo from an article the local paper had run on the animal shelter. Nola Finkle looked very different than she had that afternoon after Cade had pulled her from the burning car. She was standing beside another woman, and they were both holding cats. Her hair formed a curly mane around her head, and her eyes looked kind. Now she was dead. I couldn't help but wonder what would become of her cats.

Sloan isolated the picture in the corner of the screen and continued checking other data. "The house is paid off, and she has over $50,000 in savings," he reported. "So she was financially fit."

"Can you find out who will get her house and money now that she's dead?"

"Way ahead of you," he claimed as his fingers flew across the keys. "Here we go. Her entire estate, after expenses are deducted, goes to the county animal shelter."

"Still taking care of those cats," I whispered.

"I guess so. But more importantly it means that no one benefits financially from her death." He scrolled through several pages of information and finally said, "I've run a cross-check on Nola and the two escaped prisoners. There is no connection that I can find."

"Maybe you missed something?"

He raised an eyebrow. "Remember, I'm a professional snoop with access to all kinds of databases—even some that aren't supposed to exist. If there was a connection, I would have found it."

I sighed. "If you'll pass me the laptop, I'll e-mail Cade and break the news that he doesn't have good instincts, after all."

Sloan pushed the laptop across the coffee table until it was situated in front of me. I composed an e-mail detailing all the reasons Sloan didn't think Nola had been involved in a plot to free the missing prisoners. Then I asked, "Can I attach some of these files you've pulled up?"

"All but the tax returns," he said. "Those could get both of us put in jail."

After I attached the legally obtained files, I sent the e-mail and leaned back against the couch. "Why don't you want Cade to know you're here?"

"I've been trained to distribute information on a need-to-know basis, and Burrell doesn't need to know anything about me, including where I am." He raised an eyebrow. "How about you? Why didn't you tell him you'd be working for Drake?"

"He doesn't *need to know* anything about me either," I returned. "And besides, I knew he'd try to talk me out of it." I gestured toward the laptop. "Thanks for helping me with that. It would have taken me hours to come up with half of the information you got in ten minutes."

He gave me a bone-melting smile. "I gave you information that you could never have gotten no matter how many hours you searched."

I narrowed my eyes at him. "I said thank you. I shared my leftover wedding food with you. And I let you watch my antique television."

"I couldn't ask for anything more," he teased. "Except maybe the chance to sleep on that lumpy couch in my new home downstairs."

He is exasperating, but I couldn't be mad at him. "It was your choice to stay here. There's a nice hotel bed waiting for you outside town."

He didn't argue. "True."

Then a knock at the door startled us both. I frowned. For the second time in one night I'd had a guest arrive undetected. Sloan stood and crept to the stairs that led to Mr. Sheffield's office. Once he was concealed, I moved toward the door.

I thought it might be Cade, coming back to ask more questions. I wouldn't have been astonished if Drake had driven over just to make sure I was safe and sound, since he had appointed himself my guardian angel.

But when I opened my door, I was astonished to see Hannah-Leigh Coley-Smith Burrell standing on my tiny porch.

CHAPTER SIX

"Hey," Cade's new wife greeted me awkwardly.

"Hey," I replied in kind.

"Can I come in for a minute?"

I really didn't want to let her in. My apartment isn't great under the best of circumstances. In the middle of the packing-up process with boxes everywhere, it was, well, even less great than usual. And Hannah-Leigh is kind of woman that makes you feel fat and unattractive no matter how well-groomed and thin you are. And after a long day in the hot sun, I was far from my best as well.

But good manners required that I let her in. So I pulled the door open wider.

She stepped inside gingerly, as if afraid that my old, brown carpet would damage her expensive shoes. Then her eyes toured the room. "So, this is where you live?"

"Only for another week," I confirmed. "We're moving to Atlanta for school. And as soon as the Marines are through with my husband, we're going to Hawaii for our honeymoon." It was a prideful comment, and I knew I shouldn't have said it. And as usual, I got what I deserved.

"Oh, I love Hawaii," Hannah-Leigh enthused, not the least bit impressed by my upcoming trip. "My parents own a condo on Maui, and we go there a couple of times a year. It's on a private beach away from all the tacky tourists."

I didn't divulge that Luke and I would be renting a hotel room on a public beach like the tacky tourists we were.

She gave the sagging ceiling a glance. "I'm glad you're moving. This place doesn't look very stable."

The apartment Luke and I had rented in Atlanta wasn't a huge improvement—since we were trying to minimize costs. But I refused to apologize for my living conditions in Midway or elsewhere—especially to Hannah-Leigh—so I asked, "Did you need something?"

She laughed nervously. "Can we sit down?"

I waved at my couch. "Have a seat."

Her smile faded slightly, but she sat down, right on the edge, presumably trying to limit the amount of her dress that had to come in contact with the fabric on the old couch.

She said, "I'm sorry to drop by without calling first."

"It's okay," I lied.

Then she amazed me by saying, "It's just that it seems a shame for us not to be friends. After all, we grew up in the same community and share a bond because of Cade."

I really didn't know how to respond to this so I murmured, "Um-hm."

She continued. "Since you used to be married to him and I'm married to him now, I should probably ask you for some marriage advice."

"Watch out for drive-ins."

She laughed as if this were hilarious. "You're such a kidder." Apparently Hannah-Leigh thought that Cade's public infidelity was the kind of thing that only happened to girls like me—not girls like her.

Honestly I was too tired to muster any righteous indignation toward Hannah-Leigh, so I decided to put her in the same category as Miss Ida Jean—someone whose comments are to be ignored. And I didn't want to be her friend. Not because of Cade—I just didn't like being around her. And this was a rare circumstance where even Southern etiquette didn't obligate me.

So I said, "That's a very nice offer, but I'm working with Drake Langston for the next week or so and then I'll be moving to Atlanta. You're busy with your television career and being a newlywed so, well, I just don't see us having the opportunity to hang out together."

She was obviously disappointed. "Oh, okay. I understand. You have your life to live. I won't impose."

If she was trying to make me feel guilty, it didn't work. "I'd offer you something to eat," I told her, "but all I have is wedding food."

She gave me a tight smile. "Thanks, but I'm not hungry."

It was rude to rush a guest off, but I was tired and had Hawaiian hotels to peruse on the Internet. "Is there anything else you wanted to talk about?"

She looked down at the floor. "Oh, no, I guess not. I just don't want it to be awkward between us."

I decided to set the record straight right there. "Look, Hannah-Leigh, if you think I'm jealous because you're married to Cade, I'm not. I'm very happy with my new life and wish you the best."

She pinned me with a piercing look. "But you don't think our marriage will be happy."

She had more than asked for it, so I told her the truth. "I have my doubts about Cade's ability to limit his affections to only one woman. But he seems to love you very much so maybe it will work out."

"Well, thank you for your honesty." She stood. "And your time!" she added with a forced laugh. "I'll get out of your way now."

I walked her to the door and followed her onto the porch. Just before she descended, she handed me a business card. "If you ever change your mind and want to chat, here's my number."

I took the card, although I figured pigs would fly before I ever called Hannah-Leigh. I gave her one of my fake-nice smiles and said, "Thanks."

Then she minced down the porch steps in her expensive shoes, climbed into her fancy sports car, and sped away, spraying gravel behind her. Once she was gone I went back inside and locked the door.

Sloan stepped out of the stairwell. "It seems like everyone in Midway is determined to visit you."

"It's been a busy night," I acknowledged. "Usually I don't attract so much attention."

"I wonder who will show up next," Sloan said as he helped me pack up the wedding food.

"It won't matter," I muttered, "because I'm not answering the door again."

He grinned.

But my words proved to be a lie. We did hear the next visitor's approach in plenty of time for Sloan to hide. And at least I liked Miss

Zelda Jackson, the Baptist preacher's wife. I parted the curtains and watched as she climbed out of her minivan and walked toward the stairs. Then I waited for her to knock before opening the door.

"What an unexpected and pleasant surprise!" I said to greet her.

Miss Zelda is small but strong, so the side-hug she gave me was substantial. Then she handed me a grocery sack. "Since you're staying here longer than you expected, I thought you could use some grocery staples."

I looked into the sack. It contained a six-pack of Diet Pepsi and a box of double-decker chocolate moon pies. I grinned at Miss Zelda. "This is what I call groceries!"

She smiled back. "So your husband made it to . . . wherever it was he had to go?"

"Yes," I replied. "And he's testifying at a trial—not *on* trial—if you could clarify that for the gossipers."

"I'll do my best," she promised. "And I hope to see you at church tomorrow."

"I'm going with Madison tomorrow," I told her.

"Well, it's an open invitation. We're glad to have you anytime."

"I know. And thanks again for the food."

"Just don't tell your mother," she teased as I walked her to the door. "She doesn't like you to eat junk food."

The minute Miss Zelda was gone, I heard the door to Mr. Sheffield's office open. I turned to see Sloan emerging from the stairwell.

He sauntered over to the window and peeked outside. "What did she bring you?"

"Pepsis."

"She's an angel!"

"She's a very nice lady," I agreed.

Sloan let the curtain fall back into place and turned to smile at me. "I'll take one of those Pepsis now and another one in the morning after it's had time to get cold."

I handed him a semi-cool Pepsi. "Go to bed," I told him. "I've got a Hawaiian honeymoon to plan."

He took the Pepsi. "I'll go. But we need to leave early in the morning. I can't stand being late. Is six thirty okay?"

"I'll be ready," I promised just as my phone rang. I checked the window, and my heart started to pound. "It's Luke!" I whispered. Then I answered the call. "Hello!"

Sloan gave me a little wave and descended the stairs toward the office below.

I moved into my bedroom and closed the door to give myself more privacy just in case Sloan was trying to listen.

"Hey," he replied. "It's me, your husband."

I laughed. "Hey. I thought you weren't going to be able to call again today."

Luke explained, "I've been a good boy, so Lt. Dempsey is rewarding me with a few minutes of extra phone time."

"I'm so glad you've been good!"

"It was worth it."

"What have you and Lt. Dempsey been doing since our last conversation?"

He sighed. "Well, we ate dinner at the mess hall—chicken a la king and pudding from a can."

"Sounds awful," I said.

"It was," he confirmed. "Then we watched a baseball game, but Lt. Dempsey muted the sound in case one of the commentators mentioned the trial."

"Was that likely?"

"No, but Lt. Dempsey is very thorough."

It was my turn to laugh.

"And during a commercial I bought two plane tickets leaving the Albany airport next Sunday. After a stop in Atlanta we'll be headed to Honolulu."

Things never work out perfectly for me (I'll use the fact that it was my wedding night and my husband was four states away as proof), so I tried to control my excitement. And it didn't take me long to think of a problem. "What if the trial isn't over by then?"

"We can change the date if we have to," he assured me. "But Lt. Dempsey believes they will be finished with me by then. Now, what's been going on there?"

I told him about Sloan's arrival and his determination to sleep in the office downstairs—which he was surprisingly okay with. "I didn't like the idea of you being there alone," he said. "And that Sloan guy seemed trustworthy, being an ex-FBI agent and all."

Then I told him about Cade's visit, his suspicions that the wreck had been a prison escape plan, and his request that I look for a connection between the victim and the escapees. "It wasn't a bad idea, but there was no apparent connection between the victim and the missing prisoners. As usual, Cade was wrong."

"I don't like you working for Drake Langston, but I *hate* the idea of you working for Cade."

"It was just a quick favor and it's done," I said. "I knew you wouldn't love it, but I couldn't very well let him present his case to the Albany police chief—who is already mad at him—without any evidence to back up his theory. He would have looked like an idiot."

"He *is* an idiot," Luke replied. "But I guess it's good that you kept him from embarrassing himself, again."

"You're mellowing," I told him proudly.

"It must be all this happiness in my life."

"I hope so," I said. "And then I had a visit from Cade's lovely new wife—Hannah-Leigh."

Luke groaned. "What did she want?"

"To be friends," I took extreme pleasure in telling him. "I declined."

He replied, "Poor girl is going to need friends now that she's married to Burrell. But she can get support somewhere else. You've done your time."

He always knew just the right thing to say. "And finally I had a visit from Miss Zelda. She brought me Pepsis and moon pies. And she invited me to church."

"What did you say?"

"That I'm going with Madison tomorrow." I knew he'd be pleased that I would be attending with the Mormons since he'd made up his mind to become one.

"I should have left you my sword," he muttered.

I laughed and told him how much I loved him.

"I love you too," he said, his voice caressing me. "And I sent the receipt for our plane tickets to your e-mail so you can print it off and admire it whenever you get lonely."

"Then I'll have to print a copy now and keep it with me constantly." I carried my laptop into the kitchen and hooked it up to the printer.

"What did you find out about Hawaiian hotels?"

I loaded paper into the printer and pressed the "print" button. "That the sheer number of available accommodations is daunting. I hardly know where to start. It would be cheaper to stay inland, which appeals to me from a thrift standpoint. But I wasn't sure how you felt. Would you prefer ocean-view even at twice the cost?"

"What's the point of going to Hawaii if you can't see the ocean?"

"I figured you wouldn't be able to take your eyes off me anyway."

"You're right," he responded. "I probably won't even notice the Pacific. But just in case I glance out our hotel window, I'd like to see water instead of buildings."

Smiling, I said, "Ocean-view it is."

"Well, Lt. Dempsey says it's time to hang up. I'll try to call you tomorrow."

"Okay. And tell the lieutenant I said thanks."

"I will."

I've always found phone good-byes awkward, and that feeling was amplified by Lt. Dempsey's constant presence. Luke guessed my concerns and allayed them. "We don't really have to express our feelings for each other. You know my heart and I know yours."

After our phone call ended, I picked up the plane reservation receipt and stared at it. I tried to imagine Luke with me on a tropical island. It was enough to take my breath away. I took my laptop back to my room and set it up on my bed. I put on my pajamas and then, sitting cross-legged with my back resting against the headboard, I narrowed my search of hotels to places with an ocean view. Unfortunately there were still an overwhelming number of these to consider. I surfed through a number of possibilities until I had five reasonable choices.

I knew I'd need all my strength the next day since I had my first meeting with Drake's team and then the wrestling match at church with Madison and her evil brood. So I turned off the computer and set my phone to wake me up early.

Once I was in bed, I stared at the ceiling in the apartment over the Midway Store and Save. Luke and I were spending our wedding night apart. Apparently two bad lucks do not cancel each other out. But I clutched my phone. He was only a text away. I took comfort in that technological connection.

And Sloan was sleeping on the couch in the office below. I smiled as I drifted off to sleep. I was alone but not completely abandoned.

* * *

When I woke up on Sunday, I texted Luke a little good morning message. By the time I got out of the shower, I had one from him. He and his constant companion, Lt. Dempsey, were headed to the mess hall for breakfast and then would return to their quarters to watch more silent sports.

I texted back—*I wonder what delicacy they have prepared for breakfast.*

He promised to let me know.

Then I put on the lavender suit my mother had recommended. I hoped I looked professional without seeming like I took myself too seriously (since I had absolutely no reason to). I slipped on some low-heeled, sensible shoes and had just walked into the kitchen when Sloan knocked on the door at the top of the office stairs. I called for him to come in, and he emerged from the stairwell.

Without regard for professional appearance he was dressed in jeans and a T-shirt, as usual. And, as usual, he looked gorgeous.

I waved at my ensemble. "Is this okay?"

He winked. "Perfect." Then he opened the refrigerator and surveyed the leftovers. He took a soggy chicken salad croissant from a plastic container, and I couldn't control a shudder as he pushed it into his mouth.

I chose a couple of chocolate-covered strawberries that were past their prime but still delicious. I washed them down with one of Miss Zelda's Pepsis.

Sloan took a couple of moon pies and then read on the side of the box. "Are these things considered real food?"

"All that matters is they taste good," I replied.

He shrugged and ate one pie in two bites. "Ready to go?" he asked while opening the second pie.

"I'm ready as I'll ever be." When I opened the front door, my phone beeped, indicating that I had a text message.

"From the hubby?" Sloan asked as we walked down the steps to the parking lot.

I nodded without taking my eyes off my phone. Luke had written—*Southwestern-style cream of wheat. Don't recommend it.*

I texted back—*I'd never eat any style of creamed wheat.*

Then I walked toward my truck with one eye on my phone in case Luke responded. I was distracted from my text-watching by the arrival of Mr. Sheffield in his Cadillac. At first I was perplexed by his presence. It wasn't time for me to give him the rent money, and I hadn't sent him a maintenance request. But he didn't approach me when he got out of his car. Instead he walked straight over to Sloan. After a vigorous handshake, he invited Sloan into the office.

"Now," Mr. Sheffield said as he unlocked the door. "Mr. Langston said you would need two storage units and places to park your equipment."

"We could also use some office space. Is this available?" He waved a hand to encompass the room he now called "home."

Mr. Sheffield removed the keys from his own ring and extended them to Sloan. "The office is yours while you and Mr. Langston are in Midway." This generous gesture almost certainly meant that Mr. Sheffield stood to benefit financially from Drake's presence.

"We appreciate your help," Sloan said. "And now if you'll excuse us, we've got a meeting to attend."

I was starting toward my truck when Sloan stopped me. "You're riding with me," he said. "Company rules."

"There's a Langston Association rule that says I have to ride with you?" I demanded.

He grinned. "I'm the project manager. I can make up rules whenever I want to."

"And I can quit whenever I don't like the rules," I reminded him. Then I climbed into his truck, and we headed toward the hotel outside town.

CHAPTER SEVEN

WHILE WE DROVE, I TEXTED Luke that I was riding with Sloan to the meeting.

He answered, *Just make sure Sloan drives safely.*

I glanced over at the speedometer that was hovering near 90 mph and replied, *No worries.*

The Hampton Inn on the outskirts of Midway was small and fairly new. I had passed it many times, but I'd never had a reason to go inside until now. Sloan parked near the door and led me to the entrance. When we passed through the lobby he paused to wave and wink at a young woman manning the registration desk. She blushed in response to his attention.

"One of those ladies you could impress if you were still a secret agent?" I asked.

He shook his head. "Nah, I've just found it's helpful to be on good terms with the hotel staff." We walked into a compact conference room near the elevators. Arranged on a small table against the wall was a nice continental breakfast buffet. At the larger conference table, three men and one woman were seated with laptops opened in front of them.

I recognized Morris Pugh, the architect who had drawn up the renovation plans for Midway's library. He was perfectly groomed, like a magazine model. We exchanged a brief nod. Then Sloan introduced me to the others. The designer for the project was a very thin young woman with severely straight, white-blonde hair. Her skin was porcelain pale and she was dressed from head to toe in shades of black. The look was odd but not unattractive. She introduced herself to me simply as Catsy. (I asked her to repeat that twice, thinking I'd misunderstood.) As she extended her hand in greeting, I noted that her fingernails were bitten to the quick. This very human frailty endeared her to me from the start.

"Nice to meet you." I clasped her hand for a quick but firm shake.

"I understand you'll be giving me some design advice," she said.

I was embarrassed and feared that Drake had built up unrealistic expectations about my abilities. "I wouldn't try to advise you," I amended. "I'm just a consultant—someone to smooth your way into the hearts of Midway residents."

"That's better than advice," she told me with a smile. "Welcome to the team."

Catsy's friendliness was reassuring. "Thank you."

Newell Hamm, who looked like he had been out of college for about a week, was the team's accountant. And he didn't make a good first impression. He was a little pudgy, had a receding hairline, and adult acne. Unlike Catsy, he believed in wearing colors, but unfortunately he didn't seem to be able to pick ones that actually went together. His teal shirt with an orange tie was jarring and the royal blue (and too tight) pants didn't help. But even if he'd been more attractive, I wouldn't have liked him. He was the kind of person who when given a little authority, lets it go to his head. After informing me that he was in charge of all the money for the project, he said, "I have a check for you." He slid an envelope across the table. "I'll need you to fill out the tax form so we can send you a 1098 at the end of the year."

I nodded and opened the envelope. The check inside, written on the Langston Association account, was notated as "consulting fee," and when I saw the amount, it momentarily took my breath away. One thousand dollars for just a few hours' work. Amazing.

"Accounts payable and receivable all go through me," Newell continued in his squeaky, semiadolescent voice. "I'll need receipts and a properly filled out acquisition form if you want an advance or a reimbursement. The feds scrutinize everything we do. We can't afford to be sloppy with paperwork."

I didn't imagine I'd need an advance or reimbursement, but I nodded anyway just to show him that I understood.

The final member of the team was the lawyer, Rand Roebuck. He appeared to be around thirty-five, which made him by far the oldest person in the room. Rand was neither neat nor sloppy, colorful nor drab, friendly nor offensive. His neutrality was a relief.

I turned to Sloan and asked, "Where's Drake?"

"He's not coming until tonight," Sloan replied.

This confused me. "He told me all team members had to be at the welcome ceremony this afternoon."

Sloan waved to encompass everyone in the room. "We are the team members. He's the boss."

"I guess I misunderstood."

Sloan leaned close and whispered, "You seem awfully disappointed that Drake's not here yet. Do I need to remind *you* about your recent change in marital status?"

I smirked. "I haven't forgotten that I'm married. I'm not disappointed by Drake absence, just surprised."

Sloan raised an eyebrow as he pulled out a chair for me. Once I was seated, he asked if I wanted any breakfast pastries, but I assured him the wedding leftovers we'd eaten a little while before were a sufficient breakfast for me.

He replied, "Well, I've got to have some coffee." He walked over to the breakfast table. "Can I get coffee for anyone else?"

Everyone murmured variations of no.

Sloan fixed himself a plate of food and a large mug of coffee. Once he was settled in the chair next to mine, the discussion began. Even though Sloan was the project manager, Rand did most of the talking. It seemed odd to me, but Sloan didn't seem to mind.

"First let me say that everyone's presence is required at the welcome ceremony this afternoon," Rand instructed. "Wear a Langston Association shirt and meet in front of the city hall at one forty-five."

So much for my tasteful suit. I should have worn jeans and a T-shirt like Sloan. "I don't have a Langston Association shirt," I told Rand.

He picked up a bag and handed it to me. "Now you have several. If they don't fit, let me know. We have them in all different sizes." Then, reassured that we all knew where to be and what to wear, he moved on to more serious business.

While passing out binders to each of us, he said, "Inside this you'll find sections outlining the various projects that are included in the overall renovation. We'll discuss them one at a time."

He paused until we all had the information opened in front of us. Then Rand referred to his notes. "First we have the city hall."

Morris said, "The city hall gets a face-lift—mostly cosmetic stuff, paint, flooring, furniture, a pressure wash for the old stone facade."

"We're also completing the sidewalk repairs that we started a few months ago," Sloan said. "So we might need a little help from the sheriff's department to block traffic while we have the cement truck there."

Rand made a note. "There's not much traffic—not by my definition, anyway. But I'll talk to the sheriff and arrange that."

"We're putting in some permanent planters along with the sidewalk to hold trees and flowers," Catsy said. "That's not a big deal but will require some coordination between me and Sloan's construction crew."

"I'll let you know when we're ready to pour concrete so you can get your planters in," Sloan promised.

"Neither of these projects requires any acquisition work," Rand concluded and moved on. "The family life center at the Baptist church will be a little more involved, but still we'll be working with a sound structure on property already owned. However, the senior center and housing developments can't be started until we acquire the land." He looked up at Sloan. "When are the construction crews arriving?"

"Tonight," Sloan replied.

Rand didn't seem exactly pleased. "I was hoping they could get here early. Then they would already have their equipment organized so work could begin immediately in the morning."

Sloan shrugged. "I had to round up nearly a hundred workers on short notice. I did the best I could."

Rand was still frowning when he said, "We should have the acquisition properties finalized by noon, so put everybody on the church building first thing. Once I give you the word that we legally own the other property, you can shift some of your personnel to cover the senior center and housing development."

Rand seemed a little bossy to me, especially since Sloan was in charge of the project, but Sloan was unperturbed.

"No problem," he agreed.

I flipped to the next section of my binder—which described the housing development. This time instead of selling finished houses, the Langston Association would just be selling lots. I assumed this was because of the time restraints of the project, but when I said this, Rand corrected me.

"We do have time constraints, no doubt, but this is actually one of Drake's newest policies. We get the subdivisions surveyed and underway. Then we leave the rest to a local contractor. That gets the headaches into someone else's lap sooner."

"And the profits," Newell pointed out. "The association is all about helping the community on several different levels. If we come in and do all the work with outsiders, we rob the area of jobs."

I was a little confused. "So when you leave Midway, it won't be finished?" I didn't add "yet again," but I was sure they all knew what I meant.

"We'll be finished with the renovations and improvements to downtown," Rand explained. "And the family center at the church. But the long-term things like the subdivision will still be works in progress."

"The subdivision will have an attractive gated entrance when we leave," Catsy added. "All the interior roads will be completed along with a clubhouse and the beginnings of a swimming pool, tennis courts, and a playground too—so prospective buyers will be able to see the potential. And since the homes won't be completed, the buyers will have some input on exterior and interior finishes, which most people find an attractive option."

Rand nodded. "I love this new system because we can get in here, get things started, and then leave the rest of the work to the PR folks and the local contractors. I was never meant to be a real estate agent, and that's how it felt when we actually brokered the houses ourselves."

"We've been doing some Internet advertising and already have three tentative buyers lined up." Newell glanced over at me. "So you and Rand better get that land purchased without a hitch."

He didn't smile so I wasn't sure if he was kidding or not.

Then Rand moved around the room, talking with each team member about their area of responsibility.

I got a text from Luke and answered. Sloan noticed my inattention and called for my opinion on the project. I murmured an idiotic reply and then gave him a dirty look.

He smiled back wickedly.

I put away my phone to avoid a recurrence, but noticed that Catsy and Morris were both texting throughout the meeting. She must have felt me watching her because she glanced up. I pointed at her phone and whispered, "Your boyfriend?"

She nodded with an enigmatic smile. As the meeting progressed, I noticed a back-and-forth rhythm to Catsy's texting and Morris's. The idea that they might be a couple was forming in my mind as Rand wrapped up his discourse on Midway modifications.

Sloan turned toward me and asked, "What do you think?"

"Sounds efficient and well-organized," I said.

Newell laughed. "Oh, Drake pretty much defines efficiency and organization!"

Rand said, "I know all this is overwhelming, but your duties are really very limited. During the ceremony this afternoon just stay close to me. We'll start making acquisition visits as soon as we can get away, and I don't want to have to look for you." He turned back to the room in general. "Any comments, questions, complaints?"

Catsy said, "I don't have any complaints, yet."

"You will," Morris muttered good-naturedly.

She blushed and smiled, giving more credence to my suspicion about a relationship between the two of them.

Rand announced, "For the duration of the project we'll have breakfast every morning in here at seven."

"Now I have a complaint," Catsy said. "I hate meeting that early."

"Blame it on Sloan," Rand replied. "You know construction workers like to start at dawn."

Sloan grinned. "Yeah, blame it on me. And actually I'm about to make it worse."

"Not earlier than seven!" Catsy nearly begged.

"No," Sloan said. "But I am going to start my crews at six, which means I need to be in Midway by then. So can we hold these morning meetings at the office of the Store and Save? It will keep me from having to drive back out here—and you know we're all about efficient use of time."

"Especially on a rushed project like this," Newell agreed.

"The hotel provides us with breakfast here," Catsy pointed out. "Who will feed us if we meet in Midway?"

"I'll pick up doughnuts and coffee every morning," Sloan promised.

Rand nodded. "The storage office it is, every morning at seven." He put his file folder on the table. "Well, everyone is free until one forty-five."

"Free to get ready for opening day of the project, you mean?" Catsy asked.

Rand nodded and turned to me. "Kennedy, if you don't mind staying for a few minutes, I'd like to go over the acquisitions with you."

I checked my watch. "I don't mind," I told him. "As long as I can leave by eight thirty so I can make it to church on time."

"I'd like to show you what I've planned for the city hall," Catsy said. "But I don't want to make you late for church. So maybe you can come by this afternoon before the welcome ceremony? I'm in room 103."

"I'll come around twelve thirty," I promised, feeling sort of popular.

Newell, Morris, and Catsy left, but Sloan remained seated beside me. Rand seemed mildly annoyed by his presence, and I began to wonder if the two men disliked each other.

Rand took the seat across from me and said, "The acquisition phase of this project is going to be simple and easy. We've got seven people who own land north of town that we're offering to buy just to keep from hurting their feelings." Rand's expression eloquently expressed his opinion of this. "They don't affect the construction schedule, so if we don't get to all of them today, we can do it tomorrow afternoon."

That made sense to me so I nodded.

"Today we'll be visiting the Lebows. They lost their jobs when the tire plant closed and are about to lose their house—so selling it to Drake is a no-brainer. Then there is Mrs. Castleberry, who wants to send her grandson to law school. So both of these visits are basically courtesy calls. Then there are two others that I don't expect any problem with. The major tract of land we need is owned by Mr. Hodges, who is anxious to sell. That leaves only the four smaller properties to purchase."

He passed me four sheets of paper, one for each potential seller.

"Sometimes people are intimidated by strangers—even strangers offering lots of money," Rand continued. "We hope that having you there will make the proceedings quicker and more pleasant."

I nodded. "I'm supposed to provide a pretty face and Southern charm. Drake already told me."

Sloan raised his eyebrows again. I steadfastly ignored him.

Rand pointed at the four sheets of paper spread out on the table between us. "You can review these so you'll be familiar with the offers we are going to make to each seller by this afternoon. We'll go over them more in detail just before each appointment. But basically we'll start with some small talk—led mostly by you—to put them at ease. When I think the time is right, I'll explain the offer. At that point you step back in and watch for an opportunity to help me move smoothly to the part where they sign and I give them a check."

"That fast?" I was amazed.

"Usually it's just that fast," he confirmed. "The prospective buyers rarely refuse the deals we offer—they are *too* good. Occasionally someone wants a few days to think it over. This is inconvenient for us, but we acknowledge that it's a big decision and we don't want to rush them into anything."

"We want them to be happy with the deal," I said. I thought of the excitement Drake caused in Midway when everyone thought he was going to buy their land.

"Drake wants them to be more than happy. He wants to make their dreams come true," Rand amended with a smile. "With his money and power he could approach it another way. But he wants everything about his projects to be positive. He wants to leave the towns better places and those who sold us property better off than they've ever been. But we learned a lesson from our previous visit to Midway. For each piece of land we want to purchase, we also have a backup property. That way if our first choice doesn't work out, the whole project won't stall over one reluctant seller."

"Good for Midway!" I said.

"We don't want to pressure the sellers," Rand said. "But we are under strict time constraints. We'll make our best offer, and if they want to pass, we'll move on to our backup."

This team was not only doing good things—they were doing them well. I was glad to be a part of it all.

"Now, I've got a few things to finish before the ceremony this afternoon," Rand said. "I'll see you both there."

Once the lawyer was gone, Sloan said, "I wish I could go with you and Rand to your appointments, but I've lined up a surveyor this afternoon, and since I'm paying him double-time, I need to be there to make sure he completes the job as quickly as possible."

I frowned. "Do you usually go with the legal rep to talk to potential sellers?"

He shook his head. "But this is different. You're new to the job and you don't know Rand. I was afraid you might feel uncomfortable."

I was touched by his concern. "I'll be fine."

He checked his watch. "Go on to church with your sister. Then I'll meet you at Catsy's room around twelve thirty."

"You seriously don't have anything better to do than go around with me?"

"Let's just say I don't have anything I'd rather do."

I rolled my eyes, picked up my binder and bag of shirts, and walked toward the front entrance. "See you at twelve thirty, then."

"I'll get a pizza and we can eat while you and Catsy talk."

"Sounds good."

"What kind do you like?"

"Cheese."

He looked horrified. "Are you kidding me? Plain pizza is like a crime."

"It's what I like."

"Whenever I order pizza, I tell them to give me everything they've got."

I couldn't control a little shudder. "What if you don't like some of the 'things' they've got?"

He wiggled his eyebrows at me. "I eat pizza the same way I live life—dangerously."

"Then order yourself a dangerous pizza," I told him as I walked toward the door. "Just make sure at least one piece of it is only cheese."

I made it to the Mormon church in plenty of time to sit with Madison and her family during their services. I'm not sure my presence improved the children's behavior, but I figure it didn't hurt.

I left a few minutes early so I could go home and change out of my suit before my meeting with Catsy. While I was driving I got a text from Luke. He said, *Veggie burgers for lunch.*

I managed to respond, *Sounds healthy if not delicious*, without having a wreck.

At my apartment I put on my best pair of jeans and one of the Langston Association shirts. It fit perfectly. Then I hurried back out to my truck and headed for the Hampton Inn.

On the way Mother called to make sure I was coming to her house after church for the weekly ritual of torture—Sunday dinner. I had to break the news that I had a business meeting and could not attend. That was just one more strike against Drake in her book.

When I got to the hotel, I knocked on Catsy's door and she welcomed me into her room with a friendly smile. We settled around the tiny table near the window that overlooked the hotel's small pool to go over her plans for the Midway city hall.

She placed her phone on the table and then pushed a set of sketches toward me with one of her nail-bitten hands. "The city hall was built in the 1940s so the original details are interesting, architecturally speaking. We'd like to accentuate those details and lose all the . . . less interesting things that have been done to the space since then."

I couldn't think of anything interesting about the city hall—original or otherwise—but I nodded politely.

"We'd like to bring in more light, so we're adding a huge window in the lobby."

"I like that idea," I told her.

"We're also getting new furniture for the lobby and all the offices. These are the fabrics and paint colors we're using." She handed me a card with swatches of material and paint samples paired. Then she pointed at the red, blue, and yellow plaid. "I'm basing everything off this main fabric. In the lobby I'm using the plaid to introduce all the colors. In the other areas of the building I'll use one or two of the colors together—but not all three. I hope this will help define different areas and give the whole place a more sophisticated look. The walls will all be neutral tan to make upkeep easier. And the marble floors are in great shape."

"Sounds functional as well as beautiful," I told her.

Her phone vibrated, indicating that she had a message. Her eyes drifted toward it briefly, but she didn't pick it up. "So, what advice can you give me?"

"I don't know anything about interior design," I said. "So the only advice I can give you is about scale. Drake loves to be dramatic, but you might try to reel him in a little. Bigger isn't always better. Especially in Midway."

Catsy looked uncertain. "I'm not sure I understand."

"For instance, our library that Drake created for us and named after his grandfather—is too large."

Catsy's eyes widened and I laughed.

"I know it sounds crazy, but there really is such a thing as too big when it comes to small town libraries. We have this huge, beautiful building but very few patrons. It takes several people to operate the library so we have to reduce the hours we're open—since our circulation doesn't justify very many employee hours. A smaller place could be managed by fewer people and therefore be open more hours."

"And better serve the community," Catsy understood. "I'll remember the next time, although I'm not sure I can hold Drake back. As you say, he loves to be dramatic. And he's particularly anxious for the libraries to be spectacular because he names them after his grandfather."

"I'm not complaining about Drake or his desire for grandiose libraries," I assured her. "I'm very grateful for what he did for the Midway library and for me personally. I was just giving my opinion."

"Which I asked for and appreciate," Catsy said with a smile. Her teeth were perfectly straight and white.

"How long have you been working for Drake?"

"Three years and I love what I do. I have so much creative freedom and the opportunity to use unique quality materials. You don't find that much anymore. Instead of trying to maximize profits by cutting corners, Drake wants things done right. Whether he's working on towns or people, he believes in leaving everything better than the original."

I couldn't disagree. "Midway has a much better library now, and my life has certainly changed for the better. Even if Drake wasn't directly responsible for all the improvements, it's like he's a catalyst for good."

Catsy laughed. "He'd like that title, I think." She looked out the window at the pool. "The water looks nice. Too bad we won't have time for swimming during this project."

I smiled as I thought about the beaches in Hawaii. "Lounging by the pool doesn't hold much appeal for me anyway."

Catsy glanced at her phone as it vibrated again. "I can see why Drake likes you so much."

I was both honored and unnerved by her words. I was a married woman—one who was very much in love with her husband. My relationship with Drake was friendly but professional, and I wanted to be sure that Catsy understood that.

But before I could explain, there was a knock on the door. Catsy stood to answer it, taking her phone from the table as she walked by. She opened the door to admit Sloan. He was balancing a box of pizza in one hand and a six-pack of Diet Pepsi in the other. He plopped our lunch on the tiny table and opened the pizza box lid with a flourish. "One half is boring cheese and the other half is dangerously delicious. Take your pick, ladies."

"I'll have a slice of boring, thank you," I told him.

He put a piece of the cheese on a napkin and passed it to me along with an ice-cold Pepsi.

"How about you?" he asked Catsy.

"I'll just take a Diet Pepsi, thanks."

He passed her a Pepsi. "That means more for me."

I took a bite. "Delicious." Then I took a sip of Pepsi. "Even better."

He pulled a chair ate his multitopping part of the pizza straight from the box. "So, what have you girls been talking about?"

"Paint samples and material swatches."

He shuddered. "Glad I missed that." He picked up another piece of pizza. "Do you mind if I watch TV until it's time for us to go to the welcome ceremony?"

Catsy was texting and didn't even look up. "Help yourself."

I sat at the little table alternately watching a family with young children play by the pool and the soccer game Sloan had on TV.

At one thirty Sloan stood and turned off the television. "Well, I guess it's time to go."

CHAPTER EIGHT

I RODE WITH SLOAN TO the Midway city hall. A nice crowd had gathered for the ceremony, and it took a few minutes to find a parking space. But eventually Sloan was successful. He helped me down out of his truck, and we walked through the milling throng of my fellow townspeople. Basic good manners required that I speak to almost everyone, which slowed our progress. I sensed Sloan's impatience, but there was nothing I could do.

Finally we reached the steps, and the new mayor joined us a few minutes later. Tennison Boudreau had been chosen to replace our former mayor in a special election. He owned two Jiffy Marts in Midway and the Hardees on Highway 17. He gave me a quick hug (I get most of my Pepsis and moon pies at his establishments and he appreciates a loyal customer). Then he introduced himself to the rest of the team and thanked us for our service to the community.

A soloist from the high school choir sang "God Bless America," and then Brother Jackson said a rousing prayer of thanksgiving for Drake and his generosity. Finally the mayor took over the podium and gave what sounded more like a reelection speech than a welcome. It was all over in less than fifteen minutes, and the crowd dispersed toward their parked cars. Except for those who felt it necessary to come up and speak to me, of course.

Miss George Ann Simmons was the first. "Where is Mr. Langston?" She craned her long neck to survey the podium, presumably to make sure she hadn't missed him.

"He's not coming until tonight," I was pleased to reply.

"Well, I heard that he is reinstating the original offers he made for land when he was here before."

"That's true, I think," I replied carefully.

"I want to know if he is going to purchase my land out by the old milk plant," she pressed.

I frowned. "I didn't know he'd made you an offer for that land."

"He didn't, officially," she admitted. "But he did have one of his people look at it—which indicates interest. So I believe I am entitled to an offer."

She was almost enough to make me long for Miss Ida Jean. "You'll have to talk to Drake's legal representative." I pointed to Rand.

He gave me a look of annoyance as Miss George Ann marched over and repeated her unreasonable demands.

I barely had a second of peace before Miss Ida Jean sidled up to me. She was accompanied by Brother Jackson and Miss Zelda.

"It seemed a lot more exciting when Drake Langston came here before," Miss Ida Jean informed me with a frown.

So maybe I didn't really miss her, after all.

"I thought it was a very nice ceremony," Miss Zelda said. "And the plans for the family center sound wonderful."

Miss Ida Jean looked over her shoulder. "I'm so nervous being out here in the open with those two convicts still on the loose. The only reason I dared come was because the preacher promised me he wouldn't let me out of his sight. You should talk to Cade and the sheriff about finding those prisoners. Tell them defenseless women in town are concerned."

"I'll be sure to mention it," I lied.

Rand had managed to extricate himself from Miss George Ann and walked over to me. "We'd better get going," he said. "If you folks will excuse us."

Without waiting for their permission, Rand steered me through the crowd toward his car.

Rand looked down at me and said, "Stay close by me so we don't get separated in this crowd."

I nodded and stayed as near him as possible without actually touching as we made our way down the steps. We had only gone a few feet when Sloan walked up and joined us.

"I thought you had a surveyor to supervise," I said.

"I'm just walking you to the car," Sloan replied. "Crowds make me nervous, especially when two escaped convicts are still at large."

"Now you're starting to sound like Miss Ida Jean." I patted my purse where my father's .45 was resting comfortably. "I'll be fine. And if there's trouble, I'm ready."

He didn't look happy, but he nodded. Then he stopped walking and the crowd filled the space between us. I gave him a smile and then turned to catch up with Rand.

"You got rid of your babysitter?" he asked as we reached the edge of the crowd.

I wanted to defend Sloan without antagonizing Rand, so I said, "He's just trying to help me since I'm unfamiliar with the job and procedures."

"He's being overprotective," Rand said as he came to a stop beside a silver Altima. He unlocked the doors with the remote on his keys and we climbed into the front seats.

The roads in town were clogged with people leaving the welcome ceremony so our progress was slow.

Finally we got out of town, and he drove to a huge tract of land that decades before had been a cotton farm and would soon be divided into a housing development. I looked around at all the peace and quiet—the long grass and wildflowers blowing in the summer breeze. A bunch of houses didn't seem like an improvement to me. But I kept my opinion to myself.

"Our first visit will be with the Fondren family," Rand said. "I guess you read the sheet I gave you about them?"

I nodded. I'd known the Fondrens all my life. "They are nice people."

Rand continued as if I hadn't spoken. "The head of the home is Mitchell Fondren, who just got his master's degree and joined the throng of recent graduates looking for a job. His wife, Erin, is a stay-at-home mom. They have two kids and another one on the way. They are living in a tiny two-bedroom house they bought four years ago, and it's a miracle they haven't burst right out of the rafters already. Their only income is from Mitchell's part-time job at Lowe's, and he's got enough student loan debt to sink a battleship. I think Drake must feel extra sorry for them. He's offering almost twice the market value of the house."

Drake had a reputation for being generous, but I was impressed.

"And to sweeten the deal—as if he needed to—Drake put in a good word for Mr. Fondren with a friend of his in Chicago, and yesterday he got a job offer."

"In Chicago?" I asked.

"Right."

"So they'll have to move and actually need to sell their house."

"Exactly," Rand confirmed with a smug smile.

Suddenly I felt a little uneasy. "Isn't that kind of, well, sneaky?"

Rand shot me a look of annoyance. "Getting the man a job so he can support his family?"

"In *Chicago* so he has to move—and sell his house."

Rand waved his hand, dismissing my comments. "The Fondrens would have sold to us anyway, even without the job offer. They need the money badly. And Drake doesn't have any business contacts here in Podunkville that he could pressure into hiring the guy."

These points were valid, and I felt a little bad for doubting Drake's methods and motives.

Rand continued. "It wasn't sneaky, it was *stupid*. I tell Drake all the time that he shouldn't waste so much of his time and resources trying to help people. Especially since he does his good turns secretly and therefore gets no credit for them. No good publicity, no tax write-off—nothing. But the guy won't listen. He loves people." Rand shook his head as if this were unfathomable.

I was liking Rand less and less as we pulled up in front of the Fondrens' home. It was a small brick house with a lot of toys in the yard. Erin greeted us at the door—me with a hug and Rand with a handshake. Then she ushered us into their small living room.

Mitchell Fondren walked in and extended a hand to both of us. "Hey, Kennedy." To Rand he said, "I'm Mitch."

Then we made small talk for a few minutes. It came more naturally than I'd expected—proving that in spite of my efforts to avoid it, I am my mother's daughter. We talked about his schooling and recent degree. We talked about their children and how cute they were. Just as we finished discussing the anticipated arrival of the new baby, Rand inserted himself into the conversation.

He cleverly reminded us of the reason for the visit. The Fondrens waited with obvious anticipation for Drake's offer. When Rand finished reading off the proposal, Erin wept openly, and I saw a few tears in Mitch's eyes as well.

"This is incredible," he said. "Our situation has been pretty grim for the past few months. We were starting to feel a little hopeless."

"Mitch has worked so hard to get through school, and then not being able to find a job was so, well, discouraging," Erin added.

Mitch nodded. "But yesterday Mr. Langston's friend from Chicago called and everything started to change."

"Improve," Erin corrected. They clasped hands.

"So I have a job in Chicago, which is a good thing," Mitch said. "But we need to sell this house in a depressed real estate market and buy a house there in an expensive one. We've been worried about that. We even thought we might have to live separate for a while, which with the baby coming would be terrible."

Erin wiped her eyes. "With this offer we can get our lives back on track."

At that moment I understood what Drake meant about this being the best part of his reclamation process.

Rand leaned forward and explained, "We are trying to finish up our Midway project quickly so we'll have to move fast on this. You can have this contract reviewed by your attorney . . ."

Mitch shook his head. "That won't be necessary. We're ready to sign."

And it was as simple as that.

Once the paperwork was signed and witnessed, by me, Rand continued. "We'll hire professional movers to come in and pack up your things in a container that can be stored here and then transported to Chicago when you get a place there. And the Langston Association will pay for a hotel until you find a house."

"That is so generous," Erin whispered.

Rand smiled. "It's the least we can do since we're kicking you out of your house on such short notice."

"When will the movers come?"

"Tomorrow if possible."

I was horrified, but Erin said, "Tomorrow is fine." She put her hands on her bulging midsection. "It would be nice to get settled in Chicago before the baby comes."

Mitch nodded. "I'm supposed to start work next week, and I'd like to have my family there with me."

Rand handed them his card. "Just figure out which hotel in Chicago is most convenient, and let me know. I'll set up the reservation."

"I don't even know the words to express our appreciation," Erin told us.

Rand gave her a humble smile. "Drake Langston deserves all the thanks. And you can show your appreciation to him by being ready when the movers get here bright and early in the morning."

I looked around and realized that the tight schedule had probably condemned the Fondrens to a sleepless night. But they didn't seem unhappy about the prospect. In fact, they looked thrilled. The atmosphere in the home had changed. The Fondrens were definitely better off for their brief brush with Drake Langston and his team.

Erin and Mitch walked us to the door, still happily working out details of their move with Rand. We stepped outside and they waved good-bye. As we walked back to the rental car, I felt happy. My first acquisition experience with the Langston Association had been very positive.

When we were in the car, Rand looked over at me and smiled. "So, was that fun?"

I nodded. "It was."

"Next we'll visit the McNamaras," he said.

Jewel McNamara was a good friend of my mother's. She and her husband were both in their forties and had two teenage sons. The whole family was gathered in their living room when we arrived. There was less small talk this time. They knew why we were there and wanted to hear the offer. So after a minimum of polite conversation, Rand presented Drake's proposal.

They'd never thought about moving, but after hearing the amazing offer, they gladly agreed.

"We would like to have our lawyer to review the contract," Mr. McNamara said.

"That is perfectly reasonable," Rand said. "But we are in a time crunch here, so we'll need an answer pretty quick."

"Our lawyer is a friend of ours and he probably wouldn't mind if we brought it by his house this afternoon—under the circumstances. Then we can bring the contract to you at the hotel tonight."

"Great idea." Rand pulled out a business card and handed it to Mr. McNamara. "We're at the Hampton Inn. Just tell the clerk at the desk you're there to see me and she'll call me down."

"We'll bring them to you soon," Mr. McNamara promised.

We left after shaking hands and there were smiles all around.

"I love my job!" Rand said as we climbed back into his car.

The good mood was contagious and I found myself grinning. "We could turn this into a reality television show. A camera crew could follow us around—watching us make people's dreams come true."

Rand's smile looked more like a grimace. "That's not a bad idea. Drake could use the positive publicity."

I shuffled my stack of folders, putting the McNamaras on the bottom. The next few potential sellers had been offered attractive purchase prices during Drake's first occupation of Midway. The Scoggins Salvage Yard was on the top, marked "no sale" since, unbeknown to me, Luke had been contacted in North Carolina and had declined the reoffer. So I shuffled the files to bring one on the Castleberrys to the top. Mrs. Castleberry wanted to sell the land she owned to send her grandson to law school so there was no real negotiation involved. Rand and I were in and out of the home in less than thirty minutes.

Then we stopped by Mr. Bateman's gas station out near the land that had been in Luke's family for generations. I never would have thought I could feel sentimental about the salvage yard, but when we passed the turnoff a lump formed in my throat.

Mr. Bateman wanted to sell part of his land, but not all of it as he had originally agreed, so Rand had to do some refiguring, but they finally came up with a price that satisfied them both. While they worked, I purchased an ice-cold Pepsi and a slightly stale banana moon pie. After leaving the gas station, we drove to the Baptist church and met with Brother Jackson and Miss Zelda.

First Rand went over the construction schedule for the family center.

"We'll try to keep the mess and confusion to a minimum," he told the Jacksons, "but some disruption to your normal meetings and activities will probably be unavoidable."

"We appreciate what you're doing for the church and we'll work around you," the preacher assured him with a smile.

Rand seemed pleased by this answer. "Now let's move on to your personal property."

The Jacksons owned several large parcels of land to the north of town and the purchase price was just less than one million dollars. After all the signatures were completed, Brother Jackson took Miss Zelda's hand in his and whispered, "It looks like we will be visiting the Holy Land, after all."

She gave him a tremulous smile as tears pooled in her eyes.

I felt like crying myself. Miss Zelda had spent a lifetime following Jesus. It seemed only right that she should get the chance to walk in His actual footsteps.

Our final visit was to a small house on the south side of town. According to the file the house and surrounding two acres were owned by Mrs. Agatha Hoban. She fell into the very small category of people who lived in or near Midway whom I didn't know personally. I scanned her information to refresh my memory. She was eighty-three years old and had moved to Midway from Wisconsin two decades earlier after the death of her husband. She wanted to live near her only surviving relative—a nephew in Albany named Thorin Payne. Her house was on the far southern end of the Midway city limits. The first time Drake came to Midway, he'd had no interest in Miss Agatha's small parcel of land. This time her home was in the perfect spot for the service entrance to the new subdivision.

When we arrived at her house, Rand parked on the lawn (which was more dirt than grass) and opened his door. "Let's go use Drake's money to make Mrs. Hoban's dreams come true."

I smiled as I climbed out of the car and followed Rand up the crumbling sidewalk. The grass that couldn't seem to take root on the lawn was flourishing between the multitude of cracks in the old concrete. The wooden front porch looked unstable. Rand must have had the same thought because he tested its soundness with one foot before committing his entire weight. Then he leaned forward and knocked on the once-red door that had been reduced—by many years of exposure to the harsh Georgia sun—to a chalky pink. There was no response. So he rapped the door a second time.

Finally we heard a voice call from inside. "Hold your horses! I'm coming!" And then Agatha Hoban pulled open the door.

Since I knew she was eighty-three, I wasn't expecting a lot of her appearance. However, Agatha exceeded my low expectations. Her white hair was thin to the point of sparse and cut in a bowl shape that encircled her head right above her ears. It was a practical hairstyle, but it was not flattering. Her hot-pink stretchy pants were pulled up nearly under her armpits, and her Statue of Liberty T-shirt was tucked in so that nothing below the crown was visible. Bulky, black orthopedic shoes completed her ensemble.

"Come on in," she invited with an enthusiastic wave. I thought she was glad to have our company until she added, "Hurry or you'll make me miss Final Jeopardy! It's college week so I might actually know the answer!" She grinned and oversized dentures protruded slightly. Then she turned and walked deeper into the small house with her arms swinging at her side in an apparent attempt to propel herself faster.

Rand remained near the door, seeming completely flummoxed.

"Final Jeopardy means the game show is almost over," I whispered to him. "We'll still be able to make her dreams come true, but we'll have to wait a few minutes."

He nodded and we followed Agatha. As we walked through the living room, I noted many signs of neglect. Water stains on the ceiling, peeling paint, and cobwebs. Through the open door to the kitchen, I could see ancient appliances and several holes in the linoleum floor where the wood beneath showed through. If ever there was someone who needed Drake, it was Agatha Hoban.

We entered a den that was so crammed with furniture it made me feel claustrophobic. The room was dominated by the largest television I've ever seen. The console was so massive it covered one entire wall (and the room's only window). It was a testament to how far television technology had come, since now big screens are more compact and relatively unobtrusive.

Agatha moved some unopened mail and a mound of partially crocheted yarn off the sagging couch so that Rand and I could sit down. She settled herself into a recliner close to the huge television just as the Final Jeopardy "answer" filled the screen.

"'Good night sweet prince' was originally said to him," Agatha read out loud.

We watched the contestants write down their "questions," and as the program went to a commercial, she said, "I'm pretty sure it was Shakespeare, but I can't remember the specific play."

Rand cleared his throat. "I believe it is a line from *Hamlet.*"

Agatha beamed at him. "I think you're right." She muted the sound and asked, "So you work for Drake Langston, do you?" Without giving either of us a chance to answer, she continued. "The preacher's wife came by to see me this morning like she does every Sunday, trying to give me a ride to church since I don't drive. She said everybody is all excited about him coming back to Midway. I told her once he gets that senior center built, I'll let her give me a ride there. Who knows, I might even get myself a boyfriend."

She grinned again, exposing her oversized teeth and making the possibility of a boyfriend seem all the more unlikely.

Rand appeared to be at a total loss, so I decided it was time to earn my consulting fee. I skimmed over the boyfriend reference by saying, "The senior center will be a benefit to the whole community." Then I added, "The Langston Association is also doing renovations downtown and building a new family center for the Baptist church."

Agatha nodded vaguely and returned her eyes to the silent television.

"I guess you're a big fan of *Jeopardy!*?" I continued.

"Been watching it for over thirty years. Alex Trebec is one of the finest-looking men I've ever seen." She squinted at me. "Are you Iris Killingsworth's girl?"

I nodded. "I am."

"The divorced one or the Mormon?"

I wasn't sure which she considered worse, but I bravely replied, "The divorced one, although I've recently remarried."

I was spared further discussion of my personal life when the game show came back on and she turned the volume up. With a flourish, Alex Trebec revealed the question, "Who was Hamlet?"

Agatha congratulated Rand and he accepted her praise with a modest smile.

All the competitors got the correct "question" as well. A student from UCLA won because of his superior wagering skills.

Agatha was disappointed. "I wanted the young woman from Virginia Tech to win since she's a fellow Southerner." With a sigh she turned off the television. "We have a half hour to visit before *Golden Girls* comes on. I made a batch of brownies this morning. With real butter," she added. "Would you like some?"

Rand's eyes darted to the less-than-tidy kitchen, and I knew he was reluctant to eat anything prepared there. But I also knew we had no polite alternative. So I accepted her brownie offer and Rand followed my lead. Agatha hurried into the kitchen with her elbows swinging. She returned minutes later with a plate full of brownies.

She passed the plate to me first. I took one and tasted it immediately. It was just average, but in the spirit of successful negotiation, I said, "Delicious!"

Then she moved on to Rand. He took a brownie gingerly between two fingers as if he were touching toxic waste. He pulled a crisp white handkerchief from his pocket and wrapped it around the brownie. Then he gave Agatha a weak smile. "I'll save this for later."

I took another bite. "Some people don't like to mix business and pleasure."

Agatha nodded and sat back down in her recliner.

Rand waited until she was settled before he scooted forward to the edge of the couch. "I'm glad you're familiar with the Langston Association and the work we do in small towns around the Southeast," he began.

"I thought that stubborn old Foster Scoggins had ruined Midway's chances for improvement."

Apparently she didn't realize my connection to Foster, and I didn't feel obligated to enlighten her. "Mr. Langston had a two-week break in his busy renovating schedule and decided to come back and finish the Midway project. But this time he is locating his housing development south of town," I told her instead. "In fact, one of them will be in the cotton fields behind your house."

"So we would like to buy your property, as it offers us the easiest access to an existing road for constructions supplies and equipment," Rand said.

"You want to tear down my house to make a road?" Agatha didn't sound pleased by the prospect.

"Your property will be an essential part of a beautiful housing development," I said in an attempt to put a positive spin on her words.

Rand extended the contract to her. "You'll see we're offering you a very good price for your home and acreage—well over market value. In addition, you can buy one of the new houses we're building behind you for just what it costs us to build them. Or, you might consider a nice retirement facility."

Agatha's eyes narrowed and her cheeks turned pink. I searched desperately for something I could say to smooth over this unforgiveable breach of etiquette. I wished my mother—who always knew what to say—was there. Heck, I even wished Miss Ida Jean was there. At least her incessant (if senseless) chatter would have created a welcome distraction.

Agatha pursed her lips and asked, "Why would you think I'd want to move to an old folks' home? Do you think I'm about to die?"

Rand cleared his throat nervously. "There are many advantages to assisted living. You wouldn't have to worry about yard work or upkeep or routine maintenance. Besides, retirement homes have social activities and help would be readily available if you get sick or fall."

She leaned a little closer to him. "If you get sick or fall, you might need help too, but I don't imagine you're planning to move into a nursing home anytime soon."

Rand forced a laugh. "Of course not."

"So you're saying because I'm old I should give up my independence and move into a retirement home since I don't have long to live anyway?"

Rand was belatedly realizing his mistake—if not fully aware of its scope. "That's not what I meant."

"Well, let me tell you a thing or two, young man." Agatha pointed a bony finger in Rand's direction. "I can take care of myself and I'm doing just fine without any help from you or an assisted living facility."

I intervened before she threw us out. "I'm sorry if we've overstepped," I reluctantly included myself in Rand's stupidity. "We would never presume to tell you what's best for you and your life. Mr. Roebuck just wanted you to know that you have options."

Agatha seemed mollified. "At my age you get kind of sensitive to the mention of nursing homes and death."

Rand didn't specifically mention "death," but I let this pass. "We understand. And if you're not interested in a retirement home—please forget we even mentioned it."

"I may not be able to forget, but I will forgive you," Agatha said. "And I'll take a house in your new subdivision, in which I'll live for the rest of my life." She glanced at Rand. "Which shouldn't be long since you think I already have one foot in the grave."

"Please, Mrs. Hoban," Rand pleaded. "You misunderstood my intentions."

She waved his comment aside. "Like I said, I'll move into one of those new houses if you'll throw in a big-screen TV."

Rand blinked. "How big?"

"Fifty inches," she said. "And I want a plasma screen—none of that LCD stuff that you can't see from half the angles in the room."

"Okay," Rand surrendered without a fight. "We'll throw in a television."

Agatha beamed at him. "Then, young man, you have a deal."

Rand pulled a pen from his pocket and hastily made the adjustments to the contract. He showed Agatha where to sign and where to initial.

"When will I get my money?" she asked when they were through.

"Well, we will deduct the cost for your new house from the proceeds and deposit the remainder directly into your bank account."

"How will I know for sure that you gave me what you promised?"

Rand looked pained. "I'll bring you the receipt personally, showing the amount we deposited."

"That's all right, I guess." Agatha glanced at me. "But I'd rather Iris's girl bring me the receipt. I know she's from a good Christian family, even if she is a Mormon."

"I'm divorced," I corrected.

Agatha's eyes widened. "You're divorced *and* a Mormon!"

I gave up. "I'll be glad to bring you the receipt."

I could tell Rand was losing patience. "I'll just need a deposit slip for your checking account."

Agatha reluctantly provided one. "You take good care of this information, young man. I don't want my identity stolen now that I'm actually going to have some money."

"I'll safeguard your account information," Rand assured her.

"How soon will I be able to move into my new house?"

"It will take about a month to get your house built, but we need the road now to get construction equipment and supplies in. So we'd like to have some professional movers come tomorrow. They will pack up all your furniture and store it until your house if finished. In the meantime we'll put you up at the Hampton Inn."

Agatha frowned. "I'll bet their TVs are small."

I glanced at her monstrosity. "Not as big as yours, for sure."

She shook her head. "I don't see as well as I used to, so a small television won't do for me. And I don't want to move twice, so I'll just stay here until my house is built. But I'd like that big-screen TV now. And when you drop the new one off, can you take this one to my nephew in Albany?"

Rand got out his pen again. "Give me his address."

Agatha recited her nephew's name and his address in Albany.

After jotting down the nephew's information, Rand said, "I'll get you a new television, and I'll have this one moved. But you can't stay here. Maybe I can talk to the folks at the Hampton Inn and arrange to have your new television set up there."

"What do you mean I can't stay here?" Agatha demanded.

"Because once you sell, this house won't belong to you anymore," Rand explained with obvious annoyance.

I shot him a reproving look and then added, "There is going to be a lot of construction traffic and noise here over the next few weeks. You'll be much happier somewhere else."

Rand ignored my silent warning and continued. "If we don't have a road, we can't start building houses—including yours. So you'll have to move out. I'll hire professional movers to come pack up your furniture and things in the morning. They will store everything until your house is ready and then deliver it. That means you really only have to move once."

I thought Rand presented his case very well, but Agatha would not be swayed. "No, if I sell, then part of the deal will be that I can stay here until my house is ready. I don't want to be separated from my things for a whole month. And I don't want to live in a hotel. You can still bring all your equipment in through my property. Just go around my house."

I tried once more. "But all the construction noise and dust . . ."

"I don't hear very well so the noise won't bother me." She glanced around the cluttered room. "And I'm used to dust."

"There are also safety and legal concerns," Rand said.

"I'll sign something saying I won't sue."

Agatha was proving to be a tough negotiator, and I could see that Rand's patience was wearing thin, but I knew we'd pushed as hard as we politely could. And we'd accomplished what we'd set out to do. So I shook my head at him and then smiled at Agatha. "Well, it's all settled, then."

Agatha gave us a fake-toothed grin and shook hands with Rand. "It's been a pleasure doing business with you, young man."

Once we were back in the car, Rand muttered, "That old witch. Why did she think she could impose so many demands on us?"

He seemed really mad, which both surprised and annoyed me. I knew he didn't understand the double standard that exists between old people and young people in Midway, but he should have a little respect for his elders. "It's not your money," I reminded him. "And Drake won't mind throwing in a TV."

"He won't care about the television, but he's not going to be happy that she won't move," Rand said as we settled in his car. "Her living in that house during construction would be a liability suit waiting to happen."

"She said she'd sign something relieving the Langston Association of liability."

"Like that would stop someone else for suing in her behalf if she gets hurt or killed," he complained. "And it bugs me that she couldn't just be grateful that we were getting her out of that old house."

"That old house is her *home*." I was starting to lose patience with him myself. "She's lived there for a long time, so moving will be hard, even if she is getting a better place and a television that doesn't take up half a room. The important thing to remember is that she did agree to sell to us. Otherwise you'd be looking for a new service entrance to the subdivision."

He sighed. "I guess you're right. I just don't like to lose."

I smiled. "Now I understand why Drake is willing to pay me a fortune to go around with you on these visits."

He gave me one of his smile-grimaces. "I never claimed to be charming."

My phone rang and I checked the number. It was Drake.

"So, how is your first day as my acquisitions specialist going?" he asked.

"Pretty good," I reported. "We have signed contracts from all the potential sellers, but you are going to have to buy Agatha Hoban a fifty-inch plasma television. And she won't move out of her house until the new one is ready, so the construction crews will have to work around her."

"Sounds like she was a shrewd negotiator," Drake replied.

"She was," I assured him.

"I'd like to hear all about your day," he said. "How would you feel about eating dinner with me at the Back Porch?"

"You're in Midway?"

"I will be in thirty minutes," he said. "You can tell me all about your visits over a salad."

Since our acquisition visits were the purpose of our dinner meeting, I waited for him to include Rand in his invitation, but he didn't. After a few seconds of awkward silence, I said, "That sounds great. I'll meet you there at five."

CHAPTER NINE

WHEN RAND DROPPED ME OFF at my apartment, I had fifteen minutes to refresh my appearance. I brushed my teeth and ran a comb through my hair. I considered changing back into my lovely lavender suit before my dinner with Drake but decided this might give the wrong impression. I was a married woman attending a business dinner. Nothing more.

So I drove to the Back Porch wearing my jeans and Langston Association shirt. The Sunday evening crowd was light so I got a parking space right in front. I climbed out of the truck and saw Drake waiting outside by the front door of the restaurant. He looked gorgeous, as always, if a little tired. I was just a few yards away from him when Sloan pulled his truck in between us. He jumped out with a grin, leaving his truck blocking traffic.

"Are you joining us for dinner?" I asked him.

He shook his head. "No, I've got to fax all those surveyor reports in. I just wanted to check on you. How did your acquisition meetings go?"

"Fine," I replied.

Sloan nodded as we circled around the front of his truck and joined Drake by the restaurant entrance. The men exchanged greetings and then Sloan said, "You remember that she's a married woman now."

"This dinner is strictly friendly business," Drake promised.

"For goodness sake," I said with a frown at Sloan. "You don't need to act like my father. I'm a grown woman capable of taking care of herself."

"Yeah, you were a grown woman the day the library blew up too," Sloan said over his shoulder. Then he gave me a wink as he climbed in his truck and drove away.

"I don't know what's gotten in to him," I told Drake as he opened the restaurant door for me. "He won't take his eyes off me for a minute."

"Maybe he likes rescuing people—especially you."

"Well, he needs to get another hobby." I stepped inside and the cool air filled with delicious smells surrounded me. My stomach growled and I realized it had been quite a while since I'd had an actual meal. "I'm starving," I told Drake. "Let's eat."

He laughed as a waitress led us to a quiet corner in the back. Drake held my chair for me like a perfect gentleman. Then we both ordered salads.

Once we were alone he pointed at my shirt. "That looks good on you."

I glanced down at the Langston Association logo. "I like it too."

"I'd love to keep you on my team full-time. If you're interested, you can wear on of those great shirts every day."

I laughed. "I appreciate the offer, but I'm going to be a poor college student for the next year."

"You got your credits transferred to Emory?"

"Yes," I confirmed, although I suspected he already knew. "My adviser there said you put in a good word for me. Thanks."

He nodded. "You're a good student who deserves a great education. It was my pleasure to recommend you. Are you still planning to be a librarian?"

I shook my head. "I have found that while I still love books, I do not love all the administrative headaches that come with running a real library. Would you believe that some days I don't even touch a book?"

He smiled. "I would believe it."

"I actually find myself longing for the old trailer days."

"I'm sorry."

"Don't be! I'm not saying that a nice big library isn't a good thing for Midway," I explained. "I'm just not sure I want to pursue a library degree. So I'm going to take some general courses. I have an interest in business or even psychology. I'll just see how it goes."

"You have plenty of time to decide," he said. "And a business degree with a psychology minor would probably help you run the library in Midway if you decide to stay this course."

"Especially the psychology part!" I agreed.

He laughed as our waitress brought us ice water and a basket of cheese biscuits. While buttering one, Drake said, "So you enjoyed your afternoon?"

"It was fun," I told him. "The only bad thing is that we're finished acquiring property. Your team has everything about this renovation more than under control, which makes me . . . unnecessary. So if you want me to return your check and watch the transformation of Midway from the sidelines, I will."

I expected Drake to try to convince me that my presence really was essential to the outcome of the Midway renovation—whether that was true or not. But what he said caught me completely off guard. "I definitely want you to keep the check because involving you with my team was the whole reason I came back here."

I was surprised and confused, and the best response I could muster was, "What?"

He laced his fingers together and leaned forward so he could whisper and still be heard. "I hate unfinished business so Midway and our uncompleted projects here have been bothering me for a while. But our schedule is tight, and I have that personal policy about never returning to a town that invites us to leave. So the chances of us ever coming back were slim to none."

"What happened to change that?" I asked.

"Well, first we completed our last town renovation two weeks early—which almost never happens. Then I heard that your husband was being confiscated by the Marines almost the minute you were married. And I saw an opportunity to incorporate you into my team—even on a short-term basis—and ease my conscience at the same time."

"So you brought your team back to Midway to give me something to do and the town benefits by default. Not the other way around?"

"I'm hoping that you'll love what we do so much that once you get your degree in whatever you finally choose, you'll want to become a part of my team full-time."

I was still trying to understand what he was saying. "You weren't planning on coming here before yesterday morning?"

He grinned. "Nope. And let me tell you, marshaling all the forces necessary to accomplish even a small project like Midway was not easy on a few hours' notice."

I felt confused and uncomfortably beholden. "I appreciate your good intentions."

"I'm not looking for gratitude here," he assured me. "In fact, I was afraid you'd be mad at me. That's why I'm telling you—so you wouldn't find out some other way and feel like I tricked you. And I don't want you to feel obligated in any way. Just enjoy the experience with the team and then later—if you're interested—I'm always on the lookout for good employees whom I can trust."

"I'm flattered," I told him.

"You should be," he said. "I choose only the best people to be on my team. But my hope is that while we're in Midway you'll catch the spirit of what we do and want to be a part of it. Even while you're still in school, you could consult on other projects like this one. It won't take up too much of your time and I pay well."

I smiled. "That is certainly true. I'll talk to Luke when the Marines are finished with him and, well, we'll see."

He was obviously pleased with my reply. "Now aren't you glad I moved heaven and earth to get here so you wouldn't be bored while your husband is gone?"

"I'll have you know I had plenty to do without you. I could have been writing hundreds of thank-you notes and sorting through an equal number of useless wedding gifts with my mother."

Drake groaned. "See! I probably saved your life by coming back to Midway!"

I had to laugh. "Maybe so. But what am I actually going to do for your team, now that the acquisition phase is over?"

"I want you to come to the team meetings every morning and give your opinions on the various projects. Being a local, you have a perspective that the others don't. That alone is worth your consulting fee."

I doubted this but didn't argue.

"If anyone needs your help, they'll let you know at the meeting. If no one needs you, you're free to write thank-you notes with your mother until the next morning's meeting."

"And count wedding gifts," I added with a smile.

"And speaking of wedding presents, I heard you were planning a honeymoon to Hawaii."

"Do you seriously know *everything*?"

"That is my goal, and I have a staff in Atlanta who are well-paid to help me achieve it. But this information came without any research. Sloan told me."

I was surprised that me or my honeymoon plans were a topic of conversation between Sloan and Drake. And I told him so.

"It was just mentioned in passing," he said. "And you'll be glad it was when you hear that I happen to own a house on Oahu."

"Why doesn't that surprise me?" I teased.

He laughed. "I bought it a few years ago so I'd have a place to get away from all the stress in my life. Then I found out I don't really enjoy relaxation. So it sits empty. I'd like for you and your husband to stay there as my guests. That's my wedding present to you."

"That is a very generous gift," I said. "Too generous, really."

"Not at all," he corrected. "It won't cost me a dime so it's actually a cheap gift. And it would be an honor to do something for a soldier who has helped to protect my freedoms."

What could I say to that? "Well, then, thank you."

He pulled an envelope out of his inside jacket pocket and spread the contents on the restaurant table. "Here's the key and the security code, directions from the airport, and some pictures."

The house was spectacular, of course, with not only an ocean view but a private beach.

"The caretaker's name is Dale Kaanehe, and here is his cell number." He pointed at a business card. "He lives in a little cottage on the far edge of the property. He'll respect your privacy so you won't see him unless you call him. Anything you need while you're there—just let him know."

Staring at the pictures, I said, "I can't thank you enough." I really was overwhelmed.

"You don't have to thank me at all. I'm glad someone will be getting some use out of my unwise investment." He picked up his fork. "Now we'd better eat our salads before they wilt."

I was starving so I ate my salad with gusto. When the waitress came to ask about dessert, Drake ordered a bowl of root beer ice cream for each of us. I knew I should override him, but it's homemade and absolutely delicious. So I sat silently while the waitress rushed off to get our ice cream. By the time I had eaten the last bite, I was stuffed and my ability to fit into my bathing suit was in serious jeopardy.

Drake motioned to the waitress for our check, which he paid in cash and told her to keep the change. Then he scooped the information about his Hawaiian house back into the envelope and handed it to me.

As we walked outside together, I said, "Dinner was lovely. And I appreciate all you're doing in Midway and your job offer. And your wedding gift. Thank you so much."

"I should be thanking you for keeping me from eating alone. And tell your husband thanks for sharing you."

I didn't plan to deliver *that* message, so rather than lie, I asked, "Will you be at the morning meeting tomorrow?"

"I will."

"Then I guess I'll see you then."

Once I was settled inside my truck, he waved and crossed the street to his own car.

As I drove to the Midway Store and Save I thought about all that had transpired during the past couple of days. The wreck that had resulted in the death of Nola Finkle and the escape of two prisoners, which Cade's felt was no accident. Drake's arrival in Midway and his admission that he came just to lure me into his employment. Then I thought about my dark, empty apartment. To say it was uninviting would have been an understatement.

I considered going to my parents' house but decided I needed more than company. I needed a level-headed person to discuss everything with. I needed Luke. But he was at Ft. Lejeune, sequestered with Lt. Dempsey. My mother would listen and she is sensible, but she would tell me what to do and pout if I didn't follow her advice. Miss Eugenia had a reputation as a font of wisdom and she wouldn't pry. So instead of going into my lonely apartment, I headed for Haggerty.

* * *

Before I reached the Midway city limits, my mother called. There's no such thing as a short conversation with her so I had to hear about

Brother Jackson's sermon that morning (she said it was good but a little long), how nicely her garden was coming along (she had tons of tomatoes and was thinking that while Luke was gone I could come help her can them), and that Madison's oldest son, Major, had thrown up during Sunday dinner (I've never been happier that I missed a meal).

When she found out I was going to visit Miss Eugenia, she insisted that I come by her house too. Since I couldn't very well show favoritism toward someone else over my own mother, I reluctantly agreed. When I was finally able to end the call with my mother, I dialed Sloan's number.

"Your dinner date ended almost twenty minutes ago," he said instead of the customary hello. "I expected you to call me sooner."

I wondered how he knew the time I left the Back Porch. "My mother called me before I had a chance, and she talks forever so be thankful I was able to call before midnight."

"I'm thankful," he claimed. "Did you enjoy your dinner?"

"It was a business dinner and not intended to be fun."

"Good," he replied. "Married women aren't supposed to be on fun dates with other men."

"I'll take your word on that," I murmured.

"And I saved you a bundle by suggesting that Drake loan you his Hawaiian house. You can thank me now."

"Thanks, I guess," I muttered.

"You don't like staying in a luxurious place for free?"

"I feel a little uncomfortable about it, actually." And I was afraid Luke would be more so.

"That's ridiculous," Sloan reproved. "Haven't you been taught it's rude to look a gift horse in the mouth?"

"I have heard that saying but I'm not sure that it applies here."

"Anyway, Drake is trying to do something nice and you should let him."

"I am," I responded. "I just feel funny about it."

"So are you at your apartment?"

Apparently he wasn't watching *every* move I made. "No, I decided to go visit Miss Eugenia in Haggerty. And when my mother found out she demanded equal time. So I'll have to stop by my parents' house when I get back to Midway."

"We're still getting equipment and supplies lined up for tomorrow so it will be late before I get there," Sloan said. "I'll try not to wake you up."

"You're not sleeping in Mr. Sheffield's office again, are you?"

"I am," he confirmed to my dismay.

"We agreed that you would stay at the hotel from now on."

"You said I should," he corrected. "But with two escaped convicts still unaccounted for, I won't be able to sleep anywhere unless I know you're okay."

I wanted to deny the necessity of this, but honestly I was glad to have him there. Not that I was seriously concerned about the convicts—unlike Miss Ida Jean, who would not leave her house—but it was only sensible to be a little leery if you were a single woman living alone.

"Will you be working with Catsy tomorrow?" Sloan was asking.

"I'm not sure what I'll be doing," I replied honestly. "Drake doesn't need me anymore, and I told him so. But he thinks I'm a charity case and wants me to keep the money he paid me. He says I'm supposed to come to the team meetings every morning and if someone needs me, I can work with them. So who knows, tomorrow might be your lucky day."

Sloan was quiet for a few seconds. "You're going to help me pour concrete and hang drywall?"

"I could sit in your air-conditioned truck and admire you while you work."

He laughed. "I've always wanted a groupie."

"Dream on." Miss Eugenia's white house surrounded by incredible flowers came into view. "I'm here now so I'll let you go."

* * *

Miss Eugenia answered the door wearing an apron that said, "Kiss the Cook." Her hands were both covered with oven mitts and her little dog, Lady, was barking and running frantically around her feet.

"Kennedy! Welcome!" She greeted when she saw me. "I've got to get back to my frying. Follow me!" Then she took off toward her kitchen. Lady chased after her, still barking. I trailed behind them, alarmed by the smoke billowing from the doorway ahead.

"I think your house is on fire!" I cried.

"Not yet," Miss Eugenia replied as she walked over to the source of the smoke—an appliance full of bubbling oil situated in the middle of the table. The words "Fry Daddy" were barely visible in scuffed black paint across the front.

"There is a cooking contest in Albany on Friday night. It's sponsored by Homeland Foods and it's called 'Fry Away,'" she told me over her shoulder. "My sister Annabelle tricked me into participating. So now I have to come up with an entry."

"I see," I said with my eyes still focused on the hot oil.

"When I agreed to participate, I wasn't planning to put any effort into it. But my competitive spirit kicked in when I found out your family friend George Ann Simmons was also submitting an entry. So now I'm in it to win it!"

I studied the oil with more interest. "What have you tried so far?"

"I wanted something out of the ordinary—since you get a lot of points for originality," she said. "So I tried marshmallows. I thought they would taste good, like a campfire. I came up with a special batter using flour and sugar and cinnamon. But it keeps melting into this mess." She waved at the grease lumps on the table.

"You can't keep it in the hot grease long enough to fry it?"

"I can't keep it in the hot grease at all. It disappears immediately."

"I guess marshmallows are mostly just air—so there's not really anything to fry. Why don't you try something like corn on the cob or dill pickles?"

"I'd never win with something that ordinary!" She dismissed my suggestion. "Last year's winner was a hot dog complete with bun and sauerkraut all battered up and then deep fried."

It was enough to blow your mind. "Wow."

She removed her oven mitts and turned off the Fry Daddy. "I guess I've done enough frying experiments for today. We need to get some fresh air circulating. I'll get the window over the sink if you'll prop open the back door."

I did as I was told and soon we had a nice cross-breeze going. The smoke dissipated and Lady calmed down.

"Have a seat," Miss Eugenia invited.

I sat in a chair at the far end of her table while she took the lid off an old Tupperware cake-saver and said, "I'm going to have some of

Whit's pound cake. Would you like a piece?"

I nodded. "Yes, please."

"Do you take yours with strawberries and whip cream or plain?"

"Plain."

Miss Eugenia joined me at the table carrying two saucers with a generous slice of pound cake on each.

I took a bite and said, "This is delicious."

She smiled. "Whit knows how to make pound cake. Now, tell me about your husband. Did he make it to the Army base okay?"

"It's a Marine base, but yes, he made it there fine."

She must have heard the sadness in my voice because she said, "The time will pass."

I was thankful she didn't try to convince me it would pass "quickly," the way everyone else seemed determined to do.

Then she changed the subject. "Now tell me why I have the honor of this unexpected visit from you."

I immediately felt guilty. "I should have called."

"Nonsense," Miss Eugenia scoffed. "You probably kept me from burning the house down."

We both looked over at the pot of oil.

"I guess that's true." I took a deep breath and began. I told her about the wreck and Nola Finkle's death. I told her Cade's suspicions and that he asked me to check it out for him.

"I'm surprised that he would ask you to get involved," Miss Eugenia mused. "Most people don't trust important things to amateurs."

I lifted my shoulders. "It doesn't seem smart, I agree. But you'd be amazed the number of 'cases' I get offered. At least once a week someone calls me with investigations ranging from alien invasions to missing bicycles."

"George Ann is probably going around singing your praises since you solved the mystery of her missing barn wood. And I'm sure she's telling people that she's a close friend of your family."

I groaned. "I don't know which is worse."

Miss Eugenia didn't have to think about that. "George Ann as a friend—definitely!"

"I'm seriously considering changing my number."

Miss Eugenia laughed. "You should seriously consider taking the cases you think you can solve and charging for your services."

"What kind of cases do you think are beyond my abilities—the bicycles or the aliens?"

"Neither," she teased with a wink.

"Luke said the same thing," I told her. "Not about aliens, but that I have an interest and a little talent for solving things, so maybe I should change careers."

"This is a perfect time to change the course of your life," she encouraged.

"Maybe," I said. "But my job for Cade was a short one. Sloan has assigned himself as my bodyguard during the Midway project so he was at my apartment when Cade came by—hiding on the stairs going down to Mr. Sheffield's office so Cade couldn't see him. After Cade left Sloan helped me research the victim and the missing prisoners. There is no connection between them. Cade was wrong. Imagine that."

She chuckled. "You could knock me over with a feather."

I had to smile. Then I told her about my dinner with Drake, his wedding gift, and his job offer.

"Mr. Drake Langston seems to be paying you more attention than is appropriate," she said.

"He's never been anything but professional toward me," I assured her.

Miss Eugenia was frowning. "Just be careful where he is concerned," she advised.

"I probably shouldn't have accepted the job, but he was offering a lot of money."

"Don't fret about it," Miss Eugenia said. "Just be on your guard."

I told her about Hannah-Leigh's offer of friendship and that I politely declined.

Miss Eugenia chuckled again. "I can't imagine what she was thinking."

I shook my head. "Me either."

"But I'm glad you didn't let her pressure you into a relationship you'd be uncomfortable with."

I grinned. "Me too. Maybe next time Drake offers me a job, I'll be strong enough to resist him."

"And Cade and George Ann," she added.

I sighed. "Maybe. And speaking of Miss George Ann, she's threatening to sue Drake if he doesn't buy that wasteland she owns out by the old milk plant. Even though he didn't offer to buy it before, she says the fact that he had Sloan look at it showed 'interest' and if he doesn't buy it, he's discriminating against her."

"George Ann is just ornery enough to pursue something that ridiculous," Miss Eugenia muttered. "But that's for Drake Langston and his lawyers to worry about. You have a case to solve."

"I do?"

She nodded. "I'm not convinced that Cade was wrong about Nola Finkle. It's too much of a coincidence."

"You think she was trying to help the prisoners escape?"

"I think it's very likely."

This was not what I wanted to hear. "But Sloan has access to all kinds of information, and he couldn't find anything."

"Sloan was looking for a connection between Nola Finkle and the prisoners who escaped, but what if the plan was designed to free one of the prisoners who *didn't* get away."

I just stared at her for a few seconds. Finally I managed, "You are a genius."

"That's true, but this is just a theory. We'll have to prove it."

"When I get back to my apartment, I'll ask Sloan to check out the other prisoners and see if he can find a connection to Nola."

Miss Eugenia said, "I think it might be better to let Kate's sister, Kelsey, do the checking."

"But Sloan has access to all kinds of information that the average person doesn't."

"Kelsey is a little above average," Miss Eugenia said. "She is a licensed investigator and her information is obtained legally—which could be important if we do find evidence of foul play. Besides, I think it's best to limit the number of people who know you are still investigating."

"Limit how?"

"To just you and me and your ex-husband," she said. "And Kelsey, of course. Eventually we can include Mark if we find anything interesting."

"But not Sloan?" I asked.

"You don't really know him," she pointed out.

"He saved my life—twice," I reminded her.

"But he acted sort of suspiciously—hiding when Deputy Burrell came to your apartment and following you around with such determination."

"Surely you don't think Sloan had anything to do with Nola Finkle's death!"

"No," Miss Eugenia assured me. "But you have to be careful who you share information with during an investigation, and in this case I believe the fewer people who know, the better."

"You want me to tell Cade?"

She nodded. "He might not have been the best husband, but I think he's a good deputy, and he is unquestionably trustworthy where your safety is concerned."

Oddly this was true. I couldn't trust Cade with my heart, but I could trust him with my life.

"And since neither one of us is authorized to investigate a crime, we'll need a representative from law enforcement."

I dreaded involving myself with Cade on anything. Partly because he is so annoying and mostly because I knew Luke wouldn't like it. I explained my reservations to Miss Eugenia.

She shrugged and said, "Maybe once we get the deputy pointed in the right direction, he can handle the investigation himself."

"I doubt it, but I guess we can hope."

"Just let me have Kelsey check it out. Maybe she won't come up with anything and we can forget it.

"Okay," I agreed. "When I get home I'll e-mail you a copy of the accident report that lists the names of all the prisoners." As an afterthought I added, "Do you know how much Kelsey charges? Because Cade said until it is officially opened as a case, he can't authorize any expenses. And there is a very definite limit to the amount of my honeymoon money that I'm willing to spend trying to prove Cade's hunch."

Miss Eugenia laughed. "Kelsey will probably do it as a favor to me for now, and if it becomes a real case, she can bill Dougherty County."

I couldn't think of a reasonable objection. So I said, "I guess she's hired, then."

"And if we get some real evidence, we'll tell Mark, but I don't want to involve the FBI until we know a crime has been committed."

I felt like a huge weight had been lifted off my shoulders. "It's so nice to have a partner in crime-solving," I said. "And to repay you for your time and trouble, I'll try to think of something you can fry for that contest on Friday night."

She glared at the Fry Daddy. "I could really use some fresh ideas. I'm tired of disintegrating marshmallows."

I stood and moved toward the door. "I'd better get going. My mother is expecting me, and if I don't arrive in what she thinks is a reasonable length of time, *she'll* call the FBI. Or worse, Cade."

Miss Eugenia smiled as she walked me to her front door. "She's just being a good mother. You should appreciate her."

"I do." I stepped out onto her porch. "But she can be exhausting." I started for my truck and then turned back. "Thanks again for your help and the pound cake."

"You're welcome." She watched as I drove down the street until I was out of sight. I had the feeling that she was worried about me. Which *proves* that she is much wiser, and more intuitive, than I am.

CHAPTER TEN

MOTHER CALLED AS I WAS leaving Haggerty, and I told her I'd be there in ten minutes, assuming I didn't get caught in one of Haggerty's famous speed traps.

As soon as I escaped from being my mother's phone-hostage, I texted Luke and asked him to call me when he could. My phone rang seconds later. I told him about my visit with Miss Eugenia and her suggestion that Cade might be right about Nola Finkle.

"I guess there is a first time for everything," he teased.

"I guess," I replied. "But Cade and his one shot at correctness aside, if there was a plot to free one of the prisoners, the authorities need to know about it. I'm glad that Miss Eugenia is willing to check into it so I don't have to get more involved." I told him about Kate's sister and her investigation credentials.

"The less you are involved with Cade Burrell and crime in Midway, the better I like it," Luke agreed.

"Miss Eugenia does think I need to tell Cade," I told him reluctantly. "Since we need his badge to give our investigation authority—in case we find anything."

"I don't guess you can have Miss Eugenia call him?" Luke asked.

I laughed. "No, I think I'll have to handle that part since Miss Eugenia is doing everything else."

"I figured as much."

"And speaking of how much Miss Eugenia is doing for me, I told her I would try to think of something she could fry to win a contest on Friday night. Do you have any suggestions?"

"She could try frying chicken a la king," he responded.

"She wants to *win*," I emphasized.

"Then that probably eliminates anything they serve in the mess hall from consideration," he said. "But I'll keep thinking."

"I do have some good news." I told him about Drake's house in Hawaii and his offer to let us use it. "That will save us thousands of dollars," I concluded.

"Some things are worth paying for," Luke said. "I don't like getting any more closely involved with Drake Langston than we already are."

I wasn't surprised by his reaction, but I was a little disappointed. I had seen the pictures of that fantastic house. I had already imagined us there, walking on that private beach. "If you want me to, I'll tell Drake we'd rather stay in a hotel."

"Let's think about it for a day or so," Luke suggested.

That was one of the things I loved about him. He didn't try to force issues or make snap decisions that we might regret later. "That sounds like a good approach."

"Well, Lt. Dempsey says I've got to go," he told me regretfully.

We said our good-byes as I pulled up to my parents' house. I was surprised (and happy) that Miss Ida Jean was not out watering her lawn. But my reprieve from her annoying presence was short-lived. I had barely climbed out of my truck when I saw her standing in front of her living room window, knocking vigorously on the glass. When we made eye contact, she motioned for me to come over.

"Has Cade arrested those convicts yet?" her glass-distorted voice demanded through the window.

Standing in her soggy front yard and talking to through her window (and feeling ridiculous), I replied, "I haven't heard, so probably not."

She scowled. "Well, it's just a shame that we spend taxpayer dollars to hire a sheriff and deputies, and then they can't protect the public!"

"Just stay inside your house," I encouraged. "You're nice and safe there." Then I affixed the fake smile that I had developed especially for her. "Is Robby home?" I asked. I really needed to find out if he'd been able to set up my visit with Parnell.

Miss Ida Jean shook her head. "He took an extra shift at the prison. There aren't many men like my Robby, so hardworking and dedicated. I don't know what they'd do without him." To hear her talk, you'd think he was the warden instead of a cafeteria employee.

I was saved from any more annoying conversation by my mother. She came out the front door and greeted her neighbor politely. "Hey!"

Miss Ida Jean waved through a pane of glass.

Then my mother addressed me. "Quit dawdling out there, Kennedy. Your daddy and I are anxious to talk to you."

I gave Miss Ida Jean an apologetic smile as if I hated that I had to rush off and hurried up to my parents' porch. Mother gave me a quick hug and then pulled me inside. "I'll heat you up something to eat."

"Thanks, but I had a salad for dinner at the Back Porch." I didn't mention the pound cake at Miss Eugenia's because, strange though it sounds, it would have made my mother jealous that I ate cake there and not at her house.

"A salad!" My mother sounded appalled. "No wonder you're skin and bones!"

"I am not skinny," I objected mildly. "Where's Daddy?"

"He's gone to pick up Heaven," Mother said. "She spent the afternoon at Madison's house."

We settled in the den, and I stayed as long as my nerves would allow (which was less than fifteen minutes). Then I reminded my mother that I had to get up early the next day and therefore needed to go home.

Mother followed me out to my truck. I thought she just wanted to give me a long list of instructions, but actually she had good news. She had returned our excess Crock-Pots and other duplicate wedding gifts to the appropriate stores and the proceeds were even more than she had predicted. The cash, along with checks we received as gifts, were in an envelope, and she wanted to know if I would like her to deposit the money into my account the next day. I gratefully assured her that I would very much appreciate that. Then I dug Drake's check out of my purse for her to add to the stack.

As I drove back to my apartment, I couldn't help but smile. In a strange twist of fate, getting multiple Crock-Pots as wedding gifts had turned out to be a good thing. Who would have thought?

It was very dark, and the parking lot at the Midway Store and Save seemed a little eerie. I was thankful that Sloan's truck was there. I called him as I quickly climbed the steps.

"Are you upstairs or down?" I asked when he answered.

"I'm upstairs watching your crummy television and eating your stale wedding food."

"I won't apologize for either one," I said. "You've made your bed, so to speak, and you can lie in it."

"It's true." He opened the door to let me into my apartment. We both closed our phones simultaneously. "So, how was your visit with Miss Eugenia?"

"Fine," I replied. "She's always entertaining. Tonight she was trying to fry marshmallows to win a contest."

"That sounds . . . unappetizing," Sloan proclaimed.

"You really would have thought so if you'd seen the result," I said. "Now, I'm sorry to pull you away from my pitiful television and old food, but I'm exhausted and have got to go to sleep. And that means you've got to go downstairs to that lumpy couch you insist on using for your bed."

Sloan picked up a Tupperware container filled with finger sandwiches and headed toward the stairs. "I don't want to keep you from your beauty sleep. See you in the morning."

I barely had time to lock my door behind Sloan before Cade called.

"Why didn't you tell me you were working for Drake Langston in Midway?"

I didn't want Sloan to overhear the conversation, so I went into the bathroom and turned on the shower. "We're not married anymore, Cade," I reminded him for the millionth time. "I don't have to tell you everything."

"Well, I'm a deputy sheriff, and lying to me is illegal," he responded ridiculously.

I hardly knew where to begin. "First, I didn't lie. I just chose not to give you some information about my private life. Second, lying to you is not illegal unless you're questioning me in an official capacity, which you were not. And third, what difference does it make anyway?"

Whenever Cade knows he's wrong, he just changes the subject. "If you didn't want to do me a favor, you could have just said so."

I was offended by his ingratitude. "I did help you!" I reminded him. "I gathered information for you on Nola Finkle when I could have been sleeping. Or, even better, planning my honeymoon. What you should be saying is thank you!"

"Thank you." He didn't sound sincere. "But you should have told me about the job with Langston. Not telling me seems sneaky."

Whenever I know I'm wrong, I always go back to Cade's infidelity that ended our marriage. That's the one thing he can never defend himself against. "And you should know about sneaky—like going to the drive-in with an old girlfriend when you've told your wife you're working late."

This time he surprised me. "I do know about sneaky. And I recognize it. You purposely didn't tell me you had taken a job with Langston. There was a reason—one you don't want to admit—but I'm going to find out." Then he hung up on me.

I called him right back. As soon as he answered, I said, "Don't ever hang up on me."

He hung up again.

This time I texted, *If you want to know how Miss Eugenia and I are going to help you find out if Nola Finkle really was involved with one of those prisoners, call me.*

I made him call me three times before I answered. Then, with steam from the shower filling the small room, I said, "Miss Eugenia thinks we should check out the prisoners who *didn't* escape. She says it's possible that there was a plan, but it sprung the wrong convicts."

He was silent for a few seconds and then cursed under his breath. "I should have thought of that!"

"Yes, you should have." I was only too happy to agree. "Fortunately for you I had enough sense to discuss the situation with Miss Eugenia, and she thought of it. You can thank me again now or you can wait until I tell you how we are going to help you find out if there really was an escape plan gone wrong."

"Thanks." If possible, he sounded less sincere this time. "And how are you going to help me?"

"Miss Eugenia is getting Kate Iverson's sister to check for a connection between the other prisoners and Nola. She's going to ask her to do it as a favor for now, but if this ever becomes an official case, she'll send you a bill and you'll have to talk Sheriff Bonham into paying it."

"If this ever becomes an official case because of information she gives us, I'd be glad to pay her fee myself!"

Cade is a cheapskate so this willingness to invest his own money was surprising. "Don't get your hopes up too much," I warned him. "Kate's sister might not find any connection."

"When will she know?" he asked. "Can she find out by tomorrow morning?"

"Maybe," I said. "I'll call you."

My phone beeped, indicating that I had another call. When I saw it was Luke, I abruptly told Cade, "I have to go." Then I took pleasure in hanging up on him.

"Well, this is a nice surprise," I told Luke.

"Lt. Dempsey took pity on me," he said. "We only have a few minutes to talk, but I wanted to hear your voice before I went to bed."

Since my knees always go a little wobbly when Luke says romantic things, I sat on the edge of the tub. "So, what did you do today?"

"We sat around our quarters," he replied. "It qualifies as one of the most boring days of my life."

"Well, mine was not the most boring—of course I've always lived in Midway so I have many more boring days to compare it to."

"You've got a point there." I could picture him smiling, and I was glad I was already sitting down since my knees felt even more wobbly. "So, did you talk to Burrell?"

"I did. He's beyond excited that he might have been right once in his life."

"I guess the odds are in his favor, but I have to hope there's nothing to it. I don't like the idea of you being even remotely involved in a crime investigation—especially when I'm so far away."

"We've already concluded that Cade is not too bright and has bad instincts. So I wouldn't worry too much about a crime investigation," I replied. "Since you only have a few minutes to talk, it makes more sense to discuss Hawaii instead of Cade."

"I can't argue with you there."

"Have you given any more thought to whether we should use Drake's house?"

"I've given it a lot of thought," he said. "But I haven't formed a solid opinion yet. How about you?"

"I think we should stay at his house. It's fabulous and it will save us a lot of money. And it's not like he'll be there or anything. But if you're not going to be comfortable there, we should find something else. After all, there is no shortage of other options."

"I like having options," he said. "What are they?"

"Do you prefer a resort setting or just a regular hotel?"

"I don't like the sound of 'resort.' It brings to mind crowds of people and meal schedules and shuffleboard."

"I think you're somehow getting 'Hawaiian resort' and 'geriatric cruise' confused," I said.

He laughed. "You've got to admit, it doesn't make sense to go all the way to Hawaii to be cooped up in a resort. I'd rather walk barefoot on the beach and eat at romantic little restaurants and have you to myself."

A sigh escaped my lips. "Which is why we should stay at Drake's house."

"I thought we were considering other options before we make our decision."

"Sorry," I said. "I'll scratch all the resorts off the other options list."

"And I really don't like being a mile up in the air," he said.

"No sky-rises," I noted.

"I wouldn't mind a place that's away from the busy, touristy parts of town."

I laughed. "The entire island is touristy. But I can look for a room that is relatively quiet, low to the ground, and facing the ocean. For someone who doesn't care where we stay, you're pretty picky."

"Sorry."

"Too late. Now you have a reputation for being finicky. Lucky for you, I'm patient and have lots of time on my hands to search for the perfect place. And since no accommodations in Hawaii are exactly cheap—except Drake's house—it's a good thing my mom took back our Crock-Pot collection."

"Who knew we would have a Crock-Pot collection?"

I told him about all our duplicate wedding gifts and how my mother had returned them to the stores for us. I made sure to exaggerate enough to make him laugh. "So to some extent our exotic Hawaiian honeymoon will be financed by Crock-Pots."

"I'll appreciate Crock-Pots more in the future." After a brief pause he said, "Is it raining there?"

I glanced back at the water running in the shower. "No, that's just the shower. I turned it on a few minutes before you called."

He cleared his throat. "Well, now that I have that mental picture, we'd better hang up."

I laughed. "Call me tomorrow?"

"I will if I can. We'll be in court, so who knows."

I was sad when the call ended, but not as much as before. We already had a couple of days under out belts and time was passing. Soon we would be together in a perfect tropical setting, and that was a good reason to smile.

I turned off the shower and was walking toward my bedroom when my mother called. I wouldn't have answered, except I knew that if I didn't, she'd use that as an excuse to drive over and check on me. Since it's marginally easier to get off the phone with her than it is to get her out of your house, I answered.

She was upset with my sister Madison. From what I could glean from her heated dialogue, an incident occurred while Heaven was at Madison's house during the afternoon. (I could have told them this was a recipe for disaster—putting so many terrible children in the same place at the same time with only Madison to maintain control—but nobody asked me, naturally.)

Anyway, during Heaven's visit, Madison's baby, Maggie, got what little hair she had cut off. Major did it, he admitted, but he said Heaven told him to. So Madison said Heaven was a bad influence and wanted her punished. She said Heaven is no longer welcome in her home and even suggested that Iris make other foster arrangements for the child.

Although I didn't like to agree with Madison, I couldn't find fault with anything she had said. But I knew better than to say so to my mother.

"And what did you tell her?" I asked.

"I said they shouldn't have been playing with scissors, which speaks to a lack of supervision, so it's all Madison's fault. She was the only adult involved—or not involved, as the case may be. She shouldn't be blaming her mistakes on children."

My opinion is that Major and Heaven are both demons and probably cooked up the conspiracy to get Madison in trouble with my mother. But I also kept that to myself. In Madison's defense I said, "She does have a lot of kids and she's always stressed."

"That's no excuse for taking out her frustrations on Heaven."

There's only so much time and energy that I'm willing to invest in my sister's cause, and I'd reached my limit. So I said, "Well, it's probably best not to take Heaven over there anymore—unless you can stay yourself."

"Are you saying it's my fault?" Mother's voice rose to a higher pitch.

I was not taking any heat for this situation. "It was definitely Madison's fault," I assured her. "I was just making a suggestion for the future to keep Maggie from being perpetually bald."

"For goodness sake, Kennedy. This is not something to make light of. Now I'll have to let you go." I knew this meant she wasn't through venting so she was going to call someone else and tell them the whole thing—probably my sister Reagan. I figured better her than me.

The conversation with my mother was exhausting so I took a shower to revive myself and then looked at Hawaiian hotels that faced the beach until I couldn't keep my eyes open any longer. Then I fell asleep and dreamed of Luke.

* * *

I woke up early on Monday morning and already had a message from Luke. It said simply, *Seafood omelet.*

I shuddered just imagining his breakfast and replied with an equal economy of words: *Yuck.* I waited patiently for a reply, but I waited in vain. Finally I gave up and typed in, *Call me when you can.*

Then I pulled on a pair of jeans and a clean Langston Association shirt. I brushed my hair and teeth, applied a little makeup, and walked into my living room. Sloan was sitting on the couch.

"You're supposed to stay downstairs unless I invite you up," I scolded him.

"Sorry," he said without the slightest bit of remorse. He stood and motioned toward the door that led to Mr. Sheffield's office. "The meeting starts in ten minutes. I've got breakfast waiting."

I was starving, so I followed him below. He had the food on Mr. Sheffield's desk. There was an assortment of Krispy Kreme doughnuts, several Styrofoam cups filled with coffee, and some bottles of water. He'd gathered an assortment of chairs—including two sun-bleached lawn chairs that Mr. Sheffield keeps by the entrance—and placed them around a folding table I'd never seen before.

"Where did you get that table?" I asked with a frown.

"Out of one of the storage units," Sloan said.

I was horrified. "How?"

He pointed at the metal cabinet where we kept all the spare keys.

"You didn't!"

"I'm just borrowing it," he said as if pilfering through the private possessions people had paid the Midway Store and Save to keep safe was no big deal. "I'll put it back when our Midway project is over."

"What if the real owner comes looking for their table before then?"

He shrugged. "I'll park a piece of heavy equipment in front of that unit and tell them they'll have to wait."

I rolled my eyes in exasperation. "It's a good thing for you I'm quitting this job, or I'd insist that you put this table back immediately."

"I'm sure whoever owns this table won't mind us borrowing it—to help the cause and all." He handed me a paper plate. "Now get some doughnuts. Maybe a little sugar will put you into a better mood."

"There's nothing wrong with my mood," I muttered as I filled my plate with very fresh Krispy Kremes. "I'm just not a fan of stealing."

"Borrowing," he said as he put a whole glazed doughnut into his mouth.

"Borrowing without permission is stealing." I picked up a bottle of water and marched over to the stolen table. I had just taken a seat when the other team members arrived.

Catsy came in yawning. She was wearing skin-tight black leggings that stopped just above her ankles, black stiletto heels, and an oversized zebra-print shirt. It was an odd outfit—a lot like Catsy herself—but it worked on her. "If we're going to meet this early every morning, why don't we just get together the night before?"

"Don't give him any ideas," Rand muttered. "He'll start having morning *and* evening meetings!" He picked up a doughnut and a cup of coffee. Then he sat down in one of the chairs closest to Mr. Sheffield's desk.

Catsy took only a bottle of water from the table. I guessed that was how she maintained her skeletal weight—starvation.

Morris and Newell walked in together, and it looked like they were arguing over something. But they discontinued their conversation once they had an audience.

Sloan pointed to the desk. "Doughnuts and coffee are over there."

"I've already eaten," Morris said. He looked sleek and expensive as always, but a little out of sorts, probably thanks to his disagreement with Newell.

Newell helped himself to a plateful of doughnuts and sat by Rand. Newell had on black pants and a bright yellow shirt with a black-and-white-striped tie. While not as glaringly colorful as his outfit from the day before, this ensemble made him look like a bumblebee.

Drake walked in last, gorgeous and a little harried. He declined the offer of breakfast but did thank Sloan for getting it. Then he moved to the head of the table. His team members recognized this as his call to order and quickly settled into various seats.

Catsy sat on one side of me and Sloan on the other. I put my phone in my lap where I would immediately see any text messages from North Carolina. Then I looked up as Drake addressed us.

"Good morning, everyone," he said with a smile. "So today the renovation of Midway begins in earnest again."

There were some polite chuckles.

"We would like to particularly welcome Kennedy to the team."

I smiled, a little embarrassed. "Thank you."

Newell looked at me. "During our drive over from the hotel, Rand was telling us about your success with acquisitions yesterday. It sounds like you had a great first day."

"I didn't do much of anything," I demurred. "But we were pretty successful and I did enjoy it."

Drake said, "And because of the success with acquisitions, we can proceed as planned. Sloan, you'll add demolition at the newly acquired properties to your construction schedule?"

"I will." Sloan checked his watch. "I've got a couple of crews waiting, so if you don't have anything else for me, I'll need to get to work."

Drake nodded. "We know how to reach you if we think of anything you need to know."

With a wink in my direction, Sloan left.

Drake waved toward Rand. "I'll turn the floor over to you. Tell us what will be going on today."

Rand stood and began a lecture on all the various projects. He gave too many details and since none of it involved me, my mind wandered. I was picturing myself with Luke on a beautiful Hawaiian beach when my phone vibrated, indicating that I had a text message. It was from Luke.

He said, *I thought of something Miss Eugenia can fry. How about chicken? I'll bet it would be a big hit.*

I responded. *Ha. Although actually the other entries are so far afield going back to fried chicken might actually be unique.*

Catsy leaned forward and pointed at my phone. "Boyfriend?"

"Husband," I whispered back. "He's in the Marines."

She smiled. "Thank goodness for texting." Then she reached for her own phone. I glanced around the room. Morris and Drake were also typing onto their phones. Poor Rand. All that talking and only Newell was actually listening to him.

When the meeting finally ended, Rand rushed off to the courthouse in Albany to file paperwork on all the acquisitions. Drake had to catch a plane to Chicago for a board meeting.

"I'll be back tonight," he told me. "And I was thinking that this morning you might want to go to the city hall with Catsy and see the changes she's planned firsthand. Unless you're in a rush to get to those thank-you notes."

"I'll go with Catsy!" I answered.

He laughed and waved as he walked out.

Catsy helped me put up the leftover doughnuts. Then I rode with her to the city hall.

"Things look better already!" I exclaimed when I saw all the work that was going on. The new sidewalks were ready for cement to be poured. A landscaping company was planting a few trees. A crew dressed in rubber overalls was power-washing the building's old exterior.

"I love this stage," she said. "Seeing the transformation begin."

She took me inside, where walls were being painted in her muted-primary-color scheme. The old marble floors were being restored, draperies and blinds replaced. There were so many people working that there wasn't much room for us to stand.

"I've ordered a rug to go here," she said as she led me to a small alcove. "It's a reproduction and very similar to the one that was put here when the building was built back in 1948. I found a picture and matched it."

"That was thoughtful," I said. She could have picked any rug, but she went to the trouble to match the original.

As we walked through the building, she showed me where pictures would eventually hang. "I picked out some large framed art for the walls—prints that match the period too," she added.

"Pictures will warm the place up."

"And then there will be couches and chairs in all the sitting rooms. And new desks and chairs throughout the building—lots of dark wood to contrast with the gray marble."

"I love it," I said with sincerity. "You are an amazing designer."

She blushed. "Thank you." As we started walking back toward the entrance, she asked, "How long have you been married?"

I felt justified in skimming over my entire two-year legal association with Cade and just answered. "Three days."

She was astonished. "Why aren't you on your honeymoon?"

I explained about Luke and the trial and that he had to leave during our reception.

"That's romantic in an awful sort of way."

I nodded. "I couldn't have described it better."

"I'm planning a wedding myself," she said. "Was it hard to arrange everything?"

"Not for me," I told her. "My mother handled it all."

"I don't have any family so I'm doing it all myself. I'm hoping it won't be too bad since we don't want anything fancy. We'll just have his immediate family and a few close friends in a nice garden. Then a little reception afterwards. Very small and simple."

"Good luck with that," I said. "I was hoping for small and simple too."

She laughed and said her future mother-in-law was sort of overbearing and very hard to please so she might not end up with exactly what she hoped for either. "But as long as you get your husband in the end, that's all that matters, right?"

I smiled. "I guess you're right. And I have to admit that my wedding was very nice. It was just bigger and more public than I would have preferred."

She nodded. "I understand."

"So when is the big day?"

"We haven't picked a date yet, but I've got my dress already."

I wondered if her wedding gown was black. I wanted to ask her but chickened out.

"Will you keep working for Drake once you're married?" I asked instead.

She shrugged. "I'm not sure about that yet. I'm still trying to decide."

We reached the busy front lobby.

"Thanks for the tour," I told her.

"It was a pleasure," she said with a smile. "I've got to go over to the Baptist church and consult with the building committee about the interior design for the new family center. Would you like to come with me?"

I didn't want to go. I'd already spent enough time with Catsy— who was nice but a little odd. I didn't know her well so I wasn't really all that comfortable with her. But I couldn't think of a reason to politely refuse—especially since I was on the payroll. Just before I committed, my phone rang. I looked down to see Cade's number on the touch screen.

Under other circumstances, I would have ignored his call, but since I was looking for an excuse to get away from Catsy, I said, "I'd love to go with you to the meeting with the church committee, but this is the sheriff's office calling so I'd better see what they want."

"Do you need a ride back to your truck?"

"No, I'll find a ride. You just go on to the church. And good luck on those small and simple wedding plans!"

She laughed and, after a quick wave, slipped through the front door. I waited until I was sure she was gone and then called Cade back.

He answered with, "Where are you?"

"At the city hall," I replied.

"Can you walk over to the sheriff's department?" he asked. "There's something I need to talk to you about."

I looked out the window and saw Catsy driving away. "I'll be there in a minute."

Then I skirted carefully through all the workers and walked out of city hall.

When I reached the sheriff's department, Cade was pacing by the door, obviously waiting for me. He led me into the small office off the lobby that he liked to pretend was his own and closed the door.

"Miss Eugenia called. Kate's sister didn't find any connection between Nola Finkle and any of the prisoners—the ones who escaped and the ones who didn't."

"Well, I guess that's it for your theory." I was a little sorry for him. Even Cade deserved to be right every once in a while.

"Maybe I'm being stubborn and hard-headed, but I can't give up on Nola," he said. "I just have a feeling that there's more to that wreck than meets the eye."

I was pretty sure that what Cade really didn't want to admit was that the rude police chief in Albany had been right when he classified the wreck as an accident. But I said, "What more can you do?"

"I called the police in Templeton and notified them that approximately twenty-seven cats had been stranded by Nola's death. They said they would arrange for the cats to be picked up by the local animal shelter."

I was surprised and impressed that Cade would consider the welfare of a bunch of cats—let alone call and make arrangements for them.

"I also asked them to seal off the house as a crime scene until we've had a chance to examine it."

I was confused. "So you've established that there was a crime?"

"Not officially," he hedged. "But if we don't protect any possible evidence, we'll never be able to make a case."

"So you're going to Templeton to look around Nola's house," I guessed.

He nodded. "If I don't find anything to help prove my theory, I'll give up. I'll accept that Nola Finkle and her death and the prisoners' escape really was all just a freak accident."

"Then go," I said. "It's better to make sure now so you won't have to wonder if you made a mistake when it's too late."

His shoulder's sagged with relief. "I'm glad you agree with me."

Cade had never cared too much for my opinion in the past, so I was wary. "When are you going?"

"Now," he replied. "And I was hoping you'd go with me."

In my life there's always a catch. "Why me?"

"I need your experience and instincts."

I couldn't believe Cade was admitting he needed anyone, especially me. He must have been more desperate than I had previously thought. "That's a long drive," I said. "It will take all afternoon, and I'm supposed to be working for Drake."

"We can make it there in just a little over two hours if I drive my sheriff's car and exceed the speed limit," Cade persuaded. "And I'll bet if you ask Drake Langston, he will let you reschedule your duties for tomorrow."

"I don't have any actual duties," I said. "I'm just supposed to be available to the team members in case they need advice from a native of Midway."

Cade frowned. "What kind of job is that?"

"A pretty good one," I replied.

"But if you don't have any specific duties, you can come with me, right?" he pressed. "If we can look around Nola Finkle's house in Templeton and don't find anything, I promise not to mention it to you again."

That alone was worth a drive to Templeton. "Okay, I'll check with Sloan, and if he doesn't mind, I'll go with you. But this is it, Cade. I can't invest any more of my time in this non-case without payment."

He smiled. "Call your long-haired friend while I go tell the sheriff I'm taking the afternoon off."

I glared at him as he walked away. Since Drake was on the plane headed to Chicago, I left him a message and called Sloan.

"Hey, Kennedy, I'm kind of busy here trying to rebuild a town in less than fourteen days. So as much as I enjoy talking to you, can we save it for the evenings when we're watching your old TV and drinking Pepsis?"

I knew he was teasing, but I'll admit my feathers were a little ruffled by his remarks. "I just wanted to let you know that I'm going to be out of town for the rest of the day. If you or any of the other team members need me, I can be reached by cell phone."

"What do you mean by 'out-of-town?'" he demanded.

"I'm driving to Atlanta with Cade. He wants to check out Nola Finkle's house before he puts the case to rest permanently."

"Nola Finkle? The woman who died in the car accident?"

"One and the same," I confirmed.

"The one we agreed had no connection to the escaped convicts?"

"We still haven't found a connection, but Cade thinks there is one. The only way I can settle this is to go with him to her house. I'll be back tonight, but it might be late. So you may have to watch my pitiful TV and drink my Pepsis alone."

"I think we should talk about this," Sloan began, but I cut him off.

"I wouldn't dream of wasting any more of your valuable time. See you tonight." And then I disconnected the call.

Cade walked in just as I put the phone in my pocket.

"So?" he asked.

"I guess I'm going with you."

He smiled and handed me a stack of papers. "These are the background checks on Nola Finkle and the prisoners that Kate's sister faxed to me. I figured we could go over them during the drive to Templeton."

"Haven't you already read them?" I asked.

"Yeah, but I want your opinion."

Another first.

"Let's go before the sheriff changes his mind about letting me have the afternoon off."

CHAPTER ELEVEN

ONCE WE WERE IN CADE'S squad car headed toward Templeton, I asked, "Have those missing prisoners been recaptured?"

He shook his head. "No. It's like they disappeared into thin air."

"Well, I can't say I hope they are located anytime soon. Miss Ida Jean is afraid to leave her house for fear she'll attract their attention, and Miss Ida Jean being locked safely in her house has all kinds of advantages for me."

He smiled. "I'd like to help you out with that, but if I get a chance to arrest those two missing prisoners, I'll have to do it. I am an officer of the law, after all."

"Unless Miss Ida Jean gets you fired for dereliction of duty," I informed him. "She's pretty mad that the convicts are running free and she's stuck in her house."

"Maybe she'll cheer up when she gets her water bill," Cade remarked. "Since she hasn't been able to stand outside and drown her lawn, she's probably saved a hundred dollars."

I laughed. "That is truly a silver lining."

Then I scanned over the background checks Kate's sister had prepared. All of the convicts were residents of Georgia. All were imprisoned for nonviolent crimes and had earned the right to be part of the work-release program through good behavior.

I told Cade, "According to this, all of the prisoners had less than a year left on their various sentences. So why break out?"

He shrugged. "Maybe they just couldn't take it any longer."

I referred back to the reports. "Nola was an only child born to middle-aged parents," I read out loud. "She was a good student and got a scholarship to Georgia Tech, where she earned a degree in mechanical engineering. After graduation she took an underwhelming job at a large veterinary supply company selling cages and exam tables and doggie toys."

"It's a solid company," Cade pointed out. "She started there with a good salary right out of school."

"True, but for a Georgia Tech grad, it just seems like she would have dreamed of something . . . bigger."

Cade proved that he had read the reports by saying, "Her elderly parents were sickly and needed her to stay close to home. So she was limited in the jobs she could take."

"True." I frowned at the report. "Anyway, that explains how she owns a house that is paid for. She inherited it from her parents. But after they died, why didn't she sell the house and get a condo in downtown Atlanta so she would be closer to her job?"

"She probably stayed in Templeton for those cats," Cade said. "Since she had a house in a rural community, she could get away with having twenty-seven. If she'd lived in the city, there'd be no way to do that."

Cade's observation was nearly shrewd, but I didn't tell him I thought so.

"The report shows absolutely no connection between Nola and any of the prisoners," I continued. "Except that they all lived in Georgia and were all involved in a wreck on Highway 17 last Saturday afternoon."

"That's what it says," Cade agreed.

"And just what is it you're hoping to find at her house, besides pet dander?"

He shuddered. "I don't know. This may be a wild goose chase, and I know it wouldn't be my first dumb idea. But I can't help thinking that it's important to investigate Nola Finkle. That she deserves that much from us. And even though it doesn't make any sense, I have a gut feeling that something was not right about that wreck."

I understood that feeling all too well. "I'm not making fun of you." Well, that was mostly true. "And I think it's good that you're so dedicated to finding out the truth."

True to his word, Cade drove very fast. As we entered each new jurisdiction, he would use his radio to contact the local authorities and tell them he was passing through on official business—at an alarming rate.

I texted Luke and explained where I was and why. He texted back, *Not thrilled. Be careful.*

I promised that I would be.

Cade got several text messages from Hannah-Leigh as well, but he didn't answer any of them. Finally I commented on it.

"Why don't you answer Hannah-Leigh's calls and texts?"

"Because if I do, she'll want to know where I am and I don't want to tell her."

I didn't necessarily think that I had a *right* to know exactly where Luke was at any time of the day or night, but I was completely and totally positive that if I asked him, he would tell me (unless he was prevented from doing so by Lt. Dempsey and the United States Marine Corps). And we had only been married for three days. I felt sad for Cade and Hannah-Leigh. Even if their relationship withstood the test of time—which I doubted—I was afraid they'd never have what Luke and I had managed to achieve already in our brief marriage.

About an hour outside Templeton, Cade stopped for a hamburger. He offered to buy me one, but I was afraid this might be misconstrued as a date, so I declined and prayed that the doughnuts I'd had for breakfast would pull me through until we got back to Midway.

* * *

The town of Templeton was rural without being charming. Maybe it was the knowledge that the huge city of Atlanta loomed just a few miles to the north, but it seemed more like a suburb than a town in its own right. Or maybe it was the fact that there was no town square or even a main street to give it definition and focus. There were a couple of strip malls, some gas stations, and even a few fast food restaurants. But everything felt separate—no cohesion or sense of togetherness.

Cade had arranged with the Templeton police for both an officer and Nola's lawyer to meet us at her house. So when we arrived there were two cars parked in the driveway—a late-model Lexus and a slightly battered black-and-white patrol car.

The house was a small, single-story dwelling, painted bright yellow with green shutters. This was not a color combination I would have chosen, but it was cheerful. There were lots of flowers and plants in the yard. They weren't organized artistically like Miss Eugenia's gardens (which seriously could be a cover for *Southern Living*). But it was obvious that Nola had put forth great effort to beautify her yard. I felt a new wave of sadness for this woman I had never met.

Cade parked at the curb, and we walked up to the front door where two men were waiting for us. The lawyer introduced himself as Lester McNaughton. The police officer shook hands with Cade and nodded at me. Then he produced the keys and unlocked the door. When he pushed it open, the smell of cat urine assailed us.

Cade cursed under his breath and turned away, making gagging sounds. "I thought the animal shelter was supposed to come and get the cats!"

"The cats are all gone," Mr. McNaughton said. "But the smell is pretty strong because the house has been closed up since, well, since Nola left on Saturday."

"Pretty strong!" Cade pulled out a handkerchief and pressed it to his watering eyes. "This smell is lethal!"

Mr. McNaughton looked apologetic, the police officer looked confused, and Cade looked like he was crying. It was all I could do to keep from laughing hysterically.

"I'll open the doors and some windows," the lawyer said. "Maybe some fresh air will help."

"We need to look around quick or I'm going to be in the hospital with an allergic reaction from overexposure to cat!" Cade told me.

"What exactly are we looking for?" the police officer wanted to know.

I was still trying to control my laughter so I let Cade answer.

"We're looking for a connection between Ms. Finkle and one of the prisoners who escaped during the wreck on Saturday."

"You think she ran into the prison van on purpose to help one of them get away?" the police officer guessed.

"That's ridiculous," Mr. McNaughton informed us as he returned from opening windows. "Nola was very honest, and I can't imagine her breaking the law—let alone associating with criminals."

Cade glared at him—as well as he could with tears pouring from his red eyes. "It's just a theory we need to check out." He walked into a small bedroom that was set up like an office. "It's hard to say, but one thing's for sure—I'm not going to be able to stay in here long enough to do much searching. Is it okay if we take her computer and all these files with us?"

The police officer shrugged. "It's your case, not ours."

"I don't have any objection," Mr. McNaughton replied. I had the feeling that he was as anxious to get out of the reeking house as Cade. "As long as you return it all when you're through. We're having an estate sale, and all the proceeds will go to the animal shelter."

Cade looked appalled. "You're going to *sell* this contaminated stuff?"

The lawyer sighed. "We're going to try."

"How are you going to get into her computer without a password?" the officer asked.

"I don't think that's going to be a problem." I pointed to the hot pink sticky note taped to the side of the monitor that said "password—kittykats."

The lawyer picked up one of the files and shuffled through it gingerly. "Most of this stuff is related to her work. You might need to get permission from Universal Pet Products."

Cade nodded. "I'll call them. But right now we just need to load it all into my patrol car."

"Since you're this allergic to cats, don't you think it could be dangerous for you to drive with all this in your car?" the police officer asked.

"Maybe we can put it all in garbage bags to seal off the smell," Cade suggested. "I'll look in the kitchen."

"If the garbage bags come from here I don't see how they are going to help much," I pointed out.

"We'll turn them inside out," Cade said as he removed a big box of garbage bags from a cupboard in the kitchen. "Maybe that will help at least a little."

While the men wrapped and loaded Nola's computer and files, I walked through the house, which was neat—especially considering the number of felines that had been in residence. The furnishings were simple and functional. Nola had apparently been a minimalist when it came to knickknacks and decorations—since basically there were none. Or maybe having so many cats had restricted her indoor creativity.

And apparently Nola was camera-shy since there was only one picture of her in the entire house. It was an 8×10 color print of the newspaper picture Sloan had found on Saturday night when we first stated investigating the wreck at Cade's request. It was framed and displayed all by itself on the mantel over the fireplace (which was being used as a cat bed). I walked a little closer and looked at Nola standing beside the elderly lady—each of them holding cats and smiling at the camera.

Cade came into the room and said, "I've taken pictures of all the rooms and collected any miscellaneous stuff." He opened the drawer of the end table by the couch and dumped the contents into an inside-out garbage bag. "Let's get out of here."

He turned and went outside. My eyes were drawn back to the picture, and finally I picked it up. I walked to the front door, where Mr. McNaughton was standing. "I'd like to take this picture, if you don't mind."

"That's fine. I don't think it would sell for much," he said.

"I think the other lady in this picture might like to have it," I explained. "So I thought I'd find out who she is and send it to her."

"That was part of a newspaper article," the lawyer said. "If you look it up, I'm sure you'll find her name."

I nodded but didn't tell him I was already aware of this information.

"I'm going to close the windows," he said. "It was nice meeting you."

"Thanks for your help," I said on Cade's behalf. Then I walked out to his car where he was standing.

"What's that?" he asked, pointing to the picture in my hand. He looked like Rocky after his first fight with Apollo Creed—face red and eyes nearly swollen shut.

"It's a picture of Nola and a friend," I explained. "I want to find out who the other woman is and send it to her."

He shook his head in exasperation as he opened the trunk. "Put it in here."

I did as he instructed.

"And now you've got cat on your hands." He slammed the trunk closed.

"Do you want me to drive?" I offered, more out of self-preservation than any effort to be helpful.

"You can't drive an official sheriff's department car," he snapped. "It's against the rules." Then he climbed in behind the wheel and slammed his door shut.

Afraid he might leave me and my cat-contaminated hands behind if I hesitated, I got in on the passenger side.

"Do you need to stop at a gas station to get some allergy medicine?" I asked him as he turned the car around and headed back for the interstate.

"I've already taken something. And now that we're away from that place, I should be okay," he muttered. "Who could live like that?"

"Someone who wasn't allergic to cats," I answered in Nola's defense.

Luke texted, wanting to know about our excursion. So I delightfully spent the next thirty minutes in a typing conversation telling him all the details. When he finally said he had to go, I put my phone in my lap.

"I guess you and Scoggins have been making fun of me," Cade said. It was hard to tell from his expression if he was mad because of all the swelling, but I guessed yes.

I avoided an outright lie by saying, "There's nothing funny about allergies." Then to distract him I said, "Weren't you supposed to call the veterinary supply company that Nola worked for on the way home?"

I provided the number and Cade placed the call. He spoke with Nola's supervisor briefly and after ending the call, reported, "Her supervisor said she was a wonderful, generous person but unique." He cut his eyes over at me. "Which means weirdo."

"Not necessarily," I objected.

He ignored my remark and continued. "He says that she's been working from home ever since her parents died. He said this was an arrangement that worked out best for everyone, because even though her coworkers loved her, it was difficult to work around her." He gave me another pointed look. "Which means they had to get that cat smell out of the office."

I made a face at him. "He said everyone loved her."

"Weirdo," he repeated. "And he said all the files we got from Nola Finkle's house are duplicates. They have electronic copies."

"So did he say we can keep this stuff in the trunk?"

"He didn't actually say that," Cade hedged. "But he didn't say we had to bring it to him either."

"Then I say we keep it."

Cade smiled as his phone rang.

I glanced at the screen and saw Hannah-Leigh's name. I expected him to ignore the call as he'd been doing, but to my surprise, he answered it. He apologized for not answering her calls but explained that he was working on a case and hadn't had the opportunity.

I rolled my eyes.

After promising to be home in time to take her out for dinner and expressing his undying love, which I'll admit was a little awkward for me—and not just because he was my ex-husband. Overhearing a conversation like that is always uncomfortable. After he ended the call, he was quiet for a little while.

Then he said, "I'm sorry for how I've acted this afternoon. I know you're doing me a favor by coming along, and I shouldn't have been rude. But those cats really got to me."

I felt magnanimous, so I said, "I forgive you."

He took his swollen eyes off the road long enough to glance at me. "Do you really?"

"You haven't been that much ruder than usual today," I replied.

"No, I don't mean just about today. I mean about everything."

"Everything?" I said. "Like dating me just to spite Luke and the drive-in and the divorce?"

He nodded. "I was so immature and selfish. I am really sorry for all of it."

I could see how much he wanted me to believe him, and since I no longer had an emotional investment, I nodded. "I forgive you for everything."

His shoulders relaxed. I was surprised (and pleased) to see that my forgiveness was important to him. Then he said, "I love Hannah-Leigh."

I wasn't sure how to reply to this odd remark, so I said, "I know you do."

Clutching the steering wheel and staring at the road, he added, "But sometimes I still wonder if we could have made it work."

I shook my head firmly. "Don't go there. Don't ever even allow yourself to think about that. What's done is done. We're both remarried to people who make us happier than we ever made each other. We need to look to the future."

"You're right. I just wanted you to know."

"I appreciate that."

"And I hope we can always be friends."

I had to draw the line somewhere, and it might as well be here. "We can always be civil to each other, but we can't be friends. Even though you've apologized, the past still happened. Besides, a friendship between us would make Luke uncomfortable, and I can't do that. I won't."

He nodded. "I guess you're right."

Cade's phone rang again, and this time the name Ida Jean Baxley filled his touch screen. Cade groaned and I took comfort from the fact that I was not the only person Miss Ida Jean tormented.

"She probably just wants to know if you've caught the escaped prisoners."

With a whimper he answered the phone. Cade's side of the conversation was a lot of "no ma'ams" and "yes ma'ams." When he finally closed the phone, he complained that Miss Ida Jean was the most annoying person in the county. Apparently he hadn't really gotten to know Miss George Ann yet, or otherwise he would have declared a fair-and-square tie.

"Did she ask about the prisoners?"

"Yes, but only in passing," he confirmed. "Mostly she called to report that someone is stealing her trash."

"Trash as in . . . *garbage*?"

"I mean the bags that Midway residents put at the curb for the county garbage collectors to pick up."

"And when you say *stealing* . . . ?" I prompted further.

"She puts the garbage out the night before and the next morning, it's gone—before the truck comes by to collect it."

"I don't understand why anyone would steal Miss Ida Jean's garbage."

Cade sighed. "I'm sure there is nothing to it, but I promised to check it out or she'd complain to the sheriff. Or maybe the governor."

I would have laughed except this was a real possibility.

When we were getting close to Midway, Cade asked if he could drop all the cat-contaminated files and assorted Nola miscellanea at my apartment. "That way it will be easy for you to go through it all and search for a connection to one of the prisoners."

"I don't have time to search through all that stuff!" I objected. "When I'm not working for Drake Langston, my mother wants me to be writing thank-you notes. And for all I know, Luke might be allergic to cats. If I have all that stuff in my apartment, he might have a reaction and have a swollen face like yours during our honeymoon!"

He tried to frown. "Well, I can't do it, obviously. Maybe you could call Miss Eugenia and see if we can leave this stuff with her. She's old so she's got plenty of time to sort through it."

"She is much busier than you might imagine, and asking her to take all this would be a big imposition. But since neither one of us can keep it, I'll ask her."

"Thank you," he replied.

I called Miss Eugenia, who was eating dinner with her boyfriend, Whit Owens. She graciously agreed to accept delivery of Nola's possessions and even offered to cut her dinner date short and meet us at her house.

So Cade turned toward Haggerty. Miss Eugenia and Whit were both there waiting on us. Whit helped us unload all of Nola's things into the already crowded living room. While we set up the computer, Miss Eugenia's little dog, Lady, ran from box to box, growling.

"I think she's expecting cats to be in these bags," Whit said.

"She's going to be real disappointed when she sees it's just boxes full of paper."

Once we were done, Miss Eugenia put her hands on her hips and looked around at all the garbage bags. "Well, I declare it might take us months to sort through this."

"It can't take months," Cade replied, covering his mouth with his hand in an apparent attempt to avoid breathing more allergens. "This case is getting colder by the minute."

I frowned at him. "We know we can't expect you to drop everything else you're doing to work on this."

Miss Eugenia laughed. "I'm not doing much of anything. I'll get on it first thing in the morning."

Cade gave me a satisfied smile. Then he thanked Miss Eugenia profusely, and we said our good-byes.

"You sure were being pushy to someone who was doing you a huge favor!" I said once we got in the car.

He didn't deny it. "I know. But if we don't act fast, we may miss our chance to figure out what happened to Nola."

I couldn't argue with that, so I took out my phone and texted Luke.

When we pulled up in the Midway Store and Save parking lot, Cade noted that Sloan's truck was parked beside mine.

"So, does that guy live here now?"

"Almost," I replied. "He's sleeping on the couch in Mr. Sheffield's office."

Cade tried to raise his eyebrows, but the facial swelling prevented him from achieving much movement. "Why?"

"For security," I explained. "They are storing a lot of expensive equipment here during the renovation."

I knew it would take Cade a few minutes to process this information, and before he could think of more questions, I slipped out of the car. "I'll go over to Miss Eugenia's tomorrow and help her sort through all of Nola's stuff. I'll let you know if we find anything."

Then I waved and hurried up the stairs.

CHAPTER TWELVE

WHEN SLOAN OPENED THE DOOR to my apartment, he was eating Chinese food out of a takeout container. He pointed toward the coffee table with his chopsticks and said, "I got plenty for you too."

Generally I'm not a big fan of Chinese, but I was so hungry I would have eaten most anything. I picked up an eggroll and it tasted delicious to me. Maybe I do like Chinese food, after all.

"How was your trip?" he asked.

I had enjoyed making fun of Cade in my texts to Luke but didn't feel comfortable doing the same with Sloan, so I just said, "Fine."

"Did you find anything to suggest Nola Finkle was trying to break the prisoners out of jail?"

"No," I took another bite of eggroll.

"Told you so," he said smugly.

"We haven't found anything yet, but we brought a lot of her stuff with us, including her computer. We dropped it off at Miss Eugenia's house, and she's going to help us look through it—and hopefully find something that will at least explain why Nola was driving on Highway 17 on Saturday."

"It's worth a shot, I guess," Sloan conceded.

"How did the transformation of Midway go today?"

"Pretty good," he said. "We got all the demolition done, and now that we have a rear entrance at the subdivision, the work will go even faster."

"It's not causing a lot of trouble to work around Mrs. Hoban's house?"

Sloan looked up from his chop suey. "What do you mean?"

A little cold chill settled around my heart. "Agatha Hoban wanted to stay in her house until they finish building her new one."

Sloan shook his head. "She must have changed her mind because her house was on the demolition list. We had to delay a few minutes while the movers finished loading up her stuff, but then we plowed it over. The place was so structurally unstable that we barely even had to bump it."

"I don't understand," I told him. "She was very positive about that when Rand and I met with her yesterday."

"You can call him and ask," Sloan said. "But I'm just telling you—we tore down her house."

I didn't have Rand's number so Sloan had to get it for me from his phone. Then I called, and Rand confirmed that plans had changed. "The health department wouldn't allow her to stay there during construction. In fact, they said she shouldn't have been living there anyway. The place was unsound and full of mold so they condemned it. We talked to her nephew, and he convinced her to move into the retirement apartments temporarily."

"What about her big TV?"

Rand laughed. "I delivered it to the retirement place this afternoon. I predict she'll decide to stay there. It's nice and even though she doesn't like being called old, she is. And they are set up to take care of her needs as her health continues to deteriorate with age. As long as she has that big TV and can watch her shows—what more does she really need?"

"I guess," I replied. "And as long as Agatha is okay with it, I certainly am."

When I ended my call with Rand, I yawned and then told Sloan to take what was left of his Chinese dinner downstairs. "I need to call my husband and then go to bed."

Sloan gathered up his food and headed for the door. "Tell him I said hi."

I smirked at him, and he descended to the office below.

* * *

Because I stayed up later than I should have on Monday night talking to Luke, I slept in later than I meant to on Tuesday morning. I hate sleeping in since it gets the whole day off to a bad start. To make things worse, I didn't have a good-morning text message from Luke. I wasn't really expecting one, since he told me the night before that he would be in court first thing, but I was still disappointed.

I didn't have time for a shower so I pulled my hair back into a ponytail. I put on my jeans and Langston Association shirt straight from the dryer. I was tying my shoes when Sloan came up to get me.

He frowned. "You look like you just rolled out of bed."

"I did." I stood up and followed him downstairs.

"You're so late that all the good doughnuts are probably gone."

"Why would you buy 'bad' doughnuts?" I asked.

"I buy a variety pack," he replied. "They always stick some bad ones in—just to get rid of them, I guess."

"Oh well, I'm so hungry I'll gladly eat the bad doughnuts."

We reached the office below where the rest of Drake's team was already assembled. I was a little self-conscious about my appearance after Sloan's remark, but no one else seemed to notice. I got some doughnuts and took a seat at the table beside Catsy.

Apparently they were waiting for me because the second I sat down, Rand called the meeting to order.

"Where's Drake?" I whispered to Catsy.

"He had to go to Albany," she answered. "There's some zoning issue that's come up with the senior center."

Rand cleared his throat. Once he had our attention, he touched on each of the projects that were in progress in Midway. I tried to listen (and really tried not to doze). Then he went around the table and asked for reports, complaints, and requests from everyone.

When Rand finally dismissed us, I asked if anyone had an assignment for me.

"Drake didn't mention anything," Rand said. "But you can call him and see."

I dialed Drake's number and he answered immediately. "Nothing this morning, but I'd like to discuss business over dinner tonight if you're available."

I was available but knew the gossiping tongues in Midway would wag themselves crazy if I went to dinner with Drake again. So I said, "I'd love to, but I can't. Maybe another time."

He accepted my refusal politely and said he would see me the next morning at our team meeting.

After ending the call with Drake, I watched the others hurry on to their assignments, leaving me feeling alone and unnecessary as I put up what was left of the bad doughnuts. A few minutes later Sloan came back. He stopped in the doorway, backlit by the rising Georgia sun. His face was cast in shadows, making him seem dangerous in a good way. With his glossy black hair tucked behind his ears and his bright blue eyes, he looked like a male model at a photo shoot. And I'll admit I sighed in pure visual appreciation.

"So," he said after giving me a few seconds to admire him. "Do you want to come be my groupie today?"

Sloan was many levels of contradiction. Usually he seemed flippant and flirty, but he had a sensitive side and sometimes he allowed it to show.

"Thanks, but I think I'll pass."

"I don't want you to be bored." He didn't add "lonely," but I know that was what he was thinking.

"I won't be," I promised. "Agatha Hoban has been on my mind ever since I found out she lost her home prematurely, so I think I'll go visit her during my spare time this morning. Then I need to go to Miss Eugenia's house and help her sort through Nola's stuff."

He gave me a bone-melting grin. "Well, if you change your mind, just call me. I've always wanted a fan club. You can even be president!"

I smirked back. "As honored as I am, don't hold your breath."

Laughing, he turned and walked back outside.

I pulled out my phone and called Miss Eugenia's number. She answered on the first ring. "Hello!"

"That was quick," I said.

"I was talking to my sister so the phone was already in my hand."

"I can call you back if you're not finished talking to your sister," I offered.

"Every conversation with Annabelle ends in an argument—so you saved me from an unnecessary fight. But if you're calling to find out what I've found in Nola Finkle's things, the answer is nothing. I haven't even started yet."

"Actually I was calling to offer my assistance," I told her. "But first I'd like to go see Agatha Hoban. Do you know her?"

"I've heard the name but don't think I've met her."

"I hadn't ever met her either until I went with Rand to visit her on Sunday. Her house was on a couple of acres of land at the back of the subdivision Drake is building. They needed her property to make a service entrance for supplies and heavy equipment. He offered her a good price plus one of the houses he's building for cost. She agreed to sell but didn't want to move twice, so she made Rand promise that she could stay in her old house until the new one was ready. But Sloan told me yesterday that the health department had made her move. So she's at that new retirement complex in Millwood."

"I'd like to see that retirement complex myself," Miss Eugenia said. "Not that I'm planning to move there anytime soon, but it's good to know what your options are."

"Well, why don't you come with me to Millwood?" I suggested. "It shouldn't take long, and when we get back to your house, we'll look through Nola's stuff."

"I'll be ready when you get here."

I checked in with my mother and told her about my plans for the morning.

"I'm very pleased that you're visiting the elderly," she said. "And since Drake Langston isn't keeping you busy, you've got time to work in dinner with us tonight."

There wasn't much I could say to that. "I'd love to."

"Wonderful!" she said. "I'm making your favorite—fried chicken with creamed potatoes and fresh corn and homemade rolls. And Luke's strawberry shortcake in a bowl for dessert."

How could I possibly resist?

After ending my call, I headed for Haggerty. On the way I stopped by Walmart and purchased Agatha a house-warming gift—a home version of *Jeopardy!* Then I picked up Miss Eugenia and we started toward Millwood.

"I did accomplish one thing for Nola," she told me as we drove. "I identified the woman in that picture. Her name is Dixie Reed and she's from Graceful, Florida. She worked at the animal shelter there and that's how she met Nola—at a pet fair Universal Pet Products sponsored in Atlanta. I looked up her telephone number online, but it's been disconnected. So I asked Kelsey to locate current contact information for her."

"I appreciate that," I said. "Maybe it's silly, but that picture was obviously important to Nola, and I hope it will be to her friend Dixie as well."

It took us a little over an hour to reach Millwood. During the drive Miss Eugenia entertained me with descriptions of her failed fried food attempts. Finally she said, "I may just have to admit defeat and withdraw my name."

"Don't give up yet!" I encouraged. "I've been trying to think of ideas and I told Luke to be thinking too. Surely one of us can come up with a winning idea!"

"We can only hope," she muttered as we saw the exit for Millwood.

The town itself was small but new-looking with matching adobe-style architecture for everything from the shopping centers to the gas stations. We passed several housing developments on our way to the retirement complex. The neighborhoods seemed to be divided by size (and probably income brackets). It felt unnatural and staged. Millwood was a little *too* charming for my tastes.

The retirement complex had a Southwestern look that matched the rest of the town. It was very modern and clean. We parked and walked to the front entrance, which was flanked by large terra cotta planters filled with cactuses. The doors opened automatically and seemed to suck us inside.

"I hate nursing homes," Miss Eugenia muttered.

"I'm not a fan of them myself," I whispered back.

"But you don't have to worry about getting put in one anytime soon."

"That's true." I smiled as we entered the lobby. In my previous experience with nursing homes, they were always cramped, too warm, and smelled unpleasantly of Pine-sol. Inside the Millwood complex we found high ceilings, and the air was cool and fresh-smelling. The walls were painted a soothing tan color, and the furniture was upholstered in earth tones. We could have been in a nice hotel in Phoenix instead of a nursing home in Millwood, Georgia.

The lady at the welcome desk greeted us with a friendly smile. "Hello!" she said. Then she turned her attention to Miss Eugenia. "Are you a new resident here?"

Miss Eugenia paled. "No."

"We're both visiting," I said firmly.

The woman realized her mistake and apologized. "Oh, I'm so sorry!"

"It's okay," I said, although it really wasn't. "Can you tell us how to get to Agatha Hoban's apartment?"

She turned to her computer. "Let me check. A-g-a-t-h-a H-o-b-a-n," she spelled aloud as she typed. "Let's see, she's in the Harvest Building." She pointed to a hallway on our right. "Take this all the way through to the next building. You'll know you're there by the paint color on the walls—its called *pumpkin*," she confided. "Tell the hostess at the information desk that you're here to see Mrs. Hoban."

I thanked the lady, and we followed the instructions to the Harvest building. The walls were a pleasant light orange color. Another friendly lady welcomed us, and after we explained the purpose of our visit, she led us to suite 212 and knocked on the door.

"Mrs. Hoban!" she called. "You have visitors!" She pushed the door open and gave us a smile. "You folks enjoy your visit! I'm Mitzy and I'll be at the information desk if you need me."

Miss Eugenia and I stepped into the "suite," which consisted of a living area, a kitchenette, and a bedroom. It was attractively decorated, and Agatha was sitting on the couch facing a large television that was mounted on the wall. She was wearing sweatpants and a T-shirt just as she had been on Sunday when Rand and I had visited her at her home. Her bowl cut hair was the same too. But Agatha seemed older—like just being there had taken some of the life out of her.

I approached the couch. "Agatha?"

She turned to face me. "Are you bringing my lunch?"

I smiled. "No. I'm Kennedy Scoggins. We met on Sunday. And this is Miss Eugenia Atkins."

She squinted. "Oh, yes, I remember. You came to see me when I was still at my house."

I sat on the couch beside her, and Miss Eugenia took the nearby chair. "I'm sorry you couldn't stay there during construction. Hopefully it won't take too long for them to get your new house finished so you can move in."

"Move?" she repeated. "I thought I was supposed to stay here."

"Just until they get your house built," I said.

"I'm going back to my house?"

Miss Eugenia scooted a little closer. "You're going to a new house soon. And Kennedy brought you a present."

I had almost forgotten about the *Jeopardy!* game, but I transferred it from my lap to Agatha's. "I thought it would be nice if you could play *Jeopardy!* even when it's not on TV."

She stared at the game for a few seconds. Then she said, "Could you put it somewhere else? It's heavy."

I took the game from her hands and transferred it to the kitchen counter. Miss Eugenia and I exchanged a concerned glance.

Then I said, "I'm surprised you aren't watching that nice new TV Drake Langston bought for you."

"I don't know how to work it," Agatha told me. "The remote is different from my old one."

"Well, let's see if we can figure it out." I picked up the remote, although it was unlikely I would be better able to work it than Agatha since my television still has a dial that turns to change channels. With Miss Eugenia's help I managed to get the television on and even found a game show. It was *Wheel of Fortune* instead of *Jeopardy!,* but I thought she'd be pleased.

Agatha pressed her hands against her ears. "Just turn it off, please. It's so loud."

I turned off the television and put the remote down on the coffee table. Then I stood. "Well, I guess we'll be going. I'll come visit you again when you get moved into your new house."

Agatha nodded vaguely.

Just as we reached the door, she called out.

"Are you coming back again?"

I smiled. "I promise we'll be back." And then we walked out into the hallway. "Something is wrong with her!" I whispered to Miss Eugenia. "She was much different on Sunday—so clear and sharp! She negotiated that huge television into her home-sale deal! And now look at her. We need to talk to a doctor."

We walked around to the information desk and found Mitzy.

"I'm worried about Mrs. Hoban," I told her. "She seems groggy and confused. I'm afraid something is wrong with her medications."

Mitzy looked appropriately concerned. "I'll call the nurse and let you talk to her." Then she showed us to a little sitting room where we waited until a man wearing blue scrubs walked in.

"I'm the nurse on duty for the Harvest Building," he said. "Mitzy said that some of Mrs. Hoban's family members were expressing concern about her."

I was about to reluctantly admit that we were not part of Mrs. Hoban's family—in fact, I wasn't sure we even qualified as *friends*—when Miss Eugenia spoke.

"Yes, we are very worried about her," she told the nurse. "Agatha seems confused and despondent. We're afraid that somehow during the transfer from her house to your complex her medications got mixed up and you're giving her too much of something."

The nurse was so anxious to defend his facility that he failed to clarify our relationship to Agatha. "I double-checked her chart and her meds are being administered exactly as her private physician ordered. The lethargy you noticed is probably a side effect of her anti-anxiety medication that was added on Monday. Moving anywhere is stressful, and moving in here can be, well, traumatic. So her doctor felt it was best to give her something to keep her calm during the adjustment process. Our staff only administers the medications as written."

I was greatly relieved to hear that there was a reason for Agatha's odd behavior and that it was temporary. "How long will she have to be on the new medicine?"

"It's prescribed for a month, and her physician will reevaluate at that point."

"By then her house should be ready, and I doubt that she'll have any anxiety about moving out of here!" Miss Eugenia predicted.

The nurse frowned. "I don't think there is any expectation that Mrs. Hoban will ever move out—at least not any time soon. Her care here is paid for twelve months."

I was stunned. "I got the impression that she was leaving in a couple of weeks."

Now the nurse smiled. "Often our residents are under such delusions, and we think it's kinder to humor them. But her dementia can only be adequately monitored and controlled in a setting like this. Allowing her to live alone would be giving her a death sentence."

"Dementia?" I repeated. "Agatha?"

"The very early stages," the nurse replied.

"Well, thank you for your help," Miss Eugenia said.

"You're welcome," the nurse replied. "Is there anything else I can help you with?"

I wanted to argue, but Miss Eugenia took me by the arm and pulled me into the hallway. "Just point us toward the door. I'm ready to get out of here."

Once we were back in the car, I told Miss Eugenia, "I feel bad about Agatha. When I saw her on Sunday she was happy in her own house, watching her favorite programs all day. Now she's sedated, diagnosed with dementia, and can't even turn on her own television!"

"It's not your fault," Miss Eugenia said kindly. "The health department said she couldn't stay in her house, and her doctor felt that she needed a sedative. And if she has dementia, she doesn't need to be living alone. So your visit on Sunday might have actually saved her life."

"But on Sunday she was happy," I explained. "Now she looks miserable. What's the point of extending the length of her life by reducing the quality?"

Miss Eugenia shrugged. "I don't know. But it's not your decision to make."

"I still feel responsible," I whispered. "Agatha would have been better off if she'd never met me."

"Don't you mean if Drake had never come back to Midway?"

I turned my eyes to meet hers. "I guess that's what I mean. We didn't change Agatha's life for the better."

We were quiet during the drive home. I was racked with guilt, and I expected that Miss Eugenia was anticipating with dread the day when she might have to call a facility like the one in Millwood "home."

We arrived back in Haggerty at ten thirty. I parked my truck in

Miss Eugenia's driveway, and then we went in through her back door.

"Lady!" Miss Eugenia called. "Lady!"

The dog did not come.

"Poor thing must be sound asleep," Miss Eugenia muttered as she walked into the kitchen. "She kept me up most of the night barking at those bags full of cat hair. That's probably why I'm so cranky."

I laughed. "I don't want to be responsible for putting you in another bad mood. So if we're not finished with Nola's stuff by tonight, I'll move it to one of Mr. Sheffield's empty storage units."

"That's probably a good idea. Are you hungry? I have some potato soup I can warm up for lunch."

"Sounds good," I said as I walked on through the kitchen toward her living room. "I think I'll see what I can find on Nola's computer. Then after lunch we can sort through the other stuff."

I walked into the living room and looked around. There were no black garbage bags in sight. And the computer was not where we had set it up the night before.

"Where did you put the stuff?" I called to Miss Eugenia.

"What?" she hollered back.

"Nola's things!" I said. "Where are they?"

Miss Eugenia came walking in to join me. "What do you mean? It's all right here where we left—" She glanced into the living room. "Dear me, we've been robbed."

My fingers were trembling as I reached for my phone. I dialed Cade's number. When he answered I said, "You need to come to Miss Eugenia's house immediately. Someone has taken all Nola's stuff from her living room."

There was a moment's pause, and then Cade said, "I'll be there in ten minutes."

Miss Eugenia seemed befuddled. "They didn't take anything else. Just the bags full of Nola's stuff and her computer."

I nodded. "Yes, I think Cade now has proof positive that he was on to something with his suspicions about Nola Finkle. Unfortunately, we now have no way to figure out exactly what."

Suddenly Miss Eugenia cried, "Lady!" and ran toward the back of the house. "Lady!" she called out again. She went through the kitchen to the laundry room and out onto her back porch.

I followed right behind her.

"Lady!" Miss Eugenia tried again desperately. Then we heard a little whimper. "I think she's under the porch!"

I descended the steps and got down on my hands and knees to look under the porch. In the far corner I saw Miss Eugenia's little dog, trembling. I called her and coaxed but she wouldn't come. Finally I rocked back on my heels and said, "How are we going to get her out?"

"Run over to Kate's and get Charles," she said. "He's small enough to crawl under the porch."

I did as I was told. I hurried to the Iversons' house and knocked on their back door. When Kate answered, I explained the situation and asked if I could borrow her four-year-old.

Kate picked up her son and told Emily to stay with their foster baby. Then she followed me across the grass to Miss Eugenia's.

When we reached the porch Kate gave Charles simple instructions. He was to crawl under and get Lady unless she tried to bite him. In that case he was to come back to the steps and we would pull the wood off the porch instead. Charles nodded solemnly and then began his journey toward the corner and Lady.

Miss Eugenia, Kate, and I watched his progress through the small spaces between the wooden lattice that surrounded the porch. He reached the little dog, wisely petted her first, and then picked her up. His return trip was slower since he had to crawl one-handed. But finally he reached the steps and passed the little dog up to Miss Eugenia.

She clutched Lady to her face and wept with relief. "Oh, I don't know what I would have done if those robbers had hurt you!" she cried.

Kate helped Charles out from under the porch and pulled him into a tight embrace. "What a good, brave boy!" she praised.

I was the only one standing alone with no one to hug. And I really hated that because I felt like hugging someone. We heard a speeding car approach and screech to a halt in front of Miss Eugenia's house. Seconds later Cade ran around the corner. It was one of the few times in recent history that I was glad to see him. Fortunately my need for a hug had passed.

"So what happened?" he asked breathlessly.

"We don't know," I told him. "Everything was still here when Miss Eugenia left to go with me to visit Agatha Hoban at the retirement complex in Millwood. But when we got back all of Nola's stuff was gone."

"And Lady was outside—terrified!" Miss Eugenia added. "She must have run out when the thieves opened my door."

"No signs of forced entry?" Cade asked.

"None that we noticed," I replied.

"All of you go over and wait at the Iversons' house while I look inside," Cade directed.

For once I wasn't inclined to disobey.

We walked next door and once we were all inside, Kate locked the doors. Then we gathered around the kitchen table.

"You need to call Mark," Miss Eugenia told her neighbor.

"I already have," Kate replied. "He's on his way home."

Cade walked in about the same time that Mark arrived.

"I saved Lady!" Charles informed his father.

Mark picked up the little boy and held him close for a few seconds. Then he told Kate, "Maybe you could take the kids in the family room while we discuss this."

She nodded and led the children out of hearing range.

"Do you have any idea who might have robbed Miss Eugenia?" Mark asked Cade.

"Probably the prisoners who escaped during the wreck on Saturday," Cade replied.

Mark shook his head. "I can't believe escaped convicts were so close to my house—to my family!"

I shivered, realizing how dangerous it had been for the Iversons—and feeling guilty again. "We should never have left Nola's stuff with Miss Eugenia."

"You couldn't have known that those robbers would come and get it."

"I should have known," Cade said. "I should have trusted my instincts instead of doubting myself."

"Well, there's nothing to be gained from going on about what could have been," Miss Eugenia said sharply. "Everyone is safe, so now we can just concentrate on figuring out why Nola Finkle broke those prisoners out of jail, if that's what she was doing."

"And where they are now," Mark murmured.

"If we can figure out the 'why,'" I said, "it might help us with the 'where.'"

Cade frowned. "Unfortunately our best chance of finding out anything was from that stuff we took from Nola's house. And it's gone."

Mark turned to Miss Eugenia. "Will you call all your neighbors and see if anyone saw something or someone around your house earlier this morning?"

She nodded. "Too bad Polly is visiting her grandniece in Raleigh. If she were home, she would have seen them for sure."

While Miss Eugenia started making phone calls, I chewed my lower lip, searching my mind for something that I knew was important but couldn't remember. Finally it hit me. I grabbed Cade's arm and said, "Remember when you talked to Nola's supervisor at Universal Pet Products? He said it was okay for us to take the paper files because they were just duplicates. The company keeps an electronic copy of all Nola's records."

Cade nodded. "Yeah, I remember him saying that."

"So we could ask him if he'd e-mail all her stuff to us—the client records and correspondence, e-mails . . . everything? Then at least we'd have that much of what the robbers took."

"It couldn't hurt," Mark said, giving my idea a lukewarm endorsement.

Miss Eugenia returned and reported, "No one saw anything. Wouldn't you know? If *we* were trying to do something sneaky over here, they'd all be watching."

Mark nodded. "I expected as much. Cade's about to call Nola's supervisor and ask for a copy of her files."

Miss Eugenia took a seat at the kitchen table, and we all watched as Cade pulled out his phone and searched through his outgoing calls. When he found the number, he put the phone on speaker and dialed. His call was answered by the switchboard at Universal Pet Products, and he asked to speak to Nola's supervisor. After a short time on hold he was finally connected.

Cade wisely didn't tell the man that the files had been stolen—probably by a band of escaped convicts. Instead he told Nola's supervisor that sifting through boxes of files was going to take forever, and he was hoping they could get a copy of the electronic files—which would be much easier to search through—instead.

"I'd like to help you, deputy," Nola's supervisor claimed. "But there's no way I can give you copies of our files without a court order. Those files Nola kept were her personal record-keeping system. Our electronic files are, well, confidential."

"This could be really important," Cade pleaded. "I have had suspicions since Saturday that the wreck that killed your employee was not an accident. But unless we can figure out why she was driving on Highway 17, we can't solve the case."

"Well, I know why she was on Highway 17," the supervisor said. "She was going to Midway to see Drake Langston."

My knees felt wobbly, and I was glad I was already sitting down.

"Why was she coming here to see Langston?" Cade demanded with a frown.

"He is a good and regular customer of ours," the supervisor explained. "Whenever he renovates a town with an animal shelter, he buys equipment and supplies from us. Nola was his sales rep, and she had become concerned about some duplicate purchases. I didn't think it was a big deal. Langston Association is always doing renovations in different towns. If they ordered more veterinary equipment than they needed for one town, they could use it on the next. I just figured they'd stockpile the extras. And I didn't think it was our place to question Mr. Langston or his purchasing practices."

"But Nola did?" Cade guessed.

"Yes, she was convinced that someone in his association was overbuying on purpose and selling the surplus. She called his office several times and left messages that were never returned. I told her that was her answer—he didn't want to hear her theories. But she couldn't let it go. She thought someone was intercepting the messages. So when she called again on Friday and found out he was going to be in Midway doing a renovation, she told me she was going to drive down and talk to him personally."

The room was deathly silent as Cade thanked the supervisor.

"So Nola was coming to Midway to talk to Drake when she died?" I clarified.

"It sounds that way," Mark confirmed.

"Then Nola running into the prisoner van was the coincidence," Miss Eugenia said. "And the wreck was not a mistake."

"The thief intercepted the phone messages and realized they had to kill Nola so she couldn't tell Drake about the stealing," Cade proposed.

I was horrified. "You don't seriously think someone inside Drake's organization killed her!"

"Who else?" Cade demanded.

"It does sound a little far-fetched," Mark agreed with me. "But I think we have to check it out. She died on the way to tell Drake about the surplus purchases, and the files that contained evidence of the theft have been stolen. That's too much to ignore."

Cade looked relieved. "So you're taking over the investigation?"

Mark shook his head. "Langston has accused the FBI of harassment. My supervisor says we can't get involved with any case until he is actually convicted. Then we can dig around and try to find more—but he is strictly off limits until then."

"What does that mean?" Cade asked.

"It means you're in charge, Deputy," Mark said. "I can't be involved officially. I'll be glad to sit in on your meetings, but all my comments would be hypothetical."

"I don't feel like we have enough to go to Sheriff Bonham or the Albany police either." Cade's anxiety was obvious. "We don't have any proof that someone inside the Langston Association was stealing—let alone that they killed Nola Finkle."

"All we have is the supervisor's word that Nola was coming here to confront Drake," I pointed out.

Miss Eugenia added, "We know Nola's files were stolen—but now we're not sure who took them."

"The missing prisoners could be completely uninvolved in the case."

"If Nola didn't purposely run into the prison van to help one of the convicts escape, did the driver purposely stop to cause the wreck?"

"Either that or the witness driving the truck bumped into Nola, forcing her into the prison van and eventually the trees."

"Or maybe the wreck was just to throw us off," Cade said. "Remember how hot that fire was that burned up her car?"

Mark held up a hand. "Hold on! Too many ideas at once." He turned to Cade. "Are you saying that Ms. Finkle's car may have been tampered with?"

Cade nodded. "We assumed she had a full tank of gas, but maybe someone planted a device on Nola's car—like a gasoline bomb—and detonated it."

Mark considered this. "So it didn't matter whether she hit those trees or not—she was going to die in a car fire."

"And it would look like an accident so no one would ever check the car for the explosive device." Cade continued to plead his case. "So we need to check into the driver of the van and the truck. And we need to have Nola's car examined by a professional who might be able to detect evidence of foul play."

"That's a place to start," Mark agreed. "If you can tie one of them to a member of Drake Langston's team . . . I'd say you've got your guilty party."

Cade nodded. "Not just a burglar, but a murderer."

"Yes," Mark confirmed. "And I can help you with getting an expert to examine Nola Finkle's car. As long as there is an official case that doesn't specifically involve Drake Langston. And as long as I'm officially invited to help by the local authorities."

Cade looked sick. "I just don't know if the sheriff will open an investigation based on what we have."

"It's obvious what we have to do," Miss Eugenia said.

All eyes turned to her. "For those of us who can't see the obvious, please share," Mark invited.

"We need to call Winston," she said. "As the police chief in Haggerty, he can initiate an investigation without having to convince anyone else that it has merit."

"But Nola died in the Albany city limits—which gives their police department jurisdiction," Mark explained.

"But the burglary at my house this morning is in the Haggerty police department's jurisdiction," Miss Eugenia reminded him. "And the fact that it was Nola's things that were stolen ties this crime to the wreck and gives Winston a reason to ask for Nola's car to be examined by an expert."

"That is the best idea I've ever heard." Cade looked like he wanted to kiss Miss Eugenia.

Mark was less enthusiastic but still positive. "I think it will work. And you need to call Winston anyway, to report the burglary. I don't know why you didn't do it in the first place. After all, a crime has been committed."

Miss Eugenia narrowed her eyes at him as she picked up her phone and called Winston. When she ended the call she reported, "He's on his way over."

"We'll discuss this more when he gets here," Mark said. "At the moment security is a big concern. We don't know exactly who we're dealing with, but we do know that two prisoners are at large in our area, a burglary took place here a few hours ago, and it's even possible that we have a murderer nearby."

"How do you suggest we handle security?" Cade asked.

"I'll move my family," Mark said. "I haven't decided where to take them yet, but they are not staying anywhere near this level of danger." He glanced at Miss Eugenia. "And until this is over, you need to stay with Annabelle."

"That's so inconvenient," Miss Eugenia objected.

"Getting killed would be much more so," he replied without any sympathy. "Whoever stole the files is dangerous."

Miss Eugenia sighed. "I guess you're right."

He turned to me. "And Kennedy, since your husband is out of town, I suggest that you stay with your parents until this investigation is over."

"I appreciate your concern," I told him sincerely. "But you don't need to worry about me. Sloan is already providing security at my apartment. He's been sleeping on the couch in Mr. Sheffield's office. And he's a former FBI agent."

"He's also a member of Drake Langston's team," Mark replied, "and therefore possibly our suspect."

"Not Sloan!" I insisted. "He can't be included in our list of suspects! He saved my life! Twice!"

"We need to check out all the team members," Cade agreed with a note of pleasure. "Including Sloan and Drake himself."

"Drake is a suspect?" I asked.

Mark replied, "I think we can safely say that Langston did not steal from himself. But Sloan is another matter. We'll keep him on the suspect list along with the rest of the team—for now at least. But that means that we can't depend on Sloan to provide you with security."

"I can't stay at my parents' house," I insisted. "My mother will ask a million questions, and eventually she'll figure out what's going on and then it will be all over Midway."

"That would ruin any chance you have of solving this case," Miss Eugenia pointed out. "Maybe Deputy Burrell could even arrange for someone from the sheriff's department to drive by every couple of hours during the night."

"I guess that will be good enough," Mark said with resignation. "I can print off copies of the background checks and financial data that we collected during the FBI investigation. If we need more current information, we can have Kelsey do it."

The back door slammed open, and we all looked up to see Chief Winston Jones walk in. "Now what's this about a burglary?" he demanded.

CHAPTER THIRTEEN

MARK STOOD. "MISS EUGENIA AND Cade can show Winston the crime scene. Kennedy, if you'll wait here, I'll go print out that information. Then you can take it over to her house and explain it all to Winston while I get my family out of here."

I nodded and remained seated at the Iversons' kitchen table.

Miss Eugenia took Winston Jones by the arm and hauled him toward the back door. "Come and just see what has happened."

Kate came into the kitchen while I was waiting for Mark to print the reports. "Wow, what a morning," she said.

"Seriously," I agreed. "So, what safe location is Mark taking you off to?"

"We can't leave Georgia with our foster baby, or I'd be headed to Utah to stay with my mother," Kate said. "But given the travel limitations, he's going to have me stay at a hotel in Albany."

"If they have a pool, that might be fun."

"It might be fun at first, but it won't last. So do me a favor and help them solve this case quick!"

I smiled. "I'll do what I can."

Mark walked in and handed me a stack of computer printouts. "You and the others can go over these while I take Kate and the kids to a secure location. I should be back soon, but if you need me before then, call me on my cell phone."

"Thanks for your help," I said to him. To Kate I said, "And I'm sorry for the imposition."

"It's not your fault. I'm the one who married an FBI agent," she replied with a smile at Mark. "Now, I guess I'll go pack."

Mark pulled out his phone. "I'll call Winston to come and get you. I don't want you walking—even the short distance between our house and Miss Eugenia's—alone."

So I waited with Mark for a few minutes until Winston Jones walked over and escorted me back to Miss Eugenia's house. Cade and our hostess were waiting for me in the kitchen.

"I've heated up some potato soup for lunch," she told me. "Have a seat."

I sat down across from Cade, and she put a steaming bowl of creamy soup in front of me. "Thank you," I said to her. Then to everyone in general I added, "So, what have you figured out while I was gone?"

"No forced entry," Cade said. "Whoever broke in here either had a key or knew how to get in without leaving any sign."

I blew on a spoonful of soup for a second and then put it in my mouth. I savored the bite for a second, then I asked Miss Eugenia, "And you're sure that nothing else is missing besides Nola's stuff?"

She nodded. "That's it."

I pointed my spoon at them. "Don't you think that's a little odd? I mean if they didn't want us to find out why Nola was coming to Midway, they should have taken a lot of things and messed your house up a little so it would look like just a regular burglary—not a crime cover-up."

Miss Eugenia stopped dishing up soup to say, "That's true. If we didn't realize they contained something important, we would once they were stolen."

"But once they were stolen, we couldn't figure out what," Winston contributed. "And maybe they didn't have time to steal other stuff or mess up the house."

"Or they think we're too stupid to figure it out," Cade said. "Country cops don't get much respect—even from criminals."

Winston rubbed his temples. "I'm getting confused. Start over from the beginning and tell me everything."

So over delicious bowls of potato soup in Miss Eugenia's cozy kitchen we went through the entire series of events again. Miss Eugenia and Cade did most of the talking. I just put a word in every once in a while.

When we were finished, Winston said, "Is the overpurchasing and reselling limited to veterinary equipment?"

"I think we can safely assume that it's not," Miss Eugenia said. "However, we will need strong evidence to subpoena Langston's records to find out how big a scheme it is."

Winston asked, "So what does Mark want me to do?"

"You're supposed to call the police chief in Albany and tell him you have a crime that is related to the wreck," I said. "And you need to have Nola's car examined by the FBI."

Winston looked at Cade. "And the sheriff's department can't do this . . . why?"

I provided, "Because, like Cade said, the Albany police chief thinks they're bumpkins."

Winston's eyebrows shot up. "I'm not sure they have a real high opinion of me either."

"It's not just that," Cade inserted. "When we pulled up on the wreck scene, I was so focused on trying to save the victim that I didn't secure the prisoners. So it's my fault that two escaped convicts are on the loose. That's why I can't call the police chief."

"What we have is a lot of suspicious circumstances and one small crime," Miss Eugenia said. "The only crime happened in your jurisdiction, so it makes sense for you to take control of the whole investigation."

Winston gave her a scowl. "You're not tricking me into this mess, just so you know. I realize I'm stepping into a case full of career-ending landmines. But I'm doing it because a woman died, and if she was murdered, we need to find the person or people responsible."

Miss Eugenia nodded. "Of course I knew you'd do your duty once I pointed it out to you. That's why we called you." She stood and started collecting soup bowls. "Now I'll get everyone some pound cake while Kennedy reads us those FBI reports about the Langston Association."

I cleared my throat and read from the first page in front of me.

"Catsy had a troubled past. Her parents were drug addicts and eventually lost custody of her. Lots of arrests for misdemeanors in her youth—the specifics are not listed since she was a minor, but I think it's safe to say she was a little thug." I glanced up. "Her criminal background surprises me. Now she is very polished and stylish. You would never look at her and think 'former criminal.'"

"Go on," Winston requested.

I cleared my throat and continued. "She was only arrested once as an adult—when she was eighteen—for car theft."

"Did she actually spend any time in prison where she might have met the missing convicts or members of their families or something?" Miss Eugenia asked.

Cade frowned. "I thought the convicts weren't involved with Nola Finkle's death."

Miss Eugenia said, "We don't know that for sure, so we still have to keep that angle in mind.

"Catsy didn't spend any time in prison," I reported. "And she is so tiny and frail, I'm not sure she could kill a fly—let alone another person. She bites her fingernails, and, besides, I like her."

Winston scowled. "Are you reading us the FBI report or giving us your personal opinions?"

I fixed him with a firm gaze. "Both."

"Let's move on to another person on Langston's team," Cade suggested.

"Newell had good grades in high school but lots of trouble fitting in. There are two recorded incidents where he was bullied," I informed them.

"Which probably means there were many more that were never reported," Miss Eugenia said with obvious disapproval.

"It looks like Newell was smart but socially awkward," I continued. "He got a scholarship to Mississippi State, and his scholastic performance there was good. But he had trouble getting along with roommates and changed dorm rooms . . . twenty-four times in the four years he was in school there."

Cade whistled. "That's got to be a record."

"Sometimes he requested the change and sometimes his roommate asked for it," I added.

"But still . . . twenty-four times?" Cade said. "That's more than socially awkward. That's, well, he apparently couldn't get along with *anyone*."

"After he got out of school, he was hired three times—and fired three times. And at his last employer there were rumors of embezzlement but no proof. Then Drake entered his life, and Newell joined the renovation team." I looked up. "Drake gave him a second chance that he probably couldn't have gotten anywhere else."

"And Newell has a history of stealing from his employer," Winston said.

"It was just rumored," I pointed out.

Winston nodded. "Next."

"Rand is the oldest member of the team and the only one who has been married, although he's now divorced. He graduated from a little law school in Memphis that I've never heard of. He got a job with a big firm right after he passed the bar and worked there for almost ten years. Then he was accused of ethics violations. He lost his wife, his job, and almost lost his license to practice law."

"Let me guess," Cade muttered, "then Drake Langston stepped in and saved him—like he does everyone."

"Well, he did hire him," I said stiffly. "The last team member is Morris Pugh. His parents are filthy rich, and he lived the playboy life all through high school and college. But then his parents suddenly decided he should be responsible for himself and cut off his funds."

"So Langston saved him too," Cade interrupted. "From getting a real job!"

"Morris works hard," I informed him.

Mark walked in at this point, and after locking the back door—and reproving us for not having done so ourselves—he took a seat at the kitchen table. I offered to go back over the reports we'd already discussed for his benefit, but he shook his head.

"That's not necessary. I've already read them several times. Where are you?"

"Sloan," I said. "When Drake hired him, he was an undercover FBI agent posing as a down-on-his-luck but very talented construction worker. That fits the kind of employee Drake seems attracted to."

"Actually, Sloan fits into Langston's typical employee pattern more than you might think," Mark said. "He was an FBI agent, but one that always stayed in trouble. He would not follow the rules or report in on time. So he's like the others—well qualified and smart, but not really thriving where he was."

"But if he was working undercover, Drake Langston shouldn't have known any of that," Winston said.

Mark nodded. "I've always been suspicious that Langston knew from the start exactly who Sloan was and why he was trying to get hired."

"So all during the investigation, Drake knew Sloan was trying to find evidence against him?" I asked.

"There is a lot of wisdom in keeping your enemies close," Mark said. "And that's not a proven fact—just my opinion."

I looked down at the report—curious but feeling a little disloyal. "His parents never married. The dad was never very involved with his life, and his mother had drug problems. She was arrested several times for possession and prostitution." I understood now what he meant about not feeling at home with his parents.

"Go on," Cade encouraged.

"He did okay in school with grades but had some trouble with authority according to the principal's remarks. He had some speeding tickets and a couple of DUIs as a teenager, but nothing once he got into college. He got through Clemson in three years and applied to the FBI."

"And they took a trouble-maker like that?" Cade asked.

Mark shrugged. "Sometimes the Bureau accepts people with less than perfect records—especially for undercover work."

I stared at the reports in front of me. "They all had difficult childhoods and still carry the scars."

Miss Eugenia waved this aside. "We all have scars. People nowadays dwell on that too much."

Mark pursed his lips. "We need to figure out which one of Drake Langston's employees fell back into their old habits and decided that the best way to come up with extra cash was to steal—in this case from their employer."

"And who was willing to cover that up by killing Nola," I added. "I mean stealing is bad, but murder is so much worse."

"Give us the highlights of the financial report," Mark requested.

I shuffled the papers and, after scanning the report, addressed the group. "All of Drake's team members make good salaries. Morris and Catsy seem to spend everything they earn, so they don't have any assets to speak of." I glanced up. "But they dress beautifully."

Cade groaned. "Go on."

I frowned at him before continuing. "Newell is frugal but is still paying off student loans so he hasn't accumulated much in the way of savings. Rand was in pretty good shape financially until the divorce. His ex-wife got a lot of his money. He still has some investments, but they have all increased at a slow and steady pace. No big lump sums."

"And Sloan?"

"Sloan saves most of what he makes, and it's all carefully and diversely invested. The total amount is impressive but not—in my opinion—suspicious."

Cade reached for the reports. "Let me see that."

I passed all the reports to him and then posed the question, "So how do we choose from all these likely possibilities?"

Winston shrugged. "Sometimes it's worse to have too many suspects than not enough."

Miss Eugenia said, "All the team members had troubled pasts that should have made them poor employment prospects."

"And it's not like Langston hires the occasional risk," Mark said. "He goes out of his way to find people who are nearly unemployable."

I said, "Drake told me awhile back that he feels an obligation to help others since he has been so fortunate in his own life. He is a 'saver.'"

Mark took issue with my terminology. "Some people call that a manipulator or even a narcissist."

"He really does help people," I insisted.

Cade frowned. "We all know that you are a big fan of his."

"And we all know you are not!" I shot back. Then I looked at Winston and Mark. "You don't like him either."

"No," Mark agreed. "I don't like him."

"I don't even know him," Winston said.

Miss Eugenia said, "Since opinions about Drake Langston seem to gravitate toward one extreme or the other, what we need is a neutral party with a clear mind here. I nominate myself for the role. Your voice of reason."

I smiled. "I vote yes."

Mark shook his head. "Anyway, we need to look for motive and opportunity."

"Newell has opportunity since he handles all the money for the association," I said. "But I don't think he could possibly be the thief. He is obsessed about the books being perfectly balanced and everything being accounted for so he won't be responsible for an IRS audit or FBI investigation. I can't imagine him doing anything that would cause a bookkeeping discrepancy."

Mark nodded. "That's a good observation."

"Catsy and Sloan do the most purchasing—so that gives them both good opportunity," I said reluctantly. "Sloan has plenty of money so I don't know what his motive would be. But Catsy told me she's planning a wedding, and since she has reckless spending habits and no family to help with the wedding . . ."

"She could be stealing to finance it," Miss Eugenia interjected.

"I hope not," I said. "I really like Catsy."

Miss Eugenia sighed. "Which is why you need a voice of reason."

"And this is just a guess, but I think Morris might be her fiancé."

"What makes you say that?" Mark asked.

"It's her texting habits," I said. "She is never more than a few inches from her phone."

Miss Eugenia cut her eyes over to my phone, which was clutched in my left hand.

"I'm not usually so attached to my phone," I defended myself. "But I have a husband who has been commandeered by the Marines!"

"I know," she acknowledged. "Go on about Catsy and Morris."

"She texts a lot. And during our group meetings she blushes and seems flustered like a lovesick girl—especially around Morris."

"She could be texting someone else," Winston pointed out.

"They text in tandem," I said. "I noticed in one of my first long morning meetings that Morris and Catsy were both texting. Everyone was bored since Rand has a tendency to go on and on so I didn't realize they were texting each other. Then I noticed that one texts and then the other. And sometimes they would even look up and smile at each other."

"Sharing a joke through technology," Miss Eugenia said.

"Exactly," I agreed.

"Just because Catsy is texting with Morris doesn't mean he's her fiancé," Miss Eugenia said.

I was a little disappointed. "That's true."

"But we need to look into it. Because if they are romantically involved, they might be partners in crime as well."

I frowned. "I don't know Morris well at all, but he seems so, well, snooty. I can't imagine him getting involved in anything dirty like burglary or murder. So if it's Catsy, she's probably working alone— maybe to impress his rich family. But my favorite suspect would be Rand."

"Motive and opportunity?"

I frowned. "I can't figure out how Rand would have either one."

"Then why is he your favorite suspect?" Cade demanded.

"Because I don't like him."

Winston rolled his eyes and Mark sighed.

Cade scoffed. "Well let's talk about *my* favorite suspect, your friend Sloan! Like you said, he has perfect opportunity and just because all his investments look legit doesn't mean they are. He might have decided to help himself to some of Langston's wealth."

I glared back at him but couldn't think of anything to contradict the points he'd made.

"Realistically speaking, I think we can narrow down our list of suspects—just based on opportunity," Mark said. "I don't think Rand Roebuck or Morris Pugh did enough ordering to be behind the scheme."

I would have been happy if either one of them was the guilty party, so I was disappointed.

"That leaves Catsy, Newell, and Sloan," Cade itemized as if we all didn't know.

"So from this point out we will concentrate our investigation on those three," Mark said. "Winston, if you'll call the Albany police department, I'll get an FBI expert headed this way from Atlanta. Hopefully he can examine the car this afternoon. And I'll see what I can find out about the witness from the wreck. Then we can all meet back here tonight and see if things are any clearer."

"I'll make dinner for everyone," Miss Eugenia offered.

"I can't come until after dinner," I told them. "I've already agreed to eat at my parents' house tonight, and if I try to back out—well, it won't be pretty."

"We can meet after dinner," Mark said. "How about eight o'clock?"

"I can be here by then," I promised.

Winston and Cade both nodded.

Mark told Miss Eugenia, "I'll pick you up at seven thirty. Under no circumstances are you to come back here alone. Okay?"

"Okay," she agreed.

"I'm glad that's settled." Then I turned to Miss Eugenia. "Can I use your phone?"

She frowned. "What's wrong with that one in your hand that you check every five seconds to see if you have a message?"

"Nothing is wrong with it, but I need to call Miss Ida Jean's son, Robby, and I don't want him to have my phone number."

She narrowed her eyes. "You want him to have mine?"

I laughed. "At least if he calls here asking for a date, you're single."

"And I know how to discourage unwanted male attention," she assured me. "Something it sounds like you need to work on."

I sighed. "I was doing a good job of discouraging Robby, but then I had to ask him for a favor and I'm afraid I might have encouraged him."

"What kind of favor did you need from Robby Baxley?" Cade asked.

I felt I'd be fully justified if I told him to mind his own business. But out of consideration for the others present, I said, "I promised Luke I'd visit his father in prison while he's gone, which promise is surprisingly not as easy to fulfill as you might think. You have to get on a list and they have to check your background—and none of that could be done in time for visiting hours tomorrow. So I asked Robby to use his connections to fast-track a visit for me."

"I have connections at the prison too!" Cade claimed, as if this was something to be proud of. "You could have asked me!"

"But she asked Robby Baxley," Miss Eugenia pointed out. "And you don't have time to fool with such things! You've got a murder to solve!"

Cade looked appeased. "I guess that's true."

"So, can I use your phone?" I pointed to the cordless phone on her kitchen table.

She nodded. "Go ahead and drag me into another one of your problems."

"Thanks," I muttered as I dialed Robby's number. And he had good news for me—well, relatively speaking. At his request the warden had added my name to the visitors list for Wednesday at 9:00 a.m. I thanked him and then ended the call quickly before he could ask me on a date.

Mark stood and walked toward the door. "I'm headed back to work, after I drop Miss Eugenia off at Annabelle's. I'll see you all tonight."

Winston said, "I've got to call Albany and try to find what's left of that incinerated car."

Cade didn't look anxious to leave. "Maybe I should stay here and follow you back to Midway."

I shook my head. "You go on back to work. I'll be fine. I've got Daddy's .45 in my purse if I run into trouble—which I won't."

Cade still looked hesitant, but Mark intervened in my behalf.

"I think Kennedy can manage during the daylight as long as she's careful and keeps her phone and gun handy. But be sure and have a deputy assigned to her apartment tonight."

Cade nodded. "I'll be sure."

Then we all walked out of Miss Eugenia's house and went our separate ways.

CHAPTER FOURTEEN

WHILE I WAS DRIVING BACK to my apartment, Luke called. He was tired, having testified off and on all day. "I can't tell you what it's about, of course."

"Of course," I acknowledged.

"But I don't see how they can have many more questions for me, so maybe this will be over soon."

"I hope so," I said. Then I told him all about my day. He sympathized with me over Agatha Hoban's situation and was very concerned about the burglary at Miss Eugenia's house. "So now Winston Jones from Haggerty is leading the investigation. And you're helping him?"

"Only in the smallest way," I assured him. "Since I have at least met all of Drake's team members, I can give them a little inside information."

"It makes me nervous."

"Don't be. I've got Daddy's gun," I reminded him. "And you know Mark won't put me in a dangerous situation."

"I do feel better with Mark involved," he said. "But please be careful."

I promised that I would, and he said he call back later that night.

When I got to my apartment, I immediately noticed an unpleasant smell and a multitude of fruit flies. Apparently the wedding leftovers had reached the point of no return. I dumped them into the garbage and washed out my mother's plastic containers so I could return them to her when I went over for dinner.

I longed for a nap but knew I didn't have time for that. I took a shower instead and afterward put on a cool cotton sundress that I knew would please my mother.

When I arrived at my parents' house, I found that I wasn't the only guest. Brother Jackson and Miss Zelda were seated at Mother's dining room table. Miss Ida Jean, who had apparently decided a good meal was worth risking an attack by convicts, was also sitting at the table.

Mother rushed up and gave me a hug. "Now that you're here, we can eat!"

I was embarrassed that I had delayed the meal. "You shouldn't have waited on me."

"But you're the guest of honor," Miss Zelda said.

Miss Ida Jean piped up. "Your mother is having this little dinner to help you forget about your husband being gone."

It seemed counterproductive to invite me over for dinner to distract me and then remind me of what they didn't want me to remember.

"I don't think anything could keep my mind off Luke, even my mother's delicious cooking," I told Miss Ida Jean. "But I do appreciate Mother for making this nice meal and inviting such good company for me to share it with." I directed this last part straight toward Miss Zelda, but I saw Miss Ida Jean nod as if such a remark were her due.

Miss Zelda blushed. "Well, thank you. We were pleased to accept your mother's invitation."

Mother pointed at the only empty chair and said, "Sit down, Kennedy, so we can eat before the food gets cold." She turned to the preacher and said, "Brother Jackson, would you honor us by saying grace?"

Brother Jackson was happy to oblige. Once the blessing on the food was taken care of, everyone started passing the plates of food around. Even though I intended to eat light, I knew better than to skip a dish. So I put some of everything on my plate that I knew I wasn't going to eat just to avoid calling attention to myself. Then I picked at the food and sipped ice water, hoping I could keep a low profile—but as usual, my hopes were dashed.

"Aren't you hungry, Kennedy?" Miss Zelda asked.

"She's dieting," my mother provided for me. "She's going to be honeymooning in Hawaii soon and apparently wants to have the body of a skeleton."

I put a bite of fruit salad in my mouth and smiled. "I'm eating."

Brother Jackson said, "I sure would love to get Luke working with some of our young people once he gets back. They need a positive role model and he can provide that. In fact, it would be great if you worked as a team, showing the young folks how happy married life is."

I didn't want to mislead the preacher into thinking that Luke and I intended to be members of the Baptist church.

"When Luke comes back we'll be living in Atlanta," I reminded him. "So we won't be here to work with your youth."

"Oh, I just mean for you to be involved as you can—when you come home on weekends and such."

"I can't tell you how much it would mean to me for you and Luke to be helping with the youth of the church and sitting with Daddy and me on Sundays," Mother said. "When you're in town, of course."

Up to this point I had skirted the topic a few times, but now I felt that if I didn't tell them the truth, I'd be lying. So I said, "Luke plans to join the Mormons."

The room became deadly silent until Miss Ida Jean filled the void with a gasp of horror.

Pressing a hand to her frail chest, she said, "Oh, Lord, before we know it you'll all be Mormons!"

I was trying to think of the proper response to such an outrageous remark when my mother rounded on Miss Ida Jean. "Mormons are fine people no matter what you've heard! And if you are going to insult them, I'll ask you to leave."

"Well!" Miss Ida Jean's cheeks turned pink. "I didn't mean to offend you, Iris."

I wanted to ask exactly what her intention had been, then. But of course I didn't.

Miss Zelda entered the conversation. "You know what they say about discussing religion and politics at the dinner table."

"So if you were planning to tell us whether Luke supports the Democrats or Republicans, please don't!" Brother Jackson added and earned himself a sweet smile from his wife.

"I'm sure Luke would still be glad to come and talk to your youth about his experiences in the Marines or patriotism or something like that," I said. "On a weekend when we're home."

The preacher nodded. "Have him call me and we'll set something up."

"You're going to let a Mormon address your congregation?" Miss Ida Jean demanded.

"I'm going to let a brave soldier address my congregation," Brother Jackson said. "But anyone who doesn't want to hear what he has to say is welcome to stay at home."

Miss Ida Jean opened her mouth to speak and then closed it several times—giving us a veritable spit-string show.

Daddy said, "Iris, didn't you say you had some of that strawberry shortcake stuff Luke makes for dessert."

Mother stood. "I certainly do. Let me go get it right now."

And so the moment passed, but I had new respect for Brother Jackson and Miss Zelda and even for my mother. Southerners could also be tolerant. Who knew?

During dessert Miss Ida Jean said, "When I was at the library today, Carmella was talking on the phone at the circulation desk. And I'm pretty sure it was a personal call."

It took me a second to realize she was directing this ridiculous comment at me. "I don't work at the library anymore," I reminded her.

"But you could still call the library board in Albany and report that Carmella has been acting unprofessional."

I gritted my teeth. "But I wouldn't want to do that. Carmella is a good employee and always professional. If she was talking on the phone, I'm sure it was important."

Miss Ida Jean ignored this. "And when I asked for last year's Christmas issue of *Southern Living,* she told me she didn't have time to go look for it right then and I'd have to check back next week! What kind of customer service is that?"

"With a limited staff we can't fill all requests immediately," I said in defense of my former assistant. "And she may have been working on something for another patron."

"Well, at least she could have said she'd get it later today! And then when I tried to check out a book on eighteenth-century dentistry, she said I had to pay a *fine* first!" Miss Ida Jean's face turned an unhealthy shade of red.

"Did you turn in a book late?" I asked.

"Yes, but it wasn't my fault. It got left in the back of Robby's car, and I couldn't turn it in on time. But the fine is only fifteen cents.

She could waive that for a loyal patron like me!"

So many responses jumped to my mind. But before I could deliver any of them, Miss Zelda intervened.

"I'll pay your fine for you, Ida Jean," she said in a comforting tone. "I'll go up first thing tomorrow and take care of it. And I'll speak to Carmella about the importance of good customer service, especially for regular patrons like yourself."

Miss Ida Jean gave Miss Zelda a little nod, accepting the assistance.

Not so long ago such an exchange would have made me furious. It makes no sense to coddle a spiteful old woman—even to the point of taking her side when she is so obviously wrong. But something had changed me. Maybe it was Luke and our marriage. Maybe it was Nola and her death. Or maybe it was a combination of the two. But for whatever reason, I didn't have a desire to strangle Miss Ida Jean.

I turned and saw Daddy watching me—probably prepared to step in if I grabbed Miss Ida Jean by the throat. I smiled at him and he winked back.

After the meal everyone retired into the living room to visit. I helped mother and Miss Zelda clear the table and then told them I had to leave.

"Oh, Kennedy, please don't rush off," Mother begged.

"I'm sorry, but I've still got a lot to do tonight before I can go to bed." I let her assume I was referring to my job with Drake Langston and not a new murder case. "But dinner was delicious. Give Daddy a kiss for me."

I hugged Miss Zelda and asked her to explain my departure to Brother Jackson. I didn't mention Miss Ida Jean since I didn't care what she thought.

Of course Mother insisted on filling the same plastic containers I'd just returned with new leftovers. "Don't stay up too late working. And call me."

"I will," I promised. I carefully balanced the containers while I opened the back door. And finally I was on my way.

I stopped by my apartment to drop off the food. Then I hurried to Miss Eugenia's house. The others were already assembled around the kitchen table when I arrived. I apologized for my tardiness, but only Cade looked annoyed.

"You could have called us," he said. "With robbers and murderers and convicts running around, you knew we'd be worried."

"Sorry," I said again. "Next time I'll call. Now what have I missed?"

Winston said, "I was able to get permission from the Albany PD to have Nola Finkle's car examined by an expert from the FBI. And I even managed to locate the charred remains in their car lot. But Mark couldn't get anyone to come down here until tomorrow morning. So we don't know anything about that yet."

"And I have searched for the witness to the wreck but can't find him," Mark said.

"He's disappeared?" I asked.

Mark shook his head. "No, I can't find that he ever existed. The address and identification that he provided were both false."

"Well, that's suspicious," Miss Eugenia said.

"Yes," Mark agreed. "I'd say that means that the witness was definitely involved somehow. But finding him is going to be very difficult since we don't have a picture or fingerprints or anything."

"So what is our plan with Langston's team?" Cade wanted to know. "Are we going to confront them or what?"

"I think we're going to try and get Drake Langston's cooperation," Mark said. "If we told him about the thievery and explained that murder might be involved too, maybe he would give us access to his company records." He turned to me. "We should have the results from Nola Finkle's car by noon tomorrow. Can you set up a lunch meeting with Langston for tomorrow?"

I swallowed. "Me?" The thought of telling Drake that one of his employees was a thief and possibly a murderer—well, that just seemed way above what I was comfortable with.

"Winston and Cade will attend the meeting too," Mark reassured me by adding. "I'm still participating only as an adviser so I can't be there. But Winston and Cade and I will talk before then so they will know what to say."

"So all I have to do is ask Drake to have lunch with me and show up?" I confirmed.

Mark nodded. "Basically."

"I can handle that."

Mark stood. "Okay, then we're done here. Miss Eugenia, let's get you back to Annabelle's so I can go visit my family."

"Um, about that," Miss Eugenia said with a quick glance at me. "I really don't want to go back to Annabelle's house. I am trying to come up with an entry for the Fry-Away contest on Friday night, but I'm afraid to practice there because Annabelle is not above stealing my ideas."

"I'm sorry about the contest," Mark said. "But I can't let you stay here alone. It would be irresponsible."

Miss Eugenia had anticipated this and was ready with an alternate plan. "I was thinking that if Kennedy wouldn't mind, I could stay with her tonight. The county sheriff is already providing security at her apartment so it would be like killing two birds with one stone. If you know what I mean."

Mark shrugged. "It's fine with me if Kennedy doesn't mind."

If I'd hated it more than anything in the world, I couldn't very well have said so. Luckily I was okay with having Miss Eugenia as an overnight guest. "It's fine with me."

Miss Eugenia beamed. "Wonderful! I've already packed my overnight case."

We all walked out together, and Cade helped Miss Eugenia into the passenger seat of my truck. "I'm going to follow you home," he said. "No arguments."

Honestly I didn't even mind. I felt a little vulnerable so I nodded and said, "Thanks."

While we drove, Miss Eugenia called her sister and explained that she wouldn't be returning to spend the night. When she hung up she turned to me. "My sister is a nice enough person, I guess. But she is so lovey-dovey with her husband it's just sickening."

I laughed.

"You wouldn't think it was funny if you saw them together," she assured me. "They talk baby talk to each other."

"That sounds hilarious to me."

She smiled. "Not for more than a minute or two—believe me! And they have all kinds of little pet names for each other. They never use their real names. And they're always blowing kisses and making little heart signs with their fingers. It's not normal."

"Well my apartment is not much, but I promise not to utter a single word of baby talk."

"Then I'll love it!"

As we approached the Midway Store and Save, I could see Sloan's truck parked there. Even with the suspicions that Mark and Cade had voiced, I still trusted him and was comforted by his presence. Then we turned into the parking lot, and I saw Luke's brother, Nick, and his ex-wife, Shasta, sitting on my porch steps.

It had been a long, mostly unpleasant day, and I had the feeling it was about to get worse.

I parked my truck and whispered to Miss Eugenia. "Why don't you wait here, with the doors locked, while I see what they want?"

She nodded. "Trouble, I'd be willing to bet."

I left my truck and walked reluctantly toward the stairs. Cade got out of his car and leaned against it, watching from a distance. It was a subtle but unmistakable message of support that I deeply appreciated.

Nick and Shasta stood and met me halfway. Without wasting time on a greeting, Nick said, "Hey, we just found out Drake Langston's company is back in town and that they are willing to buy our land for the same purchase price they offered before! I can't believe we're getting another chance at this. I thought Dad and Uncle Foster had ruined it for us."

I hated to be the one to tell them but didn't see that I had a choice. "Well, actually, there isn't going to be a second chance. Luke already declined the offer."

"Declined!" Shasta cried.

"Why would he do that?" Nick asked. "Especially without asking us first?"

"Luke doesn't have to ask anyone about financial decisions regarding Heaven's inheritance," I reminded them unnecessarily. "Foster wanted Heaven to have that land. And I thought you wanted keep the salvage yard."

Nick ran his hands through his scraggly hair in obvious agitation. "Not when we can make this much money by selling it! We'd have to be crazy to turn away from a deal like this."

"Crazy!" Shasta seconded.

"I don't want the money for myself," Nick insisted. "If we sell to

Langston, we could put most of it in the bank for Heaven and just keep out enough to give her a good life."

I was losing patience. "I don't understand why you're talking to me about it. It's Luke's decision."

"Because you can call Luke and talk some sense into him," Nick said. "We'll never have another opportunity to make almost half a million dollars on that land."

"And you could talk Luke into selling," Shasta whined.

"I could, but I won't. Now I hate to seem rude, but I'm really tired."

"It's not fair!" Shasta called out. "Luke is stupid and selfish!"

Nick took Shasta's arm and tried to pull her toward their car. "Come on."

Shasta lunged at me. "Luke can't cheat us out of all that money!"

Cade was between us in an instant. Shasta stopped short and Nick was able to reestablish his hold on her.

She leaned around Cade and hissed, "You're going to be sorry for this!"

I watched Nick drag her away, still kicking and screaming. As he forced her into their car, I felt so bad for Luke—who was head and shoulders (and then some) above the rest of his family.

Cade cursed under his breath. "Those Scogginses are a bad bunch."

I looked up at him. "I'm a Scoggins now."

He had the decency to look ashamed. "Well, most of them." Cade's phone rang and he ignored it. "I was worried about those convicts and whoever killed Nola Finkle. But now that Luke's brother and his tramp of an ex-wife want to kill you . . . I'm really nervous. I think I'll just stay the whole night myself."

"I hate for you to have to do that."

"It's not a personal favor," he assured me. "It's my duty as an officer of the law."

I smiled. "Then thank you, although I am still sorry that it's necessary."

My phone rang and I looked down to see Hannah-Leigh's name on the touch screen. I turned it around so Cade could see. Then I answered it. "Hey, Hannah-Leigh."

"Hey, Kennedy," she replied. "Is Cade there?"

Cade shook his head and mouthed, "I'll be back later." Then he got into his car and drove away. I waited until he was off the Midway Store and Save parking lot before saying, "No, he's not here," so it was technically honest.

There was a little pause, and then Hannah-Leigh said, "Okay, well, thanks anyway," and hung up.

I felt a little strange about that call. I wondered why Hannah-Leigh would call me looking for Cade, and I really wondered why he didn't want her to know where he was. But I had enough drama in my own life without worrying about theirs, so I went back to the truck and held the door open while Miss Eugenia climbed out. Then I followed her up the stairs and into my apartment.

Sloan opened the front door for us, and based on his grim expression, I figured he'd heard the entire exchange with Nick and Shasta. He closed the door and locked it securely.

I pointed between Miss Eugenia and Sloan. "I believe you two already know each other."

"We do," Miss Eugenia said.

"Nice to see you again," Sloan added.

"Miss Eugenia is going to be spending the night with us," I told Sloan. "I guess you found the new supply of leftovers my mother sent?"

He smiled. "Oh yeah."

"Then it's time for you to go downstairs. I'm exhausted and I've still got to call Luke and tell him how crazy his brother and ex-sister-in-law are."

"I doubt if it's going to come as a surprise," Sloan predicted.

"I know but I hate to remind him." I walked toward my bedroom. Then I turned around. "I'm glad you're here."

"It's nice to be wanted," he replied as he opened the door leading downstairs. "If you need me, all you have to do is call." Then he closed the door and we could hear his footsteps descend to the office below.

I told Miss Eugenia, "Have a seat here on the couch for a few minutes while I change the sheets on my bed. Then we'll get you settled for the night."

"You don't have to give up your bed!" Miss Eugenia said. "I'll be perfectly comfortable right here on the couch."

I laughed. "If my mother found out that you were my houseguest and I let you sleep on my couch, I'd be in the doghouse for the rest of my life!"

"Well, we do want to keep you out of the doghouse."

"It will just take me a minute."

I had enough time to walk to my linen closet and take out my one spare set of sheets before there was a knock on the front door. I would have ignored the banging if I thought my visitor would just go away, but I'd lived in Midway long enough to know better than that.

So I put the neat little stack of clean sheets on the end of my bed and walked back to the living room. Sloan was standing at the top of the stairs with the door cracked.

"Ask who it is before you open the door," he whispered. "And if there's trouble, jump back and let me handle it."

I nodded, feeling a little anxious as I approached the door and called out, "Who is there?"

The reply was unexpected. "It's me, Hannah-Leigh."

I pulled open the door and said, "What in the world are you doing out so late at night?" I didn't add, "with convicts and murderers and my crazy brother-in-law skulking around," but I sure was thinking it.

I pulled her inside and noted that she looked different. Every hair wasn't in place and her clothes were wrinkled. (I'll admit I liked her better instantly). And this time I was positive she had been crying.

"I'm sorry to disturb you again," she said. Then she burst into fresh tears.

I led her to the couch and sat her down. "There, there," Miss Eugenia comforted. Then she looked at me. "Get us some tissue, please."

Under the best of circumstances I'm not well-equipped for weeping visitors, and since I was packing up and throwing out, all I could find was paper towels. I handed the roll to Miss Eugenia and said, "This will have to do."

She tore off a few squares and passed them to Hannah-Leigh, who then blew her nose in a most unladylike manner. Over her shoulder I could see that Sloan had the door leading downstairs opened slightly, and he was standing at the top, listening to us.

"Now, stop this crying and tell us what's wrong," Miss Eugenia coaxed.

I was prepared for a lot of things—maybe she'd been fired from her dream job at Channel 3. Maybe she'd gained a pound and could no longer fit into her size zero clothes. But her answer was beyond anything I had imagined.

"I think Cade is having an affair!" she wailed.

"Already?" I always expected the worst from Cade, but even I was surprised by how quickly he had strayed this time from the bounds of monogamy.

"Yes!" Hannah-Leigh sobbed. "I know it doesn't make any sense, but it's true."

I remembered my conversation with Cade on Monday and his words of praise for Hannah-Leigh. It didn't make sense. "What makes you think he's cheating on you?"

"He's been working late—a lot."

That did set off some alarms in my mind.

"And I've caught him in several lies—nothing big, but it's the principle."

I agreed completely.

"Then this afternoon I ran into Sheriff Bonham, and I kind of scolded him for working Cade so many extra hours while we're still newlyweds. He gave me the worst frown and said he didn't know what I was talking about. He said Cade's schedule was exactly the same as it had been for over a year."

That was it. I said, "That dirty, rotten lowlife! You need to hire a private investigator. The more proof you have, the better the divorce settlement you'll get." Not that Cade had much of anything, but taking what he did have was the only way to punish him. Obviously public humiliation didn't bother him, or he would have left the Midway area after the drive-in incident that ended our marriage.

Hannah-Leigh looked at me like I was crazy for suggesting such a thing. "I don't want a divorce! I want to get him psychological help. Anyone who would cheat on me must have mental problems."

I took a step back and remembered the role I played in this whole convoluted scenario. "I've got nothing to say."

Miss Eugenia nodded. "That's probably for the best." Then she turned back to Hannah-Leigh. "You shouldn't jump to conclusions.

Even though Cade has a history of breaking his wedding vows, there could be a reasonable explanation for his behavior."

Hannah-Leigh wiped her tears with a piece of paper towel. "Do you really think so?"

"I think everyone is innocent until proven guilty," Miss Eugenia replied.

"You should talk to Cade about it," I suggested.

"Oh, I can't do that," Hannah-Leigh said. "He'd think I don't trust him."

"You don't."

She waved the damp paper towel. "But I don't want him to *know* that. It might ruin our marriage."

I shook my head and told Miss Eugenia, "She's all yours."

"If you can't discuss it with Cade, hiring a private investigator might be a good idea," Miss Eugenia suggested. "Then at least you'll know what you're dealing with."

"I can't hire a stranger to follow Cade!" Hannah-Leigh sounded truly appalled. She turned to me. "So I was hoping you would do it."

I was shocked. "Me!"

Miss Eugenia didn't seem to think it was asking too much. "Just borrow a car he won't recognize, park by the sheriff's department when he's supposed to get off work, and follow him to see where he goes. If he goes home, you're done for the evening. If he goes somewhere else, well, find out what he's doing and then tell Hannah-Leigh."

"I could pay you," the new Mrs. Burrell offered.

I shuddered. Following my ex-husband to see if he's cheating on his new wife was awful, but getting paid for it was, well, worse. But if there was something awful to be found out, I wanted to be the one instead of a stranger. "Okay, I'll handle it," I told her. "I'll call you tomorrow with the results."

I finally got Hannah-Leigh to leave, and Miss Eugenia settled in my bed. Then I stretched out on the couch and called Luke. The one small silver lining to my visit from Hannah-Leigh was that it gave me something interesting to tell him about.

"I'm sorry for Hannah-Leigh," Luke said after I got through itemizing her suspicions about Cade. "But she should have known better than to marry Burrell."

"Now that's what I call words of wisdom."

Then he said, "I probably won't be able to talk to you much tomorrow either. We're in court early, and Lt. Dempsey expects that we'll be there all day."

"I'm going to try to look at that as progress," I said. "The sooner you testify, the sooner you can come home."

"That's what I call positive thinking."

We laughed. Then we talked about Hawaii.

After we had to hang up, I snuggled under my blanket and stared at the ceiling. And I tried to figure out how I was going to confront Cade about cheating—again.

* * *

I didn't sleep well on Tuesday night—partly because I was uncomfortable and mostly because I had so much on my mind. I didn't want my insomnia to disturb Miss Eugenia, so I stayed on the couch until six thirty. At that point I got up and took a shower. Then I dressed in the same jeans from the night before and another of my Langston Association shirts.

Miss Eugenia was in the kitchen when I came out of the bathroom.

"Good morning," she greeted. "Would you like me to heat you up some fried chicken and creamed potatoes for breakfast?"

I sat down at the table. "Sorry, I don't have much of a selection food-wise. I haven't been grocery shopping, but my mother keeps me well-stocked in leftovers."

"I don't mind fried chicken for breakfast," Miss Eugenia assured me. "In fact, I could eat your mother's cooking most any time of the day or night."

I checked my watch. "Well, it's time for me to go downstairs for the morning Langston Association meeting. They usually don't last too long, and Sloan always buys fresh doughnuts. So when it's over, I'll bring you dessert."

She smiled. "That gives me something to look forward to." Then she pointed at my laptop. "Can I use that while you're at the meeting? I should have some information from Kelsey by now."

"Help yourself," I invited. Then I walked downstairs just as the other team members were arriving. Everyone looked as tired as I felt, and I knew the project was wearing on us all.

I got some doughnuts and sat beside Catsy. Then I looked around, wondering if one of the other people in the room was a thief and a murderer. I shuddered as Rand began the meeting. It was unusually short, and afterward I asked Drake if there was anything I could do for him or the team, and he shook his head. "I'll call you if I think of something."

When I got back upstairs, Miss Eugenia was staring at the computer screen. I noticed that her fried chicken breakfast was largely untouched. I put the doughnuts I'd brought her on the table and said, "Are you okay?"

She turned haunted eyes to me. "I'm not sure." Then she pointed to the computer screen. "I got that report from Kelsey on Dixie Reed—the woman in the photograph with Nola Finkle."

"I remember who Dixie is."

"And I told you her phone in Graceful was disconnected?"

I nodded and sat beside her at the table.

"Well, that's because her house was demolished in order to build a softball field as part of the Langston Association remake of her town."

"She sold to Drake?"

"Eventually, but according to her daughter who lives in St. Louis, she originally declined. And the next thing you know, she was in a nursing home with a diagnosis of dementia and depression."

My breath caught in my throat. "Exactly the same diagnosis as Agatha?"

She nodded. "The daughter said she seemed fine but had changed doctors, and the new guy found all kinds of problems that required strong medication and made it impossible for her to live alone. She said it was a difficult time since she lives so far away, but a man from the Langston Association helped her find a nursing home and get her mother settled there."

I gasped. "Rand? You think he got a doctor to make up a false diagnosis so he could put Dixie in a home and use her land for the softball field?"

Miss Eugenia shrugged. "I don't know who, but one of them did something very much like that. So I called Kelsey and asked her to do a quick check of all the towns Drake has renovated. It's a big number—fifty-three and counting. I wanted her to see if there was anyone else who refused to sell and ended up in a nursing home."

"Was there?"

"No, but one man declined a Langston Association offer and his house burned down. Another lost his job."

I thought about Mr. Fondren getting a job in Chicago with help from Drake's team.

"And then there is Foster."

She lost me there. "But Foster was killed by Parnell and his nurse, Jenna."

"Maybe they had some help from a member of the Langston Association," Miss Eugenia said. "Or at least maybe the suggestion was made by one of Drake's people."

"This is awful," I whispered. "Do you think it's the same person who is stealing?"

"It could be but not necessarily."

"So there could be *another* criminal within the organization?" One was unbelievable, but two was unthinkable.

"It's possible," Miss Eugenia agreed. "I've asked Kelsey to go back and do a more detailed search."

I knew all these searches were going to get expensive, and I didn't want to run up a big bill just in case I got stuck with it and had to pay it out of my honeymoon money (it was selfish, I know). "What will she charge us?"

"Don't worry about that. I called Mark, and after I told him, he said the FBI would cover the cost."

"That's a relief."

"But when you go to see Parnell today, could you ask him if anyone from Drake's organization talked with them and offered any suggestions on how to convince Foster to sell or something like that?"

"Of course I will."

"And it would really help if you had a picture to show him."

"I wish I would have known sooner, and I could have taken a picture of the group at our morning meeting." Then I remembered the Langston Association brochure that had a nice picture of the whole team, except me, thank goodness. "I've got something I can show him." I went to the binder Rand had so efficiently provided and pulled out the brochure.

When Miss Eugenia saw it, she said, "That will do nicely."

I couldn't bask in my success for very long. My cell phone rang, and I answered it to hear my mother's frantic voice. "Oh, Kennedy! Family court just called and said that Heaven's parents have filed for custody of Heaven and an emergency hearing has been set for tomorrow at nine o'clock!"

I won't say I was surprised, but I was mad. Neither Shasta nor Nick had ever had any interest in Heaven until Drake had offered money for the salvage yard.

Mother continued. "Heaven is settled and doing well in school . . ."

"And getting regular dental care and immunizations," I added.

"I don't know why all of a sudden they want custody," Mother said with a sniffle.

"I do. Drake Langston has offered to buy the salvage yard property again. Foster left it to Heaven, and Luke won't sell. So if they can get custody of Heaven and her inheritance, they can sell it and spend her money, leaving her with nothing."

"That's horrible!"

"They are not nice people," I understated. "But don't worry," I said and hoped she shouldn't. "I'll call Luke, and we'll figure out what to do."

Miss Eugenia understood most of what was happening from my side of the conversation (and since my mother was screeching her side, Miss Eugenia probably heard that as well.) But I filled her in briefly. Then I said, "I never thought I would be in a situation where I wouldn't want to call Luke, but here I am."

"The sooner he knows, the better," she decreed. "So go ahead and get it over with."

I walked into the living room for a little privacy. I knew he was supposed to be in court so I expected to get his voice mail. I was trying to compose a succinct yet urgent message when I heard his voice.

"Hey, Kennedy."

He sounded so happy to hear from me, which only made what I had to say worse. "Hey, Luke," I replied. "I'm afraid I have some bad news."

"Tell me." His voice sounded grim, and I could picture him, feet apart, shoulders square, ready to accept the burden.

"Nick and Shasta have filed for custody of Heaven," I said. "Family court has set an emergency hearing tomorrow at nine o'clock."

"Because of the money." It wasn't a question.

"Yes. They came over to my apartment last night and wanted me to convince you to sell the land. When I refused, Shasta said I'd be sorry, and I guess this is what she meant. Don't worry, I wasn't in any danger," I added quickly. "Cade and Sloan were both here."

"As soon as we hang up, call Burrell and get him to help you file a restraining order against Nick and Shasta. Since he witnessed their threat, it shouldn't take more than a couple of minutes."

"But do you seriously think it will keep Nick or Shasta from coming back to see me?"

"No, but if you have to shoot them, it will help your self-defense case."

I was impressed—both that he was planning ahead and knew I would shoot if necessary.

"Hold on just a minute and let me confer with the only lawyer I know."

"Lt. Dempsey?"

"Yeah," he replied.

I could hear bits and pieces of their muffled conversation. Finally Luke was back.

"Lt. Dempsey said the first thing we'll do is file our own motion for custody. Surely any judge would consider us better parents than Nick and Shasta."

"I'd like to hope."

"Then we'll explain the situation to the judicial panel and see if they can excuse me until tomorrow afternoon so that I can attend the hearing. But if not, you'll have to handle it for me."

"Maybe Nick and Shasta will come back and try to kill me so I can shoot them and save us all a lot of trouble."

"I think I'd rather take my chances at family court," Luke replied.

"Don't worry. If you can't come to the hearing, I'll handle it."

"Thanks, Kennedy," he said. "I'm sorry being a part of my family has already caused you so much trouble. Now I've got to go."

We said hurried good-byes, and I put away my phone. Then I walked back into the kitchen. "Luke is going to file for custody and try to come for the hearing tomorrow. But if he can't make it, I'll have to plead with the judge to give Heaven to us." Talk about something I never thought I'd do in a million years. "And he wants me to have Cade file a restraining order against his brother and ex-sister-in-law."

Miss Eugenia nodded. "Wise."

I called my mother and told her Luke's plans to protect Heaven from her horrible parents.

"Well, thank goodness," she said with relief.

"I'd love to talk more," I went on, "but I've got to get to the prison to visit Parnell."

My mother couldn't argue with that, so she let me go.

Then I asked Miss Eugenia, "Do you want me to drop you off at home?"

"If you don't mind." She pushed herself into a standing position. "I've got frying to do."

I took Miss Eugenia home and got her safely inside—with the doors locked—before I continued on to the state penitentiary.

During the drive I called Cade and asked him to file a restraining order.

"I can fill it out for you, but I can't file it until you sign it," he told me.

"I'll come by when I'm through at the prison," I promised. As I hung up the phone, I shook my head. A few months ago if someone had told me I'd be visiting people in prison and getting a restraining order, I would have laughed them out of town.

I had been trained by my mother not to visit someone empty-handed, and I assumed the same rules applied for prisons. So I stopped at a convenience store and bought a bag of chocolate chip cookies. Then I drove on, more reluctant as each moment passed.

I don't like Parnell, and I hated the idea of visiting a prison. So the prospect of both at once was really unappealing. But when I arrived, I had to admit that at least from the outside, the prison was not as bad as I expected. It looked pretty much like any other institutional building—grim but not frightening. I went inside and had to walk through a metal detector and show my driver's license, but I have to do that the airport.

Then I was told by two burly looking guards that the only gifts visitors were allowed to bring inmates was a money order. So I had to leave the cookies with the guards.

The waiting room was similar to ones I'd seen elsewhere. At fifteen minutes until ten o'clock, a middle-aged Hispanic woman with a nametag that said simply "Gonzalez" walked into the waiting room and called, "Kennedy Scoggins."

I stood and walked over. "I'm Kennedy Scoggins."

"I'm your father-in-law's case manager," Ms. Gonzalez said. "I'll guide you through your visit today. Next time you come you'll just wait here until they call your name and then you'll walk down this hall to the visitors' gallery."

I had no intention of visiting again, but I kept this to myself as I fell into step beside the case manager. We passed through two metal doors and entered a long corridor, lined with small cubicles. Each room had a glass wall that faced the corridor and partitions that gave the inmate and their visitors a modicum of privacy. Two chairs were between each set of partitions.

"You have to be here fifteen minutes early," Ms. Gonzalez was telling me. "No exceptions. Prisoners are brought out on the hour and all visitors must be seated before that time. You'll have exactly thirty minutes. Do you understand?"

I nodded.

"Good," Ms. Gonzalez said. "Enjoy your visit."

I watched Parnell's case manager walk off and then, feeling conspicuous, I sat down on one of the chairs in front of the visitation cubicle. I glanced up at the clock and saw that I had three minutes before the prisoners would be ushered into their side of the visitor's galley.

So I took several deep breaths and reminded myself that I was doing this for Luke. The door opened on the other side of the glass partition, and Parnell walked into his side of their small meeting space. He was wearing the standard orange jumpsuit, which fit a little loosely, and he had circles under his eyes like he might not be sleeping well, but otherwise he looked healthy.

I didn't know how Parnell would react when he saw me. I barely knew him and what I did know was bad. He had been a terrible father and was instrumental in the death of his own brother. If it had been left up to me, he would never get a visit from anyone. I was afraid he would know how I felt, which would make the favor I was doing for Luke pointless.

I was expecting something less than an enthusiastic welcome. But when he saw me, he seemed pleased. "I didn't think I would get a visitor today since Luke is in North Carolina," he said in an almost flirtatious tone. "Especially not such a lovely visitor."

I cleared my throat. "Well, thank you. I came to represent the family, and I brought you cookies, but they took them away from me at the sign-in desk. They were chocolate chip."

He smiled. "I like chocolate chip cookies." Then his expression became more serious. "I know you think I'm a terrible person. I made a lot of mistakes. I know I did wrong by my boys. I'd make it up to them if I could."

Surprisingly I didn't want to make him feel worse. So I just nodded.

"And I never meant to hurt Foster, you gotta believe that. Jenna convinced me that it was for his own good to sell the land. And I didn't realize that she planned to kill him. I wouldn't have helped her if I'd known."

I wasn't sure I completely believed him, but there was no point in arguing about it now. And besides, that was the segue I needed to ask him about Drake's team. I pulled out the brochure and spread it across my side of the thick glass. "Speaking of Jenna and Foster, did any of these people ever come and talk to you about ways to make Foster sell?"

Parnell squinted as he studied the picture carefully. Then he pointed and said, "I think that guy came and talked to Jenna a couple of times."

I followed the direction of his finger. "Drake!" I cried.

Parnell looked startled. "That tall blond guy with the fancy suit."

I immediately relaxed. "Oh, you mean Morris."

"Yeah, I'm pretty positive he came."

This was good news. I didn't care for Morris and would happily accept him as our arm-twisting team member. "Great, thanks for your help."

For the next twenty minutes he questioned me about my future with Luke. It was a pleasant conversation, and I was almost sad to leave when our time was up. A bell sounded indicating that our visit was over. The door behind Parnell opened and he stood. "Luke and I hope to be in Hawaii next week," I told him. "But one of us will be here when we get back."

He smiled. "I'll look forward to it."

I watched as he went to the door at the back of his side of the room. Just before he walked out, he turned and gave me a little wave. I saw Ms. Gonzalez waiting at the end of the hall. Together we passed through the metal sliding doors and finally reached the entrance.

"It was so nice to meet you," Ms. Gonzalez said. "I hope you'll come back often." She gave me a visitation schedule. "I wrote my number on the back of the schedule. Just give me a call."

When I'd arrived there, I thought this would be my one and only visit. But after talking with Luke's dad, I felt an unexpected connection to him. I knew I would be back. So I thanked her.

As I was walking out, one of the guards from the desk held up my bag of cookies. "You want these back?" he asked.

I smiled. "No, you enjoy them."

CHAPTER FIFTEEN

On the way home I called Miss Eugenia and told her about Parnell's confident identification of Morris as the team member who worked with Jenna—probably to plan Foster's murder. "But we need to talk to the nurse before we make any accusations."

"Mark's right here," Miss Eugenia said. "He's tasting a fried peanut butter and banana sandwich with marshmallow cream inside. I'll hand him the phone."

"And if you were wondering," Mark said when he came on the line, "it's awful."

I laughed. "I'm sorry but not surprised."

"I'm retiring as the taste-tester effective immediately. Now what did you find out from Parnell Scoggins?"

I related the information again, and Mark said he'd find out which prison the nurse ended up in. "Then I'll get someone to go question her without drawing attention."

"Isn't that strange, though?" I asked. "If she was coached by a member of Drake's team, it seems like it would have come out during the trial so she could get a lesser sentence."

"Maybe she was afraid that if she told, what happened to Foster would happen to her."

"I guess she had reason for concern."

When I got back to Midway I stopped by the sheriff's office. Cade was in the front cubicle, leaned back in the chair and his feet propped up on the desk—sound asleep. I woke him up.

"Oh, sorry," he mumbled. "The allergy medicine I'm taking for this swelling is making me so sleepy."

I stared at his face. "It's a little better, maybe."

He pointed at a form on the corner of the table. "There's your restraining order."

I signed it and then I took advantage of the moment to talk to him about Hannah-Leigh.

"I have a question for you," I told him. "I'm not emotionally involved—I just want the truth. Will you give me an honest answer?"

He nodded warily.

"Are you cheating on Hannah-Leigh?"

He almost fell out of his chair. "No!" he denied emphatically. "No, no, NO!"

I briefly considered whether his response fell in the "protesting too much" category, but applying a literary reference to Cade was just, well, ridiculous. So I took it at face value.

"You have to believe me!"

"All that matters is what Hannah-Leigh believes!" I responded. "She says you've been acting strange lately—not telling her where you're going or saying you're working when you're not. I know for a fact that you don't answer her phone calls. And so she's come to the conclusion that you have a girlfriend."

I wanted to add *which serves you right,* but I decided to take the high road.

"I don't have a girlfriend, I swear!" He seemed so agitated that I had to believe him. "I love Hannah-Leigh!"

I didn't want to ask because I really didn't want to know, but felt I had no choice. "Why don't you want to tell her where you are?"

"Two reasons," he replied. "First, I've been using vacation time to investigate Nola Finkle's death, and Hannah-Leigh would be mad about that. When she found out you and Luke are going to Hawaii for your honeymoon, she decided we should take a Hawaiian trip too and stay at her parents' place on Maui."

"And the time you've spent on Nola's case is cutting into your Maui vacation?"

He nodded. "But the main reason is that I don't want her to think I'm stupid. If this case turned out to be a total waste of time and I was completely wrong—well, just in case, I didn't want her to know. She is so smart and successful. I don't want her to feel like she's married to a loser."

I couldn't help but smile just a little. I was the wrong person to reassure Cade about his intelligence, and I couldn't care less about his vacation plans. I felt like I was giving him a break just by not ridiculing him for saying such stupid things in the first place. But I learned something important during this little exchange. While Cade was singing Hannah-Leigh's praises, I not only didn't feel jealous—I didn't even feel inadequate. And in that moment I knew that I had truly moved on. I'd left the past behind me, and my future with Luke was bright.

Cade dragged me from my pleasant reverie. "So?"

"First, I think that Nola's case is well-established enough now that you don't have to worry about looking like a fool—at least not over this. So tell her about it. And you'd better start answering her calls and letting her know exactly where you are, or you won't ever take a vacation with her to Hawaii or anywhere else. You've got a checkered past, and she has the right to be suspicious. You have to be above reproach."

He frowned in concentration. "Does that mean *real* good?"

I nodded.

He seemed relieved. "From now on I'll answer all her calls, and I'll tell her where I am even if I know it will make her mad."

I considered suggesting that he avoid going to places he knew would make her mad, but I decided I'd done enough to save their marriage. "Good. Now I've got to go."

On my way out to my car, I made a quick phone call to Hannah-Leigh. I told her it was all a false alarm. "Cade has been working on a case—just not an official one, so he was using some of his vacation time and he thought you'd be mad. But now the case is official, and he should get back his vacation. And I've instructed him to be more honest with you from now on. So I don't think you have anything to worry about."

"Thank you, Kennedy!" Hannah-Leigh cried.

As I turned off my phone, I wondered why neither of them thought it was odd that Cade's ex-wife was in the role of their go-between. I shook my head. Only in Midway.

I needed to be at Miss Eugenia's house at one o'clock so I had an hour to spare. Against my better judgment I went by my parents' house to reassure them about Heaven and the custody hearing.

As I pulled up in the driveway, I saw Miss Ida Jean standing in her front window. From that I assumed the missing prisoners had not yet been caught.

She waved to me and reluctantly I walked over. "Did you go see Parnell Scoggins at the prison?" she demanded.

"I did. Please thank Robby again for me."

"Did you take him a money order?"

"No, I brought some chocolate chip cookies, but the guards took them away."

"Cookies!" she scoffed, as if my ignorance of prison rules was more embarrassing than her detailed knowledge of the same. "Next time bring him a ten-dollar money order for him to use at the prison store."

"If there is a next time, I'll remember that," I told her. "Now you'll have to excuse me. I'm in a big hurry." Then I walked away even though I knew that she wasn't finished with our conversation. I could hear her pounding on the glass all the way to my parents' front door.

My mother was surprised and happy to see me. I explained from the beginning that I had a very important meeting in fifty minutes and therefore could not stay long. I did let her make me a tomato sandwich and we both sat at the kitchen table while I ate.

"So, have you heard back from Luke?"

"No, he was going to be in court all day," I said.

"Oh, I hope he can come for the hearing."

My heart thudded. "Me too."

I finished my sandwich and then stood. "Sorry, but I have to go. I'll call you as soon as I hear from Luke."

As Mother was walking me to the door she got a phone call. I assured her I could see myself out. When I got to my truck, Heaven was standing by the driver's door. She was sweaty and had a big dirt smear across her forehead.

I hate to admit it, but she scares me. She's so unpredictable that I never know what to expect. Guardedly I said, "Hey, Heaven."

"My dad sells drugs," she replied as calmly as if she were discussing the July weather. "He takes them too. So does my mom. He has a lot of regular customers and some new ones who just come to the house and ask him. If you said you knew Tex, then he would sell to you."

I tried to keep my astonishment from showing on my face. "You want me to buy drugs from your father?"

"Not you," she said, dismissing my question as ridiculous. "But you could get somebody else to and then tell him that if he tries to get custody of me, you'll tell the judge and the police."

It was a beautiful, simple plan and one that should never have occurred to a seven-year-old child.

"I heard them talking last night," she said. "If they sell the salvage yard, they are going to take all the money and run away."

It was a situation that called for comfort. If I had been dealing with a normal child, I would have reached down and hugged her. But I knew a hug would not be welcome or convey the comfort she needed. So I said, "Drugs destroy people. Your parents can't think clearly anymore. They are sick. It's them, not you."

She stared at me for a few seconds, I guess gauging my sincerity. Then she nodded. "So you'll take care of it?"

Like an idiot I promised that I would. It was the first time I had felt like a true Scoggins, and I'll admit it was a little terrifying. I watched Heaven run off to play.

As I left my parents' house my mind was in turmoil. I had just agreed to entrap Luke's brother. I knew I couldn't do it alone. I didn't want to tell Luke—besides, he was hundreds of miles away and couldn't help me. I couldn't tell Cade because he would arrest Nick, and while that probably needed to happen, I couldn't be the source of it.

So my only real option was Sloan. I knew he would help me, but I hated to ask for many reasons—not the least of which was because he was a suspect in the murder investigation I was currently working on. But since my choices and time were limited, I called him and briefly explained the situation. He listened carefully (one of his best traits) and then said he'd meet me at my apartment at seven o'clock that night and we'd take care of it. I felt better immediately.

I arrived at Miss Eugenia's house five minutes early. The others were already there, so I felt late even though I wasn't. Miss Eugenia offered to fix me a sandwich for lunch, but I declined.

Mark began the meeting by announcing that Nola's car definitely showed signs of tampering.

"So it was murder?" I breathed.

He nodded. "I don't know if the intention was to kill her or just scare her—but, regardless, she's dead and someone is responsible. Because of Catsy Lanier's youthful arrests and that car theft, we investigated deeper into her past and found out that she has a former foster brother who is the right age and matches the description of the witness at the wreck. I had a couple of agents bring him in for questioning. First he said he didn't know what they were talking about. Then he asked for a lawyer. Now he's admitted that he basically planted a homemade gas bomb in Nola's car, but he wants a deal before he gives more details."

Cade frowned. "Don't give him a deal and let him get away with murder! We'll figure out the rest ourselves and convict him and the others who were working with him."

"I told them not to make a deal just yet. The fact that he's willing to make one speaks volumes," Mark said. "And in the meantime, we have impounded his truck and we'll look for evidence that he bumped Nola's car."

"I remember what that truck looked like," Cade said. "It's going to be hard to tell if he hit Nola. The paint on her car is ashes and his car's got about a million dings on it."

"We do have an expert working on it," Mark said with confidence. "And for now we'll just go on the assumption that Catsy Lanier is the thief and that she got her foster brother to tamper with Nola's car and then bump into her, causing the wreck."

I was sad about this. Even though I didn't know her well, I liked Catsy, and I felt sorry for her somehow. But if it had to be her or Sloan, I was glad it was her.

Mark continued. "And between Nola's car, the foster brother's car, and his testimony, I believe we have enough to arrest Catsy Lanier."

Miss Eugenia said, "And the most important part of all this is that based on the evidence they found on Nola's car, Mark is now an official part of the investigation!"

"Just in an advisory role, though," Mark cautioned. "Chief Jones is running the case until the Albany Police get wind of it and try to steal it away." He turned to Cade. "Winston is going to call Sheriff Bonham and bring him up to speed right after this meeting. We don't want him to feel like we are working behind his back."

"But we have been," I pointed out.

"We didn't have any evidence before, so I'm sure he'll understand why we didn't bring it to his attention until now."

"Are we going to start having meetings at the sheriff's department office or at the Haggerty police station instead of this house?" Cade wanted to know. "Now that it's official?"

"I'd rather if everyone in Haggerty and Midway didn't know that there was an investigation just yet," Mark said. "So I think we'll continue meeting here."

"And now Kennedy has some news too," Miss Eugenia said to set the stage for me.

I cleared my throat and began by telling them about Agatha, my meeting with her on Sunday, and the deal that was supposedly struck between her and Rand for the purchase of her property.

"But then on Monday I found out that her house had been demolished. Sloan said that the health department had condemned her house and she had been moved to a nice retirement complex in Millwood. So on Tuesday Miss Eugenia and I went to see her."

"And let me tell you, there is no such thing as a nice retirement complex," Miss Eugenia put in.

"Actually, I thought it was very nice."

"It was a prison," Miss Eugenia muttered. "It says a lot about a society when it locks up its old people."

I turned to her. "Are you going to let me tell this, or do you want to?"

"Go ahead," she said. "But I'm sure you won't mind if I add an occasional detail."

I looked to Mark and Winston. They both shook their heads, indicating there was nothing they could do about her. So I continued. "Anyway, we went to see Agatha in Millwood. She seemed very confused and groggy and just not at all herself. We talked to the nurse and he said that she had dementia and was on medicine for that, which was surprising because she seemed very sharp when I met her on Sunday. He also said she had been prescribed a medication to help with anxiety because of the sudden move."

"Which I could understand," Miss Eugenia provided. "If I was hauled off to a nursing home, I'd need medication too."

"We accepted his explanation for her odd behavior. But then Miss Eugenia found out today that another woman who refused to sell property to the Langston Association a few months ago is also in a nursing home with the exact same diagnosis."

Miss Eugenia just couldn't help herself. "There have also been two other instances that we found where someone refused to sell. One person lost their job and had to move and one person's house burned to the ground," she announced with a flourish. "So we think that someone on the team takes matters into their own hands if townsfolk refuse to sell."

"Is it the same person who is stealing?" Cade asked.

"It could be—we don't know for sure," Mark interjected.

"But we do have an idea of who is forcing reluctant people to sell," Miss Eugenia said. "Kennedy took a picture of Drake Langston's team with her to the prison today when she visited her father-in-law, Parnell Scoggins. You'll remember that he and his nurse were convicted in the murder of his brother, Foster."

Winston nodded. "We all remember."

"Well, Parnell identified Morris Pugh as the person who came and talked to the nurse—more than once."

"But he's not sure that they were planning Foster's murder, so Mark is going to locate what prison the nurse is in and send someone to question her," I said.

"FBI questioning is taking a long time with the car-tampering guy," Cade pointed out. "Once you know which prison the nurse is in, maybe we should contact the local sheriff and ask them to send someone to ask the questions."

"The FBI will handle it, and we'll try to work more quickly this time," Mark said dryly.

"Even if we find her, the nurse is not a great witness," Winston said. "Since she has a lot to gain by accusing someone else and probably no proof—other than Parnell's word and to say that he is a bad witness is, well, he's a real bad witness."

Mark nodded. "So instead of depending on that route, Miss Eugenia has come up with an idea to catch Morris in the act of strong-arming old people."

"Not just old people," I said. "Defenseless people of various ages."

"I stand corrected." Mark pointed to Miss Eugenia. "Tell them your idea."

"My plan will involve getting Mr. Langston's cooperation," she began. "But I don't think that will be hard to do."

"I believe he'll help us," I contributed.

"I thought if we could have a situation here in Midway where someone else doesn't want to sell, Morris will have to act. And if we're watching, we'd catch him."

I didn't like the sound of it. "But Drake has already made all the offers for land in Midway. If he adds another one, it will be suspicious."

"You know how George Ann Simmons has been badgering him to buy her worthless property out by that old milk plant where JD was killed?" Miss Eugenia asked.

I nodded. "Rand mentions her ridiculous demands in almost every morning meeting."

"Well, what if Drake says he wants to go ahead and buy the land to keep George Ann from suing him, which she is threatening, by the way."

"If he did that, Rand would make up a proposal, set up an appointment, and go visit her," I said.

"So once the appointment is made—which I'll know because you'll tell me—I'll go over to George Ann's house. She'll tell me about it because she is such a bragger that she won't be able to resist. Or if she doesn't, I'll bring it up myself. And when she tells me how much Drake is offering, I'll say if he's offering that much, it must be worth a lot more. And she'll believe that because she thinks all her possessions are more valuable than they really are."

"You'll convince her to refuse the offer," I realized.

"To hold out for a better deal," Cade added.

Miss Eugenia nodded. "Exactly. When that Rand fellow reports to Drake Langston that she has refused the offer, he'll say for Rand to offer whatever it takes and that they aren't leaving Midway without a deal. That should put Morris into action."

"Will it work?"

"I know George Ann, and if we use all her negative traits against her, it will work." There was no doubt in her mind. "And if George

Ann ends up in a nursing home, it wouldn't be the worst thing in the world."

Mark gave her a reproving look. "We want to catch the person or persons inside the Langston Association who are committing crimes, but in the process we have to keep Miss George Ann and the whole town of Haggerty safe. Since they've already used a nursing home once during this renovation, I think they'll be reluctant to try it again."

Winston nodded. "Things like that get attention eventually—especially in a town full of old people like Haggerty."

Miss Eugenia was not deterred. "So far we know of two other methods they've used—losing a job and house fire. Since Miss George Ann doesn't have a job . . ."

"We want to push Morris into setting her house on fire?" I was concerned.

"Well, we want to push him toward fire, but not for her house in Haggerty," Mark explained.

"When Kennedy and Rand meet with George Ann, I will already have suggested that she hire a contractor and make major improvements to the house on the land. I might even act like if the house is nice enough, I'll get Annabelle to buy it for much more than Drake Langston is offering." She looked around to include all of us. "In case Annabelle hasn't already told you, she's rich."

"Anyway," Winston said, redirecting the conversation back to our trap. "So this Morris guy will think that by burning down the house he'll reduce the value and Miss George Ann will be happy to sell to Drake."

"Right," Mark said. "And I think it will be best to have the actual meeting at the land—far from Haggerty."

"And far from your house," I guessed.

"Yes," he admitted. "We'll have workers there who will actually be agents providing security. We'll also have heavy equipment and big barrels that appear to be filled with fuel stacked in the barn. When Rand reports all that, a fire will be the obvious solution for our criminal to reach."

"Maybe Rand is Morris's partner," I suggested. "That would make sense."

Cade frowned. "You really want this Rand to be guilty, don't you?"

"He's not a very nice person," I said. "I don't want him to be guilty—I just wouldn't be surprised if he is."

Mark said, "After that initial meeting, we'll keep the place under constant surveillance. Our hope is that once it gets dark, Morris will come and try to burn the place down."

"Using the barrels that look like they are full of fuel," I guessed.

He nodded. "Of course they won't really contain flammable liquid."

"Of course," I said.

"Sounds good to me," Winston said. "I can use all my guys for security. And we can get more from the county sheriff."

"I'll throw in a few FBI agents," Mark said. "But only as advisers."

Everyone nodded.

"And I can provide the surveillance equipment," Mark continued. "We'll set up cameras all around the area so we can monitor what's going on from a safe distance."

"Where will we set up surveillance equipment?" Cade asked.

"We'll put a small team inside the house, but I'd like to put the main team on that clearing where Mr. Dupree used to live. If we could locate an old trailer, it should blend right in. Then we can set up our equipment there."

"I'll come up with a trailer and talk to Sheriff Bonham," Winston said. "Cade, would you be responsible for assigning positions around the property so Morris can't get away once we catch him."

"I'll handle that," Cade agreed.

"You better hope you catch him before he burns down the place or George Ann will sue the FBI to get the inflated purchase price for her worthless land," Miss Eugenia warned.

"We'll stop him before he does much damage," Mark promised.

"I'd like to be there," I said.

"No!" Cade objected.

Mark overruled him. "As long as you stay in the trailer, I'm okay with it."

I exchanged a smirk with Cade.

Miss Eugenia said, "I want to be there too."

"Nope," Mark vetoed right away. "As soon as you and Miss George Ann are through meeting with Rand and Kennedy, you're out of here and to a safe place."

"Can we stay in the same hotel with Kate and the kids?" Miss Eugenia asked. "Then at least I won't be bored."

He sighed. "I guess."

"What about Agatha and Dixie and whoever else has been forced into unhappy situations by Drake's team?" I asked. "Can we help them?"

"We can't do anything about that until we have our guilty party or parties in custody. If they realize that we're on to them, it's over."

I had to be satisfied with that. "Okay."

"Couldn't we just find out which doctor put the old ladies in the nursing homes and ask them who hired them to do it?" Cade asked.

"When you start dealing with patient privacy issues and a doctor's diagnosis—which can be pretty subjective—it gets tricky. So this is not the fastest or the quietest route to go."

"Then I guess I'm good with the other plan," Cade said. "I was just wondering."

"Asking questions is good," Mark assured him. "Questions help us find our mistakes before someone else does."

Cade smiled at the backdoor compliment.

"So now we need to set up a meeting with Drake to explain all this," Winston said. "I guess Kennedy is going to do that?"

"I don't know why I get all the fun." I pulled out my phone and called Drake's number. When he answered I told him I had something important to talk to him about and asked if he could meet me in Haggerty.

"I can be there in fifteen minutes," he said.

I gave him directions and then turned to the others. "Well, it's done. He'll be here in a few minutes."

Mark nodded. "And we'll all be waiting."

CHAPTER SIXTEEN

I MET DRAKE IN MISS EUGENIA's driveway.

"There are other people here to," I warned him as he got out of the car. "Miss Eugenia—this is her house. Also Deputy Burrell, the Haggerty Police Chief Winston Jones, and Mark Iverson."

I saw Drake raise his guard. "FBI?"

"Yes," I confirmed. "Come on in and we'll tell you about it."

He followed me inside the house, through Miss Eugenia's back door, and into her cramped little kitchen. He nodded to the room in general, polite but wary.

"Have a seat," I pointed to one of the empty chairs around the table.

He took one and I sat beside him. He was the outsider here, and I felt the need to protect him—as silly as that seems.

"Now is someone going to tell me what this is all about?" he asked.

"Kennedy, why don't you begin since you are the one who discovered the issues," Mark invited.

"Actually it was Cade." I spoke directly to Drake. "I don't want you to think that I was spying on your team while you were paying me."

"You were spying on my team?" he repeated in confusion and a little bit of anger.

"No, well, not exactly."

"There was a traffic accident on Saturday," Cade interrupted my bumbling attempt to explain. "A woman named Nola Finkle died. Does that name sound familiar?"

Drake frowned. "Vaguely."

"She worked for a veterinary supply company in Atlanta. Your organization bought a lot of equipment from them when the town you were working on needed a new animal shelter."

Drake nodded. "She was our sales rep. I talked to her a couple of times."

"Well, apparently she's been trying to get in touch with you, and you weren't returning her calls."

Drake raised an eyebrow. "I'm a busy man. What did she want?"

"To tell you that someone on your team has been stealing from you," Cade said, and I heard the relish in his voice. "Thousands and thousands of dollars."

"Impossible," Drake said flatly. Then he asked, "Stealing how?"

"Duplicating supply orders and selling the extras," I explained. "We only know about the purchases made at Universal Pet Products, but we suspect the same thing was done with other large suppliers."

Drake looked pained. "Who?"

"Catsy, we think," I disclosed regretfully. "And I'm afraid the news is even worse. Nola Finkle noticed some duplications in their orders, and when she couldn't reach you by phone, she came down here to talk to you. She was killed in the wreck before she could reach you."

"Are you saying that Catsy caused the wreck?" Drake sounded incredulous.

"Actually it was her foster brother," Cade was pleased to inform him. "He built a car bomb and put it in Ms. Finkle's car. Then he ran her off the road and, well, she died."

"I can't believe Catsy would steal money from me," Drake said slowly. "And I sure can't believe she'd kill to cover it up."

"Some of this is still guesswork," I admitted, "but I think she started stealing on a small scale at first, to be able to afford expensive clothes and shoes and purses so she'd fit in with Morris and his rich family."

He shook his head. "Why was she trying to fit in with Morris's family?"

"They are engaged," I provided.

His eyes went wide. "I didn't even know they were dating."

"With the wedding coming up and no family to help her with expenses, she probably started stealing more often," I said. "Nobody noticed so everything was okay. Then Nola Finkle caught the discrepancy and threatened to expose the money-making scheme. She thought she had no choice. So she called her former foster brother and asked for his help."

"She asked him to put a bomb into Nola Finkle's car and then run her into a tree," Cade clarified.

I gave him a reproving look. "I like to think that Catsy didn't really mean to kill Nola. She just wanted to discourage her from pursuing the duplicate purchases with you."

Drake's eyes dropped to old linoleum table in front of him. "Why wouldn't she just ask me for help instead of stealing? I could have given her a raise or something."

"Catsy makes a good salary," I replied. "She knew it was unreasonable to ask for more money. But she had to look like a rich person to fit in with Morris's family. So she took advantage of your trust and stole from you."

He sighed. "I'm an idiot."

"You're not!" I exclaimed, but I noticed that everyone else at the table was ominously silent.

"I made it too easy for her to steal. But that's it. I'm going to close down the Langston Association. My accountants beg me to every year since it takes up time I could invest in the several of my companies that actually make money. But of all my business ventures, it is the one I loved, the one that I really put my heart into."

"It would be a shame to shut it down," I said.

"But I can't go on like this—having a thief on my team. Maybe a murderer." He seemed so sad that I couldn't help but feel sorry for him.

"There's more," Cade said with a smile, and I wanted to strangle him.

Drake nodded and then turned to me. "Go ahead and tell me all of it."

"Morris has been forcing people to sell to the Langston Association even if they don't want to."

"Morris? He's not even involved in acquisitions!" Drake said. "How could he be forcing anyone to do anything?"

I explained about Agatha and Dixie. I told him there were at least two others who had sold because they lost their job and because of a house fire. And I told him that it was possible Morris had even suggested to Jenna and Parnell that they get rid of Foster.

"It doesn't make any sense," Drake said in confusion. "If plan A doesn't work, we go to plan B. We don't put old ladies in nursing homes and we certainly don't electrocute people."

Miss Eugenia cleared her throat. "Apparently someone on the team has taken it upon themselves to force plan A."

"I just can't believe it." He looked at me. "And why would Morris do this?"

"I don't know," I admitted. "I suspected Rand because he got impatient with Agatha. He wants to keep the schedule moving. He doesn't have much interest in people like Agatha and Dixie, who messed up the plans for no logical reason. But Parnell identified Morris from a picture of the team—so unless Rand and Morris are working together . . ."

"Surely it can't be my whole team."

"Let's go over it again," Mark offered.

This time I sat back and listened while Mark and Winston went over the evidence, their unproven theories, and finally their plan to trick the guilty party or parties into the open.

"We may end up giving Catsy's foster brother a deal," Mark said. "But one way or another, I think we can prove that the two of them were involved in Nola Finkle's death. Where we need your help is in proving who has been strong-arming folks who don't want to sell."

Drake nodded. "If what you're saying is true, I'll do anything I can to catch Morris red-handed."

We explained the plan, and Drake agreed to do his part.

Then he turned to me and said, "I want to do everything I can to make it up to the people who have been tricked. This Dixie lady—I'll offer her a house in the new subdivision in her town, free of charge, and give her some money. And we will get Agatha Hoban out of the nursing home immediately. I'll rent a house for her until her new home is ready."

"I think it would be better if she stays with someone at first," I said. "At least until the medication wears off."

"I'm sure Miss Zelda will be glad to have her for a couple of weeks," Miss Eugenia said.

"She might even get her to church," I agreed with a smile.

"I'll call the nursing home and find out what needs to be done to release her," Drake said. "And I'll have my staff identify the other people who deserve repayment. Then I'll have my legal department check into Parnell's situation. If there is anything that can be done to reopen his case based on facts that he may have been coerced."

"We appreciate your desire to correct the mistakes made by your team members," Mark said. "But if you would wait until after tomorrow, it would be best. If Morris finds out what you're doing, he might figure out that you are on to him. Then he wouldn't show up at Miss George Ann's land like we want him to."

"I'll wait," Drake agreed. He sounded discouraged and I felt sorry for him.

When the discussion was over, Drake stood to go. "I should probably thank you," he told us all. "But right now I just can't."

"We understand," I assured him. "But it's better to know than to just go on and not know."

He nodded. Miss Eugenia walked him to the front door, and a few minutes later we saw his car drive away.

We went over the details for the next day for a few more minutes, and then I excused myself. I almost laughed wondering what the people in Miss Eugenia's kitchen would think if they knew I was rushing home to be part of a drug deal.

* * *

Sloan was waiting for me when I got back to my apartment. I changed quickly into a black T-shirt and then we drove to the salvage yard.

"What have you been up to today?" he asked as we drove.

"Mostly hanging out at Miss Eugenia's house," I said. "Poor little old lady gets so lonely. How about you? What did you accomplish?"

He told me about the progress they had made on the various projects around Midway and I was impressed. "It's nothing short of miraculous."

He grinned. "That's me—a walking miracle."

When we reached the salvage yard, Sloan had me lie down on the floorboard of his truck. "Do not get up for any reason," he instructed. "And if there is trouble, call 911." He put a baseball cap low on his head. Then he set his phone on camera and put it in his pocket, the tiny lens barely peeking over the fabric's edge. "Are you going to give me a kiss for luck?"

I was appalled. "I am a married woman!"

"Sort of," he teased. "Okay, no kiss. Just wish me luck."

"Luck," I said.

Then he climbed out of the truck and walked up to the front door of Parnell's house. I kept low and in the shadows. He knocked and finally the door opened. It was Shasta.

"I need to speak to Nick," he said.

"Who are you?" she demanded.

"Tex sent me," Sloan said.

"Nick!" Shasta hollered over her shoulder. "It's for you."

I saw Nick come to the door and I heard some muffled conversation. Then Sloan turned and started back for the truck. Nick stood in the doorway, watching him leave. Just before he reached the truck, Sloan turned back.

"I've got bad news, Nick," he said. "I'm not a friend of Tex's, after all."

Even in the fading light I could see Nick's face turn pale. "Who are you, then?"

"FBI," Sloan replied. "And I recorded that whole transaction with my phone." He pulled it out of his pocket for proof. "I think I'll show the family court judge tomorrow and see if he thinks you'd make a good daddy."

"They won't use that as evidence." Nick tried to act brave.

"You know, that's true," Sloan said as if he'd never thought of it. "It would probably be more effective to find Tex and let him know that you are cooperating with the police, naming names. Then we can just sit back and let your suppliers and customers take care of you."

"No, man," Nick croaked. "Don't do that."

"We can make a deal," Sloan said. "You withdraw your application for custody tomorrow, and I won't talk to Tex."

"Why do you care about Heaven?" Nick asked.

"Let's just say I don't think little girls should be raised by scum like you."

Nick's head dropped. "Okay, I'll withdraw my application. Just don't say anything to Tex."

Sloan waved the camera. "I'll be watching to make sure you do."

Then he climbed in the truck and we drove away. Once we were back on the main road, I climbed up into the seat.

"It was as easy as that?" I asked in amazement.

Sloan replied, "If it isn't, then tomorrow I'll be paying a visit to Tex."

I put on my seat belt and said, "I feel bad that Nick is going to get away with selling drugs."

Sloan looked over and gave me one of his most dangerous smiles. "He's not going to get away with anything. As soon as the custody hearing is settled, I'll send a copy of our little drug transaction to the sheriff."

"I thought Nick said it wasn't acceptable as evidence."

"It's not," Sloan agreed. "But it's enough to have the sheriff set up a trap to catch Nick, along with his suppliers and customers. He can hide in the woods and pick them off one by one."

I smiled back. "You're sneaky. "

He nodded. "I've been called worse."

We were just passing the Jiffy Mart when I felt my phone vibrate, indicating that I had a text message. I hadn't heard from Luke since that morning, so I was very pleased when I saw his name on my touch screen. I opened the message and read, *I sent you a surprise special delivery.*

I called his number, and when he answered, I said, "What is it?"

He laughed. "I can't tell you. That's the whole point of a surprise."

"I'm not really all that crazy about surprises," I told him.

We rounded the corner by the Midway Store and Save, and standing on my front porch, bathed in moonlight, was my husband of four days.

"Luke!" I cried as I closed my phone and fumbled for the door handle.

"Don't you dare open that door until I'm parked!" Sloan commanded.

I obeyed him but just barely. As soon as his truck slid to a stop in the loose gravel, I was out and running toward my husband. He met me at the bottom of the porch stairs and pulled me into his arms.

I thought my heart would pound out of my chest. "Oh," I murmured against the soft skin of his neck. "Maybe I do like surprises, after all!"

His chest shook in what sounded like something between a chuckle and a sob. I never wanted the moment to end. But it did. Gently Luke pulled away, and I saw Lt. Dempsey standing on the porch above us.

"Does he still have to watch you all the time?" I whispered.

Luke nodded with a grimace. "Unfortunately, but even if the honeymoon can't start yet, I thought you'd be glad to see me." His breath was warm against my ear.

"Glad is not even close to how I feel about seeing you," I assured him. "In fact, I can't think of a word huge enough!"

Sloan walked up and held out a hand to Luke, which meant we had to separate more for Luke to accept the gesture.

The men grasped hands and shook firmly. "So, are you back for good?"

Luke shook his head. "Just until after the hearing tomorrow, but the trial is winding down. I hope it will be over in a couple of days."

Sloan smiled. "Well, I've got some work still to do so I'll give you two some 'privacy.'" He glanced up at Lt. Dempsey as he climbed back in his truck and drove off.

I felt guilty that Sloan had taken time out of his construction schedule to help me with Nick and now was having to work after dark. Then Luke's fingers laced through mine, and I forgot my guilt. I couldn't think about anything but him.

"If I had known you were coming, I could have done . . . something for dinner," I said as we climbed the stairs. I couldn't go as far as to say "cooked."

"I could have asked my mother to make something or stopped by the Jiffy Mart for hot dogs or something!"

"I've already checked out your refrigerator, and it's full of food."

"You don't mind leftovers?"

He laughed. "I've been eating at a military mess hall. Your mother's leftovers sound wonderful!"

I smiled as we reached the stair landing where Lt. Dempsey was waiting. I could tell he was a little nervous about what kind of reception he would receive from me. So I said, "Hey, lieutenant."

Lt. Dempsey nodded. "Mrs. Scoggins."

"Thank you for bringing Luke home for the hearing."

His cheeks turned pink. "Glad we could work it out, ma'am."

Luke led me inside and we sat on the couch while Lt. Dempsey went into the kitchen. Once we were sitting as close together as respectably possible, Luke said, "Now tell me about your day."

Keeping my voice low so only he could hear me, I described my visit with Parnell, the evidence that was mounting against Catsy and Morris, and how terrible it had been to break the news to Drake. I repeated what Heaven had confided about Nick and my promise to make sure her parents didn't regain custody. Then I told him how Sloan had helped me at the salvage yard.

At the last he pulled my head against his chest. "I don't know why you even want to be married to me. My family is so . . ."

"I didn't marry them," I reminded him. "Just you."

He pressed a kiss to my forehead. "You might change the way people feel when they hear the name Scoggins."

"You've already done that," I told him. "I'm just trying to build on to what you started."

Then we heard a car pull up outside.

"That's probably Miss Eugenia," I realized. Then I explained apologetically, "Mark won't let her stay at her house because of Nola's stolen stuff. She tried to stay with her sister, but her sister's too lovey-dovey with her husband and tries to steal Miss Eugenia's food-frying ideas." I paused for a deep breath. "So she's been my guest."

Luke grinned. "The more, the merrier."

"You're so nice," I sighed.

Luke went to the door and opened it. A few seconds later Miss Eugenia and Cade had both joined us in the tiny living room.

"Scoggins," Cade said.

"Burrell," Luke replied. I noted that they were still on a last-name basis, but I didn't sense any hostility between them. Luke turned to Miss Eugenia. "And how are you?" he asked.

She cackled. "Fine, soldier. Welcome home."

"It's just temporary," Luke told her. "I have to go back to Ft. Lejeune after the hearing in the morning."

She put her hands on her ample hips. "Well, if that is not the last word. I'm going to have to write my congressman about this! But if you only have a few hours together, the least I can do is get out of here and let you two have some alone time. I can stand being with my sister and her baby-talking husband for one night."

"As nice as some alone time sounds," Luke told her with a smile, "Lt. Dempsey in there has to be wherever I am."

Miss Eugenia shook her head. "That's a shame."

Luke laughed. "So you might as well stay too. And I have an idea for your entry in the frying contest. I can tell you about it if you'd like."

Miss Eugenia raised an eyebrow. "I certainly need a good idea. I've fried every kind of food in my house at least once and with disastrous results."

"The only decent thing I've had to eat the whole time I've been in Marine Corps custody were the s'mores they served for dessert last night. They used two graham crackers, chocolate, and a marshmallow—all baked in the oven until it was almost ruined but not quite."

"I'm listening," Miss Eugenia said.

"Well, I knew you were interested in frying marshmallows—so that's what made me think of the contest. But I couldn't figure out how you could fry a s'more until I saw a soldier take a big, soft cookie and wrap it around his before he ate it. That made me think if you wrapped the s'more in sugar cookie dough first and then fried it . . ."

Miss Eugenia looked ecstatic. "Young man, that is the best idea I've ever heard! If I win the hundred-dollar prize, I'll split it with you!"

Luke laughed. "If you win with my idea, keep all the money. You're the one doing the work."

"I am so anxious to try it. I'll have to make sure I get the cookie dough just the right thickness, and I'll have to figure out how long to leave it in the hot oil." She glanced into my little kitchen. "I don't guess you have a Fry Daddy or even a Fry Baby?"

"No," I told her with pretend regret. "You'll have to wait until tomorrow to try Luke's idea."

Miss Eugenia was frowning over this, and I was afraid she was about to make me call my mother (who has every cooking gadget known to man) and ask to borrow a member of the Fry family when Lt. Dempsey cleared his throat and said, "Excuse me."

We all turned to look at him.

His cheeks turned pink again. But he pressed on. "Is there any reason that some ladies in a black van should be picking up your trash this late at night?"

"Trash?" I repeated. Then I thought about Miss Ida Jean's complaint, which had sounded silly at the time. My eyes sought Cade's. "Stealing *trash*!" I whispered.

He put a finger to his lips and walked over to the window.

I motioned for Lt. Dempsey to turn off the lights in the kitchen, and he complied. Now in the darkness Cade was able to look outside without seeing his own reflection. "Well, I'll be . . ."

"What's going on?" Luke asked softly.

"Miss Ida Jean complained to Cade that someone has been stealing her trash," I explained. "But we didn't take that seriously because, well, it was Miss Ida Jean. But now if someone is stealing my trash too, maybe she wasn't just making it up!"

"It looks like they are driving around to one of your storage units," Cade whispered from the window.

"So the trash robbers are storing their . . . *spoils* here?" Luke asked with a smile.

The pun was lost on Cade. "Exactly! I'm going to go down there and check it out." He slipped quietly toward the door.

Miss Eugenia followed. "This I've got to see."

I barely controlled hysterical giggles. "Me too!" I pulled Luke by the hand.

"If Corporal Scoggins is going, then I am too," Lt. Dempsey muttered as he brought up the rear.

Cade turned around and glared at all of us. "If you're all coming with me, you'd better be quiet!"

I held up my hand in the universal "I swear" sign, and Cade looked relieved. We continued toward the last row of storage units and were as quiet as five people can be while walking on gravel. When we reached the last row, we could hear the two women talking as they opened the door to their unit. I stepped up beside Cade and peeked around the corner. I saw two smallish figures, dressed all in black, unloading garbage bags from the back of a van. A large lantern-style flashlight propped on top of the van provided the only light.

We watched them for a few seconds until Cade decided to make his presence known. He stepped around the corner and said, "Hey!"

Both the black-clad figures screamed—along with me, Miss Eugenia, and Lt. Dempsey.

"What are you doing with all that trash?" Cade continued. The rest of us came out to stand behind Cade.

A jumble of inane phrases like "oh no" and "oh gosh" came from the trash thieves.

Cade picked up the lantern flashlight and held it close to the women. As the light probed the features of the first thief, I felt like screaming again.

"Missy?" Cade whispered, staring in shock at his high school girlfriend, who was still clutching a bag full of someone's garbage.

I stared as well. The last time I'd seen Missy Lamar, she was half dressed and rolling around in the backseat of Cade's Rodeo at the drive-in.

"Is that who I think it is?" Luke whispered.

"Oh, yes," I whispered back.

Luke whistled. "Man, it doesn't get much more awkward than this."

"I declare," Miss Eugenia added.

Cade was continuing his interrogation. "Is that your sister?"

"Hey, Cade," Missy's sister, Taffy, gave him a wave and a nervous grin. She shifted the bag she was holding from one hip to the other.

"Will you please tell me what in the heck you are doing?" Cade boomed, causing Missy and Taffy to scream again.

"Well, we rented a booth at the flea market over in Putney, and it's a great way to sell things you don't need and make a little money," Missy began. "But it didn't take us long to sell all of our stuff we didn't need, and then we didn't have anything for our booth."

Taffy took over the story. "So we thought of garbage. I mean, it's really stuff nobody needs, right?"

"Garbage?" Cade confirmed.

Missy nodded. "We thought that sometimes people throw away some really good stuff. So we started going around collecting trash. We bring it here and go through it."

We all just stood there, staring at them and their storage unit full of other people's trash.

I opened my mouth several times to make a comment, but every time I closed it again, uninspired.

Finally Luke said, "Is that legal?"

"I don't know why not," Taffy said defensively. "If people are throwing it out, why would they care if we get it?"

"Because they are putting it on the curb to be collected by a professional disposal company," Cade replied testily. "Not to be picked up and pawed through by just anyone."

"You're not going to arrest us, are you, Cade?" Missy said as tears welled in her eyes. She swiped at them and smeared black eyeliner across the bridge of her nose.

"I don't know what I'm going to do," Cade said. "I've never seen anything like this in my life!"

I looked away because honestly I was afraid if I watched them for one more second, I was going to laugh and maybe never stop. My eyes settled on some bags stacked neatly in the corner of the storage unit. First I thought it was odd that bags could be stacked so neatly. Then I realized that inside the bags were boxes. I could just see the top of the box full of files poking out of the top bag, and it looked very familiar.

All desire to laugh left me and I hollered, "Cade!"

He swung around to look at me. "What?"

I pointed to the garbage bags full of Nola's files in the corner of the storage unit.

His eyes followed the direction of my finger, and the second he saw them, he sneezed. And then with a voice full of dread, he groaned, "Oh no, it couldn't be."

I nodded. "Cat-contaminated files!"

He sneezed again and my desire to laugh returned.

"Well, it sure is!" Miss Eugenia said. "Those are the bags that someone took from my living room—not the curb!"

"And they are full of worthless stuff anyway!" Missy wailed. "I told Taffy we shouldn't take them. But we were collecting in Haggerty and saw the front door of a house standing wide open. We walked up to make sure everything was okay and then we saw all those garbage bags in your living room."

"We thought you were too old to get them to the road and we'd do you a favor," Taffy claimed unwisely.

"Well, I know that taking anything from *inside* someone's house is against the law—including garbage!" Cade announced. Then he sneezed again and that was it. I started laughing and, as I'd feared, I couldn't stop.

Luke chuckled along with me for a minute or so. Then he gave me an occasional worried glance as I kept on even though I couldn't catch my breath.

"Oh, Cade, don't take us to jail! We didn't mean anything by it! We're just two girls trying to make an honest living!" Taffy rubbed her eyes and now had makeup smeared across her face too.

"Stop crying!" Cade yelled at the sisters. "And where is the computer you stole from Miss Eugenia's house?"

"We didn't take a computer, I swear!" Missy vowed. "That would be stealing!"

Cade spread his hands. "That would be stealing, but not taking garbage bags from her house? Are you insane?"

I laughed harder.

"For heaven's sake, Kennedy," Miss Eugenia said. "Try to pull yourself together."

Even that was hilarious to me. Luke shook his head tolerantly as I continued laughing. My eyes were watering and my sides were aching, but I still laughed. I doubled over, trying to ease the pain in my sides and—possibly—regain a little self-control. From this unusual vantage point I noticed a bright orange jumpsuit that was only barely hanging out of a bag on the other side of the unit. Amid my giggles my mind registered that it looked a lot like the jumpsuit Parnell had been wearing when I visited him in prison that morning. Then between waves of mirth it clicked.

I took a deep breath, swallowed my uncontrollable amusement, and rasped, "Cade!"

He turned around wild-eyed—like he was caught in his worst nightmare. "What?"

I pointed to the bag that contained the jumpsuit. "Maybe that belonged to one of the escaped prisoners!"

Cade looked at the bag and cursed under his breath. Then he slipped and slid across the sea of plastic bags until he reached the one that contained the jumpsuit. He pulled it out, examined it briefly and then said, "I need to know who this trash belongs to." He scowled at Missy and her sister. "I don't guess you categorize them by address or anything?"

Taffy shook her head. "No, but that's a good idea."

Muttering again, Cade stuck his arm into the garbage bag. "Oh gosh," he moaned as pulled out a banana peel and gagged. My laughter returned.

Luke stepped in and took hold of the garbage bag so Cade could use both hands to search. He pulled out an empty carton of milk and some wadded-up tissues. "I don't know if I can do this," he whimpered.

"Be brave," I encouraged between fits of giggles.

"Try and find something with an address on it," Miss Eugenia advised unnecessarily.

Finally he pulled out an envelope that proclaimed someone was about to get the credit they deserved. Luke dropped the bag and Cade leaned the envelope toward the flashlight.

"Ida Jean Baxley," he read. Then he looked up at us. "This prison jumpsuit came from Miss Ida Jean's house!"

"I'll bet if you keep digging, you'll find another one," Miss Eugenia predicted.

Cade looked at the garbage bag with horror. "I can't. I just can't."

"There's no need to do that right now," Luke said. "But you should go check on Miss Ida Jean."

"Maybe that's why she will barely come out of her house," I whispered. "Maybe the convicts are holding her hostage!"

Cade careened out of the storage room and said, "I've got to get over there!"

Missy and Taffy looked hopeful. "Does this mean we're not under arrest?" Taffy asked.

"Since we helped you save Miss Ida Jean from those prisoners?" Missy added.

Cade stopped long enough to point a finger at them. "I'm not going to arrest you, but stop picking up people's garbage unless you ask their permission. And don't take anything out of this storage unit! It's evidence!" Then he ran for his car.

"Should we go with him?" Miss Eugenia wondered aloud.

"I don't think we could catch him if we tried," Luke murmured.

"He'll let us know what happens." I was confident about that. "Now let's go home." Call me superstitious, but I didn't want Luke around those Lamar sisters for too long. So I took his hand and led the way back to my apartment.

"Wow," Luke said as we walked. "The only thing that could have made that worse for Burrell would have been if his wife had shown up with a news crew."

I clutched my sides. "Please don't make me start laughing again!"

Luke grinned. "I just keep remembering Missy holding a garbage bag with that glassy-eyed look on her face."

"Oh, gosh, that was priceless," I gasped.

"It was pretty funny," Miss Eugenia agreed. "But not something to get hysterical about."

I took a deep breath as we climbed the stairs to my porch. "One thing is for sure—I'll never be jealous of Missy Lamar again."

"So now were those two women really stealing people's garbage?" Lt. Dempsey asked. "Really?"

Luke put an arm around the lieutenant and nodded. "Welcome to Midway."

We went inside and I collapsed on the couch. "I never knew laughing could be so exhausting!"

"We're all tired," Luke said. "Let's figure out sleeping arrangements."

My heart pounded and I sat up straight on the couch.

"Now that we know the Lamar girls stole Nola's files, I could go home," Miss Eugenia said.

"The computer is still missing," I reminded her. "Those Lamar girls probably did steal it and just won't admit it, but just in case, you'll have to stay here."

"I'll stay," Miss Eugenia agreed quickly, "but you two will take the bedroom. I'll be perfectly comfortable out here on the couch."

Lt. Dempsey cleared his throat.

"Thank you so much for that generous offer," Luke said. "But I have to be where Lt. Dempsey can see me at all times. So you take the bed. Kennedy can sleep on the couch and I'll make a bedroll on the floor here beside her. And Lt. Dempsey can sleep there on the kitchen floor."

We all got busy distributing blankets and pillows. Luke had just finished making his bed for the night when there was a knock on the door, followed a split-second later by Sloan's entrance.

Luke frowned. "I locked that door."

"Sloan is a modern-day Houdini," I explained. "Normal things such as locks, doors, and windows don't deter him."

Sloan grinned. "Houdini. I kind of like that." Then he looked at Luke's little pallet on the floor. "Now that's just sad."

"Lt. Dempsey has to keep Luke in sight at all times. It's a Marine Corps rule," Miss Eugenia informed him. "You should write your congressman. I certainly plan to."

Sloan's smile broadened. "I know my congressman would love to hear from me." He walked into the kitchen and opened the refrigerator. "There's all kinds of commotion going on by your parents' house," he told me as he pulled out a Tupperware container filled with fried chicken. "From what I gather, those two missing convicts have been living in the neighbors' basement since Saturday. Cade was arresting them and the neighbor's son, I think."

"Oh no!" I knew that it was wrong of Robby to aid and abet escaped prisoners, but I hated that he was getting in trouble because of me. When I described my feelings, Sloan shook his head.

"Don't feel bad. He'll probably be more comfortable on the inside anyway."

I couldn't argue with this. After all Robby had stolen a flashlight not too long ago just to get back in. And if I had to live with Miss Ida Jean, I'd probably prefer prison too.

I called my mother but didn't get an answer. "They must be outside watching all the excitement," I said after leaving a message.

Sloan passed around the fried chicken, and when it was gone, I got out the strawberry shortcake in a bowl that my mother had sent. The cake and strawberries were a little mushy, but overall it was still good. We had just cleaned up after our nighttime snack, and Sloan had headed downstairs, when Cade called.

He confirmed that the two missing convicts were, indeed, in his custody. He had also been forced to arrest Robby Baxley, again, since harboring criminals was a violation of his probation and then some.

"I feel so bad about Robby," I said.

"He was the one who let criminals stay in his basement—not you. And now Miss Ida Jean won't have to stay in her house all the time or worry about convicts attacking her while she waters her lawn."

"I thought you were trying to cheer me up."

He laughed. "Oh, and I also asked the convicts about Nola Finkle. They never heard of her."

"Well, that makes our case against someone in the Langston Association even stronger." I yawned. "Thanks for letting us know."

I shared Cade's information with the others, and then my mother called. I had to listen to the whole thing again, except my mother's voice gets shrill when she's excited, so this time it was harder on my ears.

When I finally ended that call, we all settled down for the night. Once I was snuggled as comfortably as was possible on my old, lumpy couch I dropped my hand down and Luke clasped it in his. With Lt. Dempsey snoring softly in the background, I said, "This is not exactly how I pictured our first night together."

Luke laughed. "It will be a fun story to tell our children."

"How many do you think we'll have?" I asked. "Children—not stories."

"Several," Luke replied. "That part will be easy. The hard thing is going to be coming up with a good theme for their names—one that hasn't already been used by your family."

"With your military background we could name them after famous generals," I suggested. "Like Eisenhower and Roosevelt and Patton."

"Or we could go the literary route since you're a librarian," he proposed. "We could name them Hemingway and Shakespeare and Steinbeck."

"Don't make me start laughing again," I begged. "My sides are still killing me."

"Maybe we should change the subject anyway." Luke pressed my fingers against his lips. "I'm not sure it's wise to discuss our future children under these . . . limiting circumstances."

First I laughed, and then I whispered, "You're sure you won't come up here on the couch beside me?"

I heard him sigh. "No, I can't do that. We have waited this long. We can wait a little longer."

"Well, I guess we should go to sleep, then."

He closed his eyes and I watched him in the moonlight. I was planning to watch him all night until he said, "I can't sleep with you staring at me."

"How do you know I'm staring?" I demanded.

Without opening his eyes he said, "I can feel it. Now go to sleep so I can dream about our honeymoon."

I closed my eyes most of the way but still peeked out under my eyelashes at him. I marveled that I was sleeping on the old, lumpy couch with Luke on the floor beside me. I was involved in murder and mayhem—again. And I had never been happier in my life.

"You're cheating," he said.

Laughing, I let go of his hand and turned over to face the back of the couch. "Good night."

"Good night yourself," he replied.

And in seconds I was sound asleep.

CHAPTER SEVENTEEN

ON THURSDAY MORNING I WOKE up to Luke softly kissing my face.

"I think I skipped the honeymoon and went straight to heaven," I murmured.

He laughed and then pressed his lips to mine. "Time to get up."

I sat up on the couch and stretched. "I can't believe I slept all night."

"You not only slept all night," Luke said, "but you slept through all of us showering and dressing and Miss Eugenia making breakfast."

"Wow," I stood up. "I guess all that laughing wiped me out."

Luke put his hands on my shoulders and turned me toward the bathroom. "Hurry and take your shower. Sloan said your meeting starts in ten minutes."

I padded into the bathroom and took a shower. Then I went into my room and put on the lavender suit my mother loved so much. I figured it wouldn't hurt to try and impress the judge. But when I was picking out shoes, I chose a pair of low-heeled pumps because they looked motherly.

Miss Eugenia invited me to sit down and eat some scrambled eggs, but I declined.

"I'm going to be late for the meeting as it is," I told her. Then I dashed downstairs.

Sloan whistled when he saw me.

"I have to go to court today," I explained to the room in general. "So I have to look my best."

Drake gave me a smile, but he seemed subdued. I didn't think he was mad at me, but I knew we weren't friends like we'd been before. Even if I didn't do it on purpose, I had uncovered negative information about his team, which might result in the dissolving of the Langston Association. I didn't blame him, but it did make me sad.

I got a plateful of doughnuts and sat in my usual seat beside Catsy—even though I didn't want to. I felt strange and out of place. I didn't belong there anymore.

After Rand finished his daily rundown on everything that had been accomplished and what was on tap for the day, Drake stood and announced that he wanted to buy Miss George Ann's land. He turned to Rand. "I want you to draw up an attractive offer and then call Ms. Simmons to make an appointment ASAP."

Rand smiled.

Drake did not. "Seriously," he said. "I cannot have the possibility of litigation hanging over our heads when we leave here. She's anxious to sell so I don't expect a problem, but make the deal one she cannot refuse. Because no one leaves Midway until that's done."

"Hey!" Catsy and Morris both complained simultaneously and then laughed together as well.

"We're scheduled to leave tomorrow night," Morris said. "We're basically through here and need to get going on the next town."

Drake smiled. "Then you'd better hope that Rand and Kennedy can convince Ms. Simmons to sell her property right away."

After our meeting ended, Morris walked over and said, "So, it sounds like you hold my future in your hands. Please seal the deal with that Simmons woman fast. Our next town makeover is much more involved than this one."

I gave him one of the fake-nice smiles I usually reserve for Miss Ida Jean. "I'll do my best."

Rand joined us. "So when are you available to visit Ms. Simmons?"

"My niece's custody hearing is at nine o'clock," I told him. "I'm not sure how long that will last."

"I'll try to set our appointment up for eleven," he said. "If you see that you can't make that, call me and I'll change the time. I don't know what difference it will make to an old lady. It's not like she's busy or anything."

I gave him a firm look. "Don't say anything to that effect when we're meeting with Miss George Ann."

He smiled. "I want to get out of Midway as much as the next person. I'll be on my best behavior. Do you want me to pick you up?"

"Since I'll be coming back from Albany, I'll just meet you at her house."

Rand nodded. "I'll see you then."

When I went back upstairs, Luke and Lt. Dempsey were both dressed in Marine uniforms. Not the fancy version Luke had worn to our wedding, but they both looked very nice—and very official. Miss Eugenia had the kitchen all cleaned up after breakfast and was packed to go. "I've enjoyed staying with you," she told me, "but I'm ready to get home."

"You just want to start frying s'mores!" I teased.

"I do want to do that," she confirmed. "And I'm thankful that it was those silly girls who stole Nola Finkle's stuff."

"And the escaped convicts have been recaptured," I said. "So you should be safe. But keep your doors locked and ask Chief Jones to send a police car by your house occasionally."

"I will," she agreed.

Since Luke and Lt. Dempsey had to leave right after the hearing, we drove in separate cars. Miss Eugenia rode with me in the truck as far as Haggerty. Once I dropped her off, I was alone, but I kept a close watch on Luke in my rearview mirror.

Rand called just before I reached the courthouse.

"That Simmons woman will meet with us at eleven o'clock, but she doesn't want to meet at her house in Haggerty. She wants all of us to go out to the property in question, in this blazing heat, so we can risk heatstroke while we give her twice what her land is worth."

Rand was amusing in a hateful sort of way. So I laughed.

He continued his rant. "And what did Drake mean this morning about us not leaving Midway until he gets this land? Is there a gold mine on it or something?"

"He just doesn't want to get sued," I said.

"We get sued all the time! And we have a new project starting in one week that is huge! And it's in Tennessee! We need to be getting some of our staff situated there—not adding to this project, which we never should have come back to in the first place."

"You weren't a fan of the returning to Midway?" I guessed.

"I argued long and hard against it, but Drake does what he wants to whether it makes sense or not." I heard Rand sigh heavily. "But none of that matters now. I'll meet you at that godforsaken wasteland Drake is so determined to buy at eleven."

"I'll be there," I assured him.

My parents and Heaven arrived at the county courthouse in Albany at the same time we did. We parked near each other and then walked as a group to the family court area. I was expecting a big courtroom like the ones on TV, but we were ushered into a small room more like an office than something from *Law and Order*.

We made small talk for a while until the judge walked in. He wasn't wearing billowing black robes—just a slightly rumpled seersucker suit. He turned up the air conditioning and complained about how hot it always was in the old courthouse. Then he took a seat at the table and regarded all of us.

"The Killingsworths I know," he said. "And Heaven, of course. The rest of you introduce yourselves."

"I'm Luke Scoggins and this is my wife, Kennedy." He gave me a warm look and a little sigh escaped my lips.

The judge referred to some documents on the table in front of him. "You're the financial custodian who doesn't want to sell the salvage yard land. And you have recently filed an application for custody."

"Yes, sir," Luke confirmed. "I applied once before, but now that I'm married, I hope to be considered more seriously."

The judged looked up and studied Luke over his glasses. "Let me assure you, young man, that all applications are seriously considered. And just how long have you been married?"

"Almost five days, sir," Luke replied.

The judge frowned. "Did you get married just so you could apply for custody?"

"No, sir." Luke looked down at me. "I've wanted to marry Kennedy since the third grade."

"Their marriage and Drake Langston's offer to buy the salvage yard land coming at the same time was just an unhappy coincidence," my mother explained. "Then Luke was whisked away by the Marine Corps to testify at a trial right after the wedding so they haven't even had a proper honeymoon yet."

Usually I would have been annoyed at my mother for giving too much information, but at that moment all I could think about was Luke's warm hand in mine and his declaration that he had loved me since childhood.

The judge seemed to be growing impatient as he turned his gaze to Lt. Dempsey. "And who are you?"

"Lt. Hugo Dempsey, United States Marine Corps!" the lieutenant responded a little too loudly.

The judge glanced back down at the paperwork in front of him. "This is a private matter. I'll ask you to wait outside, lieutenant. And please take Heaven with you."

Lt. Dempsey's cheeks turned pink. "I'm sorry, sir, but I can't let Corporal Scoggins out of my sight. It's Marine Corps policy."

"This is my courtroom, and I'm in charge here," the judge bellowed and I nearly jumped out of my seat. "Step outside right now! I'll be responsible for Luke Scoggins until these proceedings are over!"

The lieutenant knew how to follow orders. He stood and walked toward the door. Heaven met him there, and after sizing each other up, they left the room together.

"Should we warn him about Heaven?" I whispered to Luke.

He shook his head. "He's been thoroughly trained in both survival skills and hand-to-hand combat. He'll be fine."

The judge cleared his throat. "So Corporal Scoggins, based on the timing of your application, I'm assuming that you were just trying to counter the application filed by your brother, Heaven's biological father, which I might add has since been withdrawn."

My parents were surprised and obviously relieved. Luke squeezed my hand.

"Yes, sir."

"So do you want to withdraw your application as well?"

"No, sir," Luke replied. "We still want to have full custody of Heaven."

The judge seemed surprised by this. "But you don't have any problem with the Killingsworths continuing as her foster parents?"

"No, not at all," Luke assured him. "In fact, that is what we think would be best for now. Kennedy and I will be living in Atlanta for a couple of years, going to school and, well, enjoying married life. After I get out of school and find a job we can have Heaven move in with us."

"And you're in agreement, Mrs. Scoggins?" the judge asked.

I'll admit that living with Heaven—ever—was a terrifying thought, but as long as it was sometime in the distant future, I could handle it. So I nodded in agreement.

"Well, then, based on the information at my disposal, I believe that it is in Heaven's best interest for the two of you to be given legal temporary custody. We will review the situation again in six months. Until then she is to remain in foster care at the Killingsworth home, and her biological parents are allowed monthly visitation supervised by an officer of the court," he looked at us over his glasses again, "assuming they want to visit her if there's no money involved."

Luke stood and shook his hand. "Thank you, sir."

"Being a parent is hard work, son," the judge told him, "especially with a child like Heaven. For most of her life she has seen only the worst of human nature. But if you'll stick with it, I think you'll do fine."

"We'll stick with it," Luke promised.

When we stepped out into the hall, Lt. Dempsey looked relieved. I wasn't sure if he was anxious to be rid of Heaven or if he'd been afraid that Luke, without his supervision, had climbed out a window and scaled the exterior wall to escape him.

Heaven's face was expressionless, but I knew she had to be very anxious to hear the outcome of the hearing.

"We got custody!" I told her. "From now on your uncle Luke is in charge of everything about you—not just your money."

Heaven didn't smile but instead cocked her head to one side and addressed us both. "I didn't think you'd want me, but I've heard Atlanta is pretty nice. I like it with Miss Iris and Mr. Russell, but us Scogginses should stick together."

My heart was pounding, and my mouth went dry. I thought about the little apartment Luke and I had rented in Atlanta. It was not nearly big enough for a child. I didn't know anything about the school system or if the neighborhood was suitable for children. I did know that as full-time students, Luke and I would both be very busy. And I had really been looking forward to some time for us to finally be alone.

I felt Luke watching me, waiting for an indication of how I wanted to handle this delicate situation.

I looked into Heaven's clear blue eyes. She'd never really been wanted by anyone, and I knew if we rejected her now, she might never trust again. So I smiled. "Like you said, us Scogginses have to stick together."

A ghost of a smiled played at the corners of Heaven's lips.

Luke put his arm around my shoulders and gave me a tight squeeze. Then he addressed Heaven. "The judge isn't sure that we're ready to be parents. So he said that for now you have to stay with the Killingsworths. You can spend the weekends with us in Atlanta until the end of the school year, and by then maybe he'll trust us full-time. Can you be okay with an arrangement like that?"

Heaven nodded. "Yeah, we have to do what the judge says or he can hold us in contempt."

Her knowledge of the legal process would have been funny if it weren't so sad.

My mother, who had stopped to speak to a former dental patient, joined us at that moment and enthused, "Oh, Heaven, I know you're so excited that the judge gave Luke and Kennedy custody!"

"Yeah, it's all right," Heaven replied.

"We should celebrate by doing some shopping. You need a new Sunday dress." Mother took her hand and pulled the child toward the front entrance.

Heaven looked at me over her shoulder. "When the judge lets you be my mom, I pick out my own clothes."

I nodded. "It's a deal."

Lt. Dempsey came up beside us and cleared his throat. "I'm sorry to break things up, but our plane takes off in less than an hour. We could be the ones being held in contempt if we're late."

So we started walking to the parking deck. I didn't want Luke to leave, but this time I felt more at peace. Even though we still hadn't been on our honeymoon, we had braved some life trials together, and I could easily picture us in the future together, working through whatever lay ahead.

When we reached our vehicles, Luke said, "I'd hate to leave you under any circumstances, but with all this going on with Drake Langston, I, well, I can't stand it."

I tried to reassure him. "I can take care of myself."

"You are a strong, brave person," he acknowledged. "But you're not a match for murderers. So, I lined up a bodyguard to keep an eye on you while I'm gone."

He pointed to our left, and I looked over to see my ex-husband leaning against his patrol car, watching from a polite distance.

"You called *Cade*?" I marveled.

"I didn't want to," he said. "But I kept trying to think of someone who would—and could—protect you like I would if I was here. And it always came back to Burrell. I don't like him, but I know I can trust him—with your safety, at least."

I thought Luke would die before he asked Cade for a favor. But here we were. Everything had come full circle.

Lt. Dempsey opened the driver's side door and said, "I'm sorry, corporal, but we have to go."

I grabbed Luke's forearms. "Call me!"

"You know I will." He leaned down and kissed me thoroughly.

When he pulled away I was breathless and Lt. Dempsey's cheeks were pink.

Then they climbed into the car, and I watched them drive away.

Once they were gone, Cade walked over and said, "So, are you riding with me?"

I needed to take out a little hostility and there was no one better than Cade for that. "Of course I'm not going to leave my truck in a parking deck in Albany." I fixed him with a scowl. "Besides, if I pull up at Miss George Ann's land with you, Rand might get a *little* suspicious."

"Not if we tell him I'm guarding you while Scoggins is gone."

"He doesn't think we know there is anything to guard me from," I explained slowly like I was talking to a toddler. "Is the surveillance trailer set up?"

He nodded. "Yeah, Mark and Winston have been working on that all morning."

"Then you can watch me from there." With a sigh I climbed into my truck. I left the parking deck, and I'll admit it was nice to see Cade in my rearview mirror—ready to protect me if that became necessary.

CHAPTER EIGHTEEN

WHEN I PASSED THE DESERTED building that had once housed Meyer's Country Store, I pulled in. Cade came up beside me, and we rolled down our windows. "You should wait here for a few minutes," I said. "I hope Rand doesn't see you at all, but I definitely don't want it to look like we're together."

Cade nodded. "I'll wait a few minutes and then go straight to the surveillance trailer."

I rolled up my window and drove back out onto the road. When I reached the peeling sign that advertised boiled peanuts, I turned to the left on the winding dirt road where JD had died. Before long Miss George Ann's property came into view.

I parked in the grassy space in front of the house between an old, but well preserved, Cadillac and Rand's car. Behind the house there was a bulldozer and two pickup trucks full of lumber with "Hayes Construction" painted on the side. Stacked neatly against the old wooden barn were about fifty metal barrels labeled "Fuel." And several "construction workers" were milling around.

"What is going on here?" Rand asked as he walked up to meet me.

I shrugged. "I guess we'll have to ask Miss George Ann."

He turned and trudged toward the house. My eyes trailed to the field where JD used to live. There was an old trailer positioned on the edge of his property that I knew contained surveillance equipment and a few officers of the law—soon to include Cade. Then I looked over at what was left of the old milk plant. The old cinderblock walls were scarred by bullets and blackened by fire. This area had seen a lot of sadness. I hoped that was not a bad omen for our plan.

"Are you coming?" Rand called over his shoulder.

With some reluctance I followed him.

Rand pulled out his handkerchief and wiped it across his sweating forehead. "It is so *hot* here! And it's not even noon!"

"Maybe it's cooler inside the house." I knew this was unlikely, but we could hope.

We picked our way through the tall grass littered with last year's dead leaves and the occasional broken tree limb. When we reached the house, Rand had to duck because the roof of the front porch was drooping so low. "This place is dangerous!" he hissed.

"Remember, be polite." I knocked on the door. This brief contact with my knuckles crumbled the rotten wood and several slivers fell off the door and settled around our feet.

Rand groaned. "We'll be lucky if this whole place doesn't collapse on top of us!"

"I'm due for some good luck," I told him.

Then the old door swung open—rusted hinges protesting—and Miss George Ann emerged. "Welcome," she said like a queen in her castle instead of an old woman at a hovel. "I thought we'd meet around on the patio," she said. Leading us back the way we came instead of through the house, she took us around the side and to the backyard.

Miss Eugenia was already on the patio sitting at one of four chairs that surrounded a corroded table. The patio was covered with corrugated plastic held up by metal posts. Rand tested each of the posts for stability before he stepped onto the patio and sat beside Miss Eugenia.

"You know Miss Eugenia?" Miss George Ann asked me.

"We've met," I confirmed.

"I don't think I've had the pleasure," Rand said. He extended a hand to Miss Eugenia. "Nice to meet you."

She shook his hand briefly and said, "Likewise."

"I've got key lime pie for you," Miss George Ann pointed at a pie dish sitting in the middle of the old table. "It's my prize-winning recipe."

Miss Eugenia rolled her eyes. "It's probably a melted mess after a couple of hours in this heat."

Rand stared at the pie in horror. "I wouldn't want to spoil my lunch."

"Don't mind Eugenia," Miss George Ann said as she cut us each a piece and placed them on small paper plates (that I hoped had not been in the old house for a hundred years). She gave one to each of us and we all tried a bite.

It was a little warm but good. So I said, "Delicious."

Miss Eugenia made a face and put hers aside. "You always put too much lime juice in your pies."

Miss George Ann raised her chin. "I also *always* win. You can't argue with success."

"I can't account for crazy judges either," Miss Eugenia muttered.

"Thanks," Rand said as he swallowed his first bite. Then he put his pie down as well. "Now, as I told you on the phone, Mr. Langston doesn't want you to feel slighted in any way so he has decided to make a very fair offer for this land."

"He specifically told Rand to draw up an offer that would make you *happy*," I inserted.

Miss George Ann cleared her throat. "Before we begin, officially, I think I should say that although Kennedy is a close family friend, I never let personal relationships interfere with business."

I nodded. "I understand."

Rand frowned—whether because Miss George Ann claimed to be my friend or because I wouldn't try to use my family connections to influence her, I couldn't tell.

Rand presented the offer, which was extremely generous in my opinion. But Miss Eugenia had done her job well, and when Rand was finished, Miss George Ann shook her head.

"While I appreciate this gesture, I believe that my land is worth twice what Mr. Langston is offering."

"Twice!" Rand croaked. "It's not worth half what we're offering!"

"Rand," I warned.

"Well!" Miss George Ann sniffed. "I'll have you know that I've already been notified that there is another interested buyer. Once improvements are made on the house and surrounding areas, they will pay much more than this." She waved a dismissive hand at the contract on the table. "I've hired a contractor, and he is going to begin work immediately."

"Are you sure, Miss George Ann?" I asked half-heartedly. "Is there nothing that we can say to make you sell at this price?"

"Definitely not," she replied.

"I'm anxious to see this place returned to its former glory," Miss Eugenia added brilliantly. "I always thought it was so nice."

Miss George Ann was only too happy to agree. "Daddy always thought so too. I can't wait!"

Rand looked from one old woman to the other with utter disdain. "So you're not going to sell?"

Miss George Ann shook her head. "No, I'll make the improvements and get top dollar."

Rand stood and snatched up his contract off the table. "Then our business here is done." He addressed me. "Are you staying with your family friend or coming with me?"

I stood and followed him away from the house. "She's not really a friend of my family," I said as we walked. "None of my relatives have liked her for generations."

"She is the most arrogant, short-sighted, and possibly insane person I have ever met!" Rand yelled. "She is seriously going to try and improve this!" He pointed at the scraggly landscape around us. "She actually thinks anything could make it more valuable?"

I tried to soothe him. "This land has sentimental value for her."

"Well, she just turned down a fortune, and I promise you that no one else will offer her anything close no matter how much she fixes up that old house!" He opened his car door and turned on the air conditioning. Then he pulled out his phone. "I'm about to make a conference call to let everyone know how badly this went."

I moved a little closer so I could hear.

Once he had everyone on the call, he said, "This stupid old woman refused to sell. She's hired a contractor to make *improvements* on the place and thinks she can get a better price after that!" He laughed totally without humor. "The contractor already has two loads of lumber out here along with a bulldozer and enough fuel to keep it running for a year. I say we forget about trying to buy this place and take our chance with getting sued."

There was another pause and then Rand said, "Okay," and ended the call.

"So?" I prompted.

"Drake says he wants that land," Rand reported dazedly. "He said to come up with a new proposal and present it to Ms. Simmons tomorrow." He glanced over at me. "He wants me to grovel to that insufferable old woman."

"Maybe when we come back tomorrow she will have had time to realize that it doesn't make sense to keep refusing such good offers."

Rand shook his head in disbelief. "Maybe." Then he got in his car and sped off without so much as a wave. I waited until he was out of sight and then I called Cade.

He answered with, "So, how did it go?"

"Great beyond our wildest dreams," I told him. "Miss George Ann made Rand furious, and he shared his feelings with the whole team by way of a conference call. Now everyone knows she's being difficult. It should be just a matter of time before someone acts. Although I have to tell you—I think it will be Rand who comes back to burn the place down. Morris is always so calm, but Rand takes everything personally."

"Well, we should find out who it is pretty soon. We think they'll wait until dark since that gives them less chance of being seen," Cade said. "But total surveillance starts now."

"Can we go over and watch from the trailer?"

"Yeah," Cade agreed. "I gotta warn you, though, it will probably be a long, boring afternoon."

"Believe me, I've had a lot of those in my life," I assured him.

* * *

When we met at the trailer, he said, "The police chief from Albany came by to see Sheriff Bonham this morning. He was closing the case of the missing convicts and needed the sheriff to sign off on it. He asked how we found them, and the sheriff said he'd have to speak to me since I cracked the case. It was a pretty sweet moment."

I smiled. "I wish I could have been there."

"He asked me how I figured it out, and I told him by looking through the trash. I thought he'd make fun of me, but he nodded and said, "Old school. I like that.""

"Good for you."

"I didn't tell him about Missy and Taffy and, well, all that," Cade admitted.

I didn't blame him for not mentioning that his ex-girlfriend was a garbage thief.

"And I wanted to give you some of the credit, but I didn't get a chance."

"I don't want any credit," I assured him. "And you deserve it."

"Even though Miss Eugenia isn't going to press charges, I felt like Missy and Taffy should be punished. So I've got them looking through those cat files for me," he said. "Maybe that will make them think twice before they take things out of someone's living room."

"Did they find anything yet?"

"A few invoices to Langston Association, but they don't list the person placing the order by name. The only signature on them is that Newell guy who apparently signs all purchase orders."

We left our cars parked in the woods behind the trailer and said, "Well, here we are."

The trailer was air conditioned, which was a good thing since it was a hundred degrees that afternoon. And it was larger than it looked, which was a good thing since there were ten people inside. Mark was there—just advising—along with Winston and some of his police officers. Sheriff Bonham arrived about the same time we did, and there were several tech guys sitting in front of the monitors.

For my benefit—and to kill some dead time—Mark asked one of the techs to explain the surveillance system.

"We are monitoring everything in those woods," the tech told me. "The cameras have speakers so we can pick up sound and motion detectors so we can monitor movement. They even have heat sensors so we can keep track of all the wildlife that runs through."

I pointed at one screen where about twenty red dots were distributed in a wide circle around Miss George Ann's property. "So, are those our people in the woods?"

The tech nodded. "They're wearing camo to blend in with the trees, but they each have a sensor that relays their location to us and shows up as a red dot on the screen."

"How much longer do you think it will be before Morris comes?" I felt like a child for asking, but I had to know.

"Normally you'd expect him to wait until dark, but since this place is so remote, he might take a chance during daylight," Mark answered.

"And actually a fire will be less obvious during the day," Cade pointed out.

"So it could be anytime," Mark said.

Mark's words were encouraging, but it was nearly two very boring hours later before one of the techs reported that a lone car had turned onto the dirt road and was headed our way. Excitement filled the trailer. The wait was over. Soon we would have the man who was responsible for tricking the defenseless. I was nervous and a little sad and mostly just anxious to get it over with.

We all gathered in front of the computers—each of which was attached to a different security camera—and watched the car approach. After a few seconds of observation, I said, "It's Morris, all right."

I'll admit I was a little disappointed. It wasn't that I wanted the guilty party to be Rand more than Morris. I didn't really care for either one. Rand just felt more logical.

We watched in silence as he parked his car near the line of trees that separated Miss George Ann's property from what had been JD's. Then he started walking toward the barn. It was strangely like watching a television show, and I found it hard to believe that I was seeing a real-life criminal about to commit a crime.

"He's got a small gas can," Mark said. Then he instructed the techs to zoom in with one of the cameras. Once we had a closer, if slightly blurry, view, Mark added, "In his left hand he's carrying a pack of cigarettes. And we can assume some matches."

I frowned. "Cigarettes?"

Mark replied without taking his eyes off the computer screen. "That gives a reasonable explanation for any matches that survive the blaze. And it gives the investigators an easy way to explain how the fire started in the first place—besides arson."

Winston nodded. "A construction worker throws down a cigarette, thinks it's mashed out, but during the night one little spark that survived sets some of this long grass on fire, and next thing you know—the whole place has burned down."

"And the police might not have looked into it any closer," Cade said softly.

"He's pouring gas on the grass by the barn," Mark reported.

I saw Winston tense. "Should we send some guys in?"

"Just a minute," Mark said. "We've got to prove he was going to burn the barn—not just gas it."

We all waited in silent suspense. Finally Mark nodded. "He just lit a match. Have them get him."

We watched as the red dots that represented camouflaged officers moved from the perimeter toward Morris and the newly burning fire.

"Agent Iverson!" one of the techs called out. "We've got an unidentified heat signature!"

Mark leaned closer. "Where?"

The tech pointed to a green blob on the screen.

Mark said, "Send two of my guys back to check it out."

One of the techs whispered this command into his headset.

We just had time to see two red spots reverse direction before we heard the shot. It was loud—amplified by the speakers on the cameras. And Morris fell to the ground.

"Suspect down!" someone shouted, and the trailer erupted into frantic motion. Cade pushed me into a far corner out of harm's way as Mark and Winston and several others rushed outside.

"We need to go out and see what happened," I said.

Cade shook his head. "You're not going anywhere until Mark tells me they've got the situation under control."

I turned back to the computer screens. The unidentified person was moving fast toward the road, followed closely by FBI agents.

"So the unidentified guy shot Morris?" I thought out loud.

Nobody answered.

Finally the red spots collided with the green blob.

"They got him," a tech reported.

"Fire's out," another one said.

Mark's voice squawked through a computer speaker. "The shooter isn't armed! Check the computer screens for a hot weapon on the ground!"

The computer screens filled with gridded images as the techs scanned the surrounding area systematically. Finally one said,

"I'm getting a weak register in the northeastern quadrant, about ten feet behind Agent Suarez." The area in question was enlarged so that it filled one entire screen. In the center was a tiny speck of green. A green dot—presumably Agent Suarez—turned and retrieved it.

"Shooter in custody, weapon acquired," Mark said. "All clear."

Cade pointed toward the door. "Come on."

He didn't have to tell me twice.

I had to trot alongside Cade to keep up with his long stride as we covered the distance between the trailer and Miss George Ann's property. We reached the barn, and amid the smoke from the short-lived fire I could see black-clad figures scurrying around. The sound of approaching sirens filled the warm air.

I saw Morris lying on the ground. He was covered with a plastic sheet, so apparently the ambulance was just a formality. Then I saw Mark, and he regarded me with a solemn expression. "I was just about to call Cade to tell him not to bring you over here," he said.

I assumed he meant Morris and was being sensitive to my reaction to seeing the dead body of someone I vaguely knew. Then Winston stepped up and pulled his hat from his head—a sign of respect for grief. My heart pounded. Did someone *else* die? I mentally ran through the list of my loved ones and determined that no one could have been at risk. "What is it?"

Mark shook his head. "I'm sorry, Kennedy. I really am." Then he stepped aside.

Behind him were two of the camo-dressed agents whom I'd been watching on the computer screen as red spots. Sloan was standing between them. At first I thought they had asked him to help them catch Morris. Then I noticed that Sloan's hands were pinned behind his back, and the agents were holding him against his will. Apparently Sloan was the green blob.

"Sloan?" I whispered and took a step in his direction.

He didn't answer me, just stared off into the distance.

I turned back to Mark. "I don't understand."

"The gun we found in the woods was Sloan's. It had been fired recently. And when the other agents approached him, he ran."

"You think Sloan killed Morris?" I clarified.

"I'm just going by the evidence we have now," Mark confirmed. "If Sloan has a reasonable explanation for his presence here—with his gun—I'm anxious to hear it."

I turned to Sloan. "Tell them it's a mistake."

But Sloan wouldn't say anything in his own defense, and my confusion turned to concern.

"It *is* a mistake, right?"

Cade was anxious to hypothesize. "I figure him and Morris were partners—maybe that Catsy woman too. They were all working together, stealing money, forcing folks out of their homes, and, when necessary, even killing."

This theory went against everything I thought I knew about Sloan. He had saved my life twice. He was a friend. Was it possible that he had fooled me so completely?

Winston walked up while I was sorting through the information and trying to come to a logical conclusion. He pointed at Sloan and asked Mark, "So what do you want me to do with him?"

"Since you have jurisdiction, take him to the Haggerty police station for the initial questioning," Mark said.

Winston looked nervous. "Are you going to come and supervise? I don't want to do anything wrong and have him get off on a technicality."

Apparently this was a concern for Mark too. "Just process him and save the questions until I get there."

The agents on either side of Sloan led him toward the Haggerty police car. As he passed me I reached out and put a hand on his arm. "Why?" I asked softly.

He leaned as close as they'd let him and said, "If I'd wanted to kill Morris, I wouldn't do it with my own gun, and if I'd really been trying to run, they wouldn't have caught me." And then they pulled him away.

My eyes followed as the agents put Sloan in a car and drove off. I wanted to help him but didn't know how.

The ambulance arrived and we all backed up to give them access to Morris. It took them longer to drag their equipment up the hill than it did to determine he was dead. They loaded his body onto a stretcher and carried him down to the waiting ambulance. Even though it was warm, I felt a chill.

Someone walked up beside me, and I turned to see Drake, looking miserable.

"So you saw what happened?"

He nodded. "I was with the surveillance team in the house."

"I can't believe Sloan would shoot Morris," I said, hoping Drake would concur.

But his answer didn't reassure me. "I can't believe any of this, so my opinion is worthless. I keep hoping this is a nightmare and I'll wake up."

"I wish it was."

Mark joined us. "Albany PD just picked up Catsy. Since Nola Finkle's death took place in the Albany city limits, I had to let them handle it."

I shrugged. It didn't matter to me who arrested her.

"The foster brother has already admitted to tampering with the car, so it will be easy to build a case against her." Mark gave me a sympathetic look. "This should all be over soon."

I tried to feel encouraged by this thought as Mark walked over to confer with some of the other FBI agents.

Drake hung his head. "I should never have come back to Midway."

"All this would have come out eventually," I said. "Somewhere."

"I guess." He took a deep breath.

Mark returned, and I said, "When Sloan was leaving, he said something to me that I think, well, I'm not sure that he shot Morris."

Drake regarded me with a solemn expression. "I've got my staff looking for a good criminal lawyer. If he's guilty, we'll make sure his rights are protected, and if he's innocent, we'll get him released."

"But if Sloan didn't shoot Morris, someone else did," I pressed my point. "And that other person is still free and posing a threat to everyone else."

Mark nodded. "I'll have the techs look back through the camera footage to see if they can find evidence of another unidentified observer."

I felt relieved that Mark was willing to look, at least.

"Agent, I need to find out when the body will be available for transport," Drake told Mark. "His parents live in New York State."

Mark replied in a tone respectful of the parents who had lost a child. "It might take a day or so, but we'll call you. Did you notify the parents?"

Drake nodded. "My father is on his way to see them now."

"Good," Mark said. "Because the TV news will get a hold of this pretty soon, and we don't want them to find out that way." Another agent came up and asked Mark to come over to the barn.

When we were alone again, Drake turned to me and said, "I have no choice but to close down our operation in Midway."

I nodded. "Everyone will be disappointed," I didn't add "again." "But there's nothing else you can do under these circumstances."

"But before we leave, I am going to hire contractors to finish all the work we started," he surprised me by adding. "I may need your help."

"I'd be glad to do whatever I can."

"All the blueprints and architectural plans are in the clubhouse at the new subdivision," he said. "Newell and Rand are meeting me there in a few minutes to see what we can get accomplished tonight. Are you available to join us?"

I nodded. "I'll be glad to help in any way I can."

He looked around until his eyes settled on Mark. "I'll go and make sure it's okay for us to leave."

As Drake walked away Cade rushed up to me.

"Let's get out of here!" His breathing was labored and his eyes were wide with excitement. "I need to take you to your apartment fast so I can get to the Haggerty police station in time to watch them interrogate Sloan!"

I didn't really blame him for his eagerness. This was police business, and it was natural for him to want to be there, but he was getting a little too much personal satisfaction from Sloan's problems. "You go on to Haggerty," I told him. "I'm riding back to Midway with Drake. We're meeting Newell and Rand to try and salvage what we can of the Langston Association and the Midway project."

His expression turned from exhilarated to belligerent. "I told Scoggins I'd keep an eye on you until he gets back."

"That was before all the robbers and murderers were safely in jail," I reminded him.

He still looked unsure. "Do you have to meet with Langston tonight? If he'll wait until the morning, I can come with you to the meeting."

"Drake can't wait until morning," I replied. "Now go on or they'll ask Sloan all the good questions before you get there."

The pull of a big interrogation was just too strong. "Okay, but call if you need me!" he instructed over his shoulder as he hurried off.

I rolled my eyes. "Go on!"

Drake returned in time to see Cade running for his car. He raised an eyebrow, and I had to smile, even under the grim circumstances.

"He's headed to Haggerty to watch them interrogate Sloan."

"That might not be as much fun as he thinks," Drake murmured. "Sloan is a pretty cool character—and as a former FBI agent knows a lot about interrogations."

It made me sad to think about Sloan being interrogated, so my smile faded.

"Agent Iverson says we're free to go." Drake pointed toward the woods. "I'm parked down there."

As we walked through the long grass (with me praying that we didn't run into a snake), I reminded Drake, "We need to get Agatha Hoban out of that nursing home now that," I waved vaguely behind us, "this is over. Dixie Reed too. But I feel a personal responsibility for Agatha."

"I should be able to handle that with one call to my legal department," he said. When we reached Drake's car, he opened the door for me. He was still polite, but all his flirtiness was gone—destroyed by disloyalty and grief.

Once we were headed back toward Midway, he said, "If you'll give me the name of the nursing home that is holding Ms. Hoban hostage, I'll have one of my lawyers call and arrange her release."

It would have been funny a few days earlier, but now it was just sad. "Millwood Retirement Complex," I provided.

He made a call and after a few minutes pulled his mouth away from the phone and said, "Is there someone you can send over to pick her up?"

I was startled. "Now?"

He nodded. "Right now."

"I'll find someone," I promised and he returned to his call.

I considered Miss Eugenia. I knew she'd love the drama of springing Agatha, but she was old and afraid of nursing homes, and she didn't drive after dark. Then I thought of my mother. She would be glad to help Agatha. She had no fear of anything and enjoyed driving any time of the day or night. But she already had her hands full with Heaven. Finally my mind settled on Miss Zelda. She knew Agatha as well as anyone—having tried to give her a ride to church for twenty years. She was a Christian in word and deed (which in my opinion is a rare combination). And I knew the Jacksons had a guestroom that Agatha could stay in for a few days until the effects of the medications she'd been given wore off.

So I called Miss Zelda. She listened closely to my explanation of Agatha and her plight. Then before I could even ask her, she volunteered to go get the old woman and care for her until her house was completed. "I'll take Brother Jackson with me," she said. "She might need a few prayers after all she's been through. And if not, he can carry her suitcases."

"I'm sure Brother Jackson's presence will be very useful," I agreed.

When I ended my call, Drake was talking to someone about transporting Morris's body. I didn't want to listen to that, so I tried to call Luke but didn't get an answer. So I called Miss Eugenia. She'd already heard most of the details but made me repeat them. When I got to the part about Sloan she said, "So, was he saying he didn't do it?"

"That's what I think he was saying," I confirmed. "Although it was hard to tell. He was acting strange."

"Maybe he was afraid to say too much and incriminate himself," she proposed.

"I don't know. He didn't seem like he cared what happened to him."

"He's guilty, then, and has a guilty conscience," she declared. "Well, I think I'll call Winston to see what's going on at the police station. Then I might call Zelda and ask if I can ride with them to rescue Agatha Hoban." She hung up without saying good-bye.

I'll admit I was a little jealous. I wanted to call Winston Jones myself and ask about Sloan, but I didn't know him well enough, and that would be awkward with Drake sitting beside me. And I really wanted to be with Miss Eugenia and Miss Zelda when they got to the

Millwood Retirement Complex. Miss Agatha was going to be so glad to see them.

Drake's call ended and he asked me, "So, do you have someone going to get Mrs. Hoban?"

I nodded. "The Baptist preacher and his wife—and possibly Miss Eugenia Atkins. How about Sloan and Catsy—did you get lawyers for them?"

"I don't have anyone on staff qualified to handle their cases," he said. "But I've started a search for someone who is. We'll make sure they get a fair trial."

"Right now I'm more worried about their victims than how the law will treat them."

"Don't judge them too harshly," he advised. "There are circumstances that have to be taken into account."

"Are you excusing them?"

"No, but I am standing by them. They might not understand loyalty, but I do."

I felt justifiably reprimanded.

We reached the entrance to what would eventually be the nicest subdivision in Midway, and Drake turned in. The moonlight allowed me to see many signs of progress since the last time I'd been there. The first home to the right looked nearly finished.

"That is supposed to be our model home, but I think we'll give it to Agatha Hoban instead," Drake said. "All the exterior work is done, and they will be putting up drywall tomorrow. It's conceivable that she could move in ten days from now."

I smiled. "Her and that big-screen TV."

"With the appropriate cable connections," he added.

"Of course."

CHAPTER NINETEEN

ALL THE STREETS WERE PAVED so it was possible to see how the neighborhood would eventually look. Smaller streets looped onto the large one that accessed the main road like flower petals. When houses were built, this once deserted area would be teeming with young families who would increase Midway's population and bolster the economy (such as it was). Drake drove to the center of the subdivision where the clubhouse was located. He parked in front of the simple structure and we climbed out of the car.

He led me to the back door so I could see the tennis court, which at the moment was just a rectangle of gravel, and the pool, which was just a big concrete hole. Drake unlocked the door and we walked in. He flipped the switch on a generator and instantly an overhead light turned on. Then a small window air conditioner began to whir, moving hot, humid air through the room.

There was a portable table set up against the wall like a desk. Drake sat down behind it and started stacking up papers.

"I hardly know where to start. Maybe you could make a list of all the things I need to do, and we'll cross them off as we accomplish or assign them," he suggested.

He handed me a legal pad and a pen. I pulled a folding chair up in front of his table desk, and once I was settled, he started dictating.

"I've already hired one of the contractors to oversee all of the projects, but I need to talk with all the subcontractors and let them know about the change in our chain of command so they can coordinate everything. I specifically want to talk to the guys who did the streets to make sure they plan on adding curbs."

I listed each task and numbered them.

He continued with an exhaustive list of details that had to be attended to. I was already on my third page when Newell and Rand arrived.

"I started the party without you!" Rand held up a bottle of liquor as he staggered in. "Morris's shooting is all over the television."

"I expected that it would be," Drake replied.

"Not the kind of publicity we wanted," Rand added.

Newell nodded. "We're done for here—again. We need to get out of town before they throw us out."

"We're leaving in the morning," Drake agreed. "But I can't leave our projects unfinished this time. Kennedy is making a list of everything that still needs to be done."

Rand took the legal pad that contained the list from my hands. He flipped through it and then said, "You expect to complete all that stuff by tomorrow?"

Drake shook his head. "Of course not. Everything will be assigned to contractors and we'll oversee them from a distance."

Rand collapsed into a chair. "It's your money. I guess you can throw it away if you want to. But you won't win any goodwill in this town no matter what you do. I say we just cut our losses, pack up, and get out."

Newell frowned. "I hate to agree with Rand, especially when he's in this condition, but that's true."

"It's not about goodwill at this point," Drake said. "It's about self-respect."

Newell's phone rang, and after muttering, "Excuse me," he stepped outside to take the call.

"We're also going to repay all the people who were forced to sell," Drake continued. "Rand, since you're in charge of acquisitions, you can probably remember all the people who had to be 'convinced' to sell. And just to be sure you don't leave anyone out. Kennedy has a friend who is compiling a list."

Kate's sister was not actually my friend, but I didn't feel it necessary to make this distinction.

Rand's blood-shot eyes widened. "What do you mean by 'repay?'"

"Well, for instance in the case of Mrs. Agatha Hoban from Midway, we're removing her from the nursing home where Morris had placed her because of false medical information. I'm going to give her the model home here—as soon as it can be completed—and a sizeable lump sum as well. I want her to have enough money to live comfortably for the rest of her life."

Rand looked aggravated. "Have you got a figure in mind?"

Drake quoted an amount and Rand cursed.

Then the door slammed open and Newell walked in. He looked pale and dazed as he sat down heavily in the closest folding chair. "Catsy's dead," he announced.

Shock registered all around.

"Dead?" Drake whispered.

"I thought she was arrested!" I gasped. "How could she be dead?"

"Drug overdose," Newell reported dully. "Apparently she took a whole bottle of pills right before the police came for her. By the time they realized what she'd done, it was too late. I guess she just couldn't stand going back to jail." He dropped his head into his hands.

"Poor Catsy," Drake said softly.

"And I'm sure Morris's death was a huge blow to her," I ventured, "since they were engaged."

"Engaged?" Rand scoffed. "Catsy and *Morris*? No way."

Newell raised his head, and I saw that tears were streaming down his face. "Catsy wasn't with Morris."

I'm used to being wrong, but in this case I was so positive. I guess having experienced love recently myself, I thought I recognized the signs.

"She was with Drake," Newell continued.

"Drake?" I swung my eyes over to confront him.

He didn't deny it. "Catsy and I have been close . . . friends for a while."

I was embarrassed and incensed. "Then why didn't you correct me when I told you I thought she was engaged to Morris?"

"Because you were right," Drake said. "Morris and Catsy had a secret relationship that none of us knew about, and they planned to marry."

Newell's entire body shook with a fresh wave of sobs. His depth of grief was confusing to me. Rand must have seen my puzzled expression and guessed the cause.

"Yes, Newell was in love with Catsy," Rand divulged. "And she could have saved herself a lot of trouble by becoming close friends with him instead of Drake. She wouldn't have had to steal a dime to impress Newell."

"Rand," Drake warned.

"Don't make fun of me," Newell yelled. "I did love her and I would have a least *tried* to make her happy."

My mind was reeling from one revelation to another. Drake and Catsy? Newell loved Catsy? Then I focused on the stealing comment.

Looking at Rand, I asked, "You knew that Catsy was overordering and selling the duplicates?"

Rand smirked. "Everyone knew. I figured it was Drake's way of thanking her for her *friendliness*."

I turned to stare at Drake. "You knew all along?"

Drake sighed. "I'm not sure why Rand chose to bring that up now, but yes, I've known for a while. My auditors showed me the discrepancies a couple of years ago. It wasn't enough money to worry about—just a drop in the bucket in the large scheme of things. So I looked the other way."

Rand laughed. "I brought it up because I assumed Kennedy's presence here tonight meant she was being fully inducted into the Drake Dream Team."

Drake gave him an annoyed look and then said, "You're drunk."

I frowned at Newell. "You knew it too, and you signed off on all the purchase orders anyway."

"I felt sorry for her," Newell said. "She was trying so hard to fit into Drake's world."

"That is all ancient history," Drake said. "Now let's get back to the task at hand. We need to organize everything in Midway so the work will continue as planned after we leave tomorrow."

My mind was in turmoil. Drake had known about Catsy's stealing, but when I had mentioned it, he pretended ignorance. And I believed him. Catsy and Morris were secretly in love and planning to marry—and now they were both dead. Drake had known that too. A comment Catsy made the first day I met her came back to my mind. She'd said Drake was like God—he knew everything. Sloan had called him omnipresent. It was ridiculous to think that someone as brilliant and powerful as Drake Langston was unaware of what was going on inside his association.

I turned to stare at him. His eyes regarded me with interest—waiting for me to process the information available and come to the logical conclusion.

"You've known all along about *everything*!" I accused. "You knew about Catsy's stealing and Nola's murder. You stole the computer! You knew that Dixie and Agatha were forced from their homes! You even helped Jenna and Parnell plan Foster's murder!"

Drake smiled, just the way he had so many times since I'd met him.

"It's all a game for Drake," Rand explained. "Something to ease the boredom that comes with having everything. There's no challenge in his life—so he plays with the lives of others."

I kept my eyes on Drake but replied to Rand. "We noticed that he always hires people who need to be saved. Is that to guarantee loyalty?"

"Oh, it goes way past loyalty or a savior complex," Rand said as if he were discussing someone else's problem. "He chooses us for our weaknesses and then makes us complicit. That's how he binds us to him. That's why we can never leave."

"Ever," Newell whispered between sobs. "No matter what."

"With Catsy her weakness was her desire to be something better than she was," Rand continued. "She thought if she wore fancy clothes and shoes, rich people would accept her. She was wrong. But her desire led her to steal. Drake not only let her do it, but he encouraged it by complimenting her clothing choices and suggesting new, expensive styles. By the time he confronted her, she was in to him for hundreds of thousands of dollars. She couldn't pay him back, so she either had to go to jail, which meant giving up her dream of being socially acceptable, or she could be his slave. She chose slavery."

"She couldn't refuse when Drake told her to arrange for her foster brother to kill that woman from the veterinary supply place," Newell said. "Even though she really didn't want to. Catsy was a good person. Or she could have been, if she'd never met Drake."

I heard what they were saying—and I even understood it—but found it impossible to make myself associate these horrible actions with the Drake Langston I thought I knew.

"For Morris it was his desire to be successful and admired," Rand continued. "He'd never been able to achieve anything beyond average until Drake entered his world. Then he became powerful and important—a *somebody*. If that meant he had to impersonate a doctor occasionally and commit a reluctant seller to a nursing home or burn down a house—that was a small price to pay for the respect and pride he saw in the eyes of his successful parents."

Drake sighed. "I hope you're enjoying yourself, Rand, because you will pay for this."

Rand laughed. "Oh, I pay every minute of every day." He turned back to me. "Drake stepped into my life when I got caught for ethics violations and was about to be disbarred. I thought all I had to sacrifice to keep my license was my self-respect. But of course that was only the beginning. I also had to sacrifice my family, my freedom, and eventually my soul."

Newell sniffled and Rand turned to him.

"Newell here is particularly unlucky. He didn't even have to commit a crime to come under Drake's control. Someone else in his accounting firm embezzled money and managed to pin it on Newell. So Drake saved him and, well, the rest, as they say, is history."

"We've heard enough," Drake said. "Obviously Rand is drunk and his imagination is working overtime."

"I am drunk. Who wouldn't need a drink after they'd killed somebody? But I'm not making any of this up, and I definitely don't think Kennedy has heard enough," Rand said.

"You killed somebody?" I forced myself to ask.

Rand's head lolled forward in a drunken nod. "When Drake told me I was going to have to kill Morris, I didn't know why, but I've been trained not to ask questions, so I just did it. Now I guess we know the why. It was because of Catsy. Somehow they thought they could break away, live a life separate from Drake's control. Poor fools."

"*You* killed Morris!" I cried.

"And Newell gave Catsy those sleeping pills," Rand added. "Then he sat there and watched her take them one at a time. He left right as the police arrived."

My stomach churned as I turned to look at Newell. After he'd professed his love, I thought he would deny this accusation, but he didn't.

The room was oppressively hot and I felt ill.

"Drake's favorite game is making us hurt someone we love," Rand continued. "I figure he has some plan to get Sloan out of jail so he can be the one to get rid of you. It would be his ultimate victory over our former FBI friend. Unless he's afraid Sloan wouldn't be able to do it. That's probably it. It's safer to keep Sloan in jail—where he can't help you—and make one of us do the dirty deed."

Speechless with grief and fear, I turned to Drake.

He said, "Don't worry, Kennedy. All of this nonsense Rand has been spouting is just the musing of a sloppy drunk."

But his words didn't ring true. Rand couldn't have made everything up. And Newell, who wasn't drunk, hadn't denied any of it.

"I'm like the others," I realized. "I was in a hopeless situation until you came to Midway. You built a new library and paid for my education. I thought it was pure philanthropy, but really . . ."

"He was drawing you in," Rand said. "Hooking you just like a poor, defenseless fish. And now you either become one of us or you die. It's as simple as that."

I moved way past fear to pure terror. I couldn't seem to get enough air into my lungs, and my skin was hot like I had a fever. Drake meant to kill me, and I desperately wanted to live. I wanted to walk with Luke on the beaches in Hawaii. I wanted to help him achieve his life goals and have his children and take him to doctor appointments when he was old. It couldn't all end here for me, in this little clubhouse, before we'd even had a chance to really begin.

I forced myself first to breathe and then to think. I was not defenseless. I had all kinds of people who would help me. Someone would surely come looking for me soon. I reached into my purse.

"Looking for these?" Drake asked, holding up my phone and my father's gun. "I took the liberty of removing them as were getting out of my car earlier. The gun is now unloaded and you've had some calls, but I texted back that you had a terrible headache and would call them in the morning."

I leaned back against my chair. Maybe a rescue was not imminent, after all.

"But you don't need to be afraid. While there is some truth to Rand's drunken babble, it is mostly imagination combined with exaggeration. I am not an evil mastermind, and I'm certainly not going to kill you."

"Uh-oh," Rand said. "That means you're going to have to become a part of the team, and trust me—dying would be easier and much less painful in the long run."

"I have offered Kennedy a position on our team," Drake said. "She's thinking about it."

Of course now I realized that he never intended to make it voluntary. What I didn't know was how he would coerce me. I didn't think there was anything he could say to bind me to his evil group. So I said, "I appreciate the offer, but I'll have to decline."

Rand laughed. Newell was still sniffling.

Drake raised an eyebrow. "Don't speak too soon."

"Yes, don't say no after Drake went to so much trouble to give you this chance," Rand said. "Think of all the strings he had to pull to get your husband confiscated by the Marines on your wedding day."

This new revelation fell on me like a physical blow. "*You* did that?" I whispered.

"You're perfect for the team," Drake answered obtusely. "But I needed a way to prove that to you. So I did use my connections at the Pentagon. I hope you'll forgive me."

He was saying words that both of us knew were lies. He didn't care if I forgave him, and he knew I wouldn't. It was the strangest feeling—like I had slipped into an alternate dimension where none of the normal rules applied. A place where truth was nonexistent.

I knew if I remained passive, I'd be lost. So I stood. "I'm leaving right now."

"You are completely free to go," Drake said. "I never force my team members to do anything."

Rand took another sip from his bottle and laughed. "No, Drake is a big believer in freedom. He'll make you *choose* to stay."

Nothing Drake could say or do would make me voluntarily be a part of his sick game. So I walked to the door.

He let me put my hand on the doorknob before he said, "Your husband is trained to dismantle bombs for the Marine Corps. I'll bet such a specialized skill is in high demand. And if they call him up again, he might not survive his next tour of duty."

Luke. I turned back to face him. "You could make the Marines call him up?" I rasped. "And you *would?*"

Rand laughed. "Haven't you been listening to anything I've said? There's nothing Drake won't do!"

"Everyone has limitations, even me," Drake countered. "And I don't want to ask favors of my military friends too often."

I thought he was trying to reassure me until he continued.

"I'm sure you worry about your father. Being a postal employee can be almost as dangerous as dismantling bombs. You never know when a disgruntled coworker might come in and shoot everyone."

Daddy. Tears gathered in my eyes.

"And your ex-husband is a cop, right?" Drake asked even though he knew the answer. "Cops die in the line of duty every day."

Cade. I thought I had shed my last tear over him, but I was wrong.

"Don't think that Drake is limited to your family members with dangerous jobs," Rand contributed. "You'd be surprised how many housewives get hit by cars in grocery store parking lots."

My mother and sisters. My hand on the doorknob started to tremble.

"And how many children get injured or killed playing in their own backyards," Rand continued.

My nieces and nephews. Drake was a threat to everyone I loved.

"Your weakness is that you love too much," Rand said. "That's what Drake will use against you."

"Stop!" Newell screamed. "I can't listen to any more of this. He's got you, Kennedy. Just like he has me and Rand and Sloan. You never had a chance against him, not from the minute he saw you and decided he wanted you to be a part of the team."

I didn't want to believe it was true. I didn't want to think that there was no way out. I clung with all my might to hope.

Then Drake stood. "For once I agree with Newell. We've heard enough of Rand's nonsense. Come on, Kennedy, let's get out of here."

I grappled for the door as he came toward me. But I couldn't get it open before he took hold of my arm.

"Help me!" I cried to Rand and Newell. "Surely you have a little human decency left."

"You're wrong about that," was Rand's slurred reply. "I don't care about anything or anyone. It's my only defense. And if Newell was willing to kill Catsy, his true love, why would he risk anything for you?"

There was nothing to say. I hated the feel of Drake's hand on my arm. I hated even being in the same room with him. But I allowed him to lead me through the door into the somewhat fresher evening air.

"You need some time to think," he said once we were outside. "Rand has a flair for the dramatic. I didn't force him to shoot Morris. I just mentioned that if our architect friend decided to tattle to the police about some of our less-ethical team practices, Rand, as our attorney, would certainly end up in jail."

I stared into his brown eyes. I had always thought they were so warm and sensitive. Now they seemed like windows into hell. "And Catsy?"

"She wouldn't have lasted a day in jail. Sleeping pills were by far the more humane option. And suggesting that to Newell was not even a crime. And he is guilty only of providing the means for her to commit suicide."

Drake had an excuse for everything and took no responsibility for anything. If he would just admit that he was wrong, I would have felt better. But this determination to defend or downplay his actions was unbearable. I couldn't stand to look at him for another second, so I turned away.

"I still think you'd be a good fit for my team," he said. "But I won't make you join us if you don't want to."

I forced my eyes back to meet his and asked incredulously, "You're saying that if I choose not to be a part of your team, you won't kill me or my husband or my father or . . ." I just couldn't make myself go on so my voice trailed off.

"That's what I'm saying," he claimed. "As long as you don't say anything about what you heard tonight to anyone. If you keep our secrets, you can go on with your life."

"And you can go on killing and cheating people."

"I help many people," he countered. "The few that do not come away from association with me 'improved' are what we call acceptable losses. It's a part of any business—something that is understood."

"People are acceptable losses?" I repeated.

He nodded. "And you're naïve if you believe I'm the only businessman who thinks so."

I shook my head. "How can I live with myself if I keep quiet?" And then I realized that what Rand said was true. Drake's purpose was to control me—to overcome my freewill and bind me to him forever. He could accomplish this either by my active participation in his criminal activities or through my guilt if I kept silent.

"No one will believe you if you start making outrageous claims," he said. "But your family members will pay—one by one."

I covered my face. "Why? Why did you have to pick me?"

He gave me a pleasant smile. "You're just lucky, I guess."

"I don't know what to say."

"Say that everything will just go on as before. You'll stay in my house for your honeymoon, I'll pay for your college education, and as a show of gratitude, you won't discuss me or the Langston Association with anyone."

I was trying to think of a fitting response when the door behind us opened. I glanced around to see Newell standing there. He was holding up Rand, who apparently had passed out from too much alcohol.

"What do you want me to do with him?" Newell asked.

"Drive him back to the hotel," Drake said. "I'll meet you there."

Newell just stood there, his dazed expression more pronounced than when he'd told us about Catsy's death.

"Newell!" Drake called out sharply.

He looked up. "Huh?"

"Get Rand to the hotel!"

Newell's nod barely registered in my fevered mind. I didn't know what to do, what to say. I was in my own private purgatory, separated from the rest of the world. If I told what I knew, Drake would destroy me and everyone I love. If I remained silent, all the happiness would be drained from my life. And there would be no escape. Ever.

At first a choice seemed impossible. And then I realized that there was no choice to make. My humanity demanded that I take a stand. I accepted that I would die, and I prayed only that Cade or Winston Jones or Mark Iverson or someone would protect my family. Squaring my shoulders, I said, "At my first opportunity I will tell the proper authorities everything I know about you and your corrupt association."

Drake did not seem surprised. "Then you have sealed your fate." His grip on my arm tightened painfully.

As Newell passed by, dragging Rand, a slight movement caught my eye. I turned my head and saw Sloan walking toward us. I blinked, thinking I was hallucinating. But when I opened my eyes he was still there.

"It's about time," Drake addressed Sloan irritably. "The lawyer said he would have you out on bail in no time."

"Nothing happens quickly in small Southern towns," Sloan replied, his tone dull and lifeless. "You should know that by now."

Drake's mouth twisted into a grimace. "Well, at least you're in time to deal with Kennedy. I've made her a very reasonable offer, but she won't be logical. So she's going to have to meet with a tragic accident. I'll leave the details up to you."

Sloan walked closer.

"I don't have to remind you what is at stake here?" Drake said.

"You don't have to remind me," Sloan replied.

Sloan's eyes looked dead and determined.

I never could have imagined being afraid of Sloan, but I shrank away. "No."

Drake held my arm tighter.

I pulled back with all my might. "NO!"

Newell's head jerked back around toward us. His expression had changed from dazed to fierce. He dropped Rand and let out a little growl.

"Newell." Drake's exasperation was obvious. "Ignore us and do as you were told."

"You shouldn't make us kill the ones we love!" Newell cried as he started to run at Drake.

"You can't hurt me," Drake said. Then he braced for the impact.

With a scream Newell crashed into Drake. Newell's weight combined with his running start was enough to make Drake stagger backward, but his firm grasp on my arm helped to steady him. Then he balled his other hand into a fist and punched Newell in his large, soft stomach. Newell doubled over in pain.

Drake made a little sound of disgust. "You are weak, Newell. Why would you ever think you could fight me?"

Sloan reached us and took hold of free my arm. He pulled me toward him, but Drake didn't let go. The men stared at each other across me. I was in a tug-of-war between two evils, and I wasn't sure which was the lesser.

Then, inexplicably, Newell rolled forward and hit Drake again. I felt the ground disappear from beneath my feet and thought Newell had propelled us both into the air. Then I realized that he had pushed Drake over the edge of the empty swimming pool. And because Drake was holding on to me—I was headed toward the concrete bottom along with him. I wondered if this was the answer to my prayer, a way out of the impossible situation Drake had put me in. I tried to scream, but no sound came out of my mouth. I reached toward the side of the pool, but I was too far away. Finally I closed my eyes, accepting my fate.

Then Sloan's hold on my arm tightened and he stopped my descent with a jarring yank. Drake's weight on my other arm was terrible, and I was sure my shoulders or elbows would dislocate at any second. Drake swung around and grabbed the side of the pool with his free hand, relieving some of the strain on my joints.

My stomach hit the edge of the pool so hard that I was sure my ribs were broken. I couldn't breathe, and I started to slip back down toward the emptiness below. Drake released me immediately to protect himself.

Sloan's voice came from what seemed like a long way away. "Hold on to my hand, Kennedy!"

His command marshaled strength I didn't know I had. I swung my other hand around and clung to his arm with all my might. Then slowly, painfully, he hauled me up onto the edge of the pool. He pulled me with such force that I crashed into his chest. His arms went around me briefly and I felt his trembling. Then Cade ran up and Sloan passed me to him. Cade hugged me close as Sloan walked over to Newell and Drake.

Peeking over Cade's shoulder, I saw Drake trying to pull himself up out of the pool. With nothing to press his feet against, he was totally dependent on upper body strength—and apparently he didn't have enough.

"Help me!" he called out.

Sloan stopped short, refusing to give assistance.

"Newell!" Drake screamed.

Newell crawled on his hands and knees to the pool's edge. He raised himself into a squat and leaned down toward Drake. I thought he was going to pull his boss away from danger. But instead he started peeling the fingers of Drake's left hand off the edge, one by one.

Drake let go with the remaining fingers of his left hand long enough to grab Newell by the ankle. "If I fall, you fall too!"

Newell nodded and moved to the right hand where he continued to pry up Drake's fingers.

"You don't want to die! You don't really even want to kill me!" Drake tried to convince him.

"You're right," Newell agreed. "I want you to live. But I hope you break your neck so you have to live the rest of his life as a paraplegic—dependent on others for everything." Then Newell lifted his foot and stomped on Drake's hand. Drake screamed and he let go of the pool's side. Both men fell to the bottom with a sickening thud.

I turned my head away and clung to Cade as I heard sirens approaching. A man holding a camera on his shoulder came running around the corner of the clubhouse. The red light was flashing, which indicated he was already filming. Just behind him was Hannah-Leigh Coley-Smith Burrell. She stopped cold when she saw me standing in Cade's arms.

I pulled back and Cade let his arms drop to his side.

"Sloan!" he called.

Sloan turned and stared at us.

"You watch Kennedy," Cade said.

Sloan nodded and led me to the clubhouse wall where we were somewhat out of the melee. Cade trotted over to his wife as Sheriff Bonham arrived. She started asking questions and Cade seemed happy to defer to his boss. Deputies swarmed all around us— arresting Rand, taping off the area, and escorting Hannah-Leigh and her cameraman back to the road.

Two ambulances arrived, and they loaded up Newell and Drake. Both were moving when they passed me, so I knew they were alive.

Cade trotted over. "Hannah-Leigh is furious that the sheriff won't let her interview anyone. That's the disadvantage to being married to the press. I'm going to hear about this tonight."

"How did you know that I was in trouble and where to find me?" I asked.

"Your mother called your cell phone and didn't get an answer."

I nodded. "Drake texted her back and said I had a headache."

"So of course she immediately sent your father over to your apartment to check on you."

I smiled. And to think there was a time in the very recent past when this would have annoyed me.

"I had just gotten to the Haggerty police station—and found out that Sloan's lawyer arranged bail so there was no interrogation to witness—when your father called me to see if I knew where you were. When Sloan heard you were missing, he went crazy. He asked if you had left with Langston, and I told him yes. He said we'd better get over here fast if it wasn't already too late." Cade looked embarrassed. "He said I was an idiot for letting you out of my sight, and I know it's true. You almost died."

"But I didn't." I glanced at Sloan to include him. "Thanks to both of you."

Sloan said nothing.

"He told me it would be best if he went up alone since Langston would trust him," Cade recapped. "I was waiting for him to signal me."

"That was the best plan," I assured him.

He sighed. "Well, we've got to clear this area. I'll take you home." He turned to Sloan. "Do you need a ride?"

Sloan nodded. "I need a ride back to the Haggerty police station. I've got to turn myself in."

"You're out on bail," Cade reminded him.

"And Rand has admitted that he killed Morris," I said.

Cade smiled. "That's great. Then the charges will be dropped."

"I've done other things," Sloan said slowly. "And I've lived with the guilt for too long. Tonight I am going to come clean on all of it—no matter what it costs me."

Cade started to argue again, but I put a hand up to stop him. Remembering the way I felt when Drake was trying to push me into a life of guilt, I could imagine the crushing burden that Sloan had been carrying. And I knew that it would be worth anything to be free of it.

"Get someone to take him to Haggerty," I said. "And make sure Mark Iverson is at the police station when he gets there."

Cade looked confused but called a deputy over and gave him the assignment.

"This is an arrest, deputy," Sloan told Cade. "Do it right."

So Cade reluctantly read Sloan his rights and put him in handcuffs. It was painful to watch, but I could feel Sloan's relief. Even being arrested was better than living a lie.

As he passed by me in the deputy's custody, he said, "No matter what Drake said, I would never have done anything to hurt you."

Then he walked away with the deputy. Cade put his hand on my arm and led me to his car. "I'm taking you to your mother," he said.

I didn't even argue. While we were driving, I got a text from Luke. It said, *How's your headache?*

I couldn't bear to go into all of it at that moment, so I just replied, *Better.*

* * *

My parents were standing in the driveway when we pulled up. Mother led me to my childhood room and tucked me into bed. She had the doctor make a house call (yes, such things do still happen in the Deep South) and he checked my ribs. None of them were broken but several were bruised. So he prescribed some pain medication and rest.

After everyone left I could hear the phone ringing constantly. Instead of being irritated, as I might have been a few days before, I was thankful that so many people were concerned about me.

CHAPTER TWENTY

ON FRIDAY MORNING I SLEPT IN—something my mother rarely permits, so I knew how worried she was about me. I was planning to call Luke and tell him everything that had happened on Thursday, but when I checked my phone, I had a message from him saying he was coming home. They had declared the military equivalent of a mistrial, and he was headed to the airport. Lt. Dempsey had kindly changed our flight reservations, and we were now scheduled to leave for Honolulu from the Atlanta airport at three o'clock that afternoon. My flight from Albany to Atlanta left at one.

I forced myself into a standing position even though I was very stiff and sore. A warm shower soothed my aching muscles but did nothing for the multitude of bruises on my stomach. Fortunately I hadn't been planning to wear a bikini in Hawaii.

By the time I walked into the kitchen, I felt refreshed and was barely limping.

Mother had a delicious breakfast waiting for me. I ate with relish while she and my father plied me with questions. Once their curiosity was satisfied, I told them that Luke was on his way.

"That is wonderful news!" Mother said. "But I wish he was coming here instead of meeting you in Atlanta. That way we'd get to see you off."

"They've delayed their honeymoon long enough," Daddy said. "The sooner they get on with it, the better."

I smiled at my father. Then I asked him to call Cade.

"I need to know about Drake and Newell—not much, just whether they are alive. And I want him to arrange for me to visit

Sloan. I was thinking maybe you could take me by there on the way to the airport."

"Isn't he is in jail?" Mother asked with a frown.

"Probably, but I want to see him anyway."

Risking my mother's wrath, Daddy nodded. "I'll call Cade and see where Sloan is and if he can have visitors."

"If that is not the very last word," Mother complained. "At least drink your juice while your father calls the jail."

I gulped down my juice while Daddy had a short conversation with Cade.

After hanging up, he reported that both Newell and Drake were alive. "The two guys who fell in the pool are in serious but stable condition at Memorial Hospital in Albany."

"And Sloan?"

"He's at the Haggerty police station at the moment, but they'll be transporting him to Albany soon for his arraignment on a variety of charges. Cade is checking to see if you can visit him there."

"Oh, Kennedy," Mother said. "I wish you wouldn't. There has been so much trouble already. Can't you just stay here where it's safe and quiet until its time to go meet Luke?"

"I'm sorry, Mother," I said. "But I need to talk to him."

"Don't you have packing to do?"

I shook my head. "Nope, I'm all packed. But while we're waiting for Cade to call, we can work on thank-you notes."

This seemed to cheer her up. I was working on my fifth note (and contemplating a pain pill that would render me unconscious) when my phone rang. It was Cade's number, but when I answered, it was Sloan.

"I appreciate your concern," he said. "But I don't want you to come here."

A gulf of misery had opened between us that in person I might be able to bridge. Over the phone it was going to be difficult if not impossible to reach him. But I tried. "I wanted to thank you and tell you that I understood. Drake put people in impossible situations."

"Difficult but not impossible." He sounded so sad. "I see that now. I did a lot of things that were wrong. I lied and falsified and protected Drake from the FBI investigations, but I promise I never killed anyone *or* bullied an old lady."

"I believe you," I said, thankful for the confidence I felt.

"I'm going to pay the price for my mistakes and hope that when I'm done I'll still have enough time to find happiness."

"I hope so too," I told him. "And once you get . . . settled, I'll come see you."

"I hate to think about you coming to prison—especially to see me."

I laughed. "It's getting to the point where I have as many friends in prison as out."

He didn't laugh along with me, but he sounded a little less sad when he told me good-bye.

I was on thank-you note number nine when Miss Eugenia arrived, and I was so happy to see her that I hugged her neck—which hurt my ribs—so I was smiling through my tears.

"I just wanted to check on you," she said. "And hear all the details."

She sat down at the kitchen table, and I told her everything that had happened. My parents both listened to the whole thing for a second time.

When I got through, Miss Eugenia said, "I could strangle Cade and Sloan for almost letting you fall into that pool!"

"They saved my life," I corrected her. "What almost killed me was my foolish decision to trust Drake."

"I tried to warn you," Mother said.

I nodded. "Yes, you did." Then I asked Miss Eugenia, "So did you get Agatha all settled at the Jacksons' house?"

"Oh, yes," Miss Eugenia replied. "She was a little nervous when we left, but I'm sure that was just confusion caused by the medication. She'll be well enough to complain in no time."

"I'm not sure what will happen now with the model home and all," I said. "Since Drake is hurt and a criminal—I don't know if she'll get her house."

"If not, I'm sure the church folks can help her get a place to live." Miss Eugenia didn't seem worried. "And Mark finally found out what happened to that nurse of Parnell's—Jenna. She was in a federal prison in northern Georgia, but an appeals judge overturned her conviction based on a technicality and now she's free—whereabouts unknown!"

This wasn't much of a surprise, considering all that I had learned about Drake Langston. "So she didn't implicate Drake's team because he'd promised to get her off—later when no one was watching."

"Exactly," Miss Eugenia confirmed.

"So Drake really was behind everything?" Mother asked.

I nodded. "It certainly does look that way."

Miss Eugenia stood. "Well, I need to go so you can get to the airport on time. Mark said to thank you for all your help. And according to Mark, Cade may be a big hero before it's all said and done."

I smiled. "His instincts really picked a great moment to improve!"

She waved and my mother walked her to the door.

Daddy and I were discussing what time we needed to leave for the airport when Mother returned. "You have a visitor, Kennedy," she said. "It's Hannah-Leigh, but she won't come in. She asked if you would step out on the back porch."

I considered refusing in hopes that Hannah-Leigh would eventually go away, but I knew this would upset my mother. So I stood and hobbled to the backdoor.

Hannah-Leigh was lovely as usual, but her eyes were puffy from crying. "Are you okay?" I asked.

"You can quit playing games," she said. "I saw you and Cade hugging last night. I know you've been meeting him behind my back, trying to steal him away from me."

Nothing she could have said would have astonished me more. I was speechless.

Apparently translating my silence as an admission of guilt, she continued. "I understand that it's hard for you to let him go. He is the most handsome, wonderful man in the world."

I thought about Cade the last time I'd seen him—his face peeling, his eyebrows singed, and his eyes swollen from the cat allergies.

"But I'm not going to let you have him," Hannah-Leigh went on. "I'm going to fight you for him. Because I love him."

And I began to hope that Cade and Hannah-Leigh might just make it. Because after that horrible moment in the drive-in—when I realized that Cade and Missy Lamar were in his Rodeo right beside us—it never occurred to me to fight for him. Our marriage was over. Apparently I didn't love him the way Hannah-Leigh did.

"So I'm going to ask you to stay away from him," she said. "He's my husband and you can't have him."

I thought of many responses. I could have told her that Cade and I had been working together on a case. I could have told her the last thing I wanted was to have Cade back. But I decided the best thing was just to nod and say, "Okay."

Her shoulders sagged in relief. "It's better this way, really."

I nodded. "I think you're right."

She took a deep breath and said, "Good-bye, then," and walked away. So much for us being friends.

* * *

Mother and Daddy drove me over to my apartment so I could change clothes and pick up my suitcase. When I came out of my bedroom wearing the sailor sundress my sister had gotten for me, Mother held up the envelope Drake had given me with the information about his house in Hawaii.

"This looks so nice," Mother said.

I shook my head. "I would rather sleep in the Honolulu airport than in Drake's house."

Mother looked concerned. "But where will you stay?"

"It doesn't matter where we stay, as long as we're together."

On the way to Albany we passed the spot where Nola Finkle's car had crashed. I stared at the scorched trees, amazed at all that had happened during the past week. In a very real way, Nola—with a little help from Cade—had brought down the great Drake Langston and his corrupt association. I hoped that wherever Nola was, she knew that.

My parents walked with me as far as the security checkpoint. Then they gave me careful hugs and waved as I headed down toward my gate. I only made it a few steps before I turned back to look at them. They were standing hand in hand, watching me leave to start a new phase of my life. And I hoped that the day would come when Luke and I would be just like them. I didn't want to cry, so I gave them one last, quick wave and then hurried to the plane that would take me to Luke.

* * *

When I got off the plane in Atlanta, Luke was the first thing I saw. Dressed in perfectly pressed fatigues, and grinning for all he was worth, he was standing right by the ticket counter. I ran toward him and he caught me up in his arms. It was a moment I know I'll always remember.

"So, do you miss Lt. Dempsey?" I asked, breathless after his welcome kiss.

"Oddly, I do a little," he replied, equally short of breath.

He put me down and we hurried to our gate. While we waited to board, I told him about everything that had transpired over the past twenty-four hours. He was tense and sometimes angry but mostly just relieved that it was over.

"I'm glad we won't be living in Midway after our honeymoon," he said.

"I am going to have to figure out what the future holds for me now," I said. "Since Drake won't be financing my education . . ."

"I've got some ideas about that," he said as they announced that our flight was boarding. "We'll talk about it once we get on the plane."

We waited our turn in line, but when we actually walked onto the plane, the flight attendant took our tickets and said that our seats had been reassigned.

I frowned. "What do you mean?"

She pointed to a pair of seats in first class. "Two of our first-class passengers gave up their seats so you two could use them." She looked at Luke. "They wanted to thank you for your service to our country."

I was touched and could tell that Luke was as well. "Can we thank them?"

The flight attendant said, "They wanted to remain anonymous, but I'll pass your message along. Now sit down! We're blocking traffic."

Feeling conspicuous, we slid into our luxurious seats. "Too bad you're becoming a Mormon," I whispered. "Because they will probably offer us free champagne!"

Luke laughed. "I wouldn't drink it even if I wasn't about to be a Mormon. I want to keep a clear head and remember every minute of this trip."

We put on our seat belts, and I ran my hand along the soft leather armrest. "I've never flown first class. Have you?"

He laughed. "Yeah, right." He stretched his legs out into the ample space in front of him. "But I could get used to it."

The flight attendants went over air safety and then brought us appetizers that consisted of cheese and olive shish kebabs. When they asked what we wanted to drink, we both ordered ginger ale. They brought it to us in fancy goblets.

After we toasted to "happily ever after," I asked Luke if he was disappointed that we wouldn't be honeymooning in a multimillion-dollar mansion.

He shook his head. "I never felt comfortable with that anyway."

"Maybe one of our fellow passengers will be so thankful for your military service that they'll give us their hotel room," I suggested.

"I wouldn't count on that." He slid a shish kebab off the spear and into his mouth.

"What did you mean earlier when you said you had a plan for my educational future?"

He put his goblet down and turned to face me. "The Marines want me to come to Lejeune and train special ops teams full-time," he said. "They're offering me a commission. That means I'd be an officer—entitled to on-post housing so Heaven could live with us sooner. The Corps would pay for me to finish my degree while I'm earning a salary so we could afford to pay for you to get a degree in whatever it is you want to do."

It was a lot to digest all at once. "Wow."

He laughed. "No pressure, just something to think about."

"What do you want to do?" I asked.

"I love my country and the Marines. I think I'd like to accomplish my personal goals and help other soldiers who are going where I've been."

"Then it's settled," I said with conviction. "Marine Corps, here we come."

Luke kissed me soundly.

Then I said, "I can't wait to tell Heaven."

He raised an eyebrow. "Are you so anxious for our honeymoon to end?"

I pulled his face close to mine. "I don't plan for our honeymoon to ever end, soldier."

* * *

We both slept during most of the flight and arrived at the Honolulu airport just as the sun was setting. As we left the plane Luke said, "You realize that we have now slept together twice—and nothing else."

I laughed. "Maybe your luck will change soon."

"I've been saying that all my life," he teased.

We walked outside and were greeted by beautiful girls in hula skirts. They put leis around our necks and welcomed us to Hawaii.

While waiting for our luggage, we did an Internet search and located a hotel. It did have an ocean view, but unfortunately it was also a high-rise, and it wasn't cheap. But Luke didn't want to keep searching so we made our reservations.

"You only live once," he quipped as I stared at the obscene amount it was going to cost us to stay there for seven days. "Or at least we'll only be in Hawaii once—probably."

"Definitely at these prices," I muttered.

We got our luggage and rented a car and finally were headed toward the hotel. As we drove, we discussed our options.

"We can go straight to the hotel," I said. "Or we can stop along the way and get something to eat. We could even go for a walk on the beach."

Luke nodded. "I plan to eat a lot of good food while I'm here and I look forward to walking on the beach. But right now I have unfinished business with you, Mrs. Scoggins, so I vote that we head straight to that expensive hotel."

I leaned across the seat to kiss him on the cheek. "We can't get there too soon."

MORE MIDWAY RECIPES

MISS EUGENIA'S S'MORE COOKIES
(deep-frying is optional—and really not recommended)

    1 sugar cookie mix (prepared according to package directions)
    1 sleeve graham crackers (broken into pieces)
    1 large Hershey bar (broken into pieces)
    2 cups mini-marshmallows

Heat oven to 325 degrees. Lightly grease a cookie sheet. Add graham cracker pieces, Hershey bar pieces, and mini-marshmallows to sugar cookie dough. Stir. Spoon onto cookie sheet and bake for 12–15 minutes. Cool and serve at room temperature.

MISS ZELDA'S MILLION DOLLAR PIE
(since she's about to come into some money)

    10 oz. Cool Whip
    1/4 cup lemon juice
    1 cup sweetened condensed milk
    1 cup chopped pecans
    1 cup crushed pineapple (drained)
    1/2 cup chopped cherries
    2 graham cracker crusts

Mix Cool Whip, lemon juice, and condensed milk. Add nuts, pineapple, and cherries. Stir well. Divide into graham cracker crusts. Refrigerate for 2 hours. Serve cold.

MISS IDA JEAN'S EASY MEXICAN DIP
(perfect for unexpected guests)

    1 lb. sausage, cooked and drained
    2 cans Ro-Tel diced tomatoes (mild)
    2 8-oz. pkgs. cream cheese

When sausage is cooked and drained, add Ro-Tel tomatoes and cream cheese. Cook on medium-low heat until cheese is melted. Serve with tortilla chips.

MISS IRIS'S LEMON CHICKEN
(a favorite for Sunday dinner—especially if the preacher is invited)

    5 Tbsps. butter (divided into two equal pieces)
    4 chicken breasts (rinsed, dried, and cut in half)
    1 cup flour (on a plate)
    1/4 cup honey
    1/4 cup lemon juice
    1 Tbsp. soy sauce

Preheat oven to 350 degrees. Melt one portion of butter. Dip chicken pieces into butter one at a time. Then roll pieces in flour and arrange them in a casserole dish. Bake for 30 minutes. While chicken is cooking, combine the following in a small sauce pan: honey, lemon juice, and soy sauce. Add other portion of butter. Stir until mixed. After 30 minutes remove chicken from oven. Pour sauce over it and then return to the oven for an additional 10 minutes. This chicken is good served alone or with rice.

MISSY'S TACO SOUP
(great for a night when you have to scrounge up dinner)

    1 lb. ground beef, browned and drained
    1 medium onion, finely chopped
    1 pkg. dry Hidden Valley Ranch dressing mix
    1 pkg. dry taco seasoning
    1 large can ranch-style black beans
    1 large can pinto beans
    1 large can white corn
    1 large can stewed tomatoes
    2 8-oz cans Ro-Tel, diced (1 mild, 1 hot)
    (Serve with tortilla chips, sour cream, grated cheddar cheese.)

Mix beef, onion, Hidden Valley mix, and taco seasoning. Simmer until onion is tender. Add a small amount of water if necessary. Add remaining ingredients and simmer on medium-low for 1 hour. Serve with tortilla chips, sour cream, and grated cheddar cheese.

ABOUT THE AUTHOR

BETSY BRANNON GREEN currently lives in Bessemer, Alabama, which is a suburb of Birmingham. She has been married to her husband, Butch, for thirty-two wonderful years, and they have eight children, one daughter-in-law, three sons-in-law, and eight grandchildren. She is a Sunday School teacher in the Bessemer Ward and works for Hueytown Elementary School. She loves to read, when she can find the time, and watch sporting events—especially if they involve her children. Although born in Salt Lake City, Betsy has spent most of her life in the South. Her writing and her life have been strongly influenced by the town of Headland, Alabama, and the many generous gracious people who live there. Her first book, *Hearts in Hiding,* was published in 2001, followed by *Never Look Back* (2002), *Until Proven Guilty* (2002), *Don't Close Your Eyes* (2003), *Above Suspicion* (2003), *Foul Play* (2004), *Silenced* (2004), *Copycat* (2005), *Poison* (2005), *Double Cross* (2006), *Christmas in Haggerty* (2006), *Backtrack* (2007), *Hazardous Duty* (2007), *Above and Beyond* (2008), *The Spirit of Christmas* (2008), *Code of Honor* (2009), *Murder by the Book* (2009), and *Murder by Design* (2010).